THE ACCUSED

Constance BRISCOE

EBURY
PRESS

3 5 7 9 10 8 6 4 2

Published in 2011 by Ebury Press, an imprint of Ebury Publishing
A Random House Group Company

The Random House Group Limited Reg. No. 954009

Addresses for companies within the Random House Group can be found at
www.randomhouse.co.uk

A CIP catalogue record for this book is available from the British Library

The Random House Group Limited supports The Forest Stewardship Council
(FSC®), the leading international forest certification organisation. Our books carrying
the FSC label are printed on FSC® certified paper. FSC is the only forest certification
scheme endorsed by the leading evironmental organisations, including Greenpeace.
Our paper procurement policy can be found at: www.randomhouse.co.uk/environment

Printed in the UK by CPI Cox & Wyman, Reading, RG1 8EX

ISBN 9780091940928

To buy books by your favourite authors and register for offers visit
www.randomhouse.co.uk

To Darley Anderson and Tony Arlidge.
I have a great deal to thank you both for.

Chapter One

Leticia Joy had to die. She had no choice in the matter.

The stained-glass window illuminated the church with hues of magnificent sapphire. Pools of light cast a glow around Leticia as she sat slumped forward in a pew, lost in a moment of private contemplation. All of a sudden she felt herself jerked backward, out of her prayers. Her eyes snapped open as she struggled to make sense of what was happening to her.

A sharp blade travelled across the front of her neck, exposing the soft contours of her throat. The blood oozed out of the wound, falling in steady drops onto the front of her cream silk blouse. The blade continued on its journey in a circular motion across the front of her gullet. When it sliced through her artery, there was a sudden gush of blood.

As she began to lose consciousness, images of her fiancé, Tom, danced before her eyes. She fancied she saw the face of Christ above her. And as death lingered like a taxi waiting for a passenger, an angel approached her. Pale, beautiful and ethereal, the fair creature placed her hand against Leticia's face. Leticia smiled through the pain as the tallow candles flickered in the darkness, casting shadows on long-dead Christians.

The stranger reached forward and touched Leticia's wound, pressing the edges closed. Even in her semi-conscious state, Leticia could feel her own blood seeping between the stranger's fingers. The angel fell to her knees. And that was when Leticia saw the knife in her hand.

'Bless me, Father, for I have sinned,' the stranger whispered, and Leticia Joy's last thought before she died was that perhaps this was not an angel after all.

Chapter Two

It took the police forty-one minutes to arrive at St Mary Magdalene's Catholic Church in Camberwell. The police had received a phone call from a man named Sexton, who claimed to have seen a woman standing in the church door covered in blood. It could be nothing but, equally, in this part of South London, it could be anything.

First, the police secured the church; when they were satisfied that all exits were covered, they made their approach. Detective Chief Inspector Paradissimo was long past his prime, but he still saw himself as an alpha male, a natural leader. The church was in total darkness and there appeared to be no signs of life. Edging forward, he pushed the door open and stepped inside. As he did so he spotted the victim sitting in a pew immediately facing the statue of Christ on the Cross, and realised at once that this was no crank callout.

It looked like she had been praying, but the devil had answered.

Paradissimo moved swiftly to her side and saw that the victim's legs were crossed at the ankles and she was sitting with her head thrown back, which exposed her neck wound. The killer had severed her carotid artery and there was blood everywhere. Automatically, Paradissimo felt for a pulse, even though it was clearly already too late for the young woman. She appeared to have been dead for some time.

Calling for backup, he turned to his left and noticed that, sitting between an elaborate candelabra and the collection box in the corner, there was another young woman, slightly older than the first. She was pale, blonde and fragile-looking. At first Paradissimo presumed she was a second victim, luckier than the first in that she was still breathing, although her face was streaked with blood. But as he approached her motionless form, he saw that she held a large knife in her left hand; a knife with the tip of its blade missing.

Instinctively, he knocked the weapon from her hand and pulled her roughly to her feet. While he handcuffed her, one of his constables collected the knife and placed it in an evidence bag. The woman seemed dazed and confused but unharmed. The blood on her face and hands didn't appear to be from any obvious wound; Paradissimo therefore presumed it was the victim's. He asked her name but she seemed unable, or unwilling, to respond, so he simply informed her that she was under arrest on suspicion of murder.

The suspect's shoes were then removed at the scene for later forensic examination, and she was provided with a pair of plain white paper slippers. Her clothes were also removed, and she was forcibly dressed in a large white paper bodysuit. She was escorted into a police van and taken to Camberwell Green Police Station, where the custody sergeant booked her into cell number 18.

A call was immediately placed to the Forensic Medical Examiner. The Scene of Crime Officers certainly had their work cut out: a large expanse of the church was splattered in blood, as the killing had been particularly brutal. The victim was formally pronounced dead at the scene and, once the SOCO boys had completed their fingertip search of the premises, the as-yet unidentified victim was taken to a morgue, where the exact cause of death would be determined.

The police had more luck with the other woman, their suspect. They soon found her handbag in a pew close to the victim, and her driving license revealed her to be one Elizabeth Johnson. It was then a matter of minutes before they established that she had form.

As far as DCI Paradissimo was concerned, it was case closed.

Chapter Three

'Members of the jury, all twelve of you are the final judges of fact. You decide whether the charge laid against Miss Elizabeth Johnson has been proved beyond reasonable doubt. She stands accused on one count of murder, and it is the case for the prosecution that she is guilty. Don't allow any sympathy for the victim to prejudice your mind. Elizabeth Johnson is presumed innocent until you, the jury, decide whether or not she is guilty.'

Judge Certie peered over his glasses as he addressed the jury. His triple chin bulged over the starched white bands of his winged collar. His weather-worn hands were creased with age, and his wedding band cut deep into the flesh of his solid ring finger.

'Leticia Joy was reported dead by the police at St Mary Magdalene's Church in Camberwell on Saturday the third of July, 2010. Elizabeth Johnson, known to the police along with her friends and associates as Icey, was discovered at the scene of the crime with the murder weapon in her hand. Subsequent forensic testing revealed that she was covered in Leticia Joy's blood, and also that she had been drinking alcohol.

'The defence claim that she in fact came to Leticia Joy's aid, which is how she came to have the victim's blood on her. They also maintain that she did not know the victim nor have any reason to kill her, and that she picked up the knife instinctively.

Elizabeth Johnson claims she is not guilty. You, the jury, must decide.

'Miss Johnson has chosen to tell you that she has been convicted on several occasions for being a common prostitute. She also has a number of past convictions for violence, dishonesty and drug and alcohol abuse. The defence maintain that, while she has been a petty crook, she is not a cold-blooded murderer. Bear that in mind. If you think that her previous convictions demonstrate she has a propensity for violence, you may take that into account in determining the charge of murder.

'It is for you to decide whether the prosecution has proved guilt beyond reasonable doubt so that you are sure. And if you are, return a verdict of guilty.'

Chapter Four

Sam Bailey turned into Old Bailey Street. The jury had been out for two days and still seemed no closer to reaching a verdict. She didn't know if that was good or bad but she couldn't get the judge's words out of her head. Elizabeth Johnson – Icey – was her oldest friend. She had been on remand in custody for exactly seven months and had spent Christmas inside. Surely the jury would deliver a verdict today?

Pulling her navy blue coat around her petite waist, Sam tugged the belt through the loop and double knotted it. As she sidestepped black pools of rainwater, her gold stilettos clicked on the wet pavement in a staccato melody. She was too preoccupied to notice the heads that turned as she walked by. Unrealistically hopeful, pot-bellied men sought her out with their appreciative gazes. Even after no sleep and seven months of stress, Sam Bailey was heartbreakingly beautiful. She was a black beauty, impossible to ignore; she had been attracting attention – mostly unwanted – since she was seven years old.

If Sam had stopped to think about it, she would have realised that it was already too late for twenty-five-year-old Icey. The prosecution had portrayed her as an immoral tart who had never done a legal day's work in her life. They'd painted a persuasive picture that she didn't give a flying pair of knickers about anything, as long as she was able to continue working her way through various layers of sexual depravity.

No, the jury had already made up their mind for sure, and time had run out for Elizabeth Johnson, former thief, con artist, alcoholic and prostitute.

There was nothing Sam could do except wait . . . and hope. She had no choice but to place her trust in the twelve members of the jury.

But they had no real notion of what Icey had been through in her life. They had been presented with certain facts, but how could they even begin to understand that she was one of life's tragedies? Icey had confided in Sam years ago about the sexual abuse she'd suffered at the hands of her mother's sick boyfriend, Jack Billings. He had started raping Icey when she was just nine years old, and her prostitute mother had thought it more important to keep her new boyfriend happy than to listen to what her daughter was constantly trying to tell her about Uncle Jack's behaviour. Barbara Johnson would never hear a word said against her darling Jack.

Sam also knew that when Icey was thirteen, she'd finally taken matters into her own hands. She had waited until her mother was out tomming, and Jack was drunk enough to be welded to the sofa for the night. Then she'd poured a bottle of cheap brandy over his sleeping form before setting him on fire with his own lighter. By the time the fire brigade and ambulance arrived, Jack Billings had suffered sixty per cent burns. He spent three weeks in intensive care but never regained consciousness. Finally a decision was made to turn off the life-support machine.

The police investigated the matter and, although the death prompted questions, Jack was well known for being a heavy drinker and a heavy smoker, so it was eventually concluded to be a stupid, tragic accident. No one – aside from Icey's mother – ever suspected Icey. By all accounts, she had got on well with her mum's new partner; and at the time of his accident, she had been out with her best friend, Sam Bailey. Sam would swear to that fact on a stack of Bibles. Icey had been unable to assist the police with their enquiries. She'd remained mute until the investigation was closed.

Sam wondered what this jury would make of Icey's 'violent tendencies' if they'd known that she'd burnt Jack Billings to a crisp and smiled while she did it, even if she had cried in Sam's arms for hours afterwards.

But Icey had had very good reason for wanting Jack Billings dead. As far as Sam was aware, Icey had never even met Leticia Joy. And while Sam knew that when Icey was drinking heavily, she could get loud and obnoxious – and had got into the occasional fight as a result – she had never turned violent without good reason.

Sam also had a theory about why Icey drank. Icey might claim it was to forget the abuse she'd suffered at Jack's hands, but Sam suspected that the truth was she felt haunted by what she had done. Even if Jack Billings had deserved to die, Icey – raised a Catholic – on some level still regretted her actions.

That was one of the many reasons Sam was convinced in her heart that Icey couldn't have killed Leticia Joy, despite one of the biggest problems with her defence being that Icey simply couldn't remember anything that had happened on the night of Leticia Joy's murder.

From the moment Sam had dropped her at St Mary Magdalene's Church, to the moment she was arrested . . . nothing.

Chapter Five

The entrance to the Central Criminal Court was on the right of the building through a small brick arch. Every day for the last six weeks of the trial, Sam had made the same journey, arriving at the same time, to take up her position in the exact same seat as she waited for the day's proceedings to begin. She had sat patiently, willing the lawyers to ask questions that were obvious to her but apparently not to the professionals. She had held her breath when Icey lost her temper with the prosecution barrister; and now, for the first time, she had to admit that Icey was not the only one in the dock.

She was too.

While Icey had been physically remanded in custody, Sam had served the sentence. Sure, she had not been incarcerated behind bars, but she had served her own time.

Today was judgement day for both of them.

Outside the main entrance, hordes of people had gathered, milling around. Today, of all days, the entire tourist industry seemed to have formed a disorderly queue to get into the latest London attraction: Court Number One of the Old Bailey. There were at least fifty people ahead of Sam; most were Chinese, with a few Americans. They talked openly about the ladykiller as though she had already been convicted. Icey's case had attracted an enormous amount of publicity, and the press had followed each and every gory detail.

Sam pushed her way to the head of the queue. No one objected, but they all noticed and recognised the beautiful but anxious-looking black woman with unusual sea-green eyes, wearing striking gold stilettos. As she finally arrived at the front, the whispers from the crowd seemed unanimous in their view that Icey was guilty. Sam tried to ignore them but her irritation was obvious.

As she entered Court One, Sam was full of nervous energy. The jury had to find Icey not guilty. Her friend was capable of many things, but not murder. As Sam walked to her seat at the front of the public gallery, a terrible feeling of despair overcame her. It started in the pit of her stomach and rose up at the back of her throat. But there was nothing she could do except wait.

She unknotted the belt from around her waist and removed her coat. The courtroom felt colder than usual; she could feel goose pimples rising on her arms, despite the warmth of her black Chanel suit. Underneath it she wore a pink silk blouse. It was an outfit that made her look older than her young years, albeit that she looked smart, elegant and cultured. Irma, her former boss, had contacts in the fashion business and all of Irma's girls wore designer clothes, purchased for a fraction of the price. Sam still had a wardrobe full of expensive outfits she'd bought for a song.

As Sam composed her thoughts, her throat felt dry and constricted. It had crossed her mind not to wear black, given the significance of today, but she had put the suit on all the same. Her stepmother would have said she was dressed for a funeral, but a long time ago someone had told Sam that black was the colour of wisdom. Black had always been, for her, a lucky colour; and today she and Icey needed all the luck they could get.

Chapter Six

Unable to tune out the crowd, Sam finally gave up and opened her eyes, looking down into the well of the court where she spotted Mr Frizzel, Icey's solicitor. She knew now that it had been a mistake to use him, but both girls had felt they owed him a debt of gratitude for all of his help in the past. He had represented them both on their first and all subsequent court appearances. In fact, he'd been the duty solicitor when they first appeared at Camberwell Magistrates Court for a string of shoplifting charges in their teens.

Sam and Icey had been best mates ever since they met in their final year at St John's Primary School. As Sam had entered her new classroom for the first time, she'd noticed a small girl with ice-blonde hair. She was sitting at her desk and had made a rude gesture at Sam. Sam had pulled a rude face back, and instantly got into trouble. She was forced to make up with the girl who had started it. Her name was Elizabeth Johnson, but even then everyone called her Icey, because of her distinctive colouring.

After school, Icey challenged Sam to a fight, and won. Sam conceded defeat, but the following day at school she almost scalped Icey in the playground, using a technique she had seen her father perform on her stepmother countless times before he finally got sent down. After this incident, they were isolated from the rest of the children, though rather absurdly in the same room. They soon discovered that they had a lot in common: each had a father in prison, a mother – or, in Sam's case, a stepmother – on smack and on the game.

And both, although they didn't discover this at the time, were suffering horrific abuse in their own homes.

As a result of the not-quite-solitary confinement, they became friends and then, out of growing mutual respect, best mates. From that point onwards, they always looked out for each other.

By the age of thirteen, they had skanked up and down the length of East Street Market in South London. They had become professional weekend thieves, with Icey acting as lookout and Sam's nimble fingers lifting anything they thought they could flog to make a quick profit. Between them, they could easily turn around several hundred pounds a week in stolen goods. Their aim even back then was to save enough so that they could get a flat together, but after a couple of years their luck ran out and they were caught. Both girls were held in juvenile custody for a week. That was when they first met Mr Adrian Frizzel.

Even at that time he'd had a fat belly that overhung the waistline of his trousers, and a bad habit of dressing in ill-fitting suits and brown suede shoes. However, he was very friendly and had always treated the girls with respect. He turned out to have a clever way of pulling on the old judicial heart strings of District Judge Novo, explaining as best he could that Icey had gone off the rails because of the horrendous, tragic death of the man who to all intents and purposes was her stepfather. Little did Frizzel know that Icey herself had been the cause of that 'tragedy'.

Whatever Mr Frizzel said, though, had seemed to work. The judge had taken pity on both of them and ordered the girls to perform 240 hours' unpaid work with supervision for a period of twelve months. He'd warned them that if they committed any further offences, he would send them to a Young Offenders' Institution. Standing in the dock back then, a teenage Icey and Sam were glad to be free.

Chapter Seven

It had only been a matter of weeks before the two teenagers were up to their old tricks again. Twice a week they would visit Soho to skank. The area had an abundant, exotic mix of people: Chinese, West Indian, Latin Americans. Young fashion-conscious men completed deals in the pungent alleys, while always looking over their shoulders. Young girls in provocative dresses stood ominously close to the edge of the pavement as hope gradually ebbed away.

It was there that the girls met Ishia McGinty. She was standing on the corner of Brewer Street. She was not exactly pretty, but she was slim with striking features. There was something about her which made her stand out, and not just because of her burgundy-dyed hair and her preference for very short micro-skirts. On the day they'd first met her, Ishia's pale bare legs had stuck out like matchsticks beneath a mini-skirt as she perched precariously on top of five-inch, red peep-toe stilettos . She had been wearing a cream lace tank top and large clip-on flower earrings. Her heavy foundation didn't quite mask her bad skin, although her grey eyes were pretty and clear.

Ishia had spotted them before they'd spotted her. With fists raised in striking mode, she'd marched over to Sam and Icey and invited them in no uncertain terms to bugger off if they knew what was good for them. She'd worked long and hard to secure her patch, and she was not prepared to give it up to the pair of fresh, pretty newcomers. It took some persuasion before Ishia accepted that they were not a pair of toms looking for business.

Ishia spoke with a deep Liverpudlian accent. She was twenty-one, which made her seem terribly grown up and sophisticated to seventeen-year-old Icey. She said she was on the run, from what or whom she wouldn't say. She didn't give away a lot of information about herself, and Icey knew better than to ask. She knew only too well about secrets – she had enough of her own already.

Ishia disappeared just after nine o'clock that evening, and returned with a bottle of red wine and three plastic cups. Time passed as they supped the wine and Ishia – while telling them little about her past – relayed funny stories about life on the street, making fun of her punters. Although she'd tried hard to mask it by telling anecdote after anecdote about the stupid men she had to deal with, she'd clearly been on edge the whole time, looking around her constantly.

Before the girls had departed, arrangements were made to meet the next day . . . and then the next. The summer passed in a haze of wine and funny stories. A couple of nights a week, Sam and Icey would make the trek into Soho and meet up with Ishia. If she wasn't working, she would take an hour's break or two, heading off if business picked up, but always coming back to find the two younger girls when she wasn't turning tricks.

Then one Friday night when the girls arrived shortly after eight o'clock, eager to swap more stories with their new-found friend, Ishia wasn't there. The night was warm; a light breeze danced around the streets of Soho. As they stood at their usual meeting place, both were conscious of how many other young girls in short skirts and high heels were already plying their trade.

Icey slipped away and purchased a bottle of red wine. When she returned, Sam was engaged in conversation with a West

Indian man. She spoke to him through the open window of his beaming black Mercedes. He claimed that he was looking for his sister, called Ishia, which seemed unlikely given that Ishia was white and this man wasn't. Handing his card to Sam, he promised a reward for any information leading to his being reunited with his beloved sister.

As he drove off, Sam showed the card to Icey. There was no name on it, just a telephone number. Ishia might well have just been off somewhere with a client, but the girls both had a very bad feeling and sensed that Ishia was in danger. They talked to a few of the other working girls – and even a few of the men they'd recognised as regulars – but no one had seen her.

Sam also had a bad feeling about Icey. While she herself enjoyed the wine they usually had with Ishia, Sam could take it or leave it. But for Icey, it was becoming an everyday necessity rather than something to be shared and enjoyed. Icey constantly claimed not to care about what she had done to Jack Billings, but Sam knew better. Icey was a good girl at heart. Killing a man didn't rest easy on her conscience, even if that man had deserved to burn in hell for what he had done to her.

Hanging out in Soho Square on a warm summer evening, it hadn't seemed a good time to raise the matter. When the wine was gone, the two girls headed for home. They would return another night in the hope of catching up with Ishia.

As they'd crossed the road to catch the bus home, a smart black car approached and stopped suddenly in front of them. The driver exited the car, followed by a man and a woman climbing out of the rear of the car. Icey and Sam glanced in their direction but continued on their way. One of the men blocked their path by standing in front of them. The other removed a pair of handcuffs from his coat pocket.

Chapter Eight

Detective Constable Green grinned. He hated kerb crawlers. He hated the toms as much as he hated pervs. Tom-watching was really beneath a detective constable, but if things were slack he liked to take a couple of uniformed constables, WPC Elliott and PC Henslow, out on his own personal mission of zero tolerance.

'You're under arrest, the pair of you,' DC Green announced.

'What for?' said Icey.

'For soliciting.'

'When?' replied Icey. 'When were we soliciting?'

At a nod from the plain-clothes officer, young PC Henslow cuffed Icey's wrists together behind her back.

'We've been keeping observations on the toms in the area,' DC Green informed her as she was being restrained, 'and you two are becoming regulars. And we saw you tonight with a punter. Nice car, that Mercedes. What's the matter – didn't he fancy a threesome? Don't worry, darling, I'll make sure you get all the company you want back at the police station.'

'You've got a cheek, officer,' Icey declared hotly.

'Detective Constable, actually; and I have two, as a matter of fact. You can smack my cheeks any time, darling, but let's get you into a cell first.'

All three officers began to laugh and the WPC slapped cuffs on Sam.

'It's not that bad,' the older policeman continued. 'Just think of it as a day of rest.'

Sam didn't struggle as the handcuffs were fastened around her wrists. She was self-possessed, almost serene, and her composure slightly unnerved her arresting officer, the young WPC. Icey, however, was beginning to lose her temper and aggressively attempted to strut past the older detective constable.

'You don't have to say anything but anything that you do say will be taken down and may be used in evidence against you,' said PC Henslow, following drill.

'I would like an answer to my question,' Icey snapped, ignoring the young officer and addressing DC Green.

'What's that?'

'When?' said Icey. 'When were we soliciting?'

'As I've already told you, you've been observed on several occasions over recent weeks hanging around with known prostitutes, and tonight both of you have been observed approaching a number of cars.'

'We were trying to find our friend.'

'You've got a lot of friends. You're so lucky, and all of them male? If only I had the same luck with women. You must tell me your secret when we get to the station,' DC Green said, sarcastically.

They were driven to Soho Police Station and booked in by the custody sergeant, who reminded them of their legal right to contact a solicitor of their choice. Both independently requested Mr Frizzel. Before they were placed in separate cells, they were both searched. It was then that their real problems began, as both were in possession of stolen credit cards.

They were detained overnight and presented at the magistrates' court the following morning. Mr Frizzel came to see the girls in the cells beforehand. The matter of whether they had been soliciting was now irrelevant; evidence of their theft was stacked against them, and he advised them to plead guilty.

This time there was no sympathetic Judge Novo. They were up before a no-nonsense district judge, worn down by the countless criminals who had appeared before him over the last seventeen years. Mr Frizzel put up his usual good show, but the judge had heard it all before and didn't want to hear it again.

The judge had described them as ambitious, single-minded and short-sighted. A short, sharp shock was what was needed to bring this pair of professional thieves to their senses. He rejected Mr Frizzel's submission that they were really on a collision course with justice and needed help. So, at the ages of sixteen and seventeen respectively, Sam and Icey both received their first prison sentence together – six months' youth custody – which they served at a Young Offenders' Institution in Kent.

For three months, the girls shared a cell. During their time there, they only received one letter between them, addressed to Icey from her father, who was currently serving eight to ten in Wormwood Scrubs for armed robbery. It was short and not so sweet, reading simply: 'WELCOME TO THE FAMILY BUSINESS.' Icey handed the letter to Sam in disbelief.

After their release, they swore that they would never again do anything to make their fathers proud of them.

Shortly afterwards, Icey severed all ties with her family. Sam had lost contact with her own dad over the years, and with her stepmother through choice; and, although she'd wanted to re-establish contact with her sister, her letters to her were always returned unopened.

After leaving the YOI, the two girls spent several months in temporary accommodation – a shabby, five-storey hostel which served as a halfway house for newly released young prisoners. Sharing a room once again, they remained inseparable.

However, the opportunities for young, pretty, uneducated girls were not vast – especially those with a record. It was inevitable, almost, that, having tried their fathers' profession of thieving, Sam and Icey would then follow their mother and stepmother into the oldest profession of all. They had already been falsely accused of it, now they really were going on the game.

Neither had seriously wanted to – it was hardly a job young girls aspired to – and had it been a question of walking the streets, soliciting for punters, Sam doubted that either one of them would have considered it. But Sam had met Irma – in Battersea Park, of all places – and Irma, seeing a pretty girl down on her luck, made a more palatable suggestion of how Sam could make some easy money.

In truth, it wasn't easy, and Sam had needed wine more than Icey the first time she'd had sex for money. She had just turned seventeen and had had little positive sexual experience. But at least she was working at a brothel under Madam Irma's watchful motherly eye, with security on the door to weed out the more violent perverts, and a maid to look after her. While it could never be considered safe, at least it was safer than a Soho street corner.

Eventually Icey also started working for Irma, but a trial period catering for Madam Irma's more specialist clientele resulted in disaster. Icey proved too sadistic even for the most servile masochists. Clients complained, and Icey was retired from special duties for all but the most hard-core punters.

Even without 'added extras', Icey still proved as popular and in demand as Sam; but, given the differences in their appearance and temperaments, the girls appealed to different types of clients. Icey was as pale as Sam was dark. Icey would kick off at the slightest upset. Her actions belied her name.

Sam, on the other hand, was usually the cool one – ice cool. What you saw was what you got with Sam. And she never threatened; she only ever promised. She would kill you with her bare hands if she had to, but she'd make sure she did so without so much as chipping the polish on her fingernails.

The girls became very good at their jobs, but it was purely a means to an end for both of them. They planned to work hard and save well until they had enough money to quit. And at least they'd never walked the streets like Ishia and their own mother and stepmother.

Chapter Nine

There was a stirring of excitement in Court One. The usher had received a note from the jury. During the recess, Icey had been waiting in the bowels of the court. Now the security guard told her she was wanted upstairs. She was nervous and excited at the same time. Moments after she arrived back in court, the judge and lawyers took their seats.

The judge read out the note. The jury wanted to know why they had not heard in person from the man who claimed to have seen the defendant at the door of the church with blood on her. Where was the witness who had called the police? They wanted to know.

'Members of the jury, the witness Mr Sexton was not called because he was too ill to attend. His statement has been read. In it, let me remind you, he said he was passing St Mary Magdalene's and saw Miss Johnson come to the west door of the church. He had been at school with her and recognised her. He stated that he thought she had blood on her face. He saw her go back into the church, and he called the police. That is the full extent of his evidence. Please continue with your deliberations and let me know when you have reached a unanimous verdict.'

The jury were led out of court to their private room. Icey was taken back down to the cells. Sam remained seated, motionless, in the public gallery, pondering the event. At the sound of coarse laughter, she scanned the faces around her and spotted an all too familiar figure wearing red lipstick and a fake leopard skin coat. Their eyes met and Sam willed herself not to be the first to look away. For long moments they held eye contact, unspoken messages flashing between them.

Eventually she turned away, forcing herself to concentrate on watching Icey go back down the stairs towards the cells. A feeling of despair clawed at her. All she and her friend had ever wanted to do was find some way of leaving their former lives behind them; but there were reminders, like this unspeakable woman, everywhere. All their plans were coming to nothing; it seemed they could never be free of the past.

It was a past that made Sam's skin crawl, and she wanted out. All her life Sam had been a loner, plagued by insecurity and self-doubt. She wanted to be loved, but she had come to believe she was unlovable. She wanted to be normal but didn't know how. Her 'uncle Pete's' idea of love she had tried to forget. She wanted to be nice, but she was born wicked. That is what her stepmother had told her and, as a child, she had believed it to be true.

Sam had found it hard to have normal relationships with men, even to make friends. Icey was the closest friend she had, and without her by her side Sam felt more alone than ever.

The only man Sam had ever loved had called her Duvet. At first in affection because of her habit of taking up so much space in bed, but later because that's what he claimed she was: warm and inviting on the outside, but hollow on the inside, too damaged to have a meaningful relationship. He had called her a tart and claimed he'd done her a favour when he picked her up and fucked her that first time. Their last time together, he'd thrown money on the floor, instructing her to pick it up.

'You're nothing but a dirty little whore.' Previously he'd

always sworn that he didn't care how she made her living. He knew she was working to quit, and that was enough for him; but it soon became clear that he wasn't as secure in their relationship as he claimed. She should have realised that was the case. After all, theirs had been a relationship conducted largely in secret since they'd first met in a bar. Sam had been looking for Icey, whom she hadn't seen for a few days. Instead she'd found a tall, darkly handsome older man who'd made her forget her own rules about getting seriously involved.

She'd been honest from the start about her working life, but she'd been shocked to discover what he did for a living – they were at opposite ends of the law. He was also much older than her, a fact that bothered him more than Sam (although Sam had read enough women's magazines and seen enough trashy TV to know that some would say she was looking for a father figure). Whatever their differences, the relationship had worked for a while, even if Sam never met any of his work colleagues or family. She in turn had never tried to introduce him to Icey, sensing neither would approve of the other.

After a few hot and heavy months, an argument about nothing had blown up out of all proportion. He called her a tart, so she presented him with a bill for services rendered. She had never seen him so angry and, while she had immediately regretted her actions, it was too late. He walked out, never to return, and her love life had been a complete no-man's-land since. She'd always joked with Icey over the years that it was a pity neither of them were gay as it would have been an ideal solution relationshipwise. She never tired of spending time with her best friend. But neither of them was hardwired that way. Sam still liked men and wanted a relationship, whereas Icey was only prepared to see men on a cash-only basis.

*

So many men; so few who had given them anything but pain and trouble. Now Sam watched as another man in their lives, Harry Kemp, limped into court and whispered something to Frizzel.

Dear old Harry. It was he who had first suggested they open, of all things, a detective agency. Sam and Icey had been saving like crazy and making all sorts of plans for when they could go straight. They'd started thinking of setting up in business together – a legit business this time – and had started throwing around ideas of what the business should be. When Harry first suggested they become private investigators, Icey had fallen into fits of laughter. It was a ridiculous idea. They had no training. What did they know about detective work? And who was ever going to hire a pair of ex-toms as investigators?

It was Harry who convinced them both that they were ideal for the job. Having been their probation officer during their wayward teenage years, he knew them very well and was remarkably persuasive about why it was the perfect business for them. Apart from possessing an invaluable degree of female intuition, he told them, from their personal backgrounds they knew exactly what the world was about. If they encountered any hiccups, he could give all the advice they needed, he'd added, and no one would ever suspect they weren't experienced detectives.

Sam and Icey had first been assigned to Harry after being released from the Young Offenders' Institution. At first, his relationship with them was just routine. He knew all about criminals. In his previous life as a police detective, he had hounded tarts like there was no tomorrow. But age had mellowed him, and his own background wasn't so very different from that of his new 'clients', as they were called.

Harry Kemp was born on the back streets of Peckham, the

only child of a whore. He was taken into care when Social Services slapped a Child Protection Order on his mother. He knew very little about his past – only what he'd read about in his own file. From the age of two, he had been cared for by foster parents. His birth mother had died when he was nine, of a drug overdose, which he found out later was probably administered by her pimp – Harry's father. He'd never met the man – rumours were that he'd gone underground. He was certainly never seen in the area again. Despite everything, Harry gained a place at a good grammar school in Camberwell, and left with three A levels, which allowed him to join the police force. Pimps, prostitutes and drug dealers became his speciality.

His time as a beat officer didn't last long. With his qualifications, he moved up the career ladder until he became a detective inspector. At the age of twenty-eight, he was assigned to the newly formed murder squad at Trident and remained there for the next eight years. That was before he took very early retirement, on the grounds of ill health.

Harry took a bullet, which shattered his kneecap. It took the best part of three years for him to recover enough to walk without a stick, but the limp was permanent. The thought of a desk job in the police force didn't thrill him. He wasn't yet forty but he was done with the job – or, more accurately, the job was done with him. Harry allowed himself to be pensioned off.

Since then he'd resigned himself to serving a life sentence. He was good for absolutely nothing apart from giving advice, so he requalified as a probation officer, supervising offenders released into the community on probation. He also started studying part-time for a degree in criminology and psychology at the South Bank University.

As a probation officer, his job was to supervise newly released cons and to enforce the terms of their order. He was required to maintain contact with his clients through office, home and field visits. He was also required to perform drug tests, motivate them to attend counselling, write court reports and testify in court on occasion. He hadn't expected it but Harry found that he was good at his new career, and it gave him a reason to get up in the morning.

When he was assigned to Elizabeth Johnson and Sam Bailey, he'd had mixed feelings. They were very young but, he suspected, already hardened by their experiences. Yet, in spite of his preconceptions, he found himself liking them. They were clever, funny and Harry genuinely enjoyed their company.

As the compulsory probation period came to an end, they had asked it they could keep in contact with him. Harry had been delighted. Even before his knee was shattered, he had never thought of himself as that attractive to women. He wasn't conventionally good-looking. The best that could be said about his face was that it looked lived in. He'd never married – never come close, in fact. He was an intensely private man and now, with his limp, he doubted himself even more when it came to the opposite sex. His only joys were vintage cars (which he couldn't afford) and classical music.

He had been disappointed but not surprised when the girls had started working for Irma. He worried about them, especially Sam, for whom he'd developed a real soft spot over the years. She seemed to regard him more as a mentor, a father figure, whereas if forced Harry would have had to admit that the feelings he had for Sam in return weren't always that paternal these days.

Sam had leapt at Harry's suggestion that they should become detectives. Secretly, she'd always wanted to be a private investigator. As a child, she had read every available book about Nancy Drew, a fictional eighteen-year-old amateur detective.

Even now, she devoured crime novels by the score and loved nothing more than spending a quiet evening watching police dramas, or sitting in a cosy pub with Harry regaling her with stories of his days as a copper. Eventually Sam's enthusiasm had worn Icey down, and she'd agreed to enter the partnership.

The irony was that it was only when they tried to go straight that they got into real trouble.

The night of Leticia Joy's murder, Icey had been visiting God's house to ask for forgiveness. She'd told Sam she wanted to start their new life with a clean slate. But no one really knew what had happened after that, not even Icey, who had suffered severe memory loss and only remembered fragmented snippets of the night in question.

But Sam believed the police had never bothered looking for the truth. Icey was too easy a suspect to pin down. Now Sam felt that God could take his forgiveness and stick it where the Christians go blind.

She had been left to start Fleet Investigations by herself. Though the name had been one of the last things they decided on together. They had liked the way it sounded, but it was also an in-joke, a nod to their time on the street where being nimble and fleet of foot kept them one step ahead of the police. It also gave a sense of two people coming together to work as one and here she was on her own; and the first seven months had passed with her partner in crime facing a possible life sentence for a murder she couldn't even remember committing. They had yet to take on their first case, and Sam couldn't wait to have Icey home so they could start looking for business. Just like the old days.

Only this time, they'd be on the right side of the law.

Chapter Ten

After what seemed like an eternity, the usher silenced the courtroom and instructed: 'Be upstanding in court.'

Sam opened her eyes. The courtroom was now packed and a low hush of expectation descended and stilled the cool air. Sam struggled to her feet with the rest of the crowd. Even the barristers stood to attention as Judge Certie strolled into court and took his place on the bench. No one spoke as the jangle of keys unlocked doors to the cells beneath the court.

Icey was brought up into the dock again. Sam tried to attract her attention with a tentative wave but Icey looked dazed, her pale blue eyes glazed over as she focused on the judge alone. She looked tired and as anxious as Sam felt. Her usually shiny ash blonde hair was flat, greasy and clumsily scraped off her face.

Dressed in prison runners and a grey top, she also seemed to have dropped at least a stone since her arrest, which was about a stone more than someone as slight as Icey could afford to lose. Sam noticed that her face was drawn, and when she looked closer still, she saw that Icey was shaking slightly.

The jury filed in, and not once did they look at the dock. There were eight men and four women; three blacks, one Asian and the remainder white.

Sam looked for any sign of their conclusion, but there was not a flicker of emotion from them. They looked straight ahead –

not a glance at Icey – and Sam could hear her heart pounding as though it was trying to tear through her chest.

'I will take the verdict,' said the judge. Peering over his spectacles, he blinked rapidly as he absent-mindedly stroked his bushy eyebrows into an orderly manner. The clerk of the court rose.

'Would the foreman of the jury please stand.'

In the front row, a compact man with a stoop rose to his feet. He was in his late-to mid-fifties with thinning hair, dressed in a white shirt, green pullover and dark grey suit. In his hand, he held a piece of paper. Staring at the judge, he nervously buttoned up his jacket as he waited for further instructions.

The clerk of the court stood up. 'Members of the jury, have you reached a verdict on which you are all agreed?'

'We have,' the foreman replied.

'Do you find the defendant guilty or not guilty?' the clerk asked.

Icey finally met Sam's gaze as they both held their breath, and waited.

The judge picked up his pen and dipped it into his inkwell. In this – as in most things – he was a stickler for tradition, and would no more sign his name with a common or garden biro than he would pour milk before tea into his cup. Pressing the nib gently onto the blotting paper, he looked up at the foreman. He was now ready.

The foreman looked momentarily confused as he glanced at his fellow jurors. They nodded their approval and returned their gaze to the judge, who was waiting patiently for the verdict. Taking a swift gulp of air, the foreman at last replied, 'We find the defendant guilty.'

Chapter Eleven

Icey swayed as the verdict reached her ears. The female security guard leant forward and pressed a warning hand into the small of her back. Icey's legs buckled against the dock. Sam stared at the foreman and shook her head in disbelief. Icey looked deathly pale. The public gallery was a flutter of excitement as the tourists murmured their agreement with the foreman.

'Silence in court,' said the judge as he turned again to the foreman. 'And that is the verdict of you all?'

'It is,' the foreman replied, looking at the paper in his hand. 'It is the verdict of us all.'

Sam stared at Icey in complete disbelief, her mouth falling open in shock.

Then she turned to glare at the jury. Twelve complete fools. Ever since the trial had started, she'd spent a great deal of time watching their every move. The prosecution had pretty much savaged Sam during her own testimony, undermining her credibility because of her colourful past, and the jury had seemed to relish her discomfort. She hadn't been able to offer anything helpful about the night of the murder, as she'd simply dropped Icey off at the church. But she'd hoped at the very least to provide a strong character witness for her friend, emphasising the progress she'd made in her life; but clearly these people had made up their minds about both of them, and dismissed every shred of positivity Sam had offered.

During the proceedings, some members of the jury had returned Sam's scrutiny, even holding eye contact with her; now they were all seemingly preoccupied. Not one of them was prepared to look her in the eye. Sam was boiling over with rage and watched powerlessly as Icey too looked at the group of twelve people who had determined her fate, and then back at the judge, and finally towards the public gallery in similar disbelief.

'You . . . what?' said Icey in a loud voice. 'Guilty of what, you dick head?'

The judge was quick to respond. 'Madam, you will behave and if you cannot I will have you removed.'

'Go on, then, remove me. Better still, I'll remove myself!' Moving towards the front of the dock, Icey found the lock and pressed the release catch. The security guard pulled her hand away as Icey's barrister, Mr Percival, hurriedly made his way across to his client.

'Take your hands off me!' shouted Icey as she glared at the guard, who swiftly released her grip, hoping to defuse the situation.

'Icey,' said Percival calmly. 'I know this is a shock but you have to behave, otherwise the judge will have you removed.'

'Sod off.'

'Icey,' said Mr Percival more firmly, 'we can always appeal later, but you are not helping yourself here.'

'Not . . . helping . . . myself,' Icey enunciated precisely. 'Do you call getting me sent down, helping me, you tosser!'

'Mr Percival,' said the judge 'can you please have a word with your client, or I really will have no choice but to remove her.'

Sam watched in horrified silence as Icey exploded.

Judge Certie calmly banged his gavel, ignoring the clamouring press, who were having a field day with the defendant's dramatics and scribbling furiously in their note-books. The jury sat awaiting further instructions as prosecuting counsel Mr Alfred Roma buried his head in his hands.

'I appreciate that you may be under a great deal of stress,' the judge said, addressing Icey gravely when the court was finally brought to order, 'but you will kindly control yourself in my courtroom or I will have you removed and sentence you in absentia.'

Icey glared back at the judge but remained silent as he continued, 'You have been found guilty of the murder of Leticia Joy. You pleaded "not guilty", so you will get no discount for an early plea. You slaughtered a woman whose only crime was that she was in the wrong place at the wrong time. You have shown absolutely not one ounce of remorse since your arrest. Mr Percival?'

'My lord,' Icey's barrister responded formally.

'I don't think there is any need for a presentence report in this case. As you know, the purpose of such a report is to assist the court with the appropriate sentence, but there is only one possible sentence for a crime of this nature, and that is a life sentence. I know more than I need to about your client. I am, however, troubled by the fact that, on the night of the murder, your client by her own admission as well as confirmed by the police reports had consumed a large amount of alcohol.'

'My lord,' Mr Percival repeated deferentially, standing up and rubbing his round sweaty face with his bulbous fingers, 'I hasten to reassure that is a thing of the past. My client has had prior problems with alcohol but is seeking help for her addiction. She is also admirably attempting to start a new life for herself, and is now a partner in a new business venture, Fleet Investigations, a private investigation service.'

During her testimony, Sam had talked about Icey's changed

behaviour, but she hadn't gone into detail about their future plans for the agency, and some of the jury looked startled by the announcement that Icey was to turn detective. A middle-aged lady whispered to the man next to her. Sam glared at her in frustration and, once again, doubted the intelligence of the jury members. What was their problem? It made perfect sense for an ex-tom to be an investigator. As Harry had always said to them, they knew what made the world work. They knew what it was like to live in hope and die in expectation; and, given the chance – and with Harry's help – they would both make good investigators.

'Well, she won't be able to do that for a very long time,' said the judge. 'A very long time,' he repeated as his furrowed brow creased into an even deeper groove. Icey stood motionless.

'My lord, my client maintains her innocence. She intends to appeal her conviction.'

'Have you advised her about this? She has been convicted on overwhelming evidence.'

'I have, my lord,' Percival squeaked in response.

'I'm sure there is no need for me to remind you that she was found with the murder weapon in her hand, and the dead woman's blood all over her,' roared the judge.

'My lord, I appreciate all of that, but my client has consistently maintained her denial.'

'All she has said is that she had no recollection of what happened!' the judge interjected. 'It seems to me that this was a particularly brutal murder committed on a random victim. The sentence must reflect that.'

Defeated, Percival sat heavily in his seat and the judge invited Icey to listen. She brushed her fringe away from her eyes as she looked over at Sam. A faint hint of a familiar cool smile crossed her lips, and Sam knew that, whatever was about to happen, Icey was ready.

'Miss Elizabeth Johnson.' The judge's voice boomed as he addressed the court. 'The jury has convicted you on the clearest possible evidence of the cruel murder of Leticia Joy. She was a beautiful and intelligent young woman with her whole life ahead of her. She was about to get married. You chose to slaughter her in the very church where she was to be wed.

'You claimed that you were in the church to confess your sins, yet on your own admission, this was the first time you had chosen to attend confession in some years. I believe that, for some reason you have not shared with us – be it jealousy or some perceived slight on your person, or purely because you were the worse for drink – you followed that young woman into the church to murder her. What is worse, from the forensic reports it's clear that you toyed with her before you finally dispatched her.

'This was a sadistic murder. One can hardly imagine the stress her parents have had to endure in this courtroom, hearing how their beloved daughter met such a cruel death. There is only one sentence I can pass by law, and that is life imprisonment. I am, however, also required by law to fix a minimum period before which you cannot apply for parole. The starting point in this case must be thirty years. And that is the period I fix. Take her down.'

Icey had remained calm, apparently unmoved throughout the judge's remarks. As she turned to go down to the cells, though, she turned and addressed the court.

'My lord, ladies and gentlemen of the jury, I'm innocent and you can all sod off!'

And with that, she walked defiantly down the stairs to the cells to start her life sentence.

As the court emptied, Sam sat rooted to her seat, but she was not alone. Mrs Barbara Johnson, Icey's mother, had attended her daughter's trial every day and had followed the proceedings keenly. She'd sat in the front row, pressed up against the barriers of the public gallery, becoming an all too familiar sight in her fake leopard skin coat, brassy clothes, blood-red lipstick and bouffant hair. Shifting anxiously in her seat, she no doubt gave the appearance of an overanxious mother, but Sam knew her better. Babs had come for her own sort of justice.

Mrs Johnson had a thousand regrets about her daughter, but chief among them was the fact that she hadn't ended Icey's life when she'd ample opportunity to do so. She heard the judge say 'thirty years', and the anger that had been burning inside her for years simply exploded. As far as she was concerned, Icey had taken from her the only man she'd ever loved, not just once but twice. First, she had stolen Jack's attention by being younger and prettier than Babs could ever hope to be again. Then she had cruelly arranged his death. Babs had never believed the police verdict on Jack Billings' death. As far as she was concerned, her daughter Icey was as guilty as sin. She'd got away with murder once but now she was getting everything she deserved and more.

Standing up in the public gallery, Mrs Johnson began a slow hand-clap.

'Thirty years and not a day too long!' she shouted. 'I hope you rot in prison. It's not your first time, is it, you murdering bitch? Why don't you tell the jury about Jack Billings?'

Riled up already by Icey's outburst, two burly security men wasted no time in taking hold of Mrs Johnson and threatening her with arrest for contempt of court. She fell silent instantly, but still found herself ejected from the court building.

Sam waited for ten minutes before leaving the court herself, but as she walked down Fleet Street, it was with a heavy heart. The only person she still cared about was banged up for life for a crime that had been proved beyond reasonable doubt she had committed.

Chapter Twelve

Judge Certie felt every one of his sixty years as he walked back to his private chambers. He closed the door behind him and, as he crossed the room, he threw his wig at the desk in the corner. It landed on a copy of the 'Sentencing Guidelines'. Casting a passing glance at himself in the dusty mirror that had hung on the wall for the past nine years, he looked closer to seventy than sixty. The wrinkles around his eyes had long since started to join up with the wrinkles around his mouth. He looked like a giant wrinkle. He looked like what he was – a grumpy, grey old man. Sighing, he removed his gown and placed it in his small suitcase. Then he retrieved his wig and placed it on top. He was still deep in thought when the landline phone rang.

'Certie speaking.'

'My lord, I believe it's your wife. She says it's urgent.'

It was very unusual for Margaret to bother him during the day. 'Did she say what it was about?'

'No – just that it's urgent.'

'All right, I'll take the call.'

Replacing the receiver, he waited for the call to be transferred. On the third ring, he picked up the phone. The voice he heard chilled him to the bone and he hung up immediately. When it rang again, he ignored it; but a second later, his mobile phone rang and, reluctantly, the judge answered it.

'I told you not to call me here,' he said at last. A short, blunt request followed.

'And if I don't agree, what then?'

He waited for a reply, but there was silence, just the sound of breathing. Judge Certie visibly paled. Nausea washed over him like a putrid smell. As he put his mobile down abruptly, he was overcome with emotion. His case was packed. He snapped it shut but his hands were shaking. He caught sight once again of his reflection in the mirror. What little colour he'd had was gone; he looked lifeless, which was apt. His life was already over.

He picked up his case and closed the door on the way out. Turning left, he exited via the emergency doors. Using his security pass, he moved through the second set of doors, his progress picked up by the CCTV cameras, which lined the hallways of the court. Making his way to the top of the stairs, he turned right and then right again, finally making his way up to the roof of the building.

The fresh February air was cold against his face as he looked up to see her above him. The only lady he had ever really cared for was staring down at him. He'd had enough. Stepping through the trap door, he made his way to the feet of the golden statue of Lady Justice; and, looking up, he discovered that for all of his legal life he had made a terrible mistake. She was not blindfolded.

He had always assumed that justice could never be swayed by bias and prejudice, when in fact he was quite wrong. In a way, though, the sudden knowledge made him feel more certain of the task in hand. He took his robes and wig out of his bag and donned them. He looked one more time at the woman he had admired for so long, stepping back briefly to do so. Then he wrapped his gown around him and made his way once more to the edge of the roof. With his arms outstretched, he closed his eyes, and jumped.

Chapter Thirteen

Icey made it to the bottom of the stairs and then collapsed. She was dying for a drink. Following the red wine of her teenage years, vodka had become her tipple of choice. But at the moment she'd settle for either. All she could hear were the words 'thirty years' echoing in her head. She couldn't be in prison for three decades. She knew she would be dead long before she completed the sentence the judge had just dished out. Or would want to be.

Her body began to shake as the reality of the sentence hit home. Her life had always been tough, but she'd survived before, and with Sam by her side she had always believed she could do anything. But now all her plans and dreams were on hold, if not completely destroyed.

It took a while before she was back in her cell. First, she was allowed a conference meeting with her solicitor. Mr Frizzel fussed nervously with his papers as he entered the basement conference room. He had not expected the sentencing to take that long. He too was dying for a drink, and he'd already discreetly emptied his hidden hip flask. It was just after midday and Icey could smell whisky on his breath. There were days when she was sure he had the shakes, but then it probably took one alcoholic to recognise another.

'I'm going to be in prison for the rest of my days.'

Mr Frizzel patted her arm distractedly and replied, 'Difficult times, dear girl, difficult times. Keep your nerve. Percival says we must appeal.'

'Percival can keep his advice to himself! He told me that the jury wouldn't convict on the evidence. He said it was all circumstantial! But you heard what the judge said: "over-whelming evidence". No one told me the case against me was watertight! And I still can't remember what happened. But I know I didn't kill that girl. Why would I?'

'Dear girl, we have every faith in your innocence. We must keep our nerve,' Mr Frizzel repeated with a cough, and a new cloud of alcohol fumes enveloped Icey. 'This is plainly a miscarriage of justice. I want you to wrack your brains to see if there is anything else that might throw light on what happened. What we really need is some fresh evidence which will cast doubt on the jury's verdict. I'm going straight back to my office and will talk to Sam.'

Icey nodded slowly, and watched Mr Frizzel as he moved his papers around the table. Half of them were covered by doodles and the other half seemed to be from a different case entirely. She couldn't help but wonder if employing Percival – and Frizzel in particular – had been a good idea. Once upon a time he'd helped them, but not this time. She still wasn't entirely sure what they each did, but whatever it was, it had failed.

She was now a convicted murderer. A feeling of dread sat heavily in her stomach.

Chapter Fourteen

This was not the first time Sam Bailey had been disappointed by the verdict of a jury. Her first visit to court wasn't during her teenage encounters with the law; the first time she'd set foot inside a courtroom was actually at the age of five.

She was her father's only natural child. She didn't remember her prostitute mother, who, according to her dad, had done a runner with one of her clients when Sam had been little more than a baby. He'd married again when Sam was two, and Sam gained both a stepmother and a stepsister, who was three years older than her. While her father made a token effort at first with Molly, there was never any doubt that Sam remained her father's favourite daughter.

There were times when his treatment of his new stepdaughter was all too obviously harsh. When he was around, he showered Sam with presents – pretty dresses and toys, as well as hugs and kisses. Molly didn't get anything like the same attention.

It was hardly surprising, then, that her stepmother took against her from the start. The second Mrs Bailey, Violet, had a ferocious temper not helped by her many addictions. In time, Sam only had to walk into the same room as her new mother and she would develop an instant nervous rash. As Sam grew older, she realised that nothing she could do would change the way her stepmother felt about her. So they held each other in mutual contempt. Sam had her father's love and her stepmother's hatred. This obviously affected the relationship between her parents. There were constant rows and her father's own temper often erupted into violence. He called it 'having a domestic'. The police called it battery. When he was eventually sent to prison, Sam suffered her first broken heart.

She constantly asked the only mummy she had ever known exactly when her beloved dad was coming back. One particular day, she wouldn't let it rest but kept asking the same question over and over.

'Mummy, Mummy, when will he be home?'

But Mummy ignored her. The very sound of Sam's voice maddened Violet. Refusing to answer her stepdaughter, she simply turned her face in Sam's direction and glared at her.

With tears in her eyes, Sam spoke again quietly to her stepmother. 'I want my daddy.'

Violet didn't speak or appear to register Sam's presence until she raised her right hand above her head, slicing through the air to catch the left side of Sam's face. The blow forced her backward and Sam's cheek burnt with pain.

'So you miss your father? Well, I can promise you that after tomorrow you will never feel that way. Now clear off before I really lose my temper.'

Sam left the room swiftly as her stepmother turned away from her to rest her head on her duck down pillow. For the rest of the evening, Sam kept out of her way.

The following day Sam was cosy in bed without a single desire to get up when Molly popped her head round the door.

'Mum said you have to be up and dressed,' she said matter-of-factly.

It was early morning and there was nothing in her tone to indicate that speed was of the essence. Forty-seven minutes later and Sam was still in bed when she turned over and found herself unable to breathe following a blow to her upper ribcage by her stepmother. Sam caught her breath as Violet Bailey stood over her.

'I'm not going to tell you again,' she said as she walked out of the room.

Sam didn't need a second reminder. She was up and dressed and waiting for her stepmother in the sitting room. In silence they travelled to Hither Green by bus and then tube. They walked for twenty minutes away from the station until eventually her stepmother turned off and led her up a long gravel drive. Then she spoke for the first time since leaving the house.

'You're going to stay with Uncle Pete for a few days. I want you to be a good girl until I come back for you.'

'Come back – come back from where?' Sam had asked as the door opened and 'Uncle Pete' appeared. 'I don't have an uncle called Pete,' she added, bewildered.

'Well, you do now,' her stepmother told her.

Three vicious Rottweiler-type dogs were barking and pulling on their leads as Uncle Pete tried to control them. They were large dogs with a substantial build. Their powerful jaws snapped at Sam. She was scared and tried to run, but her stepmother held her firm and pulled her into the house. The front door closed abruptly behind them. Sam heard the crack of the whip and the yelp of the dogs as they were beaten back out of the dingy hallway into a back room. She remembered hearing a door slam somewhere before Uncle Pete reappeared.

Sam had never seen him before in her entire life. She felt sure he wasn't her uncle – at least, she knew he wasn't her father's brother. He was tall, much taller even than her beloved dad, who was six foot. Pete was wearing a string vest and stained jeans. Sam didn't like the look of him at all. When he smiled, he frightened her. Some of his upper teeth were missing and the rest were badly chipped and stained. Uncle Pete held his arms wide open. 'Who's a pretty little girl?' he said, as he brushed his hand through her hair. Sam stepped back towards her stepmother, who pushed her forward.

'Say hello to Uncle Pete. He's a friend of your dad's and he's going to take real good care of you this weekend.'

Sam looked beyond 'Uncle Pete'. She could hear the dogs were scratching at a door. They were in an agitated state.

'Take no notice of them,' Pete said, taking her by the hand. 'They're just a bit overprotective and suspicious of strangers. They'll settle down.'

She was steered into a living room. Her stepmother followed behind. It was shabby and dark; the furniture sparse. Walking over to the mantelpiece, Pete picked up an envelope, which he handed to her stepmother. Sam could see it was packed with money. Much later she would realise that it was the first time someone had paid for her. And little girls did not come cheap. Her stepmother always said she was a very expensive little girl.

'Be good for Uncle Pete. I'll be back on Sunday.' That was all Violet said before she turned around and walked out.

Her visits to Uncle Pete became regular after that. At first Sam was glad. She looked forward to seeing her uncle Pete. It was a time when she could escape from her stepmother's drug-addled, critical gaze, from the thrashings and the cold baths. Uncle Pete seemed very nice. He was not married and seemed to have endless patience with her.

The three young Rottweiler dogs – Tilly, Millie and Pansy – were his pride and joy, and although they grew used to her, they still barked and growled. And even when they didn't, Sam was still fearful of them. They were very aggressive dogs. Uncle Pete banned them from wandering through the house. They had to be on a lead at all times, and Uncle Pete had to be present wherever they were.

Sam was under strict orders not to let them out of their room and never to play with them. They were guard dogs not pets and very dangerous. Pansy, Millie and Tilly's favourite food was duck pâté. Uncle Pete fed them on the stuff when they were puppies. As they grew up, he continued to treat them on special occasions – or when they were poorly – to a large helping of the gourmet dish.

On one occasion Sam helped Uncle Pete to feed the dogs. Millie ate her pâté and then savaged Tilly for hers. Uncle Pete had to separate the dogs with a large stick. When Tilly was eventually rescued, she had a large wound to her throat that required stitching. There were several occasions when the three dogs fought and drew blood.

Unlike her stepmother, Uncle Pete was kind and gentle. Sam – starved for affection at home – was guaranteed lots of hugs and kisses and more hugs. Uncle Pete made Sam feel special. She was his favourite little sweetheart. Sam wasn't to know exactly what that meant to him.

The first time Uncle Pete popped into her bedroom to kiss her goodnight, she was so happy.

'Come here and give Uncle Pete a kiss,' he said in his deep voice.

Sam threw herself at him. He was so wonderful and kind – not at all like her stepmother.

'Uncle Pete, I love you lots and lots.'

'And I love you, too, and do you know what?'

'What, Uncle Pete?

'You're my favourite little sweetheart. There will always be a place in my heart for you. And do you know what else?'

'What, Uncle Pete?'

'Come here and give Uncle Pete a kiss,' he said again, playfully.

Sam put her arms around his neck. He scooped her up in his arms and pressed her body close to his. For a little girl still missing her daddy, it was the best feeling in the world.

Several weeks later, Uncle Pete surprised her. He bought her a beautiful pale blue cardigan. He went to the trouble of having it gift-wrapped with layers of cerise tissue, tied with a beautiful deep blue ribbon. It was waiting for her in her bedroom. Sam was so excited when she carefully unwrapped yet another present from Uncle Pete.

'Don't tell that stepmother of yours. It has to be our secret.'

'I won't, Uncle Pete. I will never tell.'

Sam loved having secrets from her stepmother. Uncle Pete couldn't do enough for her. When he discovered that Sam was afraid of the dark, he took immediate action. He brought an extra pillow into her room and tucked himself up in her bed.

'Don't you worry about me. I'll just wait here until you're asleep and then I'll go into my bedroom.' He was so thoughtful.

'Uncle Pete, you don't have to stay,' Sam would protest, encouraging Uncle Pete to go to his own room; but he wanted to look after her. She was so lucky. Once or twice Sam discovered Uncle Pete still in her bed the following morning. It was so funny. Sam always laughed as she woke him up.

'Uncle Pete, what are you doing in my bed?'

Rubbing his eyes, Uncle Pete would look around him and then jump up out of bed, all surprised.

'Oh no. I fell asleep. Sorry. It won't happen again. Don't tell that stepmother of yours.'

'I won't, Uncle Pete. I'll never tell.'

It took a while before Sam realised that Uncle Pete had moved permanently into her bedroom and into her bed. It was shortly after this that he started touching her. She told him not to, but he continued anyway. When Sam complained about Uncle Pete's behaviour to Violet, her stepmother slapped her face and, dragging her to the kitchen sink, washed her mouth out with soap and called her a vindictive liar.

'Repeat after me, "I am a dirty little liar." What are you?' said her stepmother.

'I am a liar,' Sam said.

Her stepmother then grabbed a wooden spoon from the draining board and hit Sam across the head with it.

'I am a dirty little liar,' Sam managed between blows.

'There you go, that wasn't too bad. If Uncle Pete wants to show you affection, it's no different to the cuddles and kisses you were happy to share with Dad. You're just a selfish bitch,' her stepmother said. She kept her off school until the bruises disappeared. After that, Sam was a very good girl. She never complained to her stepmother again, and she kept her uncle Pete's little secret.

Eventually Pete was caught with images of young children on his computer. Social Services and the police were involved. They eventually interviewed Sam and, after much coaxing, she finally told her story to a sympathetic social worker. Pete was prosecuted. Sam gave her evidence and was called a liar by everyone she knew. Her stepmother took the stand to say that her stepdaughter was a habitual liar. Pete blamed a housemate for the images. He was acquitted. Sam's trust in the police, in social workers and in courts and justice, vanished instantly.

And now Icey's verdict had just cemented all of her fears.

Chapter Fifteen

Sam continued walking up Fleet Street and then turned into a narrow alleyway called Deveraux Court. It was named after the Earl of Essex whose house was in nearby Essex Street. Next to Server Chambers was a small door, which bore the gold letters FLEET INVESTIGATIONS. Tonight should have been the official opening. But now there would be no celebration; not until Icey was free.

Above the gold lettering was another title – A.R. FRIZZEL, SOLICITOR OF THE SUPREME COURT. They had rented half of Mr Frizzel's office space ten months ago. He was a sole practitioner who had fallen on hard times. Sam had entrusted Icey's case to him primarily because of his past record in helping them, but also because he was already their office neighbour, which made things handy. In any case, there hadn't exactly been a host of solicitors beating a path to their door to defend an ex-tom for murder. Sam was aware that Frizzel had an alcohol problem, but he had always served them well in court before.

Now Icey was serving life and there was only one person to blame.

Sam.

Sam believed that she herself was completely responsible. Icey had trusted her to get the best lawyer available, and Sam had instructed a washed-up old drunk. It was Frizzel who had suggested Percival for their QC, and he had proved equally useless. The depth of Sam's surprise and upset at the verdict was really a reflection of the extent to which she believed she'd failed her only true friend. She felt a tear run down her face and brushed it way. Life was too short for tears, and she had work to do until Icey was free. Only then would she rest in peace.

She opened the door of their office and switched on the light. The room was painted ash grey; the desktop was burgundy leather and there were two matching chairs. They had installed soft low lighting to put clients at their ease – at a time when they presumed they'd have the luxury of clients, of course. Sam set her bag down on the desk and picked up the phone, holding the receiver to her ear. Putting on her posh voice, she said, 'Fleet Investigations, Sam speaking,' and then, before she could stop herself, gave a slightly hysterical laugh. They were up the proverbial creek without a paddle and she was talking to herself. She knew Icey talked to God when she was alone, but Sam had never been a believer. And where was Icey's God when she needed him? He was asleep on the job, it seemed. It was down to Sam to sort it out, and she couldn't do that playing telephone like a child.

Whatever the tabloids might make of Sam and Icey's past, and despite all that had happened to them, Sam knew that up to now she and Icey had been the lucky ones. They had survived. Some of the girls she'd gone to school with had never even lived to see their twenty-first birthdays. They had been killed by pimps, jealous boyfriends or lost a battle with HIV, drugs or alcohol, or both. Not all their school friends had been as lucky as to have ended up at Irma's, and life on the streets was a lot tougher than life in a house, even a house of ill repute.

Fifteen months ago, Ishia McGinty's skeletal remains had

been discovered. What was left of her had been found dumped on a landfill site. The police identified her from dental records, but they had yet to find her killer. Not that Sam thought they were looking very hard for the murderer of a long-dead whore. She'd been livid at the casual way in which Ishia's death seemed to have been investigated. Even the press had only given brief mention to human remains being found and identified as Ishia McGinty, twenty-one, known prostitute and missing since 2002.

They had a saying on the streets: 'Once you're a tart, you're a tart to your grave.' Ishia's murder had played on Sam's mind and about a year ago she'd wanted to quit. She had been twenty-four, and Icey twenty-five. It no longer mattered that she and Icey were working in the relative safety of Madam Irma's. Sam wanted out.

Harry had tried to find out what he could about Ishia's death on Sam's behalf, but even his old colleagues who were still serving in the force had little to say about this coldest of cases. Sam had even been tempted to contact her old flame – now a DCI himself – to see if he could be of any assistance, but he wouldn't take her calls. In desperation she had sought out Mr Frizzel to see if he could help her force the police to investigate Ishia's death properly, but he refused. He said he didn't have the time and, more importantly, he was not prepared to work without funds. He did, however, allow Sam to come into his office for two hours to pursue any investigation she thought appropriate.

It was Harry, though, who ultimately proved to be her saviour. Having drawn a blank with his former work colleagues, he nevertheless managed to pull some information on Ishia, and also used his past knowledge of Soho's street life to find other women who'd worked alongside Ishia back in the day. He helped Sam gather together what she knew of Ishia's past – the snippets Ishia had shared, and what Sam could remember of the man in the car who had been looking for her friend all those years ago. It wasn't much, but what they found out they passed over to the police – and the media. It was the press interest in the story that eventually persuaded the police to continue their investigation, albeit without much success as yet.

Frizzel, having initially shown little interest, was impressed with what Sam had achieved and agreed that she could help him case-manage some of his other cases.

Sam only hoped that the skills she had learnt helping out in his office would now help her prove Icey's innocence.

Chapter Sixteen

Detective Constable Haydn was pushing fifty. He wasn't exactly God's gift to women, but he would be the first to admit that he came close. His eyes were blue, he still had his own fair hair and a well-toned body, but his vanity came at a price – a failed marriage and a trail of dissatisfied lovers. Eighteen years in the police force and, prior to that, ten years in the army, and not a single day went by when he didn't look in the mirror and wonder how he could fall in love with anyone other than himself. No one else measured up. He trained three times a week; he had the stamina of a man twenty years younger.

In the force, he was well respected by his colleagues. Unlike Detective Chief Inspector Paradissimo, he had no desire to climb any higher up the ranks. He liked being a working copper, out on the streets getting his hands dirty. When promotions came his way, he'd ducked and dived sufficiently over the years that his bosses had got the message and now they left him to get on with what he did best.

Haydn was good at his job, he was discreet and got results, which was more than he could say about his private life. His last relationship had ended a few weeks earlier. The split was acrimonious and ever since he'd tried to keep a low profile. Even so, he knew he was currently the subject of a whispering campaign. Rumour had it that his stamina did not extend to the bedroom. He was intensely upset by the gossip. The fact that the gossip was true made his pain all the more excruciating. Not even his boyish good looks, physical presence or manly charms were enough to keep his women happy in bed. It was all superficial, and he had been exposed.

He had been pleased when the call came in that he was to lead a new investigation. Despite his relatively low rank, his experience and the respect of his colleagues qualified him to head up the case. He would report to someone more senior but, as the Officer in Charge, he would be out on the streets doing the legwork. Haydn was pleased that he'd be spending much of his time out of the office, hence avoiding the gossips.

An Old Bailey judge had apparently just committed suicide. It wasn't every day that judges threw themselves off the roof of the most famous court building in the land. It had been reported that the judge had just dished out a life sentence moments before his death, and there was speculation that the two might be connected. Haydn's superiors indicated that he was to be given a free rein and a team of two officers to investigate the matter to a satisfactory conclusion.

Suicide – even a high-profile suicide – didn't usually merit so much police attention, but it was clearly not good for the public morale to have a judge in one of the highest courts in the land take his own life. In the several months preceding his death, Certie had also put several well-known criminals with ties to organised crime behind bars for varying amounts of their natural lives. Foul play and revenge couldn't be ruled out.

At best, Certie's suicide demonstrated a gross lack of judgement, and every convicted crook that had been sentenced by him in recent years would now want to appeal on the basis that the judge's mind had clearly been disturbed. His judgements would be deemed unsound, and doubt would be cast over his sentencing. DC Haydn needed answers quickly if a public outcry, and chaos within the criminal justice system, were to be avoided; and the first question had to be: What was it that pushed the judge to the edge? By all accounts, his death was unexpected. He had left no suicide note and it seemed unlikely that a High Court judge would have had any money worries.

Haydn was quickly at the scene and, on arrival, found that the uniformed police had already cordoned off the whole of Old Bailey Street. Judge Certie was long dead, but his body still lay gruesomely splattered on the pavement, with his wig partially on top of his head. A forensic tent was in the process of being erected, but until then the gathering tourists, eagerly pressing themselves up against the police tape for a better view, had another unexpected attraction. Camera flashes danced like lightning on the pavement around the newly dead judge. Without uttering a word, the young beat officer approached the feasting crowd and ushered them further along the pavement. The flash of cameras faded and decency returned to stake its claim on Old Bailey Street.

News, however, had already travelled fast. The guards at Old Bailey reception had informed their superiors that the judge had breached security in a final, fatal way. It hadn't taken long for gossip to carry on the idle lips of the ushers waiting for excitement. Whispers danced a merry jig down the corridors of justice to Court Two, where the Recorder of London, the most senior Old Bailey judge, had been in the middle of trying a triple contract murder. The clerk of the court passed him a note and, as he read it, he brought the proceedings to an abrupt adjournment.

'I am afraid,' he said to the jury, 'that I am going to have to rise for a few moments. I will let you know when I am ready to resume.'

The court usher was all aflutter when she hissed the first whisper into the ear of prosecuting counsel. Stunned, he asked her to repeat it, and she did, first clearing her throat before speaking in a stage whisper loud enough for all the other ushers to hear.

'It's Judge Certie,' said Lilian Weatherby, known to her colleagues as Acid Lil. 'He's only gone and topped himself by jumping off the roof!'

Chapter Seventeen

Judge Certie's suicide delayed the departure of the prisoners, but they were given no explanation. Icey was handcuffed to a short, round, black prison officer, who had a soft face and a boxer's neck. Picking up her belongings, Icey followed her as she was led out of the building and into the inner yard, a solid drab concrete area with high walls and razor wire. At the far end of the yard were the prison vehicles. Parked bumper to bumper, the regulation white vans waited for their human cargo. Inside the individual cubicles, security guards checked for unauthorised substances. The heavy-duty door ensured that the prisoners stayed put. They could sit and enjoy the lack of scenery until arrival at their ultimate destination.

There were in total seven women returning as guests of Her Majesty. Icey was dazed. She looked a mess. Her make-up had been washed away by the intense atmosphere in the intestines of the Old Bailey. As she rested her weary body on the seat in her cubicle, she felt close to tears but they wouldn't come. Much more than the relief of tears, she wanted to die. Closing her eyes, she leant her head against the side of the van and prayed for a better life that she would never know.

The other ladies were escorted into the van. Icey recognised the large black African woman. Her name was Meme and she was quite clearly off her rocker. Everyone in Holloway knew what she had done – killed her young daughter because she thought she was a witch. Now, as her guards tried to manhandle her into the van, she hopped from foot to foot, praying for her God to curse those who damned her. She was busy telling her invisible listeners that the child was a witch and had deserved to die. Icey kept quiet. The bitch wanted a good lumping. She had heard that the decomposing body of Meme's daughter had been found in a large industrial fridge in an abandoned factory. It was a horrific killing. And there was one murder Icey would readily commit if Meme did not shut up.

The last to enter the van were two drug mules. They had been convicted of bringing in heroin from Jamaica. They had befriended Icey in Holloway. When they saw her, they started to laugh. Sandra slumped her heavy body into one of the cubicles and clapped her hands. Jean even seemed pleased to see Icey. Icey would have been happy not to see either one of them again if it had meant she was free. The guards looked on, stiffened their necks and looked away. Light humour was within the prison rules.

'Hey, innocent Icey, I thought we'd seen the last of you,' teased Jean. 'How comes you innocent and we did nothing wrong and we both here?'

Icey did not see the joke. It was not a laughing matter.

'How long you get, girl?'

'Life with thirty years before I get parole,' said Icey as matter-of-factly as she could manage.

Jean slapped her thighs and gave another laugh. 'For someone who did nothing, you sure get a lot!'

Sandra started to join in again too; her shoulders convulsing. 'Hey, Icey, how comes you kill a woman in God's house and you say you did nothing? You would have been better off running self-defence, girl.'

'I did nothing wrong,' said Icey defiantly.

'Sure you did, you just got caught with the knife in your hand,' Sandra replied. 'Should have run when you had a chance, girl. I hear that you just lay down and sleep. What's that all about, huh? The cops had to wake you up before you got busted.'

'Is that right, girl? You fell asleep on the job?' asked Jean.

'I'm innocent,' Icey repeated as she felt her eyes well up again with raw emotional frustration. 'I didn't do anything.'

Jean's voice softened as she teased Icey. 'I know the feeling, love. Every now and then I feel innocent, but I let it pass over me.'

'Don't worry yourselves. I'll get out on appeal,' Icey insisted softly, with more conviction than she felt. Her voice was as cold as ice, but deep inside her tired and abused body, the flame of hope had not yet disappeared completely.

'We're going to start a campaign for you,' Sandra called out to her as the guard moved her further along the van to her individual cubicle. 'It's called the ICEY IS INNOCENT Campaign, but in the meanwhile we're on our way back to the prison of the innocent. We're all not guilty in here!'

Before Icey could respond, two guards entered the van with a big box of provisions. Just before it was ready to move, each female prisoner was given a high-energy chocolate bar and a carton of orange juice. As the van pulled away, Icey tried to lose herself in her own thoughts, zoning out the world around her, but all she could hear was Sandra chanting mockingly, 'Icey is innocent!'

Chapter Eighteen

The security van advanced forward slowly. The press were waiting. They surrounded the vehicle and pointed their cameras at the blacked-out windows, hoping to get at least one decent photograph. The flashes bounced off the side of the vehicle until it sped away on its final journey.

When the van finally arrived back at Holloway, Meme was still protesting her innocence. As the meat wagon approached the steel shutter, it wound open and the van drove in. Once inside, the gates rolled shut behind them and a heavy-duty security mechanism sprung into action.

Icey turned to study the place she'd call home for the next three decades of her life.

She had never truly noticed the vastness of the prison before. As a remand prisoner, it had felt temporary to her – and she'd hoped that's exactly what it would be – and she tried not to think about the gloom of her surroundings. It had never crossed her mind that she would be 'promoted' to a serving prisoner.

The Young Offenders' Institution where she and Sam had served time had been like Butlins compared to this. The reinforced razor wire around the perimeter wall, and high, steel-mesh fence, was exactly how she'd imagined prison. Holloway lived down to her expectations. It was now after seven o'clock and still she hadn't fully taken in the words of the judge. She had not slaughtered anyone. It didn't matter what she could or couldn't remember. No matter what the judge said, she was innocent.

The meat wagon came to a halt in the holding bay for the prisoners to be unloaded. Picking up the black plastic bag containing her belongings, Icey was handcuffed to a female security guard and escorted into the building together with the other women. All of them were quiet, apart from Meme. Her voice was now quite coarse and shallow. Whoever she had been praying to clearly hadn't answered her in any meaningful way. Her argument with her maker was now getting personal.

'If I am guilty, strike me down now!' she hollered. 'Let God Almighty be the only one to judge me.'

Stepping off the van, Meme started to get difficult with the guards, which they refused to tolerate. She asked why she was being detained. She knew the answer. Everyone knew.

'Why me?' she demanded. 'Why me? What have I done? Tell me why!'

Rose, another prisoner on the wagon, had been quiet through the entire journey. She had a lot to think about. Her grey hair hung over her pinched face and she'd kept her red eyes firmly fixed on the steel floor. She had got four years for the manslaughter of her abusive husband, and thought that it was time well served. She had spent so long on remand that she had almost completed her sentence. The jury had acquitted her of murder, but by ten to two had convicted her of manslaughter. In less than twelve months, she would be eligible for parole. Her four children had given evidence about their father's violent behaviour, and the neighbours had all agreed that he was better off dead. The sentence Rose could manage, but she missed her children dreadfully; and Meme, quite frankly, was getting on her tits. In the shared holding cell, Meme sat down beside Rose and waited to be processed.

'What did I do?' she said, turning to Rose.

'You killed your kid,' said Rose, as she raised her steel-cold eyes to display a hidden fury of pure hatred from deep within.

'But how, why?'

'You put her in a fridge, after you had beaten and starved her because you thought she was a witch. Don't you remember?'

'But, why? How?' Meme pleaded.

Sandra now stepped forward, her plump body straining against the grey jersey prison suit. 'The best thing you can do is shut it, bitch, and keep your trap closed and your head down.' Meme was silent. 'Just remember, you killed a kid and everyone in here will know it. Some of the homies will say you're due for a bitch slap.'

Meme looked up, her face frozen in worry. She had killed her child because she was a witch. She was possessed. How could anyone doubt her sincerity? She noticed that the women prisoners were looking the other way, but that was after they had all made a mental note of her face. Each one of them knew that duty had called. There was honour among thieves; even murderers and inmates were known to be fair but brutal. When it came to a convicted child killer, no allowances were made for gender when it came to exacting punishment.

Chapter Nineteen

Sam sat on the floor of the office kitchen in the dark. She was still dressed in her courtroom gear as she swigged Chateau Neuf du Pape straight from the bottle. She wasn't a heavy drinker; in fact, she hardly had a drink at all after having watched her stepmother's abuse alcohol. She also made a point of rarely drinking around Icey, even if Icey insisted she shouldn't change her behaviour on her account. But Icey wasn't here and the mean bleakness of the early evening, and the shock of the verdict, meant she needed something to take the edge away.

Ironically, she'd bought the wine the day Icey had been arrested, wanting to celebrate the opening of the office with Harry and Icey. Now she wasn't celebrating but drowning her sorrows.

As she took a long drink, she thought she heard a noise next door in her office. Clasping the heavy bottle in her hand, she stepped into the other room. Her heart missed a beat as panic took over. In the dark she could see a larger-than-life figure sitting on her desk. The silhouette was black against the grey shadows. She stifled a scream as she realised she knew the outline well. It was Mr Frizzel.

Composing herself, Sam allowed her breathing to calm and then felt pure unadulterated anger welling up from within. She wanted to pull his heart out and crush it with her bare hands. Only then would he understand the depths of her despair. A wave of loneliness washed over her as she sighed mournfully into her bottle of Chateau Neuf du Pape, taking another swig before placing it on her desk and glaring at her visitor.

Mr Frizzel was still dressed in his court clothes too: his well-worn three-piece suit. The buttons of his waistcoat were bulging open under a heavily stained jacket.

'We're not open,' Sam told him curtly.

He turned to look at her. 'Oh, it's you, Sam,' he slurred, obviously drunk.

'Who else would it be?' she replied. 'This is my office.'

'I am so sorry, my dear, to have startled you. Even more sorry that Icey was convicted. I intend to give the appeal my full attention. I have already instructed Mr Percival to draft grounds . . .'

He tried – and failed – to shift himself off the desk to shake her hand.

'As far as I am concerned, Mr Percival can take a running jump at himself. He was completely useless. I don't want him doing the appeal,' Sam snapped.

'Very good reputation in the appellate courts. Always best to keep trial counsel. We've got to file an appeal in twenty-eight days,' Mr Frizzel muttered.

Sam leant across and grabbed him by the collar. Mr Frizzel did not wait to be ordered to his feet. He heaved his heavy buttocks up off her desk and walked with a very unsteady gait to the door, assisted by Sam.

'I should never have trusted you. I repeat: we are not open, Mr Frizzel. You will have to come back tomorrow.'

Mr Frizzel stumbled and fell forward as Sam urged him out of the office. His fall was broken by the wall on the opposite side of narrow passage. He staggered back into his own dingy office, and Sam slumped into her chair, her heart beating wildly with adrenaline and wine. Next door she could hear Mr Frizzel crashing and banging about. Sam grimaced as she imagined the mess he'd be creating. Looking around her own office, she was satisfied that she and Icey had done their part to improve the premises, however small they were.

The main attraction was the beautiful floor, which they'd discovered when they'd taken up the old carpet. Although there were a few chips here and there, the burgundy marble tiles they'd uncovered were still a vast improvement on the '70s carpet they'd ripped up. It gave the office the appearance of being much larger and grander than it actually was. Sam felt at home here. Her desk was big and opulent, topped in burgundy leather. The previous owner had discarded it in favour of a minimalist modern look. Nothing had cost very much, as they'd got almost everything from a recycling yard, but it looked expensive and well loved after a good scrub and polish.

Sam and Icey had both qualified for a start-up grant, which would pay the rent for the year. Harry Kemp had provided invaluable help with their entitlements. They had enough saved to pay bills and expenses, and Sam had spent hours budgeting so that they would just about survive without income if the agency took time to get established. But for Icey's conviction, all would have been good. They had arrived, but it had never been Sam's intention to arrive without Icey.

It was painfully ironic that the first case Fleet Investigations would have to investigate was that of one of the founding partners.

Chapter Twenty

'Chin up, love; it could be worse,' said the prison clerk. 'If they hadn't got rid of capital punishment, they'd be cutting you down now.' Smithy had a sing-song voice overflowing with maternal love. 'Can I give you some advice?' She carried on before Icey could reply. 'You might not want it, but I give it to all my long-term prisoners. Keep your head down. Don't get into trouble. Whatever you do, don't get into a confrontation with the screws, they have long memories. Before you get depressed about your sentence, book yourself onto a course and get a degree and masters. Just think, you could leave prison a professor!'

Icey was still in a daze. She wasn't listening. She gave the clerk her paperwork and stared at her pale hands as the lady continued to talk.

'Religion?' she asked.

'Catholic,' Icey replied.

'Are you on medication?'

'No.'

'Are you feeling suicidal?'

'No. I'm a Catholic.'

'We get all sorts in here. Any children?'

'No.'

'Now, who is your next of kin?'

Icey paused. She wanted to name Sam but was unsure as to whether they'd accept someone who wasn't a blood relation, even if Sam was like a sister to her. 'Can I think about it?'

The clerk looked up kindly. 'Yes, and we need the names and phone numbers of the people you can call on your prison phone card, and that doesn't include your legal team.'

Icey felt on surer ground. 'Can I put down Sam Bailey?'

'Yes, what's her relationship to you?'

'My best friend.'

'Anyone else?'

'Can I think about it?' she answered again.

'Right, please remove your clothes for inspection and hand them to me,' Smithy instructed, pointing at a cubicle.

Icey stepped into it and pulled the plastic curtain around her, though she could still see the outlines of the other inmates. Although she wasn't one to be prudish about nudity, she felt vulnerable in the sterile grey room so she turned to face the wall. She removed her clothes and then handed them to the prison officer outside the curtain. Next the officer entered to make sure she was not carrying anything she should not be – drugs, mobile phone and SIM cards were valuable commodities in prison.

'Touch your toes, please,' the lady barked.

Icey looked over her shoulder at the officer. She was as tall as she was wide, with scrunched up features and blonde shoulder-length hair. She was wearing gloves.

Icey did as she was told. She cleared security and was handed a prison uniform of blue underwear, a tracksuit and a T-shirt. She pulled on the clothes under the discomfiting stare of the officer. She was given her bedding: one blanket, grey; one sheet and one pillow.

'You're moving cells now that you're a convicted prisoner,' the officer said, her eyes lingering on Icey's face. She'd heard about Icey's outburst in court and was expecting trouble, but was very surprised at the extent to which she was now compliant. 'Before you start shifting your stuff, I have to tell you that we run an equal opportunities policy with our cell allocation, and you're going to Trinidad.'

'Trinidad?' said Icey.

'Yes.'

'What's Trinidad?' Icey hadn't heard of that at all during her time here on remand.

'It is between Jamaica and Croatia and across the way from St Kitts. Block eight, third floor, cell four.'

The officer waited with her hands folded across her enormous chest while Icey gathered her belongings. As she turned to lead the way, Icey couldn't take her eyes off the woman's bottom. She had the mother of all arses. In her previous life, Icey had known people who would pay good money for an arse as big as the map of the world.

She picked up her few belongings and followed the officer. Until now, she'd been a remand prisoner; now she was a convicted murderer and she would spend her time on a wing for convicted prisoners.

Outside reception, they waited until a large steel door moved slowly sideways. Stepping into the small area, they waited again until the doors moved back, locking them inside the holding bay. Once the door was secured behind them, a matching door in front of them rolled open. Icey followed the officer out and was made to wait again until that door had closed before they could proceed into the corridor area leading towards the inner yard.

Icey was functioning on autopilot. The bulging key ring at the officer's side held at least fourteen keys. As she opened and closed the inner doors, they finally made their way to the third floor. Cell four was on the west side of Block eight, an oblong block of cells with a central open space.

'Cell four,' the officer said, ticking Icey off her list. Checking her keys once again, she inserted a large key into the steel cell door, and it swung open. She then double-checked her notes and wrote Icey's name on the small blackboard at the side of the door.

'This is mine,' said Icey flatly as she looked around the room. In the bright manufactured light she could see it was off-white with a tiny barred window. There were bunks to the left and a desk table immediately to the right. Someone had already taken possession of the top bunk. She could make out a slim, sleeping form. Icey put her belongings on the bunk below.

'It's en suite,' said the screw with a grin, pointing to the sink and toilet. The table and chairs were secured to the floor by large bolts. The screw checked Icey in and then closed the large metal door and locked it shut. The sound of the bolt closing was ominous. Outside the bars on the window, Icey could see only darkness. The wardrobe was part of an alcove and the toilet area reminded her of the toilet in her first primary school. There was a strong smell of disinfectant that didn't quite mask the underlying stench of bodily fluids.

Icey lay down on the bottom bunk. The mattress on the bed was barely visible. It felt like cardboard. She realised she should try to sleep, and closed her eyes, but she knew from her time here that the pink lights from the hallway were permanently on in case of prison disruption. The bright glow made sleep impossible for her.

Icey lay awake in her bunk. Her back was stiff, both legs had cramp and she couldn't filter out the smell in the room of stale piss from the dirty toilet. She rolled over onto her side, facing the wall. She wondered how in God's name she was going to prove her innocence because she sure as hell couldn't survive in prison for the next thirty years.

Chapter Twenty-One

When Icey had first been arrested seven months ago, Sam had arranged with Mr Frizzel that she would keep herself busy by working for him three days a week typing, filing and answering the phone. She had already been unofficially helping out in his office for a few months, managing some case work, after Frizzel had been so impressed with her investigations into Ishia's murder. Now he agreed to pay her a minimal wage but enough money so that, what with their start-up grant as well, she could keep her head above water and also continue to add little bits to their savings.

It also gave her time now to work on Icey's case. Fleet Investigations could open as planned, too, although in a limited capacity. All of her energy and attention was focused on Icey. Plus, Sam's early confidence about getting clients had faded fast in Icey's absence. Her past was not exactly a glowing advert to attract legitimate clients, she acknowledged; without her best friend at her side, she began to doubt herself all over again.

With Mr Frizzel having let Icey down so badly the day before in court, Sam realised now that she should have kept a closer eye on Icey's solicitor. He had failed them as much as Percival had. When he'd told her he was off working for Icey, she now suspected that he'd actually been in the pub drinking. She should have been fighting for Icey herself, Sam thought angrily. Her trust in Frizzel had been misplaced, but she could hardly complain since she had hired a drunk to represent her best mate; and, what a surprise, he had behaved like one.

Sam was learning fast, but not fast enough to save Icey from a life sentence.

Still, one advantage to Mr Frizzel being the solicitor for Icey's case was that Sam had free access to all of the paperwork. Little did Mr Frizzel know that, as he slept off his hangover in his office next door the following morning, Sam was sitting at her desk with all of Icey's case files in front of her. It was Saturday but she intended to spend every spare second of her time from now on working on her friend's case, until she was free . . .

She started by going through the prosecution papers in meticulous detail. Even Sam had to admit that the police and the prosecution had a strong case: Icey had been apprehended at the scene, covered in the victim's blood. The police had found her fingerprints on the murder weapon – no surprise, though, as she was found holding the knife. Icey had also had a bead in her pocket, which the prosecution claimed came from Leticia's broken rosary necklace.

The prosecution had struggled to come up with a motive for Icey's alleged attack, but had put forward various suggestions: that it was a robbery gone wrong; that Icey, in a drunken state, had become violent and Leticia was merely in the wrong place at the wrong time. However vague the motives, they were absolutely clear in their assertion that Icey had murdered a stranger and had been caught red-handed. They even had a witness who put Icey at the scene – covered in blood, standing at the church door.

Reading the statement of the witness, Mr P Sexton, Sam was struck again that he claimed to know Icey from school. Sam didn't remember him at all, but it could have been from before she knew Icey. She jotted down her query on a notepad, next to the witness's name, and continued reading. In his statement, Sexton placed Icey outside the church at 11 p.m., which obviously put her at the scene close to the time of death. Not that they had contested the fact that Icey had been present in the church at the time of Leticia's death.

Sam checked through the papers for Mr Frizzel's notes on the witness, and was horrified when she found only doodles and more of the same. He hadn't even highlighted the memo that said Sexton wouldn't be in court due to illness. Frizzel's files – even with Sam's admin help – were a mess. Sam realised she would have to start totally from scratch.

First, she checked the prosecution file for contact information on Sexton. As a witness, surely his details would have been included. The details were missing. Checking through an online phone book, Sam found fourteen listings for Sextons in the London area. The site also told her that the name Sexton derived from the Middle English 'sexteyn', and that it meant 'church official'. The sexton traditionally made sure all candles in the church were lit.

Sam began to wonder if her Sexton was merely a witness or a potential suspect. He had clearly never been under suspicion by the police, who seemed to have immediately latched on to Icey as the obvious perpetrator. But if this Sexton had been at St Mary Magdalene's at the time of the murder, he could just as easily have been inside the church as passing by. She needed to make contact with him and ask the questions they had been unable to ask in court. St Mary's was in South London, and if Sexton had been at school with Icey and passed by the church on the night of the killing, then it was reasonable to assume that he lived close by or was associated with that area. This supposition narrowed the field down to just five P Sextons who lived within a five-mile radius.

Picking up the phone, Sam dialled each number in turn. The first two were unobtainable. The third was not at home, and voicemail clicked in; Sam declined to leave a message. The final two Sextons were female with no 'Mr Sexton' at home, so she discounted them as her witness and crossed them off the list. Broadening the radius to within ten miles of the church, Sam then worked through the extended list, making a note against each one that could be readily identified. After an hour she had removed another seventeen from the new list of twenty-eight names. Two had passed away. A further eight were females living on their own. That left the final three that she couldn't account for – including Mr Answer Phone – and they would all receive a personal visit from Sam.

She went back to the case files. There were other issues that she needed to investigate. In the case papers there was virtually no mention of Tom Padfield, Leticia's fiancé, other than a reference in Father Luke Armstrong's statement that Tom had been due to marry Leticia, and that both had come to him for instruction. Sam didn't remember seeing anyone who looked like he might be Leticia's fiancé in court, which was surely odd in itself. Leticia's grieving parents had been there, staring angry daggers at Icey the entire time she had been in the dock. But they had been alone.

The police had assumed Icey's guilt from the start, and didn't appear to have looked to any of Leticia's friends, relatives or loved ones for another suspect. Strangely, Tom Padfield hadn't been called as a witness, nor could she find any transcript of a police interview with him, let alone a mention of an alibi for the time of the killing. It was curious, though, that he hadn't attended the trial of his dead fiancée's 'killer'. Sam found one of Mr Frizzel's rare notes stating that he'd tried to call Padfield but had no response.

It was a puzzling omission from the case. Sam decided to call Harry and ask him why he thought the prosecution had not called Tom Padfield as a witness.

'I don't know,' he said. 'It's strange. Even if they know nothing about the night in question – can prove they were nowhere near the crime scene – the prosecution usually like to call in a relative to gain the jury's sympathy. I'm surprised they didn't think a grieving fiancé would be even better than grieving parents. Maybe the prosecution thought they didn't need him. Or maybe he's too cut up to leave the house. There could be something off about him, of course, making them think he wouldn't make a good witness.'

Sam sympathised with Padfield's loss but both she and Harry agreed that they needed to interview him themselves. When Sam hung up the phone, she made another note on her pad: *2 – pay Tom Padfield a visit.*

As part of her legwork for Mr Frizzel, Sam had cold-called the houses closest to the church in the weeks after Leticia's death. But the process had yielded nothing. She had covered all homes in the vicinity of St Mary Magdalene's Church. Leaflets had been dropped through every door with an opening. At the time, Frizzel had said she shouldn't worry about carrying out a follow-up drop to a wider vicinity, despite there still being a whole box of leaflets left, but now she was in charge Sam would make sure the expanded drop took place.

She would hand deliver each and every one.

Chapter Twenty-Two

Icey's first day as a lifer started with breakfast in the hall – tea, toast and a choice of porridge or one of a selection of dry-looking cereals, followed by a cooked breakfast of eggs and bacon. Icey could barely swallow her tea.

Although she'd been locked up for almost seven months already, this time it felt different – it *was* different. At the beginning, she'd had a reason to believe in justice and freedom. Now there wasn't an end in sight. Just thirty years within these walls. The other women had already fallen into a routine, and Icey envied them. But no one was conscious of Icey. She was just another con who had come in overnight.

As she waited in the queue to collect her food, she noticed that Rose was several paces behind. Poor old Rose – she always looked miserable even when she was happy. Icey observed her discreetly. She looked like she had been in a fight with thunder and had been struck by lightning. Icey smiled and Rose tried hard to smile back, but it was more like a glare, then she turned her head abruptly away. A heavily tattooed woman barged past Icey and went to the head of the queue. No one stopped her. The inmates collected their food and made their way to the long table. Rose came and sat opposite Icey without saying a word. A large woman came and sat to Icey's right. Icey looked up and was surprised to find that it was Meme.

Sipping her disgusting tea, Icey spat it back into the cup. It must have been stewed overnight. It was molasses in colour and tasted bitter. The room fell silent. Meme was not eating her food. She was oblivious to the gaze of those who watched her. Breaking her bread into small pieces, she arranged twelve pieces in a pattern on the table. She mumbled incoherently to herself as she hit each piece with the back of her fork.

'What you doing, Meme?' asked Icey.

She ignored the question.

'Voodoo? Are you mad?' Icey asked

Meme didn't reply as she placed her plastic knife in the middle of the bread and span it round. The bread scattered and the point of the knife came to rest pointing at Rose. A portion of broken bread landed in Rose's lap. Rose wasted no time. Picking the bread up, she stamped on it twelve times before reaching over and spinning Meme's knife. It stopped when the blade was pointing at Meme. One by one the other ladies got up, picked up their plates and moved to another table. Icey did not move. Meme was frantic. The voodoo spell she had sent to Rose had been returned to her. Meme was furious.

The rest of the day was made up of induction classes. Icey was given a choice of jobs that were available, and opted for the library or kitchens. Everybody wanted the kitchens. No one wanted the gardens – working outside in the cold weather wasn't much fun. In order to work in the library, Icey had to do literacy and numeracy tests. Although she'd never had much time for school, she was surprisingly good at those.

As part of the induction, all the new prisoners were shown around the prison, despite the fact that many of them had been on remand in the same place. The 'go' and the 'no-go' areas were pointed out. The punishment for breaching a prison rule varied from a loss of days, which were added on to the end of their sentence, to time spent in the isolation wing.

Lunch was some kind of meat stew – it was best not to enquire what kind – followed by apple crumble. The food reminded Icey of the meals she'd had when she was at school, and she wished she could go out and order cod and chips wrapped in paper with salt and a dash of vinegar, like she and Sam used to do when they were flush. Icey couldn't afford that now, though she had eight pounds in her prison account. There were many things that she desperately needed like toothpaste, a toothbrush, credit on a phone card and personal hygiene products.

After lunch, Icey was told she had been appointed to the kitchens, where her weekly wage was eight pounds and fifteen pence. She was not eligible for the library this time round, because there were better-qualified inmates than herself. She'd been up against a teacher who'd had an affair with an underage pupil, and a mercy-killer nurse.

In the late afternoon, Icey turned up to start the evening shift in the kitchen. She was put on vegetable preparation, which she enjoyed. The kitchens were very modern, full of stainless steel. There was a large cold room where perishables were stored. The isolation of the job meant that she could think and clear her head of her personal suffering that at times overwhelmed her. She was disappointed to see that both Meme and Rose were also allocated to the kitchens. They studiously avoided each other and worked in silence.

At the end of dinner, one of the screws told Meme to take the excess food back into the cold storage. She gathered up as much as she could carry in her bulbous arms and walked towards the walk-in freezer. Rose appeared to be preoccupied sweeping the floor and wiping down the tables. No one noticed when Meme failed to reappear. Everyone assumed that she had gone straight to association time.

Meme's frozen body was found next morning. The police were called to investigate the death. Everyone was interviewed, including Icey. The police recorded that there was no foul play. It was a tragic accident. On the day that the police concluded their investigation, Rose was standing in the kitchen slicing bread rolls. Breaking a roll into twelve small pieces, she placed each one strategically around the edge of her chopping board in a circle. As she spun her knife against the work surface, the blade stopped pointing in the direction of the cold storage room.

'She can't do no more harm now,' said Rose as she winked at Icey.

Chapter Twenty-Three

Sam stood outside the church, handing out yet more leaflets to passers-by and members of the small congregation. The sun was shining and, even though it was a weak, wintry afternoon sunshine, the stone building shone beautifully and gave even Sam some faith. Dressed in a sharp business suit with thick black tights and a crisp white blouse, and wearing a pair of modest earrings, she looked professional, friendly and approachable. Her hair was styled with a side parting, and her make-up was subtle but still made her green eyes shine. She was pleased when the walk-bys went out of their way to take a leaflet. For the first time since Icey's arrest, she felt like she was doing something constructive, however simple.

As she neared the scene of the crime, though, Sam's mind accelerated into overdrive. Walking up the Camberwell New Road, she headed round to the back entrance of the church and carefully retraced Icey's steps on the night of the murder. St Mary Magdalene's was a Victorian church, overtly Gothic in style. It was an impressive, rather foreboding building; a relic from a bygone age. Sam had always thought it was rather ugly, despite its pretty stained-glass windows and ornate pillars. She noticed now that there were thirty-two steps to the back door, but only eighteen to the front. Why had Icey entered through the back of the church? It didn't make any sense.

She was suddenly aware of someone behind her. The footsteps were distinctive, heavy, with a sense of purpose. Sam stopped abruptly. The footsteps fell silent. Looking over her shoulder, she appeared to be alone so she carried on. Entering the church, Sam paused in the doorway. Icey had said in her initial interview that she remembered trying to leave by the front door, but that she had heard a noise – Leticia Joy being attacked – which had made her retreat back into the church.

Making her way up the aisle to the front of the church, all of a sudden Sam knew that she definitely wasn't alone. The pitter-patter of steps followed her. Sam stopped again and discreetly looked over her left shoulder as something – someone – darted from right to left into one of the church's alcoves. Sam forced herself to continue on her way until anxiety took over.

Turning her head to the left, Sam looked again and saw, hiding in the alcove, a woman she recognised from court as Iris Walker. She was one of the most devoted members of St Mary Magdalene's congregation, and had been there earlier on the night of Leticia Joy's murder, arranging flowers on the altar as per her usual routine. Now as Sam walked towards her, the woman evaporated into the blackness of the church.

Stopping again, this time at the front of the building, Sam realised that the outer doors of the church were set back from the street, and it would not have been possible from the road to see someone just inside the doors. Sam paused. That meant that it would be impossible to have seen Icey from the position Sexton claimed in his statement. But then, equally, Icey couldn't have seen him – not that she had claimed to.

It was one of the many things Icey couldn't remember about the night in question. Sam had become increasingly intolerant of her friend's excessive drinking, and the truth was that she didn't know whether to believe that Icey really did have a blackout that night. She'd certainly had experience of how easy it was to take the life of another.

But with Jack Billings, Icey had had reason to kill. Sam was still no clearer as to any possible motive Icey might have had to murder Leticia Joy, even if she had to admit that her friend had previously demonstrated the capacity to kill. It was all very confusing. Sam had never seriously doubted her friend's innocence; she knew instinctively that Icey couldn't have committed this crime. Yet there were puzzling aspects to the case which she simply couldn't fathom, and both the police's biased and Frizzel's totally useless investigations had left her with a huge amount to unravel. She desperately needed to find answers.

Sam piled the left-over leaflets thoughtfully into her handbag as she retraced her steps back to the feet of Christ. It was here that the slaughter of Leticia Joy had taken place. The statue of Christ smiled down at her as she tried to compose herself, her mind still racing as she tried to assimilate her surroundings and work out what had happened here.

'Don't turn around,' a harsh voice whispered in her ear. It was impossible to tell if it was a man or a woman. Either way, Sam froze. 'You're not welcome here, and if you know what's good for you'll go now and won't come back!'

'Who are you?' Sam cried out, sufficiently unnerved to obey the instruction and stand stock-still. But the voice didn't answer. By the time she'd summoned up the courage to turn around, there was no one there.

'Who are you?' repeated Sam at the top of her voice. She didn't wait for an answer. She ran from the church, her heels clattering against the flagstones.

Chapter Twenty-Four

Back at her office, Sam calmed herself with a cup of tea before resuming her vigil at her desk with renewed determination. She didn't think to report the incident at the church to the police. Frankly, they'd been no help so far, and Sam thought she'd be far better off working things out for herself. Starting at square one, she removed from her file the transcript of Icey's original police interview.

Transcript of statement by Elizabeth Johnson
Date: Sunday, 4 July 2010
Time: 9.23 a.m.

My full name is Elizabeth Johnson, but most people call me Icey. On the evening of Saturday, 3 July 2010 I went to confession at St Mary Magdalene's Church in Camberwell. My business partner dropped me off at the church. We were about to launch our business and make a new start in our lives and I wanted to take confession. When I came out of the confession booth, I stayed in the church for a short while to . . . to pray, but I saw some bloke and a girl over by the foot of the statue of Christ. He was attacking her. When he saw me, he stopped and came after me, so I ran back into the confession box. He tried to get in. I held the door and jammed it with my foot. I waited until the coast was clear and then I crept out. I saw that the girl was badly injured but still alive. I crawled towards her in case the man was still in the church and saw me. I knelt over her and I could feel her breath. She was bleeding heavily. I tried to help her. She was trying to say something. I couldn't hear so I pressed my ear closer to her and she whispered something. I can't remember what it was or what happened next. I think I must have . . . blacked out. It's happened before when I've been drinking. The next thing I remember was the police coming and arresting me in the church. I don't remember anything else . . . But I know I didn't kill anyone . . .

DCI PARADISSIMO: Miss Johnson, you were found at the crime scene with the victim's blood on you and a knife in your possession that my colleagues have now proved is the murder weapon. Your blood was also found at the crime scene in far smaller quantities, and you have some superficial wounds, which have been attended to. I'm suggesting to you that you killed Leticia Joy but were too drunk to make good your escape.

JOHNSON: There was a man. I remember that much. He attacked her. And then he attacked me . . .

DCI PARADISSIMO: If you ran away, how did Leticia Joy's blood get on you?

JOHNSON: I went to help her . . . I must have got her blood on me then. There was a lot of it . . . her throat was cut.

DCI PARADISSIMO: How did your blood get on the inside of the confession box?

JOHNSON: I told you, he was attacking me so I ran back inside.

DCI PARADISSIMO: Or was it Catholic guilt, eh? Did you go back in afterwards to confess that you'd killed her?

JOHNSON: No, I did not.

DCI PARADISSIMO: Well, let's talk about the murder weapon. We found it in your possession. How do you explain that?

JOHNSON: I don't know. I don't know how it got there. I must have picked it up after the killer left . . . I don't remember.

DCI PARADISSIMO: By your own admission, you'd been drinking heavily throughout the day. But I don't buy your loss of memory act for a moment. You killed Leticia Joy and now you're trying to cover your tracks by acting as if you've had some kind of blackout.

JOHNSON: No, why would I?

DCI PARADISSIMO: Leticia Joy had a rosary, didn't she?

JOHNSON: I don't know. I don't know her – I'd never seen her before. She might have done. Most Catholics do.

DCI PARADISSIMO: Her rosary was broken and there's a bead missing, a bead we found in your possession – in your coat pocket. What happened? Did she fight back and the rosary got broken in the process? Is that when you sustained your own injuries or did you self-inflict them to cover your tracks?

JOHNSON: I don't know what you're talking about . . .

DCI PARADISSIMO: Why'd you pick up the bead from her necklace? Did you want a memento from the murder, a trophy?

JOHNSON: I told you I didn't kill her.

DCI PARADISSIMO: The only thing I don't understand is why you stayed put after killing her. Were you really too drunk to even leave the crime scene? Find some communal wine and decide to make a party of it?

JOHNSON: I told you . . . there was a man. He attacked her. I ran away from him and then I tried to help her but . . . I don't remember.

DCI PARADISSIMO: Leticia Joy's broken rosary has traces of your blood on it. If that didn't happen in a struggle with you then how do you explain how both yours and Leticia Joy's blood got on her rosary?

JOHNSON: I don't know . . .

DCI PARADISSIMO: The point is that, if it wasn't you, someone must have put a rosary, covered in your blood, back into her pocket after they had slaughtered her. Do you know who might have wanted to do that?

JOHNSON: No.

DCI PARADISSIMO: Do you have a similar rosary?

JOHNSON: I have a rosary. I don't know if it's similar.

DCI PARADISSIMO: I need you to take a look at this evidence bag. Is there anything about this rosary that's unusual?

JOHNSON: No.

DCI PARADISSIMO: Have another look.

JOHNSON: It's just a rosary.

DCI PARADISSIMO: It's a rosary that is identical to the one you say you had at the church?

JOHNSON: It's not my rosary. It looks like mine, but it's not.

DCI PARADISSIMO: Now, there is nothing to distinguish this rosary from the one found in your pocket after you had been arrested, except of course that the rosary in your pocket was not broken.

JOHNSON: Yes, that is correct.

DCI PARADISSIMO: But the one found on the deceased had a missing bead. If you count up from the cross do you see there are four beads?

JOHNSON: Yes.

DCI PARADISSIMO: Well the fifth bead is missing.

JOHNSON: And what has that got to do with me?

DCI PARADISSIMO: Quite a lot. The rosary you have identified as identical to yours belonged to the deceased. Did you kill her and then get confused as to which rosary was which?

JOHNSON: No, that's not correct. I told you I don't know how that bead got there.

DCI PARADISSIMO: Give it your best shot, Miss Elizabeth Johnson. Just tell me how you came to be in possession of a bead from Leticia Joy's broken rosary?

JOHNSON: I don't know . . . I don't remember . . .

Sam closed her eyes – she had read enough. She had been there when Mr Frizzel had originally examined the two rosaries at the police property store, and he had not mentioned a broken rosary or a missing bead. Nor had she spotted it, but then she hadn't handled the necklace herself and she knew nothing about rosaries. He had missed the fact that the rosary was broken until the prosecution brought it up at the trial, when the importance of the missing bead became apparent for the first time, and by then it was too late. It was obviously not something he had given much thought to, and yet it had helped secure the conviction of Icey. It was another strike against Mr Frizzel in terms of how ineffective he'd been throughout this whole nightmare situation.

And yet, as Sam pondered some more, she realised that there was no evidence at all that the rosary bead found in Icey's possession was the actual bead from Leticia Joy's necklace. In the trial, the prosecution assumed that the two were connected and the jury went along with it. They assumed that Icey had killed Leticia Joy and broken her necklace in the struggle, then dropped the necklace into the deceased's pocket, not realising that she'd left traces of her blood on the rosary. They claimed she'd taken the missing bead with her as some kind of trophy of her crime. This was a significant plank in the prosecution's case against Icey.

This was evidence that had helped to convict Icey, and Mr Frizzel and Mr Percival should have been aware of its significance. Both of them had missed it. How could Sam have been so stupid? She should have been more involved from the beginning. She'd trusted them, and she'd been wrong to do that. She wouldn't have missed this; she knew that.

Well, if the rosary had convicted Icey, maybe it would also help set her free.

Chapter Twenty-Five

The next morning, Sam's alarm went off while she was in the middle of a terrible dream in which Icey was being marched to the gallows. Her heart was pumping hard by the time she managed to sit up and thump the alarm silent. She caught a glimpse of her reflection in her dressing table mirror. Her wild hair and tired eyes made her look like a mad woman. She checked her clock in disbelief. It was eight already and she had no recollection of even getting into bed.

Throwing back the covers, Sam leapt up and ran to the bathroom, where she turned both bath taps on full. Although she was now her own boss, she had her standards. It was Sunday morning but, even so, work was nine to five and it was unacceptable to saunter in when she felt like it. She jumped into the bath while it was still running, and fifteen minutes later she was washed and dressed. It only took her ten minutes to eat breakfast and she was soon waiting to catch a bus to Oval underground station. Despite the rush, she still looked like it had taken her hours to get ready. Her pink suit fitted her perfectly and her warm, woollen coat was smart and elegant. She hadn't had time to put on any make–up, but she had grabbed her artificial pearls, which now draped from her neck.

As she took her seat on the tube, she felt a discarded magazine under her backside. It was a Sunday newspaper supplement but from the previous weekend. On the cover was a picture of a stunning young woman, leaning forward to show her cleavage to advantage. It said her name was Ros Holliday. She was very beautiful, but Sam had never heard of her. Sam flicked inside. There she was again under a big A for actress. It was part of an 'A to Z' article on the twenty-six most up and coming professionals. On the opposite page, under a large B, was a picture of a barrister in wig and gown.

Ashley Towers was in his late thirties. Single. Ruthless. Specialised in murder trials. Never lost a case. His female colleagues said he reminded them of Johnny Depp. To Sam he sounded like a man to know if you were in trouble, and she smiled for the first time in months. She just wished she'd heard of him before. He should have been briefed instead of that old dodderer Percival; Sam could have done a better job herself. Tucking the magazine into her bag, she decided she'd add Mr Towers to her list of things to do and look into him later.

Arriving at Temple station, she checked her watch. It was 9.35. She ran along the pavement but soon realised that was not a good idea in high heels. With every second step, one of them snagged in the cracks between the paving stones; and her skirt was too tight to allow any latitude should she fall.

Crossing the road, Sam slowed her pace to a brisk walk as she made her way up to Middle Temple Lane and down the alleyway to the Fleet Investigations office. Her keys were at the bottom of her bag and she struggled to find them. Hot and bothered, she undid her coat and, sitting down on the step, spread the contents on the ground. A couple of female barristers entering Server Chambers made a deliberate point of stepping over her. They were both polished and well presented – thirty-something professionals with immaculate make-up and neatly plucked brows. They glared at her curiously. She was clearly not one of them. No barrister would arrive at the Temple in a pink and white check suit and stilettos that she could hardly walk in.

Rushing into the small reception area, Sam stopped to catch her breath. Her office was dark and empty – just as she'd left it the night before – and she suddenly felt stupid for rushing. Icey wouldn't know if she opened half an hour late. She probably wouldn't really care, either, as Sam was the one who was a stickler for good time-keeping. The thought of Icey focused her, and she pushed aside her depressed thoughts. She didn't want anything taking her attention away from Icey's case.

Sitting down at the desk, she noticed a flashing light on the phone indicating a message. She played it back and immediately recognised the warm, rich tones of her former boss.

'Madam Irma speaking. What do I hear about Icey? Anything we can do to help? Please ring.'

Madam Irma was the mother Sam never had. Far more than simply the madam who'd hired her, over the years she'd become a firm friend. Both Icey and Sam had worked for Irma in her home before moving with her to her new premises in Soho.

Sam didn't hesitate. She pressed the return call button. It seemed an age before the phone was answered.

'Madam Irma speaking.'

'It's Sam.'

'Sam, I've been expecting you. How are you?'

'Oh, Irma. It's all dreadful. Icey is doing life. No one believed she's innocent.'

Irma waited with the patience of a mother as Sam described the final day of Icey's trial, growing increasingly distressed as she relived those awful hours. When she managed to regain her composure, Irma spoke in affectionate tones.

'We have to work on the appeal, and you need to deal with that fool of a man you call her brief.' Sam listened intently while pulling a tissue from her bag and blowing her nose, thinking wryly that it was a good job she hadn't yet put on her make-up. 'From what you've told me, he's let our Icey down,' Irma said bluntly. 'I've been thinking, which is why I called. You're not alone – you obviously need some help over there. You can have Oriel and Flick to work with you for the appeal. They're two of my best girls. You can trust them, and you will always have me.'

Sam welled up with gratitude. It had been a mistake not to get Irma involved earlier, but she hadn't thought for a second that Icey would get convicted. Plus Irma had her own problems; given her line of business, that was perhaps inevitable. There had been a recent crackdown on brothels, and the boys in blue were always buzzing around Irma's place these days, harassing her guests. On top of which, Sam had heard that one of Irma's best girls had recently quit, and Irma had yet to find a suitable replacement. The desertion had no doubt stung, coming as it had after Sam and Icey had also quit the business.

Irma prided herself on running a happy home, and it was rare for one of her girls to just up and leave without a word. If they were fed up of the life – like Sam and Icey had been – Irma had always done her best, albeit reluctantly at first, to help them change profession. In fact, Irma had always been Sam and Icey's greatest supporter. It made sense that she would now lend her Oriel and Flick to help her try to free Icey.

'I don't know how to begin to thank you, Irma. To be honest, I feel overwhelmed by all of this. I've made a start, and Harry's said that he's going to help me, but there's so much work to do. Our defence all along has been that Icey probably picked up the knife in an instinctive reaction, and that Leticia Joy's blood could have got on her when she went to her aid. But I've been reading the police transcripts of Icey's interview, Irma, and there's this question about the victim's broken rosary with the missing bead found by the police in Icey's pocket. I just can't explain that – why she picked it up. Although it has occurred to me that there's no proof that the bead Icey had is the one from the broken rosary. I think we might need to get expert help with that. I need to find out more about rosaries, for sure.'

Irma laughed. 'Leave that with me. I'm sure I can find someone who can help.'

Chapter Twenty-Six

Ashley Towers was sitting at his desk in Server Chambers. He was reading his recent profile in the press when he heard someone crying. As he walked over to the open window, he listened carefully, and waited. She was at it again.

Word had got round the chambers that the new occupier of the detective agency downstairs was a former tart on a rehabilitation mission. It was the last thing he needed. Some old tart with an office full of screaming whores for clients – after all, whom else could she hope to get business from? The current loud-pitched wailing gave him every reason to be concerned. Closing the window, he pulled down the blind and looked at his watch. It was another fourteen minutes before the wailing ceased.

He made a note in his diary out of habit; however, he decided against complaining. If it happened again, then perhaps he might make a formal complaint. Ashley was always one for an easy life and, who knew, as unlikely as it might seem, Fleet Investigations might provide a source of work in due course. Besides, he of all people should know better than to listen to gossip.

Reclining in his seat once again, he reread his recent profile in last week's *Sunday Times*. It was almost true that he had never lost a case. He would be the first to agree that he was flavour of the month, although he harboured a belief that he had been for quite some time. The article was penned by a man called Ian

Hamilton-Smythe. Ashley knew him well. They had attended the same prep school: Spittle Downs. He'd lost touch with Ian when he went to Cambridge. It was a chance meeting at Daly's in Essex Street that had resulted in the complementary article. Picking up the phone, Ashley dialled through to *The Times'* help desk. Mr Hamilton-Smythe was about to become his new best friend.

The taxi pulled over in front of the High Court and June 'Oriel' Tomescu and Felicity 'Flick' Peasey stepped out on to the pavement. Reaching into her pocket for cash, Oriel pulled out some loose change.

'You don't need to worry. It's on account,' said the taxi driver as he stared at Oriel's substantial assets.

'Thanks,' said Oriel in her impeccable if heavily accented English, 'but it's just a tip. Our pleasure.'

'Believe me, the pleasure is all mine. If you two are ever stuck for a lift, here's my card.'

Flick nodded politely, took the card and slipped it into her pocket. 'Thank you very much. We just may need your services.'

The taxi did not move off immediately. He waited and watched as Oriel and Flick crossed the road and disappeared down Devereux Court. He wanted to see if the rear view was as good as the front, and he was not disappointed. How on God's earth, he wondered, could he have allowed them to walk off without at least attempting to get his leg over later? He must be getting old.

June 'Oriel' Tomescu was not ordinary; she was far from that. It was not just her 34-DD bust that made her stand out in the crowd. She was exceptionally pretty, with tanned skin and blue eyes. At five foot ten with Amazonian curves to match, she had a penchant for short skirts, high heels and bright colours like the purple soft leather coat she currently wore that barely reached her hem. Heads turned as Oriel strolled elegantly past, and the sober lawyers in the vicinity couldn't help but wonder how she could stand upright, let alone walk, in six-inch heels.

By contrast, 'Flick' was short and slight, a petite 5'3" and just seven stone. She looked fragile and waif-like. Her little-girl-lost looks appealed to a lot of men. In fact, Flick was strong and supple; she could flex and bend in any direction, an agility that had won her an army of devoted clients. Her hair was shoulder length and jet-black. She looked like a pocket Burberry model. Her make-up was beautifully applied with all the expertise of a make-up artist on a *Vogue* shoot. She had one major flaw: ever since she was a child, she had struggled with an eating disorder. At the slightest bulge of her stomach on her slight frame, she would resort to making herself sick. Flick had everything going for her except emotional stability.

Turning into Middle Temple, they were both aware of the attention they attracted. They had that rare quality that money couldn't buy – natural good looks. They were also aware that, while their looks might open doors, their chosen profession, if it became known, could see those same doors slammed in their faces. They were high-class call girls who looked more like fashion models on a shopping trip than working girls, but that just made them very good at their job. Madam Irma catered to a very high class of client; as a result, her girls were always special in some way – and always drop-dead gorgeous.

Flick and Oriel were excited to be helping out Sam. Although they'd never met her, Irma always spoke very fondly of Sam and Icey. Moreover, they were curious to meet someone who had seemingly turned her back on turning tricks. They also wanted to see if Sam was as beautiful as Madam Irma – and the girls who'd worked with her – said.

Sam was waiting for them in the reception area of her office. Flick stepped through the door first, followed by Oriel. Under her arm, Flick carried a present from Irma.

'This is for you,' she said, handing it over, after they'd all introduced themselves.

'Oh, what's this?' Sam eyed the huge book with interest.

'Irma said you'll need it. It's the Directory of Barristers and Chambers. She borrowed it from one of our regulars. Irma did some research among some of our clients in the know, and flagged up barristers with a good reputation.'

Sam nodded and took the directory and flicked through the flagged pages. 'Well, well,' she said, 'great minds think alike.'

'Why do you say that?' asked Flick.

'Because Irma has flagged Ashley Towers, and I had him in mind as well. I saw an article about him. I think that's a good sign.'

Sam ushered the girls into the kitchen at the back of the office, and put the kettle on. She made a pot of tea and placed it on a tray with a jug of milk, sugar and three mugs. Because the office only had two chairs so far, they all sat on the floor. Sam used the opportunity to check out her new – albeit temporary – staff.

'How did you two end up working for Irma?' asked Sam, pouring the tea.

'I was training to be an accountant,' Flick began easily. 'Three days before my finals, my boyfriend dumped me and I failed my exams. After that I needed some way to pay the mortgage on my own and, well . . . It was never my intention to get into the sex trade,' Flick concluded with a wry smile.

Sam turned to look expectantly at Oriel, but she appeared more reluctant to discuss her past.

'This is not confession, Oriel. You don't have to tell me

anything you don't want to,' said Sam. 'I'm just curious, especially as we're going to be working together. I ended up working for Irma after my best friend and I served time for credit card fraud. We had all these plans to go straight and get proper jobs, but there aren't that many people looking to hire young offenders! It seemed like an easy way of making money at the time.' Sam stopped, although there was a great deal more she could say on the subject. She didn't regret her time working for Irma, but all the same she was glad to be out of that life. Conscious, though, that the two other girls were still 'working', she kept her negative thoughts to herself.

Oriel remained silent at first as she composed herself, and when she spoke at last her voice was cold and without passion. 'I am from Romania originally. My boyfriend had a job earning good money over here; he persuaded me to join him. I was reluctant to come at first. I said that I would miss my little sister Rala but he agreed to pay for both of us to come to this country. It was our intention to get married after we saved enough money. I believed that I was coming here to make a good life with Hunor.'

'So how did you end up as a working girl?' Sam asked.

'I arrived on a cold and wet day. My sister was to travel one week later so I could make sure everything was ready for her arrival. Hunor was waiting at the airport with a large bunch of flowers and the keys to our apartment. He was with another man who did not speak. He just looked and nodded at me. He did not stay very long.'

'Then what happened?'

'I was so happy and in love. Our apartment was a wonderful flat just off Sloane Square. That first night Hunor asked me to sleep in the guest bedroom and I did not think anything about that. We were both tired. The following day he came into my room and told me that he had found a job for me and it was necessary for us to recover our expenses and that it was not good to start our married life with debt. I agreed. We travelled to China Town to a five-storey house. There was no lift. We walked up three flights of stairs and it was then that Hunor asked for my passport to show my new employer. I did not question him. There was no need. He had arranged everything.

'In the room there were four other women and three men. One of the women was crying. The man I had met at the airport the day before was there. It was then that I learnt that Hunor had sold me.

'The airport man approached and told me to remove my top. I said, "No". He asked again and I refused again. Hunor left the room. That was the last time I saw him, and the last thing I remembered of that first night was a blow to the side of my face. When I woke up, I discovered that my clothes had been removed by the female guard, and the man on top of me was one of many who had paid to have sex with me that night.

'I was kept in a mostly drugged state and watched constantly for the first couple of months. There were lots of men who raped me. Then I was taken to a whorehouse in Hendon, where I was beaten, raped and forced to have sex for money every day. I was told that I had to repay the cost of my fare. After ten months I managed to escape but by then I was already pregnant.'

'That's awful,' Sam commented grimly. 'And what happened to your sister?'

'She arrived. That much I know but I have no idea what happened to her after that or where she is now. I hope every day that she is alive and we will be together again. I hope that she is not in one of those awful houses where I worked but I think it is likely. God willing, I will meet with Hunor again and

I will exact upon him a fate worse than my ordeal.'

'Do you know where your ex-boyfriend is?' Sam asked.

'No, I never saw him again after he sold me.'

'And you had the baby?' asked Flick, who had been listening intently to Oriel's story. 'Why would you want to give birth to a child fathered by your rapist?' she queried bluntly.

'It just did not occur to me that abortion was the right option. When she was born I called her Rala, after my little sister. I worked the streets for a while then but I hated it, then I met Irma and she helped me get back on my feet. I may still be a whore but at least it is my choice to be so. And the money I earn is mostly mine. And it's enough to support my daughter and me. It was a lucky day when I met Madam Irma,' she said, allowing herself a small smile.

Sam smiled back at her new help and, while she didn't want to say anything to give Oriel false hope, she resolved there and then that when Icey was free, they would both help Oriel find her little sister. And, just maybe, track down the man who had betrayed them both.

Chapter Twenty-Seven

'Do you think your friend did it?' asked Flick, with what Sam was coming to realise was characteristic bluntness.

'She can't have done,' replied Sam without thinking. 'She didn't even know the victim. She had no reason to kill anyone. She was only there that night by pure chance.'

'It happened in a church, didn't it?' Oriel said, gesturing to Flick to hand her a notebook and pen. 'Which one was it again?'

'It was St Mary Magdalene's in Camberwell,' Sam told her. 'I tried to dissuade her from going there, especially that late on a Saturday night. I don't believe in God but she kept banging on about wanting to make a fresh start before we opened our new business. So I told her to go and get her confession out of the way, if it meant so much to her.' Flick reached into her handbag and pulled out two notebooks and pens. She handed one of each to Oriel as Sam continued, 'I went to the office to get ready. We were planning to celebrate opening our business. You can imagine how I feel about that now . . .'

'Who was it that was killed?' asked Oriel.

'It was a young woman called Leticia Joy. She was going to get married. She was going to see Father Luke at the church for instruction. He gave evidence in court supporting that. Leticia had apparently started going to the church quite regularly.'

'Was her fiancé there at the time, then? Do you think this

Tom Padfield could have done it?' Oriel asked thoughtfully.

'He wasn't called at the trial. I don't even remember seeing him in court. I don't know. In her police statement, Icey talked about seeing a man attack Leticia. Tom Padfield is a potential suspect in my book. We'll have to follow that up,' Sam confirmed, nodding to her two new employees. 'Leticia was found dead under a statue of Jesus Christ. She had been stabbed, loads of times. Some of them were just jucks: repeated, shallow stabbing, designed to inflict pain. But one severed an artery.'

'You said Icey was found with the murder weapon in her hand?' queried Flick.

'That's right, and she had Leticia's blood all over her.'

'How did Icey explain that?'

'She didn't. She couldn't remember anything. Her memory has been very badly affected.' Sam paused but realised she had to try to be honest with the two girls. 'Icey's had problems in the past with alcohol, but before the night of the murder she'd been sober for months.'

The two girls exchanged glances. 'Sober!' said Flick loudly.

'Well, not completely.' Sam smiled ruefully. 'But she was trying and things had improved significantly.' Icey had assured her that, once the business was opened, she would stay on the wagon; but she'd never had a chance to make good on her promise. 'She'd been drinking on the day of the murder. We had wine at lunch. She said it was a special occasion.' Sam had always suspected that Icey had been drinking alone on that day as well, and when her blood alcohol level was admitted as evidence in court, she'd realised that her suspicions had been correct.

'So if she didn't kill the girl, who did? Do you think Icey was set up by the real murderer?' Oriel pressed.

'Icey was in the wrong place at the wrong time. She has suffered from blackouts in the past when she's been drinking heavily, and she'd drunk a lot that day – far more than I realised at the time. She's also an ex-con and an ex-prostitute. Let's face it, she's an easy target – the obvious suspect, even leaving aside her being found in the church covered in the victim's blood. It wouldn't have been difficult to frame her.'

'So who do you think did do it?' Oriel asked again. 'Do you have any suspects other than Leticia Joy's fiancé?'

'There was a guy called Sexton who said he saw Icey outside the church with blood on her. He said he saw her go back into the church. But he didn't give evidence in person – they had a statement read out. They said he wasn't well enough to attend. He may not be an actual suspect yet, but I think that is definitely suspicious. We need to check him out, too, as well as Tom Padfield.' Sam sighed heavily. 'Look, I need all the help I can get. Our lawyer Mr Frizzel will file an appeal within twenty-eight days, or Icey can apply for her own appeal; but if we don't find some fresh evidence, there's simply no point. She won't ever be released.'

Chapter Twenty-Eight

Sunday morning, Icey woke up with a stiff neck and a heavy heart. The light that beamed into the cell didn't help, nor did the noise. She didn't move from her bunk but allowed her mind to drift back to a time when it had just been her and Sam against everyone else. Sam was an early riser. Icey realised that, out there in the real world, her friend would be up and out of bed already. Sam was also a survivor; she might miss her but she would manage, and that thought was something Icey had yet to come to terms with.

Lights out in prison was really a signal to chat between the cells, and last night had been no different, with two of the homies talking loudly about absolutely nothing, shouting across the hall at each other. It was only when some of the other lifers complained and threatened serious violence that the conversation stopped in the early hours of the morning.

It wasn't until Sunday late afternoon that Icey finally talked to her cellmate for the first time. She was a young girl accused of the manslaughter of her man. She was no more than twenty, doing a straight six on a plea of diminished responsibility. She'd killed him when she was blind drunk, and then hid his body. She didn't want to talk much after they'd traded the prison basics of name, age, crime and sentence, which was good because Icey didn't know what else to say.

At five o'clock, the horn sounded three times. It was the start of association time, which meant that the prison doors were unlocked for a period. The women were allowed to mix with the other prisoners. After only two days as a convicted murderer, Icey was already clinging on to habits and routines. But then she'd already had months to get used to life inside. She wanted to fit in, find her way round her steel cage and keep her head down. She walked up the landing and down the other side.

The entire balcony was connected by steel lace netting that hung across the width of Block eight. It was there to prevent the inmates jumping to their deaths or causing themselves serious harm, but was more commonly used to stop them throwing fellow prisoners over. But with the netting in place, the furthest they could fall, jump or be pushed was one block down.

Icey came across Sandra and Jean in the TV room.

'How you doing, girl?' said Sandra. She was sitting on the one soft chair, braiding Jean's hair.

'Just fine,' said Icey, sitting down next to her and bringing her knees up under her chin.

'Still here, then?' Jean said from under her hair. 'I thought you told me that you were innocent.'

Icey wished she'd change the record. She studied the other woman coolly before replying, 'I am.'

'Well, don't worry about it. We're all innocent in here – until proven guilty, that is.'

Sandra started to laugh, but stopped abruptly when she saw Icey's distraught face. 'What wing are you on?'

'Trinidad,' Icey told her, 'and you?'

'We are on the Jamaican wing.'

Icey frowned. 'There isn't a Jamaican wing.'

'Yes, there is. That's where they send all the mules. My bloke's on Jamaica wing, too – only he's in Brixton,' said Sandra.

'What is he in for?'

'Drug smuggling. He's a stuffer and packer himself.'

Icey nodded, and then grimaced. 'Do you mean he swallowed condoms full of drugs?'

'No, that was too dangerous, he said,' Sandra replied, handing Icey a piece of Jean's hair to hold.

'Well, how did he bring the drugs in?'

'He was stuffed,' Jean chipped in from her under her hair.

'Where?'

'Up the rear end,' Sandra explained. 'He brought in a half kilo.'

'How on earth did he get half a kilo up there?' Icey asked, smiling for the first time in what felt like years.

'You don't want to know.'

'Well, he must be pleading guilty?' Icey said.

'No,' Sandra told her. 'He says he didn't know that he was carrying the drugs.'

Everyone started to laugh.

'Go on,' said Icey, 'tell me, what's his defence?'

'His defence is that when he got off the plane, he was wearing his African roots robe and he went to the toilet after the plane landed.'

'Yeah?' said Icey, wondering where Sandra's story was going.

'He was followed into the toilet.'

'Yeah?' repeated Icey. 'This is getting better all the time.'

'Well, when he was in the toilet he noticed another man who had followed him in and he was behaving very suspiciously.'

'Yeah?' said Icey again, handing Jean's hair back to Sandra to braid.

'Yes, it was only when he went to the toilet that he realised the man was behind him and the next thing he remembered was coming round and feeling very constipated.'

'Definitely not guilty,' said Icey, with tears of laughter in her eyes. 'I just want to know one thing: how was this mystery man going to get his drugs back, assuming that it was him who stuffed your boyfriend?'

Sandra thought about it and started to laugh. 'I'll have to ask him when I next see him.'

Icey smiled back and it felt good. It had been a while, seven months perhaps, since she'd properly laughed, and she was glad she had Jean and Sandra as friends inside. It didn't mean she missed Sam any less. Not seeing her every day was really hard, and the thought of thirty years without her promptly sobered Icey up.

Sensing a change in Icey, Sandra asked, 'So what's next for you?'

Icey looked at Sandra. 'I have a chance of an appeal. My solicitor is drafting it now.'

'I wouldn't trust a lawyer,' said Jean, looking up from underneath a mass of hair. 'They are a bunch of bloodsuckers, money-grabbing liars. They say they will do this and they do that. When it all goes wrong, all they have are excuses. They're a waste of time. Girl, if I was you, I'd do the appeal myself.'

'They are lazy and expensive,' added Jean. 'We've both put in a request to be deported – so we can go back home and serve our sentences near family – but the request has been turned down.'

Sandra added, 'I'm still hoping that an appeal will work, but Jean isn't too sure.'

Icey understood their frustration and wished she could help them in some way. If her appeal worked, then maybe Fleet Investigations could help these two. She'd thought all along that she and Sam wouldn't attract conventional clients, but maybe among criminals and ex-cons they would find their own niche. She started to tell them about Sam and their plans for their detective agency. They listened, surprised, but impressed all the same. They'd both suspected there was something different about the beautiful English girl.

After association, Icey went looking for God. She had tried to talk to him twice since the murder and she reckoned that she still had some unfinished business with him. She had been told on her induction that the Catholic service was at midday, and she had decided she would go. It was time to give God one more chance to help her. At the very least, it was a way of getting out of her cell.

Chapter Twenty-Nine

Sam decided to put Oriel's legs to good use. She had narrowed down her list of P Sextons through the process of dogged telephone pursuit until she thought she had got her man. Oriel could confirm in person that it was the right Sexton, while Sam concentrated on finding Tom Padfield and interviewing him.

In fact, Oriel's legs caused quite a stir on Streatham High Street. She was wearing a very short, tailored skirt with an inverted pleat at the rear, along with a pale blue cashmere top and a leather jacket over the top. The address Sam had given her led to a small row of Edwardian houses off the main road. They were only two up two down, but smart and well maintained.

The house she was looking for was set back behind a small garden dominated by a mature wisteria. Oriel knocked on the black door and stood back to wait, assessing her surroundings as she did so. It was not so much that the house was rundown, it just looked tired among its smarter neighbours. The paint was beginning to flake but had yet to peel.

The door was eventually opened by a woman in her mid-forties, with tight, dusty, mother of pearl curls, skin that was wrinkled beyond its natural elasticity and a body that was significantly swollen past its natural reproductive cycle. She was wearing a plaid skirt, a chunky-knit cardigan and slippers. The crusty-stained apron that hung around her neck was as diverse as any government policy. Here was a full complement of majority and minority stains. None was more prominent than what looked like an old red stain that was splattered across the front of her chest in glorious Technicolor – a multi-coloured splash of shocking red fading to dark red, almost black, smear marks. It looked like blood.

'I am looking for a Mr P Sexton,' Oriel began, a little apprehensively, in her perfect English.

The lady looked her up and down before she spat the words, 'You ain't his minder, are you?'

'Minder? Definitely not. Why does he need a minder?'

''Cos he's a loony. You're wasting your time, love, whatever you're selling or want him for. He's not here.'

Oriel stepped forward and placed her hand on the door as she smiled understandingly. 'When did you last see him?'

'Don't know,' the lady replied, glaring at Oriel's hand. 'Last night, night before, maybe the night before that. When I see him, I call the police and they come and collect him.'

'Where is he now?'

'In the lunatic asylum, where he has been most of our married life.'

'Where is that?' Oriel asked in her best 'you poor dear' tone of voice.

'Somewhere in Kent. Tranquillity House – it's a secure unit, only it can't be that secure 'cos he keeps getting out.'

'Is your husband a religious man, may I ask? Does he go to church?'

'Every day,' Mrs Sexton said with a bitter laugh. 'Practically lives there. Him and God are real close. If you ask me, that's what sent him over the edge. He's a loony – a religious nut!' She started to laugh again and then she stepped back and closed the door. Oriel moved her hand quickly out of the way before the rough wood swung towards her.

As she walked away from the house, Oriel could still hear the woman's laughter ringing in her ears. Sitting back in her car, Oriel made a note: 'Religious nut.' Before moving off, she wound down the window and adjusted her mirror. She put the car into gear but before she could pull off, she was startled by Mrs Sexton forcing her head through the open window.

'If you find him, you'll tell him that he ain't welcome round here.'

As Oriel caught her breath, she confirmed that she would tell him, but she had a feeling that Mrs Sexton would waste no time in telling her husband herself.

Chapter Thirty

Sam slipped into her ostrich-grey two-piece suit. The soft material felt good against her skin and the suit fitted well. The dress was sleeveless, with a Peter Pan collar. The hem was not indecently short, resting just above her knee. The jacket was nipped in at the waist and complemented her womanly curves. Overall, she felt as good as could be expected.

She never could get the hang of putting on her wonder-lash mascara without smudging or clogging her lashes. No matter what she did, it never worked, and today was no different. Looking down, she swiped the smudge of black from her upper lash with a tissue and stared at her reflection again in her hand mirror – not perfect, but it would just have to do. She added a slight touch of rouge and a copious amount of lip gloss. Clipping on her mother of pearl earrings, she then slipped into her heels. She was ready to fulfil item number one on her to do list for the day.

She was at the doors of Holloway Prison two hours before the official visiting time, but the queue was already impossible. Walking back from the gate to take her place in the line-up, she clutched her visitor's order. Despite the long, warm woollen coat she'd pulled on over her suit, the wintry early morning air chilled her, and Sam felt a little tense and apprehensive. She was anxious to know how Icey was dealing with the blow of her sentencing, and how she was bearing up after a weekend back inside.

As she finally reached the visitors' centre, her heart sank to see that the area outside was crowded with relatives eager to see their loved ones. Even the line for security checks to enter the prison wrapped all the way round the outside of the building, and Sam wished that she'd worn lower heels. It was going to be quite a wait. The amount of people was crazy and there were at least a dozen children wandering in and out of the line. It was exactly how Sam remembered visiting hours from all those years ago, when she and Icey had briefly spent time in the Young Offenders' Institution. Although then, both of them had been on the inside, and visitors had been rare.

As she joined the queue, she checked the VO Icey had left for her once again, out of habit. It had her name, address and date of birth printed on it. Sam had brought her driving licence with her as identification, and she reached into her bag to reassure herself that it was still there.

Clearing security was an impossibly slow process. First she had to produce her ID to show that she was who she claimed to be. The queue at the reception counter was fifteen deep. Once cleared through there, she was led into a glass holding bay with a dozen other visitors before proceeding to the next stage, which was effectively the other side of the counter. Here, Sam had to produce her identification again. Once she'd passed through second clearance, a fingerprint and digital photo were taken. The whole process took twenty-two minutes precisely before she was allowed to move on to the next room.

It was a plain municipal room painted more off-than pure white. On the floor by the wall on the right-hand side there were three painted circles about the size of hula hoops. They were in a straight line, approximately three feet apart, one green, one red and one yellow. The prison officer was standing at the side of the three circles and beckoned the visitors forward. Sam was second to go. She stepped forward into the red hula hoop, and held her head high. She had nothing to hide.

In front of Sam, crouched by the feet of the prison officer, was Lucy, a Cavalier King Charles Spaniel. The little dog scampered along the line and until she reached a young woman with beehive hair, wearing skin-tight trousers, where she promptly sat down and remained dutifully still in front of the visitor. The woman was carrying a newborn baby and started to kick off when the dog refused to move away.

'What? What?' was all she could say when she was asked to step aside.

Sam watched as security confirmed that Lucy had picked out Miss Beehive. Additional guards arrived in quick time to conduct a search of Miss Beehive, who became increasingly agitated.

'That dog is picking on me,' she screamed, 'I've done nothing wrong. I've not got nothing on me. Nothing!'

She was right. She was clean when she was searched, but when they asked her to loosen the baby's clothes, she kicked off again.

'What about my baby's rights? You are violating his human rights,' she said to the officer as he removed the baby's cardigan and then his baby-grow. The baby was wearing a double disposable nappy. Inside the outer nappy was half a kilo of cannabis wrapped in cling film.

'How did that get there?' said Miss Beehive.

'Don't know, but you will get an opportunity to explain later. You don't have to say anything, but anything you do say may be taken down and given in evidence. You are under arrest for possession of drugs with intent to supply.'

Lucy trotted past Sam and then back again, evidently deciding against standing in front of her. Sam was allowed to step out of the red-painted circle and proceed to the next room. It was time for her pat-down. Inside, outside, legs, arms and back, hair and shoes. When they found nothing, Sam was finally cleared to see Icey.

She had fourteen minutes left of her allotted visiting time.

Chapter Thirty-One

The visitors' hall was a vast gym-type room with chairs and tables, all of which were bolted to the floor, set out in five rows. The prisoners sat on the left. Their 'guests' were directed to the right-hand side of each table.

At the top of the hall, on a large raised podium, was a larger table. Security sat there and observed the visit to make sure that nothing was passed between the parties. Other security officers also observed from surveillance points and via CCTV. No touching was allowed, no matter what the gender. Such contact would automatically bring the visit to an end. As the notice instructed: NO TOUCHING. NO KISSING. NO PETTING.

Despite these warnings, the prison was awash with drugs, and while everyone knew that bent screws could be relied on to bring in gear, they were rarely caught. The main entry point for drugs, though, in spite of Lucy and the body searches, was on the visits. Searches of prisoners were conducted before and after each visit. Anyone caught was put in segregation and would lose seven days, minimum.

As Sam entered the hall, her eyes scanned the bustling room until she spotted Icey, sitting on the left, wearing regulation clothing. She looked like she'd lost even more weight, and Sam's heart constricted as she studied her. She didn't look well. The prison tracksuit swamped her figure and grey was never a colour that did her pale complexion any favours.

The prisoner on Icey's left wore a similar tracksuit, but with a stripe all the way down the right- and left-hand sides of the trousers and top. She was a runner. She'd tried to bolt it out of the prison, but she had been caught and striped.

Icey smiled and seemed in good spirits as Sam approached her table. If was only when she sat down that Sam realised it was all a show. Icey was fidgety and on edge. Sam wanted to hug her friend, but she knew that she couldn't. She also wanted to tell her that everything would be all right, but she wasn't sure that it would be and she didn't know if she could carry off the lie.

'I never did it, Sam. It's a stitch-up,' Icey said immediately. 'Thirty years in this place will drive me mental.' Her voice was low and sorrowful, brimful of regrets.

'I know you didn't do it. Just tell me what happened, Icey. Have you remembered anything more?'

Icey ignored the question, asking instead, 'When's the appeal, Sam?'

'I don't know, but Frizzel is working on it. And I'm now working on your case, too, and Irma's lent me a couple of her girls to help out. I'm hoping we can find some new evidence, but I don't want to say too much unless it all comes to nothing. I think we'll have good grounds for appeal, though.' Sam smiled with more confidence than she felt.

'I don't know, Sam. I'm not sure about anything any more.'

Ignoring her friend's uncertainty, Sam leant forward. 'This man, Sexton – the witness who saw you that night in the church – what do you know about him?'

Icey thought for a moment. 'Sexton and I were at primary school together. His parents used to live round the back of the church, but that was a long time ago. There was talk at the time that his family were a little odd, but he always seemed fine to me.' Icey held her head in her hands and Sam could see she was shaking. 'What am I going to do, Sam? I shouldn't be in here.'

Sam looked closely at her friend. Her once bright, healthy hair was limp and lifeless. Her face was drawn and she had visibly aged. Shocked at the change in her old friend, Sam knew exactly what to do.

'We're going to clear your name. That's what we are going to do. Firstly, I need to know, do you remember Sexton's first name? He's listed in the court records as P Sexton. I've got one of Madam Irma's girls tracking down a likely address, but I don't know yet if it's the right one.'

'I'm not sure. It was a long time ago that I knew him . . . Peter, I think it was.'

'OK, good. That's something. Secondly, can you tell me: before the night of the murder, when did you last see him?'

'I don't even remember seeing him that night! Before that? I haven't a clue.'

'Did you have any problems with him?' Sam pressed.

'Not that I can remember. It was such a long time ago, Sam.'

'Does he have a reason to set you up, Icey?'

'Not that I know. Honestly, I haven't seen him in years.'

Sam nodded at her friend and tapped her fingers on the plastic table. 'The funny thing is, his statement was read out for him at trial because he was supposedly too ill to attend in person. I think that's a bit suspect. Then there's Tom Padfield.'

'Who's he again?' Icey asked, her expression puzzled.

'That's the man Leticia Joy was about to marry before she was killed. No one seems to have even interviewed him.'

'Oh. Sam, I didn't kill her,' Icey insisted again, quietly.

'I know, but you only get one chance of an appeal and I want to keep more control of your case this time. That way I can make sure it's investigated properly. I've also found you a potential new brief,' she told Icey, making her voice sound deliberately positive.

'Who's that?'

'His name is Ashley Towers. I read about him in the paper. He's good, Icey. He always wins. If you give me the go-ahead, I'll approach him and get him to take your case.'

'Sure, go right ahead and instruct him. Right now what I need is a miracle,' Icey said starkly.

'From what I've read, Ashley Towers sometimes performs them as well.'

The two women smiled at each other, and momentarily fell silent, the reality of the situation really hitting home.

'Sam, this whole business has got me down,' Icey said after a few moments, 'and I just don't know how much more I can take. I'm going mad in here. What do I do if they knock back the appeal? I can't do thirty years. I just can't . . .' Icey held her head in her hands again.

'They're not going to knock back the appeal! We're going to make damn sure that they don't. Come on, Icey. Dust yourself off and get over yourself. You've got to stay strong. But you didn't answer me before – have you remembered any more about that night?'

'No,' Icey said in a downbeat tone.

'Come on, stay strong, Icey,' Sam urged again. 'We'll get you out of here.'

Before Sam could tell her more about her two new helpers at Fleet Investigations, the visit was over. Getting up, she was about to embrace her friend out of habit when she remembered that touching was not permitted, unless Icey was prepared to lose another seven days of her liberty. There would be plenty of time to talk and hug when Icey was free, Sam told herself.

But first they had to achieve the impossible and overturn the guilty verdict at her appeal.

Chapter Thirty-Two

The picture Detective Constable Haydn was putting together of Judge Certie was that he'd led an unremarkable life. He went to work and then he returned home. Occasionally, he would go to a work-related function, but there was nothing obvious in his past that indicated why he might have taken his own life. And everything seemed to point to suicide.

Haydn had learnt that the judge's wife was a committed Christian. Margaret Certie spent most of her time involving herself with charities. Her favourite was the NSPCC and she also volunteered two days a week at the Trinity Hospice, mainly involved with raising money for their end-of-life care services. She knew of no reason why anyone would have wanted to harm her husband – and certainly no reason, she said, that he might have been driven to suicide. They had been married for thirty-six years and their two children had left home several years earlier. Their eldest, James, was a lawyer on secondment in Hong Kong. Maria was a university lecturer. Their large family home in Chelsea was tastefully decorated. The mortgage had been paid off many years ago, and they had no financial worries.

Staring at the file again, flicking through his notes, Haydn was baffled. Why would a successful judge commit suicide? This was a question to which he didn't yet know the answer, but he felt sure someone did. Sooner or later he would find the right person to talk to; someone who would provide the last piece of the puzzle of Certie's life. Having already talked to the judge's family, he was now moving on to question Certie's colleagues and peers.

DC Haydn presented himself punctually at the judges' entrance to the Old Bailey, at his appointed time. So far, he had not made much progress with his interviews at the court. Everyone had closed ranks. He had tried repeatedly to loosen the lips of the powers that be, and had been rebuffed in the politest of judicial terms. The judges were not about to snitch on a fellow judge. Haydn just hoped that he would have better luck with the Recorder of London, the most senior permanent judge of the Central Criminal Court as well as a man renowned for his straight talking and no-nonsense approach.

The porter was a shrivelled prune of a man, who had dried up years ago. He looked as dusty as the security equipment that he monitored, and not particularly pleased to see Haydn. He didn't exactly go out of his way to welcome the detective constable. Perched on his high stool, the porter barely looked up as Haydn held out his ID. Instead, he kept his gaze firmly fixed on the green flashing lights of the security scan machine.

'The Recorder of London is expecting me,' DC Haydn announced.

The porter reluctantly peered at Haydn before nodding.

'Yes, sir. Just sign here and put the time in the second column, and right you are,' he instructed dourly. 'The Recorder said you'd requested to take another look at where Judge Certie jumped from. We'll go up in the lift. If you would care to follow me, sir,' he invited, leading Haydn towards the lift.

The lift arrived, the doors opened and they both stepped inside. As they made their way up to the roof, the porter sighed heavily, evidently deciding that if he had to escort Haydn, he may as well make the effort to talk to him. 'Rum business this, sir. Wouldn't be surprised if there was a woman involved.'

Haydn listened but didn't comment. He waited for the porter to say more, but as they exited the lift the porter led him to the left.

'He would have gone through this door, sir, and up those stairs to the balcony. Must have been pretty determined to top himself, if you ask me.'

They ascended the stairs and came out on the balcony beneath the Statue of Justice. Haydn looked up at her and smiled wryly. He was not one for the niceties of the law – just got on with the business of catching villains. He looked down and felt a distinct sensation of vertigo tingling up and down his spine. His stomach rose at the thought of moving closer to the edge; of Judge Certie jumping off it.

'That'll be enough,' he said. 'I'd like to see the Recorder now, please,' he said, fighting nausea.

The porter nodded and led him back down the way they had come.

The Recorder of London had a modern office. He was seated but stood up as the porter knocked and opened the door to allow DC Haydn to enter the room. On the shelf behind the Recorder's large desk, Haydn noticed ornate framed photos of what he presumed to be the judge's wife and children.

'Morning, morning,' the Recorder said, cheerfully enough, stepping out from behind his desk to gesture Haydn into the room. 'Do come in. Would you like some tea, or maybe coffee?' He appeared refreshingly youthful to hold such a senior position, and was jolly and somewhat overweight, with very few grey hairs and a boyish smile.

Haydn looked around the office before replying. 'No thanks, sir, I'm OK as I am.'

'Welsh?' the judge inquired.

'Yes, sir.' Haydn had lived most of his working life in London, but the lilt to his accent was still evident.

'We have some Welsh judges here, you know,' the Recorder told him chattily. 'We are very diverse.'

Haydn looked surprised as the Recorder laughed to indicate it was a joke. He didn't join in. The Recorder pointed at a man sitting in the corner.

'By the way, this is my Common Serjeant. He's my number two. I asked him sit in on our meeting, in case he could help.'

'Good morning,' said the Common Serjeant, in clipped tones. 'You're a sergeant yourself?'

'No, sir. I'm a detective constable,' Haydn corrected.

'Soon to be promoted, no doubt.'

'I doubt that very much, sir, unless I solve this case, of course.' The judges permitted themselves a restrained smile in response. 'If you don't mind me saying so, sir, yours is a curious title,' Haydn commented, addressing the deputy judge.

'Yes, it's an ancient title. Serjeant is spelt with a "j", of course. It simply means an advisor,' he explained. 'Part of my job is to give advice to the Common Council of the City of London.'

'Shall we get on?' suggested the Recorder impatiently, his initial jovial mood vanishing.

'Well, sir, first of all, I'd like to get some idea of what Judge Certie was like,' Haydn asked.

'Rather a bluff fellow,' said the Recorder after a brief pause. 'Not really one for socialising or emotional outbursts. Rather surprising thing for him to do, considering . . .'

'The porter downstairs—'

'We call them redcoats,' the Common Serjeant interjected with a condescending smile. Haydn shifted his stance uneasily.

'Well, sir, he mentioned he thought there might have been a woman involved?'

The Recorder and the Common Serjeant exchanged glances.

'Not that we know of,' said the Recorder. 'Of course, experience shows that still waters run deep. And most people don't like to advertise that sort of thing.'

'He'd just been told that he was to be made a High Court Judge,' revealed the Common Serjeant. 'We're both Circuit Judges like him. That's a rank below the High Court, though our offices do hold similar prestige.'

The Recorder smiled broadly. His teeth were remarkably white and perfectly straight.

'Between these four walls,' added the Common Serjeant, 'some of us were rather surprised at his appointment.'

'He wasn't the sharpest card in the pack,' explained the Recorder. 'Rather old-fashioned, even for a judge.' He gave another slight smile. 'Not up to date with the latest developments. But maybe that is what they like.'

'You have to apply these days to the Judicial Appointments Board,' clarified the Common Serjeant. 'Between you and me, they're a lot of do-gooders who know nothing about the law. We did wonder if, when he heard the news, Certie perhaps thought he was not really up to it. That might just be behind it.'

Haydn made a note but privately thought that a man who didn't think he was up to promotion always had the option of turning it down rather than taking his own life. 'His wife, sir. What's she like?' He had no intention of mentioning that he'd already interviewed Margaret Certie and formed his own opinions on the grieving widow.

There was another slight pause.

'A bit colourless,' said the Recorder. 'Didn't offer much in conversation. Very religious. Did good works.'

'The wives don't play a big role here,' said the Common Serjeant.

'They do go to the city dinner,' said the Recorder, glancing at his deputy.

'Any other thoughts, sir, which might help?' DC Haydn asked, his gaze flicking between the two judges before settling on the face of the Recorder.

'Not really, it is all very puzzling.'

'Well, sir, if you do think of anything . . .' Haydn allowed his words to trail off meaningfully.

'Of course.'

The redcoat was summoned and Haydn was escorted back down the stairs to the judges' entrance. He asked the redcoat about his earlier hint of a woman's involvement.

'Just a guess, sir. A hunch. Nothing concrete.'

Frustrated, Haydn left the Old Bailey. He was getting nowhere here, but he did know that he was more prepared to buy the porter's theory than the view expressed by the Common Serjeant.

Chapter Thirty-Three

Sam had sat hunched over papers for far too long. Her neck was stiff and she had cramp in both her legs, but she was determined not to quit until she'd read the forensic report again. The first time she read it, she didn't understand it. The second time, she worked through it more methodically, Googling the unfamiliar medical terms on her laptop, so it had been a little clearer. Harry Kemp had agreed to meet up and look through all the trial papers with his ex-copper's eyes, and Sam wanted to read everything thoroughly before they did so.

As she settled down to read the papers for the third time, she noticed a tall figure walk past the detective agency's open outer door. She looked up and could have sworn that it was Ashley Towers. She recognised him from the magazine article. Craning her neck, she tried to get a better look, but he had gone. Curious, she quickly strode outside to take a look, just in time to see whoever it was disappear up the flight of stairs outside.

Sam paused, then followed. She needed to find out if it was indeed Towers, and, if so, persuade him to take on Icey's case. She had tried to leave a message for him, but had got no answer from the number listed in Irma's directory. Reaching the offices upstairs, she checked the clear glass sign that ran down the side of the closed double doors. It bore a list of all the members of chambers in bold print, and there in the middle of the board was Mr Ashley Towers.

'Unbelievable,' she murmured to herself.

Back in her office, Sam quickly thumbed through the directory that Irma had given her. It gave a different address for Towers' chambers, but then she noticed that the directory was a year out of date. Frustrated, she walked back up the stairs and found the telephone number at the bottom of the sign, along with the contact details of the senior clerk. Sam made a mental note of the number before hurrying back to her own office. She repeated the number in her head as she dialled it.

'Good afternoon. Server Chambers. May I help?' A well-spoken lady answered the phone.

'Yes. My name is Ms Bailey, and I would like to speak to Mr Towers, please.'

'Is Mr Towers expecting your call?'

'No, he's not.'

'May I enquire as to the nature of the call?'

'Yes, I'm next door and I'd like to—'

'When you say next door,' the refined voice cut in, 'what do you mean?'

'I mean that I work at Fleet Investigations and—'

'Oh, you're that woman.'

'I'm sorry? What woman might that be?' Sam enquired, beginning to feel irritated.

'I think we both know the answer to that, don't we?' the prim voice declared.

'I'm a private investigator.'

'Yes, and I am the Queen of Sheba. You want to speak to Mr Towers? In your dreams.'

The phone went dead. Obviously her neighbours must have heard something about her previous line of work and were judging her accordingly. Sam sighed heavily. Still, forewarned was forearmed, and maybe she could use the woman's prejudices against her. She waited until the automated recording invited her to replace the receiver, hung up and tried again. The phone was picked up instantly and Sam recognised the same voice.

'I would like to speak to Mr Towers,' she repeated with icy politeness

'He's not available.'

'I think he is. And trust me, darling, he'll want to speak to me.'

'Who shall I say is calling?'

'His favourite tart.'

'What's it in connection with?'

'Let's just say it's personal, and you really don't want to know.'

'Just one moment, madam.'

Several moments later, Mr Towers was on the line. His voice was crisp, educated and he spoke with a determination to end the conversation as soon possible.

'It's Ms Bailey, I understand? How may I help?'

'Mr Towers, we've never met but I have been asked by a dear friend of mine to contact you with a view to instructing you in her appeal.' Sam came straight to the point.

'I'm afraid I'm really very busy.'

'You may have read about it in the papers. She was convicted of the so-called Magdalene Murder. She would like to appeal and she would like you to represent her.'

'What's your friend's name again?'

'Elizabeth Johnson.'

Towers had heard of the case. It had attracted a lot of publicity, but the woman had already been convicted. He didn't like taking on another barrister's client at the appeal stage. It was always messy, lots of hard work and with no significant financial reward. There would also be hardly any publicity left in it for him by this stage, and Towers – like most briefs – thrived on press coverage and column inches.

'I am very sorry, Ms Bailey, but I really am snowed under. I don't think that I will have the time to get the appeal up to scratch. I'm going to have to say no.'

'Mr Towers, Elizabeth Johnson is innocent.'

'I'm sure she is, but I really cannot help, now if you will excuse me . . .'

'Wait. Mr Towers,' said Sam frantically, 'your secretary may not have mentioned it but your chambers are next door to my office. I would welcome the opportunity to tell you more about the case. I'm sure that once you have heard all the evidence, you will want to be involved in the appeal.'

'Interesting, Ms Bailey. You say that you're next door. Next door where?'

'I'm a private investigator and I run Fleet Investigations from the same building as your offices.'

Sam could almost hear Ashley Towers' spark of recognition. He'd probably also heard the gossip about his neighbours downstairs – spread by his vicious receptionist, no doubt. But maybe he'd be intrigued enough by the idea of former prostitutes running a legitimate business to at least hear her out.

'Tell me more about the case,' he instructed.

Sam smiled to herself. Bingo, she thought; she had an opening at least. She started at the beginning and told him all she knew.

Once Towers had listened to Sam's doubts and the evidence discrepancies, she could tell he was still in two minds about accepting the case. But she knew that he'd be attracted by the possibility of more publicity; and she also hinted that there would be the chance of more work in due course. And while a man like Ashley Towers might feel he was above dealing with an ex-tart, she knew he'd overlook any principles at the thought of cold, hard cash. Barristers, she was learning, might be expensive but they could be hired as easily as any high-class whore. She knew enough about men to know how to tempt him to take the case, and she could tell that she had him hooked. She kept her excitement to herself and continued to talk professionally to Towers. She agreed to arrange for him to be sent the appeal brief, and made a note to do it straight away.

When she put down her phone, she almost laughed herself silly. Mr Towers was a typical lawyer: seduced by the prospect of money and press coverage. Sam punched the air and grinned. She had him.

Chapter Thirty-Four

Sam rushed to tell Mr Frizzel immediately of the new developments, wondering how he would react to news of Ashley Towers coming on board; but when she turned the handle to open the door to his office, she found him curled up on his desk fast asleep, despite it being late in the afternoon. He looked so old and dishevelled that, as she watched him, she was overcome with a profound sense of sadness.

He looked half-dead, despite his skin being almost constantly flushed as a result of alcohol addiction. He was asleep now, but when he was awake he usually had no idea whether he was coming or going. Frizzel rarely went home these days. His preference was to sleep in the office, preferably on his desk or in his chair.

For him, the case was a nice little earner. Legal Aid paid well in murder cases. He was still billing Icey's case and getting paid to read the statements and study the forensics, and this did nothing to encourage him to prepare the case for appeal. It all made Sam's blood boil. But given what she knew about the man, she was as ever torn between killing him with her bare hands and taking him under her wing.

Those who knew Mr Adrian Frizzel from his heyday as a lawyer spoke of a man with a razor-sharp intellect. He had graduated from Cambridge University with a first in Latin, followed by a double first in law from Oxford. As a qualified lawyer, his success had been swift. He'd been involved in every celebrity case that landed on his desk, and he fought all with equal passion and determination. He would instruct counsel at a very early stage, and between the two of them they would work out the strategy of the trial and he would win. These glory days, however, had all come to an abrupt end some years before.

He had represented the defendant in what the press termed the 'Sweet Dreams' murder case. Accused of killing a number of women while they slept, this notorious client had been defended so successfully by Mr Frizzel that he'd won the high-profile case against all odds. Then on a warm summer's night, when the air was thick and the stars glistened in the grey-black sky, the husband of one of the Sweet Dreams victims came to Frizzel's house armed with a Colt 45 and blew out the brains of Mr Frizzel's wife and only child, before turning the gun on himself.

The killer left a note, blaming Frizzel for the dedication with which he had defended his client. He had helped free a serial killer. In his mind, Frizzel was guilty too and it was only fair that he should experience the loss of a loved one or two. Maybe then he would reconsider the appropriateness of representing monsters with dogged determination.

Adrian Frizzel sank from celebrity lawyer to recluse overnight. He vanished from the legal scene and hit the bottle, hard. When he finally returned to court twenty-three months later, he was a different man. Gone were the razor-sharp brain, the instinct for killer tactics and the fearlessness that set him apart for other lawyers. Frizzel was now dishevelled, incoherent and addicted to alcohol. He wasn't willing to talk to anyone about what had happened to his family. He was also a coward. He wished he had the courage to join his wife and child, but he didn't. Every day was just a reminder to him that he was a dead man walking.

In the early days, most people who knew about his tragic personal circumstances were sympathetic; but as time wore on and the days turned into months and the months into years, patience and sympathy became thin on the ground and Adrian Frizzel was yesterday's man. Since that dreadful day when his family were wiped out, he had mostly chosen to sleep in the office rather than face an empty house. He was haunted by the nightmares of a past life, and it was killing him, albeit too slowly for his liking. Unable to go forward, he was too terrified to look back. His former colleagues still had a huge amount of sympathy for him, but newer lawyers and barristers who didn't know his story regarded him with contempt.

Sam Bailey didn't want to judge him too harshly. He'd always been there for her and Icey. And he had never judged them. He had once been committed and brilliant, and she preferred to remember him that way. She'd known him before he had lost everything. Then, he had commanded her respect. She decided she would continue do her best to move him on from the trauma of his past. Sam understood a bit of his pain and the need to numb his feelings. He and Icey were very similar in some ways. And all three of them, in fact, had suffered as victims of a past from which they couldn't escape.

Sam had been honest with him when she and Icey had signed the lease for the office premises. He obviously knew all about their pasts, given that he'd defended them on more than one occasion. It was regrettable that he was unable to share his pain with her or accept her offers of help, but at the end of the day, she was not his keeper. It was also made more difficult now that Sam realised he was one of the greatest obstacles in Icey's appeal. She knew she would have to work doubly hard for the both of them.

Sam even suspected that Mr Frizzel would have been happy if Icey abandoned the appeal altogether. Then he could spend most days in the Frog and Duck getting drunk. Provided he had a steady income, which meant enough to keep him supplied with alcohol, then Frizzel was happy. But Sam and Icey needed him, so she worked hard to keep him in a semi-professional mode and ready for the appeal.

While Frizzel slept on, Sam reorganised his office around him. She filed away the briefs he claimed to be working on, and then she very discreetly got rid of the bottles hidden in the office. She had thrown out four bin liners full and still she kept coming across more. At least he'd had the good sense recently to increase her pay. Most of the days when he was incapable, he would simply drink himself into a stupor and direct his clients next door to Fleet Investigations, where Sam would take copious notes and instruct any prospective clients in serious need of a lawyer to come back when Mr Frizzel might be more sober. Although those days were getting fewer and farther between.

Chapter Thirty-Five

Martha Lewis was a pretty girl – blonde, slim and toned – but at the moment she looked ugly. It was Thursday night, almost the end of the month, and it was pay day – and that meant only one thing: getting legless. Martha wasn't an attractive drunk. She was nasty, spiteful and loud. But she'd had a very good night and now she was on her way home alone.

It had crossed her mind to go via Clapham Junction, which was closer to her flat, but for no better reason than that she happened to be nearer to a tube station, she had decided instead to travel to Clapham Common on the Northern Line and walk home from there.

As a chilly February wind blew down the street, Martha pulled her coat around her. Earlier it has seemed like a good idea to dress to impress in the latest fashion: a white playsuit, worn with white stilettos. Her long legs, gracious gait and 'sit me down' rear end had made sure she got all the attention she needed. She knew she was fit. And until she'd drunk too much, every available man wanted to buy her a drink. But now she was freezing and couldn't wait to be home as soon as possible. Walking up the road past the Pepper Tree restaurant, she crossed over from Clapham South Side onto the Common, and decided to cut straight across it rather than along The Avenue.

Drawing her coat more tightly around her shapely figure, Martha suddenly knew that she was not alone. Walking past a cluster of trees, she noticed a shadow to her right. She walked into the centre of the path, refusing to look back. As she approached the football pitch on the left, she noticed that the person behind her was now walking on the path. She could see their shadow behind her, bobbing over her left shoulder. It was not like Martha to get nervous about nothing in particular. She was a Londoner, born and bred, and she could handle herself; plus she had walked this route on many occasions when she was equally drunk. But even so, it didn't feel right; Martha was glad that she only had fifty metres to go until she reached the main road.

As she increased her pace, she noticed that the shadow had disappeared. Taking a deep breath, Martha continued to walk and concentrate on the footbath ahead of her. The end of the path was in sight and, looking over her left shoulder and then her right, she inhaled slowly. Whoever it was had vanished. Maybe it had just been her imagination. Turning left by the football pitch, Martha kept close to the path. As she looked up into a remarkably clear sky, she saw the stars twinkling. She felt a lot better. It was funny how she never really noticed the beauty of the sky at night, unless she was out late and a little bit worse for wear. But as Martha stopped briefly to marvel at the stars, she realised far too late that she had made a big mistake.

Chapter Thirty-Six

Clapham Common North Side was a row of splendid Georgian houses facing the open space. It consisted of five-storey buildings in a commanding position with views across the Common. The only traffic was cars heading, normally at speed, to the Common or to Stockwell. The houses were set back from the road. The gardens were over fifty metres long, beautiful and immaculate, and there the very rich and the would-be rich lived comfortably and anonymously in the very heart of the old town.

It was an area with an interesting history, as the numerous blue plaques attested. Most notably, on that very road over a century ago, Wilberforce and his friend Edgely, along with other socially conscious Claphamites, planned the campaign to abolish slavery. This year, however, its current residents were more concerned with a spate of break-ins, to the extent that they had employed a security firm to patrol the area each day, doubling up guards over the weekends when many of the residents departed to their second homes in the country, leaving their London pads at the mercy of opportunistic thieves.

The overnight security attendant was almost asleep in his car when he took the call from a resident on Clapham Common South Side. She reported that a light was on at the football pitch, disturbing her sleep. Promising to investigate the matter, he took two more calls from other residents in quick succession, each expressing the same annoyance. Putting his phone down, he made a note of the time and the name of the complainants, and then he called Head Office to report. They told him to ignore the complaints; lights were not part of their security contract or his job description.

At 6.30 on Friday, four hours after the original call, the night security man took another call from a lady on the West Side of the Common. She claimed the lights on the pitch were now flashing intermittently on and off.

Rachel Hall was a wiry old woman. Some would say she was a nosy parker and an interfering old cow. But since the death of her husband, and needing less and less sleep as she got older, her main occupation was people watching. She had not slept all night. She had twice called the night security firm to complain about the floodlights on the nearby football pitch. So far they still had not sent anyone out to turn them off.

Now she could see a strange man standing at the scene, and she'd had enough. At 7 a.m., Rachel Hall rang her local police station to complain about anti-social behaviour. On her third attempt, she was connected to a person, not a machine. She was provided with a crime reference number and a promise that a police officer would go and investigate. Rachel Hall replaced the phone and looked out of the window across the road. He was still there.

Chapter Thirty-Seven

Detective Constable Anne Cody was in plain clothes, sitting in an unmarked car. She was tired and worn out by the constant demands of her duties, but for the first time in her entire life she was in love. It was not something that had just crept up on her. She had known for a while now that she was falling. What to do about it was another matter.

She had almost got fed up waiting for Mr Right. She was, after all, thirty-six; and although she was not the prettiest picture in the force, she wasn't unattractive. She had a good body that she worked on when she could get to the gym.

It had taken all her courage to call him. She had been thrown when it went to voicemail, but she'd pulled herself together to leave a message asking him to call her. As she drove back to the police station in Kier Road, she thought about the message and smiled. She had left him in no doubt that she was available if he was. She laughed to herself as she realised all she wanted was for DCI Paradissimo to recognise that she was a real person with feelings. She had been aware of them for some time but she'd tried to ignore them. She was never one for dating other coppers, and had always tried in the past to keep her private life separate from the job.

It was bad enough with all the gossip and sexist comments that were seen as everyday, normal banter. She wanted to be taken seriously. She was not just a bit of skirt; she was a first-rate cop with a good reputation and a level of seniority. But pulling Paradissimo was a chance worth taking. She had waited for him to make the first move, but when it didn't happen, she had finally decided to do it herself. And now that she had, she felt excited.

It was 7.40 on Friday morning when the call came out over the radio stating that a suspicious person had been spotted on the North Side of Clapham Common. The report also said that floodlights had been going on and off all night on the football pitch. DC Cody had five minutes until the end of her shift. No one would make a comment if she didn't answer the call and knocked off slightly early. However, full of nervous energy, and always ready to demonstrate her commitment to the job, she answered the call, switching on her engine immediately and heading to North Side.

On the way there, Cody didn't turn on her blue siren. The incident was probably nothing, but she didn't want to alert any potential suspects as to a police presence. Arriving at Clapham Common, she drove slowly along the North Side and past North Road. Nearing the bright lights, as reported, she spotted a man walking towards her. He was just a random male and it wasn't so early in the day for his presence to be suspicious, but her brain was working overtime. She parked her car quickly on Long Avenue, and got out to approach him, but he swiftly crossed the road and walked away in the opposite direction. Cody crossed to the North Side and followed him.

She quickened her pace but as she turned the corner, the street was empty. She walked back to where the floodlights illuminated the football pitch.

Even before Cody approached, she could see that this was not a simple matter of anti-social behaviour. The lighting looked like it has been rigged so that one solitary light flashed on and off, illuminating the centre of the field. As Cody approached the entrance to the pitch, she saw an image that would remain with her for the rest of her life.

A young blonde woman was spread-eagled in the centre of the pitch. All of her clothes had been removed and they were neatly arranged in a pile to the left of her head. She was lying on her back with her arms outstretched, legs wide. Her head was facing west and her arms were outstretched north and south.

Cody approached the naked body with caution, her stomach churning with adrenaline. Training told her she needed to check for a pulse, even though it was obviously already far too late. The victim's throat had been so deftly split that she was very nearly decapitated. It wasn't an ambulance that was required here; it was a body bag.

She spotted immediately that the girl had put up a fight. The defensive wounds across the palms of her hands told their own story. At some point before she died, the victim had tried to resist. Two of the fingers on her right hand were severed to the first joint. There was substantial bruising, which suggested she'd been beaten before death; the array of knife wounds to her torso also suggested a prolonged, torturous attack. Cody noticed that the victim's pubic hair was neatly trimmed in the shape of a heart. But most shockingly of all, protruding from her vagina was what looked like a crucifix. Cody was no expert but that, together with the nudity and the bruising to the top of her legs, clearly indicated a strong sexual element to the attack, although they would need the coroner to confirm her worst suspicions. The religious overtones were also unsettling, but lots of freaks and perverts seemed to get off on crosses and the like.

DC Cody used her radio to call back to the station and request an ambulance, SOCO and the coroner. She stood looking at the victim as she waited for them. She couldn't help but feel sorry for the unknown woman. The lights continued to flash on and off, but until they'd dusted for prints and searched for other forensic evidence, there was nothing she could do about that. It seemed likely that it had been the killer who had rigged them to do that. He wanted to show off his victim. It was as if he was proud of his handiwork. Under the lights, the victim's face shone and her body was ghostly white, albeit lying in a pool of congealed blood. She must have died in the most excruciating pain, Cody realised as she checked her watch again, longing for her colleagues to arrive. Hardened police officer she might be, but she felt sick just imagining what her unnamed victim must have endured.

Chapter Thirty-Eight

It was 8.30 on Friday morning when Flick took the escalator towards the exit at Clapham Common Station. She was tired from working for Irma all night, and was looking forward to sleeping that morning before going to help out Sam for a couple of hours after lunch. So far she had enjoyed her time at Fleet Investigations, and she was determined to do all she could to help Sam in her quest to get her friend released. Flick would give one hundred per cent commitment towards that goal.

Feeling a little woozy from lack of sleep, Flick decided to walk across the Common to save time. Crossing over from the South Side to The Pavement, she was surprised by all the activity. On the North Side of the Common, past Orlando Road, she saw police lights flashing in the distance.

As she approached Macaulay Road, Flick could see that a white tent had been erected close to the edge of the Common. A small group of rubbernecks had stopped to watch the police activity. Flick turned right into The Chase just off the North Side and walked the final twenty metres or so to her own front door. Plunging her hand into her bag, she pulled out her key. But as she turned it in the lock, she stopped dead on the threshold. Something was wrong; something significant was happening back there on the Common, and she needed to know what. After all, it wasn't every day she saw police swarming about near her home. Her instinct told her to go back, and the years spent in her line of work had taught Flick always to listen to her instincts. She closed the door and retraced her steps. Sleep would have to wait.

The police had cordoned off an area surrounding the white tent with their blue and white tape, marking an obvious crime scene. The Scene of Crime Officers, dressed in their pristine white overalls and face masks, moved silently between the tent and the mobile forensic laboratory. Walking round to the far side of the cordon, Flick spotted a lone young officer. She checked her appearance and was glad that, beneath her coat, she still had on her work gear of short skirt and silky blouse. She undid her coat as she approached the man, and readied a smile; but he simply raised his hand, ordering her to halt. She stopped and caught the officer's eye before his gaze drifted to roam lazily over her petite but shapely body.

'Officer,' she said smoothly, ' I live off Clapham Common North Side. Do you know how long before all the activity dies down here? I work nights and . . .'

The officer looked at Flick and smiled appreciatively.

'Can't say, but there has been an incident and I'm sorry we're keeping you up, miss.'

'Oh, how terrible. I guess you'll be here a while, then?'

'We will be here for some time, yes.'

'I hope you got here in time?' Flick purred seductively. She moved closer. The officer was young, fresh-faced and eager.

'No, I'm afraid we were too late. The victim was dead before we arrived. SOCO – I mean our Scene of Crime Officers – are with her now.' He had a strong masculine voice but sounded a little nervous.

'How did she die?' Flick probed.

'I'm sorry, miss, but I can't reveal that information.'

'Of course,' Flick acknowledged smoothly. 'Well, I hope she didn't suffer too much.'

The young policeman's look told Flick all she wanted to know on that score.

'Oh! How awful!' Flick said. 'I think, officer, I'll just go for a walk on the other side of the Common to clear my head until the police activity dies down.'

The young officer studied her beautiful face and replied, 'I don't advise that, miss. I suggest that you go home. There is a killer on the loose.'

Flick nodded and smiled as she stepped away towards the undergrowth. Moving slowly, she watched as one of the white-suited men – SOCO, she deduced – approached the young officer she'd just been talking to. Darting behind the trunk of a great oak while their attention was distracted, she listened to their conversation.

'How much longer do you think?' said the young officer, rubbing his hands against the early morning chill.

'We'll be here a while yet,' his colleague answered.

'So it's definitely murder. I haven't seen the body.'

'Yes, without a doubt,' replied the SOCO. 'Whoever killed her did a very thorough job. They removed her clothes. Must be some kind of religious freak. He rammed a crucifix up inside her.'

Flick stood absolutely still. The words 'religious freak' had stopped her in her tracks. Not wanting to give away her presence, she hid there for several more minutes before making her way to the front of the cordon. Once she was at a safe distance, she reached for her mobile and called Sam on the office phone. When Sam didn't pick up, Flick left a message and then tried to call her mobile. There was no answer. She kept trying as she walked the short distance home, this time letting herself straight into her flat and changing swiftly into a tracksuit and trainers before returning to the Common. She hoped her jogger's disguise would help her blend in more easily as she observed events and waited for Sam to call her back

Chapter Thirty-Nine

Sam kicked off her shoes and stretched out her legs. She'd been working in her office since the early hours, unable to sleep, and now her mind buzzed with Icey's case notes. Moving her feet from under the desk, she noticed with dismay that the left leg of her tights was snagged, with large holes the size of conkers. The ladders ran the whole length of her thigh and made her smart dress look dishevelled and cheap.

Sighing, she leant forward and hunted through her desk drawers until she found a spare pair of tights, and tucked them into her bag. Then she went to the building's communal ladies' toilet to change and freshen up, glad that it wouldn't yet be too busy with people arriving at work. She knew that if by any chance a potential client came in to the office, she owed it to Icey to look presentable and professional.

As she returned to her desk, she noticed the red light flashing on the right-hand side of the phone. Lifting the handset, she dialled the number to retrieve the message. Anyone who knew Sam well would know it was pretty pointless to leave messages on her phone because she rarely picked them up. She preferred to talk in person. But these days she always hoped it might be someone with news that might help Icey's case; maybe someone who had read one of the leaflets she'd distributed three weeks ago and come forward with new information. Mostly, all she'd had to deal with so far were crank messages. This time, though, the message was from Flick, and as she listened to the girl's words panic set into Sam's heart.

A second woman was dead, and Flick was convinced there could be a connection to the murder of Leticia Joy.

Grabbing her coat and bag, Sam rushed out of the detective agency. She arrived at Clapham Common twenty minutes later, and went in search of Felicity Peasey.

As she headed down Long Road, one hand desperately rifled through her bag for her oyster pink mobile phone, which she pulled out and flipped open to call Flick.

There was no answer at first, so she redialled, again with no response. Cursing, Sam crossed the road at a run, heading for Trinity Church on the edge of the Common. Expecting to find the murder scene in or at least close to the church, she was fleetingly disappointed as she realised the heavy police presence was in fact further along the Common. Flick's message had been brief but Sam had automatically presumed that the second murder would also be in the vicinity of a church. It seemed the similarities between Leticia Joy's murder and the new victim weren't as close as Sam had assumed. Or indeed hoped.

'Excuse me,' she said as she approached the police cordon and pushed through the growing crowds. Bending down, she started to step underneath the tape, but a burly police officer stopped her.

He held up his hand authoritatively. 'Sorry, miss, but this is a crime scene. You're not allowed in here.'

Sam took a deep breath and smiled in apology. 'I am sorry,' she said confidently. 'I'm a private investigator and I'm looking for my assistant. She left me a message to meet her here.'

'Well, miss, I can assure you that she is not here now. If you would like to make your way back behind the cordon, I'd be most grateful.'

'She must be here. Do you mind if I look?' Sam moved forward, but was again stopped by the officer, who this time glared at her.

'I suggest you go home. Someone was murdered here last night, and no one is allowed on the pitch, not even a private investigator,' he said, somewhat scathingly.

On hearing this, Sam cannily saw an opening. She gasped loudly, clutching her throat, pretending to come over all dizzy. Partially falling against the officer, she whispered, 'Murdered? You say that someone was murdered. Who? I mean, male or female?'

The office looked shocked and then uncomfortable as he held Sam. 'Er, a female.'

'No!' Sam took a deep breath and a calculated risk, pretending to swoon. The officer caught her before she fell to the floor. As she 'came round' she gasped and began to wail – loud howls that would have chilled the souls of the dead. She slumped into the officer's arms, confident that her waterproof mascara would hold up under a little fake sorrow for a 'friend' who was no more.

'Miss, we don't know who the victim was yet. If you think you know her, we'll have to take a statement,' said an approaching female officer.

'Do you think you know her?' asked her male colleague, still supporting Sam.

Sam realised the gig was up; there was only so much she could bluff without outright lying, and she didn't want to do that. She broke free from the officer's reluctant embrace with a semi-apologetic smile. The WPC summoned another female colleague and together they started to escort Sam away from the crime scene, each firmly taking hold of an arm.

But as they were walking her away, one of the WPCs received a call and turned away to answer it. On finishing the conversation, the officer nodded to her colleague and gestured towards the murder scene. It was evident they were needed elsewhere. Issuing instructions to Sam to stay where she was until they could return to question her, they both left her unattended. Sam remained perfectly still for a moment. As soon as she thought she was not being observed, she ducked under the police tape and made her approach to the white tent. She strode towards the entrance with all the confidence of someone who belonged, as if she didn't expect to be challenged by an officer standing inside the entrance – a young, fresh-faced copper who nevertheless displayed steely determination.

'You can't go in there, miss,' he declared as he placed his arm in front of Sam to form a barrier. 'How did you get through the cordon, anyway?' Sam tried to dip under his arm, but again he stopped her by holding on to her wrists. 'I've just told you that you can't go in there. If you want to get yourself arrested, you are certainly going the right way about it. I suggest that you go home.'

Sam stood still and looked up at him. He was only a couple of years younger than her and he looked uncomfortable with her stare.

'Who's the victim? Do you know?' she asked pointedly.

'None of your concern,' he replied, blushing slightly as the beautiful young woman glared at him. 'Please go about your business.'

Sam considered her options. She did not wish to get herself arrested, so she turned and walked away, right into the arms of one of the WPCs who'd approached her earlier. She'd evidently come looking for her potential 'witness' and took hold of Sam's arm, firmly leading her away from the police cordon. Only when they were at a safe distance did she release Sam's arm.

'I don't know what your game is, love. Reporter, are you?

Whatever, if you come back here again, I'll arrest you on sight,' the WPC told her brusquely.

'What for?' said Sam, scowling.

'For obstructing a police officer in the execution of their duty. Now clear off!'

Sam didn't look back as she walked calmly away from the police, searching in her bag once again to grasp her mobile. Brushing her hair off her face, she sensed before she checked her left ear lobe that something was missing. Her favourite ruby earring was gone. She felt around her neck, but it was not there. It hadn't got caught in her dress or her jacket, either. She hoped she'd taken the earrings off in the office and hadn't remembered, but her right earring was still in place. Sam pulled it from her ear and placed it safely in her coat pocket. She took a deep, steadying breath. The earrings were a gift from Icey when Sam turned twenty-one. She had to find the missing one. She put her bag on the ground and began frantically checking her clothes again. As she looked inside the pockets of her coat, she heard her mobile ring.

'Fleet Investigations, Sam Bailey speaking,' she snapped, her eyes still scanning the ground as she spoke into the phone.

'Sam, it's Flick.' The girl's voice sounded distant over the phone and Sam bent her head in concentration to hear properly. 'I'm here, by the great oak.'

As Sam looked around to find Flick, her eye was caught by a red glow in the mud. Forgetting about Flick on the other end of the phone, she fell to her knees and began to swipe the ground with her bare hands, digging her nails deep into the mud. After a few seconds, Sam pulled free her hands and then her missing earring, which was caked in mud. She scooped up the earring and smiled.

'There it is.'

Flick didn't comment on Sam's slightly dishevelled appearance. Fearing arrest, Sam suggested they talk as they walked away from the crime scene. She was shocked as Flick told her what she had learnt. Maybe this murder hadn't taken place in a church but there were distinct religious overtones. There just had to be a connection; it was too coincidental, too similar to the murder of Leticia Joy.

This time, however, the killer had left a crucifix rather than a rosary behind, violating his victim in the most brutal and intimate way.

When Martha Lewis did not return home on Thursday night, her flatmate Clare was not overly concerned at first. She had shared a flat with Martha for nearly two years now, and she was still no closer to understanding what the other woman was about. She knew that Martha sometimes stayed out all night if she got lucky; once, she had even been gone for several days. Still, in most ways she was an ideal flatmate – good job, paid her rent and her full share of the bills on time. She was usually very considerate, too, apart from those weekends when she'd had too much to drink and went out on the pull. But Clare had never felt seriously concerned before when Martha failed to return home. Sometimes, when Martha was in a responsible mood, she would call Clare, or at least send a text, when she knew she wouldn't be home. She hadn't this time.

Her flatmate's silence wasn't unusual, but for some reason this morning Clare was worried. It was nothing that she could put her finger on – just a gut feeling that all was not well with Martha. She'd called her flatmate's mobile twice but it had gone straight to voicemail. The third time she called, the recorded message reported that there was a fault on the line. It was only when Clare looked out of their living-room window and saw the white tent outside that she realised that something might be very wrong indeed. Martha often took the short cut across the Common, Clare recalled. She had prevaricated for too long. Reaching for her phone, she dialled the number for the police. She wanted to report a missing person. She hoped against hope that this was all Martha really was – missing.

Chapter Forty

Detective Chief Inspector Gilbert 'Gil' Paradissimo was a sour and warped man. At the age of forty-three, he had much to be bitter about. He had given his life to the force and he had been rewarded by rejection. Three times, he had been turned down for the rank of superintendent. If that was not humiliating enough, those promoted instead of him were all idiots, in his opinion; plodders who, between them, couldn't even investigate a blocked sewer. He was convinced his colour had held him back.

When he'd joined the force twenty-three years ago, things had been very different. The racism had been more blatant, of course, but you knew where you were with people. He always harked back to the good old days when it didn't matter how you got results; before paper chasing and bloody forensics took over from detection. The Met was now full of anoraks.

In his day, you sniffed out the scum, picked out the bastard and then beat the shit out of him until he owned up to something. His governor in Stratford East had been old school, and had taught him how to smack a villain hard enough to make him cough up blood but without leaving a trace on his body. You didn't wait for DNA and modern highfalutin concepts to point you in the right direction. Nowadays, you had to be far more circumspect and fill in a slew of bloody forms to prove you had balls. The truth was, Paradissimo was bored. It was time to move on but it was too late for him to start over. He was drinking too much, eating too much junk food and not looking after himself.

Paradissimo was six feet two of pure muscle and grit. He kept himself fit with a regime that would bring tears to the eyes of lesser men. His lousy diet had not yet caught up with him, but it was only a matter of time. Although he was beginning to grey at the temples, this simply gave him an air of distinction. His short, close-cropped hair and dashing brown eyes made the ladies pay attention. He was handsome and he knew it. But he hated his name like he'd begun to hate the force.

He had been plagued all his life with stupid jokes about it. It was a slave name, though which slave master had conjured up this cruel joke he would never know. He was a smallie, the name given by other West Indians to those who came from small islands. His was Grenada. This caused Paradissimo further embarrassment whenever he was forced to give his name, given his height.

So his face did not fit. He would be the first to admit his limitations. Paradissimo was an old-fashioned copper and what was wrong with that? Ask him and he would tell you that there really was a glass ceiling for the likes of him – 'darkies from bongo wongo land', according to some of his less-enlightened colleagues, although they rarely voiced such comments to his face these days. No matter how good he was at his job, that's how some of his colleagues would always see him. Although Paradissimo wouldn't ever acknowledge that he had played the same game: dished out violence when it was uncalled for; laughed at sexist jokes and fitted up criminals when it suited him. But still, he was not one of them. The truth was, he never would be.

Then, last night, he'd got the call.

He had been shortlisted.

Twenty-three years, three months and four days after joining the force, he had finally been shortlisted for superintendent. He'd opened a bottle of bourbon. He deserved a slug and he took it in one draught and then another. Unsure of what to do with the news – he had no loved one to tell –he'd switched on the television and relaxed into the soft folds of the sofa. Closing his eyes, Paradissimo crashed out of consciousness and there he stayed in a stupor until he noticed the flashing light on his answer phone. Rolling over onto his side, Paradissimo reached forward and pressed the play button to listen to his messages.

He had one: from DC Anne Cody. She sounded clear-headed, but her voice was strained. She wanted him to return her call urgently. He could tell when a woman was coming on strong and right now, he was her rash. She'd be all over him given half the chance. He laughed. What had taken her so long – that's what he wanted to know. She wasn't the first and she certainly wouldn't be the last. She could call it whatever she liked – supper, dinner, drinks. It made no difference to him. He understood what she wanted – a piece of his equipment. Well, his dick would have to freeze over in purgatory first. He reached forward, pressed the delete button and went to bed.

He was woken when the phone rang with a call from despatch summoning him to Clapham Common. He could barely make sense of what he'd been told, but he knew it was big – another murder case.

Rolling out of bed, he realised that he had slept in his clothes from the previous night. It was becoming a habit. Grabbing his jacket, which lay crumpled on the floor, he barely paused to brush his teeth and throw some water on his face before making his way out of his front door. A police car was waiting outside his house. He buzzed the windows down as soon as he took his seat in the back. He needed to sober up quickly before he compromised the crime scene. He needed to be seen as a natural leader.

Stepping out of the car as it pulled up, Paradissimo fell forward, partly onto his knees, but retrieved himself sufficiently well to pass it off as an unfortunate stumble. The crime scene was already a hive of activity, he noted, and around him his colleagues bustled in great numbers. As he moved forward to make his presence known, the last person he expected to see was a slapper from his recent past with what appeared to be an even younger model in tow.

'Ladies,' he greeted as he approached them, his voice heavily ironic as he checked out his ex. She was dressed in a smart coat but she looked tired and her hands and knees were covered in mud. Despite that, she was as attractive as ever and Paradissimo could see that he was not the only one who thought that. He registered that several male officers were checking her out. 'Busy night? I hope you were paid well. I guess, as the saying goes, "Where there is muck there is brass".'

Sam had frozen when she'd heard Paradissimo's voice but now she turned around to glare at him. He had been assigned to Leticia Joy's murder, too, of course, but while he'd been in court to give evidence, they hadn't spoken; and when she had on occasion met his gaze, he had looked away first, evidently having no plans to acknowledge their far from romantic history.

'Detective Chief Inspector,' Sam replied now, as coolly as she could manage.

As he came to stand in front of her and Flick, Paradissimo nodded his appreciation in Sam's direction. She'd always had the ability to take a man's mind off the job in hand. As ever, he thought of what might have been if she had been a few years older, perhaps. Or he a few years younger. And if he hadn't been a cop and she wasn't an ex-tom, she could have been his ideal woman.

'Duvet,' he said without thinking, before becoming extremely embarrassed.

Sam averted her eyes and clasped her hands together. He still remembered. She didn't know what to do with this information, but then she remembered Icey and why their paths were crossing again. Sam needed to remain completely professional.

'That's not my name. It's Miss Bailey to you. Sam, if you must,' she replied, ignoring Flick's curious look.

'Of course it is. Forgive me.' He didn't look at all apologetic. 'What brings you here?' he said, still directing his attention at Sam.

'Can you confirm that a young woman was murdered here last night?' Her question threw him and she allowed herself a moment of satisfaction.

'I'm not confirming anything,' he said coldly.

'Does this mean that you still have a killer on the loose, detective?'

Paradissimo started to walk away and then changed his mind. 'What are you doing here?' he said to her quietly.

'Elizabeth Johnson is serving life for an offence that she didn't commit. I've heard that there's now been a second victim – a woman knifed to death by some religious freak, just like Leticia Joy was.'

He answered by reaching out to grab Sam's arm, and then thought better of it. 'If you don't clear off right now, I will have you and your friend here arrested and I'll make certain that you will both spend the night in a police cell. Now the choice is yours. Am I making myself clear?' he told her aggressively.

Sam stood there staring at him for a few seconds before replying. 'I hear you, Detective Paradissimo.' Despite everything, she felt a familiar pang of desire at his rough touch. She tried to ignore the feeling.

'Not so long ago you were a tom; now you're a private dick, I hear. Who'd have thought it? Why don't you stick to what you're good at and leave the investigation to the experts, eh? Now clear off, if you know what's good for you.'

DC Cody stood by the great oak on the left-hand side as she watched the exchange, after which the beautiful young woman walked away. There was something about her that made Cody uncomfortable. Paradissimo had referred to her as an ex-tom but she was not a typical slapper. She looked a lot younger than Paradissimo, a lot younger than Cody, in fact, and she had class, real class. Despite the muddied edges of her clothes, she could see that the woman's dress sense was flawless.

Cody also watched Paradissimo as he too watched Sam retreat. Perhaps in hindsight she should have told him face to face about her feelings, instead of leaving a message last night. As she walked over to him, she ran her fingers through her hair and pursed her lips. Cody felt her blood chilling. There was obviously a history between Paradissimo and this woman. She knew he was the type of man used to female attention, but she hadn't expected his taste to run to much younger women, or to have to compete for his attention with a former tart. She walked up to him.

'Did you call her Duvet?' she asked, before she could stop herself.

'Yes, it's a nickname, a private joke.'

'You know her, then?' she asked, unable to keep the jealousy out of her voice but trying to hide it with a coy smile.

'Used to.'

'She's very young. How well did you know her?'

Paradissimo ignored the question. He was in no mood to explain himself to anyone. 'Let's get cracking, Officer Cody, we have a murder to investigate.'

Chapter Forty-One

Next morning, the papers were awash with stories about the body on the Common, the tabloids typically hyping up the alarm. All reports confirmed what facts were known: that the naked body of a young woman was discovered on the Common; that her throat had been cut and that she had been stabbed multiple times while walking home. Several made much of the fact that a crucifix had been found on her person, though the police had not given precise detail as to where the item had been found.

The victim had not been formally identified at the time the papers went to press, but there was much speculation that she had been raped, although the papers did mention that the police had yet to confirm it. One carried an interview with a witness who claimed she'd seen a man washing his hands in the pond on Long Road in the early morning when she was walking her dog.

Most of the papers carried a quote from Detective Chief Inspector Gilbert Paradissimo, the officer in charge of the murder investigation, appealing to the public for anyone with information about a man seen acting suspiciously in the area on the morning after the attack. Only one of the papers spelt his name correctly.

Chapter Forty-Two

Ashley Towers was enjoying a rare Saturday morning at home, which currently involved him lying on his made-to-measure sofa in his expensive flat with its even more expensive view of the Thames. He had the morning papers spread out on the floor at his side – the broadsheets as well as the tabloids. He liked to read them all in case he got a mention. The hairs on the back of his neck prickled as he came across the story of the Clapham Common murder. Paradissimo was the OIC. Ashley cross-referenced the reports in the *Mail*, *Mirror* and the *Sun*. All three led with the story on the front page, with a more detailed piece inside.

Picking up the phone, he scrolled through the address book for Mr Frizzel's telephone number. He dialled it and waited. The phone rang out. Redialling the number again, Ashley was about to terminate the call when a muffled voice answered.

'Yes.'

'Frizzel?'

'Yes.'

'Have you seen the news today?'

'My dear boy,' said Frizzel, suddenly sounding louder, 'is that you?'

'Yes, it is me, Ashley Towers. There has been another killing, on Clapham Common this time. A young female victim was stabbed and there's a religious element. There's a reference to a crucifix in all the papers.'

'What are you saying, dear boy?' Frizzel asked, and Towers heard a rustling then a clinking noise.

'Well, nothing at the moment, but the case does bare some similarity to ours.'

After a pause, Frizzel said, 'We must have a conference. What do you say – the Frog and Duck tomorrow?'

Mr Frizzel was barely coherent and obviously already drunk; Ashley didn't have the heart to suggest elsewhere. He knew Frizzel's past and the man deserved a little leeway now and then. He had, after all, suffered enormously with the loss of his family.

'Fine,' said Ashley. 'The Frog and Duck it is. Let's say two o'clock?'

Terminating the call, he paused and kept the phone in his hand. Then, smiling to himself, he scrolled through the address book on the handset again and dialled the number of prosecuting counsel.

'Hello, Alfred Roma speaking.' He sounded distant.

'Hello, Roma, it's Ashley, Ashley Towers.'

Alfred Roma paused before asking, 'What can I do for you, Mr Towers?'

'Well, not a lot really, but I thought you might want to look at the front pages of today's tabloids.'

Sensing something suspicious, Roma said. 'Why, what are they about?'

'There's been another murder.'

Roma, the pompous man, was silent. Ashley knew exactly what was going through his mind. 'Was a rosary involved?' he asked tellingly after a few seconds.

'No, not that I'm aware of,' Ashley told him, 'but the killer stabbed his young female victim multiple times in an area of South London not a million miles away from Camberwell. And he cut the victim's throat. Also left a crucifix on the body.'

'Well, that is certainly a little unfortunate, but a crucifix is hardly a rosary, is it? The police haven't said there's any evidence that the two cases are connected, have they?'

'No,' said Ashley. 'Not yet.'

Chapter Forty-Three

Detective Constable Haydn was getting nowhere with the evidence he had so far. Due to the unusual circumstances of Judge Certie's death, the SOCO boys had taken the extreme step of dusting the stairs leading to the roof. It was clear from their findings that there was only one set of recent footsteps leading up to the roof, and none at all that led down. Certie had been alone at the moment when he jumped off the roof. The forensics had also proved beyond doubt that Certie had stood at the edge of the roof and had on at least one occasion moved back from the edge as if he'd had a moment of doubt. But there were currently no suspicious circumstances to his death. It looked like he had simply jumped.

Even so, the coroner had recorded his death as the result of a misadventure – a sop to the judge's widow, Haydn presumed, aware from his investigations that the coroner had been to the same public school as Certie. Clearly it was suicide more than misadventure of any kind. All the pieces of evidence fitted seemingly perfectly into place, but there was just something about the case that still did not feel right.

As Haydn arrived at the office that morning, a set of telephone logs was handed to him. The traffic evidence at first seemed unremarkable. All the calls received by Judge Certie's mobile had hit the telephone mast close to Burgess Park, which meant very little. Those calls could have been made anywhere from as far apart as Crystal Palace to the Elephant and Castle. What was interesting was that several of the numbers were untraceable. Meaning that the phone making the calls was not registered when it was purchased.

The last call – made just before judge Certie died – hit a different mast. The telephone experts had not considered it relevant to find out where the call was made from. It was only after days of dithering over the finance were they able to identify the mast.

Haydn read the report with interest. The mast was based in the East End and covered the area of the Central Criminal Court. He got up and studied the white board holding the cell site maps – on the Old Bailey mast and on Burgess Hill. That meant the caller who phoned Certie shortly before his death would have been in the local area when he'd called the judge.

'Bingo,' said Haydn to Cody, who was sitting next to him. She was working on her own case, the Clapham Common murder, and trying to tune him out as he talked. 'It means that the caller could well have been standing in the crowd outside the Old Bailey when Judge Certie put his justice gear on and jumped to his death. Now why would he want to do that?'

Haydn stood up and started pacing next to his desk. He knew that someone had phoned the judge's landline moments before the mobile call was received. The judge's clerk claimed to have put though a call from the judge's wife, but that it hadn't lasted long. When he'd questioned her, Margaret Certie said she didn't remember calling her husband that morning; she said that her husband didn't like her calling him when he was at work. Haydn's phone boffins had confirmed that it hadn't been Mrs Certie's landline or registered mobile that had made the call. So who had phoned the judge?

Haydn's experience had led him to believe that the most

common reason why people had unregistered phones was to make calls that they didn't want appearing on a regular bill, which their loved ones might see. Maybe the judge had been involved in an extramarital affair with someone who also had something to hide, or maybe he was being blackmailed. It felt dodgy, to say the least.

Margaret Certie was boxing up the last of her husband's clothes to go to Trinity Hospice Charity Shop. Some of the clothes she hadn't seen for several years. The dark brown tweed suit had once been a favourite, and hadn't been discarded even though it was well worn. They just didn't do tailoring like that any more. She had fond memories of that suit. Jonathan had worn it when he was still a nobody and she was just a young girl in love.

The final suit at the back of the wardrobe was the most expensive and the one that he'd worn more often than the others. He had last worn it only two days before he'd died. Mrs Certie loved that suit. She also loved her husband more than anything else in the world.

When she'd married him, she reflected now, she'd had no idea how far he would go in his chosen profession, or indeed what it would be like to be married to a judge at the Central Criminal Court. It had meant effectively signing a death warrant on any normal life that they had enjoyed so far. She had not realised that she would lose her own identity. As long as she was his wife, then she would be respected. She had dedicated herself to him – cooked, cleaned and even nursed his wounded pride when the Court of Appeal gave him a judicial bloody nose.

Pulling the final suit out of the wardrobe, Margaret placed it in the last of the charity boxes. When they had all gone, she would have exorcised the ghost of her late husband. All that was left in the back of the wardrobe now was a cardboard box, itself containing old mobile phone boxes her husband was accustomed to keeping. She checked the first two, which were empty.

The third box was a little heavier than the others. Checking inside it, Margaret was surprised to find the phone still in it. It was quite a recent model but not one she recognised as having belonged to her husband. Upon pressing the button to switch on the phone, she was astonished to discover that it was still partially charged. She watched the screen. Three missed calls flashed up. Then, before her very eyes, the missed call tally went wild, hitting seven and then ten and then fourteen.

When the phone finally settled down, there were twenty-one missed calls with no messages. Margaret called up the detail option on the last call. It was not a number she recognised. Spontaneously, she pressed the redial button and waited. The automated speaker said the phone was no longer in service. She scrolled through the list. It became apparent that all the missed calls were made from the same number. They stopped on the third of July, the day of his death. He evidently had not had this phone with him when he'd jumped from the roof of the Old Bailey, though the last call made to it was seventy minutes before his death.

Margaret Certie sat on their bed and closed her eyes. Her mind felt dizzy and she didn't know what to do with her findings. She couldn't deal with this alone. She didn't want to. She needed to talk to someone.

As Detective Constable Haydn leant across his files to pick up the handpiece of his old office phone, his right arm strayed across the front of his coffee and knocked it over. Hot liquid sloshed and steam rose, and DC Haydn used the sleeve of his jacket to contain the worst of the damage. The phone continued to ring and, picking it up, he snapped his response in irritation with himself.

'Yes.'

A quiet voice asked, 'May I speak to DC Haydn, please?'

'Who is this?' Haydn asked, still frantically mopping.

'This is Margaret Certie.'

Haydn stopped mopping up the coffee and picked up a pen as Judge Certie's widow began to talk.

Chapter Forty-Four

Harry Kemp knew his way around the Temple area. When he was in the force, he often attended conferences with counsel in Queen Elizabeth Building. Fleet Investigations was set back from the road to Middle Temple Gardens. It was in a small, bow-fronted building. Harry pressed the buzzer and walked through the door into reception. He had an appointment with Sam and had promised her that he'd help her go through the court files from the trial; that he would, in fact, help her in any way he could to free her best friend. Mostly, though, they needed to discuss the recent murder on Clapham Common and the impact it might have on Icey's appeal.

As ever, Harry was looking forward to seeing Sam. She intrigued him. Part of it was that he wanted to understand more about her former world so that he could understand his own past and the path that his mother had chosen in life. Sam was a link to all that – a former whore who had turned her back on that whole world to make something better of herself. He wanted to know how Sam had survived while the same sort of life had dragged his mother under. But Harry also realised that he liked spending time with Sam for her own sake. She was easy on the eye and great company for a middle-aged ex-copper. He liked her rather too much, he realised.

She greeted him warmly and walked him through to the back of the office, watching him limp slightly. She was looking as stunning as ever, dressed in a chocolate brown trouser suit. Harry settled down behind the highly polished desk. Together they went over the Saturday newspapers that Sam had bought on her way to the office that morning.

'What do you think, Harry?'

'Well, we obviously need to find out more about the Clapham killing.'

'I just know it's connected. Sure, the two murders are seven months apart but it's the same type of victim, same multiple stab wounds . . .'

'From what you've said of the crime scene, and what your girl Flick overheard, I have to say it feels a little different than the first murder.' Sam started to protest loudly. 'No, hear me out,' Harry responded swiftly, his voice as soothing as warm brandy laced with honey. 'I'm not saying it's not the same killer, but it's more violent, as if the killer is moving up a gear. That's quite common, especially if the killer has waited a while before attacking again.'

'There's also the religious overtones, don't forget . . . The rosary necklace and the church in Leticia Joy's case, and the crucifix found on the second body.'

'Inserted inside her,' Harry corrected. 'The police haven't released that piece of information to the press. But this second murder seems more overtly sexual. I always wondered if Icey interrupted the real killer at the church. That might be why the first murder was less sexual, though still quite a frenzied attack. She interrupted him before he could do what he really wanted to do and he had to cut to the chase, as it were,' he speculated.

As soon as Sam heard Harry's theory, she realised that he could well be right. 'Harry, I don't know what I'd do without you . . .' She leant over and kissed him on his cheek.

Harry blushed a little but smiled to cover it. 'Well, my theory is all well and good but I'm not sure how we prove it, and we need hard evidence to get Icey out. Just because we say it's connected doesn't make it so. You have to think like an investigator. Your confidence alone won't free Icey. We need more than that.' He sounded flustered. 'Let's concentrate on the evidence. Look at the killer's MO, see if there are any similarities.'

'MO?'

'Yes, his modus operandi – his method of operating,' Harry explained when Sam still looked at him a little blankly. 'What has he done to both victims? I guess I'm also wondering if a killer as assured as this might have killed before. I can talk to some of my old mates on the force – in London and outside – and see if I can get them to do some rooting through cold cases.'

'Why outside of London?' Sam asked, puzzled.

'Can't guarantee that our killer's always been in South London. People move around, and that includes killers. Also, I suspect if there was anything similar in London, some eagle-eyed reporter would have spotted it by now and made the connection. Got himself a front-page exclusive. But if our guy's struck outside of London, it might not have been picked up, especially if the victim wasn't . . . well, media-friendly.'

'What do you mean?'

'Well, look at Leticia Joy, innocent bride slain in church. Media field day. Do you think if she'd been older or homeless, for example, it would have received the same coverage?'

'Or a whore, of course . . .' Sam added, unable to keep the bitterness out of her voice.

Harry looked flustered. 'Well, I wish I could say all cases receive the same priority, but you know that's not the case. Look at your friend, Ishia,' he reminded her, guessing the direction of her thoughts.

'I suppose,' Sam acknowledged thoughtfully. She hadn't

forgotten about Ishia; her mysterious death still upset her, but she had to concentrate on Icey for now. 'So what's our next step?' she asked Harry, determined to focus.

'We need to get all the evidence we can that casts doubt on Icey as Leticia's killer, and that includes proving there's a connection between her murder and the Clapham Common case.'

It was a tall task but soon they were both buzzing with ideas. Sam explained what she'd tried so far, and Harry made suggestions and comments, which Sam wrote down, and then they put together a plan of action. Sam felt so relieved to have Harry to lean on. Without him, she knew she'd be lost. Harry caught her looking at him from over her file of papers and smiled curiously at her. 'What?'

'I was just thinking how lucky Icey and I are to have you, Harry,' Sam said honestly.

'Nonsense, happy to help. This is like my good old days on the force – before I got shot,' Harry responded wryly. 'You're making an old man feel useful.'

'You're hardly old, Harry. Or at least you're not quite pushing up daises yet!'

Mr Frizzel didn't put in an appearance until one o'clock, and when he arrived he was wearing the same clothes he'd had on the previous day. His personal hygiene was becoming a serious issue, but Sam didn't wish to offend him or give him reason to sack her from the work she did for him alongside her own detective agency. She needed Frizzel in the same way that Icey needed her. Without him, she would not have been able to launch the agency. Fleet Investigations was created in part as a result of his generosity. Apart from that, she was now in essence driving the appeal in the case of Icey, although admittedly that was down to Frizzel's ineffectiveness and failure to remain sober. As she spied him coming through the doors, Harry sensed her disapproval and gently put his hand over hers in a consoling way.

'He has a lot to deal with, Sam.'

'Don't we all,' she replied a little more sharply than she intended.

'He lost his family overnight and he blames himself. If he hadn't been so committed to his job, they would probably still be alive – that's what he thinks. This is the only way he can survive. Give him a break. After all, he gave you and Icey a break when most people would have said he that he was mad.'

Sam looked at Harry with affection. Frizzel had not been the only one to give them a break. Harry was proving to be a knight in shining armour, as far as she was concerned; even if the armour in question was somewhat rusty.

'Spot of lunch?' Frizzel said, hovering in the doorway.

Sam turned to look at him. She really wanted to tell him where to stick his spot of lunch, but when she looked at him she could see the pain and loneliness in his eyes. He was not an alcoholic because he wanted to be. He was an alcoholic because he thought he had no choice.

'That would be lovely,' she said, standing up and smoothing down her trousers. They were a little tight around the backside, as she hadn't worn this suit since she'd stopped working at Irma's. It had fitted her then like a dream, but now she was in her mid-twenties she'd filled out where it mattered. 'I would love a fry-up.'

'Jolly ho,' said Frizzel, 'Jolly ho, old girl, come along.'

Sam collected her coat on the way out and said goodbye to Harry. He'd declined the offer of joining them in favour of following up with his ex-mates. Sam was a little disappointed –

she'd much rather have lunch with Harry than Frizzel, but they'd talk again soon. Although, as she faced Icey's solicitor, she felt her compassion ebb away. As much as she sympathised with his past tragedy, there were times when she was just as certain that she could kill him.

Chapter Forty-Five

During her last telephone call to Ashley Tower's office, the clerk had assured Sam that Mr Ashley Towers was not 'dodging' her, as Sam had suggested in irritation, but would return her call as soon as he was back from court.

Now two weeks had passed since she'd given Percival notice and briefed Ashley Towers in his place, but with no further word from the high-profile barrister, and she had concluded that Ashley Towers was indeed avoiding her. He had shown her disrespect, she thought angrily. Icey had been sentenced to life and since then her legal team seemed to have closed down. She, like Icey, had thought there would be an automatic appeal. It seemed that they had assumed wrong, and Mr Frizzel didn't appear to be able to answer her legal questions. She needed Towers.

As soon as Sam got back to the office from lunch, she decided to write a further plan of action. She was just about to put pen to paper when the phone rang.

'It's Ashley Towers.'

'Finally!' Sam exclaimed in exasperation.

'I'm very sorry that I've not been in touch, but I'm afraid I've been busy in court and I really wanted to think about the best course of action.'

'So you're still going to take on Icey's case? You're not backing out?'

'I'm still on board, Miss Bailey. I've got a meeting scheduled with Mr Frizzel tomorrow, and I think we have a fair chance. An appeal will certainly get past the single judge.'

Sam tapped her pen against the desk in frustration. All she wanted was a straight answer. 'Are we going to succeed in an appeal or not?'

'Well, I can't say,' said Ashley, 'but I will give it my best shot. Thank you for sending up copies of the newspaper clippings about the Clapham killing. I was already aware of it, of course. And Mr Kemp's theories make for interesting reading, too, but we need to find out more. There's a gap of some months between the two murders. We need solid evidence if we're to link them together.'

'I will find you more, Mr Towers, but in the meanwhile are you going to apply for bail?'

'Yes and no,' said Ashley succinctly. 'You can sometimes apply for bail if you have a good reason, but the reason will need to be exceptional. In Icey's case, I don't believe that there are exceptional reasons why she would get bail.'

'Does that mean you're not even going to try?' Sam asked angrily.

'No.' He paused for effect. 'I mean that she won't get it. It is almost unheard of in these circumstances and, whether you like it or not, she has been convicted of murder. That conviction is valid unless it is overturned by the Court of Appeal, which has not happened and may indeed never happen.'

Sam thought about it for a moment and then she asked the question she most feared the answer to. 'Are you saying that Icey might have to serve almost thirty years before she gets out?'

'Yes, as it stands at the moment, unless we overturn the conviction. We have twenty-eight days to launch an appeal from the date of conviction or sentence. Then we just have to wait and see what happens. The single judge might grant leave to appeal, or he might refuse. As I say, I'm fairly confident we won't have any trouble at that stage, but we can't take it for granted. In the meantime, you and your Mr Kemp can try and find any additional evidence.'

Sam inhaled deeply. 'What happens if they refuse leave to appeal?'

'We appeal that decision.'

Sam sighed. 'Is there any message you have for Icey? I mean, as her new barrister. I'll be seeing her soon.'

'Yes. Tell her I shall be in to see her within the next couple weeks to explain the appeal process to her. In the meantime, I will draft the advice and grounds of appeal and we can discuss them nearer the time. Of course, do let me know if you find out anything useful out.'

And with that, Ashley Towers ended the call, leaving Sam more conscious than ever of the mammoth task ahead of her.

Chapter Forty-Six

Harry Kemp, with his ex-copper's instincts, had told Sam that he was convinced the second murder could be Icey's passport to freedom. Sam needed to get inside the head of the killer, although exactly how to achieve that she had no idea. Standing now on Clapham Common, surveying the vastness of the open space, she was still lost as to where to start.

Something was puzzling her: the victim was murdered where she fell, and the killer did nothing to hide their crime. Indeed, by all accounts they had drawn attention to it by rigging up flashing lights. Why? Wouldn't they want to be more discreet?

Sam was still convinced that the police had missed some vital clues during the case of Leticia Joy, and she was determined it was not going to happen again. Icey deserved better than that. The gaps in evidence had left her friend wide open to the guilty verdict. There were times when even Sam had not known what to believe at the trial. If she hadn't known Icey so well, maybe she too would have believed that she'd committed that terrible crime. But she did know Icey, and if Icey said that she was innocent, Sam believed her; even if all the evidence against her friend was damming and there were so many gaps in her account.

Sam thought about Harry's idea that the killer might have struck before Leticia Joy. She wondered if he'd discovered anything of interest, but she knew he would call her the moment he did. Harry was one of the few men she'd ever met who was always reliable.

She started walking towards the crime scene area. As she approached, she could see the tent that had been placed over the body the previous day. The SOCO boys were still moving around, still collecting evidence. The light wind gently stirred the leaves of the trees that lined Avenue Walk. The afternoon sun was already fading and the scene looked almost tranquil, until Sam remembered why they were all here.

She had convinced herself that the clue to Icey's freedom must lie somewhere on the Common. Walking towards the tent, Sam noticed that one of the male officers was looking considerably bored. She'd not seen him before and, as she approached, he was so uninterested that he even turned his back on her. Glad she had on her smart chocolate brown trouser suit, and could pass for someone with legitimate authority on the case, Sam held her head high.

'Can you update me, officer?' she snapped at him.

'No, ma'am, I can't. I'm just on security duty.' He was quite young, and up close he looked nervous. She stood still and waited. For a moment, she wondered if he'd know instinctively she wasn't a copper, and braced herself for his scorn. He looked at her as though he knew her, and as he took a step towards her she stepped back, just in case she needed to make a swift escape should he try to arrest her.

'I was here yesterday,' she said sternly. 'My team are investigating a similar murder. I had hoped to discuss the similarities between this case and the other with whoever is in charge.'

'I am so sorry, ma'am. I didn't recognise you. The Officer in Charge is with SOCO.'

'The odd feature about these two murders is the religious overtones. The same modus operandi was employed in the case I am investigating.' She felt pleased with herself for slipping one of Harry's phrases into her act. She liked the way it sounded.

The officer paused thoughtfully and then, recognising his chance to prove his detective skills and to suck up to the beautiful detective, said: 'This one had the crucifix forced into her . . . erm . . . private parts.'

Sam tried to appear unconcerned. 'Yes, we'd been told that. Do we know who she is?'

He shook his head solemnly. 'Not yet.'

'When will the post mortem take place?'

'Later today, I believe.'

'I see. Thank you for your help, officer,' Sam said briskly, keeping up her act.

She took out her diary, trying to look official, and made a note to arrange a meeting with the coroner. Looking around, she then studied the area of the crime scene. She hadn't had a good enough look yesterday, and remained baffled as to how the killer could have escaped without being seen. The football pitch was not obvious from Avenue Walk, but was accessed from Long Road. The killer wouldn't have had many options once they'd struck, as, given the ferocity of the attack, they must have been covered in blood. They must have had previous knowledge of the area, but there was always a chance that someone somewhere would have noticed something. One of the papers had mentioned a witness. And maybe they'd be more likely to talk to a pretty woman than to the police.

Walking back to the pitch from Long Road, Sam checked the time it took – four minutes to walk to where the road diverted. If the victim had been followed, she would have known. There was nowhere for the killer to hide their approach until the turn-off from the road. He or she would have had to act swiftly, and then go in search of the trip switch to set the light. Could the victim have been killed elsewhere and then carried to the point where she was found? The fact that the SOCOs were still at the scene indicated otherwise.

The killer had gone to a lot of trouble to make their crime apparent. Harry had discovered through an old Met contact that the victim's body had been found illuminated under a floodlight, which they'd rigged to go on and off. They had clearly wanted to put the victim on display. The killer was playing games. Sam had previously assumed that the woman killed in St Mary Magdalene's Church was chosen for a reason, probably known only to the killer, but maybe she had been wrong about that and Leticia Joy had just been in the wrong place at the wrong time, just like Icey.

The woman on the Common seemed to have been chosen at random as well. Leticia had been at the church because she was due to get married. Icey had gone there because she was about to turn her back on her previous life. The latest victim seemed to have been taking a short cut across the Common. Was there a connection here somewhere? If she was to prove Icey's innocence, Sam had to find one.

Harry had quickly disabused her of using the term 'serial killer'. Even if they could prove it was the same killer, two murders apparently didn't make a serial killer, just one sick individual. There must be some hard evidence that would link the two deaths. Harry had said that certain killers develop their own ways of killing – a signature. She needed to prove that the killer's signature at St Mary's was the same as here on the Common. To do that, Sam needed to go back to where it all started, back to St Mary Magdalene's Church.

Chapter Forty-Seven

It was no good, Sam couldn't sleep. Her nightmares seemed as though they were there to stay. Every time she closed her eyes, she saw her 'uncle Pete'. Despite the chilly winter air, pearls of sweat gathered on her forehead as she waited for fear to move on. She knew exactly when she had felt like this before. It was when Pete had last come into her bedroom, as he often did, to give her one of his special 'bedtime stories'. He always insisted it was to be their secret and, at first, she'd been too terrified to tell anyone what he did to her. It was then that Sam learnt an important lesson – that she was never safe, not even in her own bed. Ever since, when she slept alone, she always wore thick layers in bed, thinking of it as some kind of protection. Old habits die hard.

When she was a little girl, she had frequently endured restless nights, tossing and turning in bed, often falling into the crevice between the bed and the wall. Confused and terrified, she would lie there with her eyes wide open, waiting for the familiar sound. If she heard the slightest movement on the stairs, she would squeeze herself into the narrow space and hold her breath for what felt like an eternity.

Now, as an adult, she lay in her king-size bed in her own flat, but the fear was the same. Once again she was lying awake in the dark, curled up like a child, hugging her nightdress over her knees. Still a prisoner of her past in her Victorian nightdress with frilly, ruffled lace. If the memories weren't so real and relentless, Sam might have laughed at herself as she hid in a frumpy gown waiting for ghosts to settle.

As her heart rate slowed, Sam realised it was no use; she would never get back to sleep. Pulling herself back into the centre of the bed, she lay there for a few seconds, listening to the sound of her own breathing before deciding she would give up on sleep and just get up and start her day early.

It was 5.30 a.m. when she tugged off her nightie, showered and quickly dressed. She put on her designer stretch jeans, pulled the zip up and grabbed a soft cotton long-sleeve top. Her new duck-blue boots were by the side of the bed, along with her sea-green cashmere cardigan. She finished dressing in the hallway in the dark, too scared to turn the light on, just in case the ghosts became real.

As she pulled the front door closed behind her, Sam turned up the collar of her grey mohair coat against the chill February air and started walking towards the bus stop. The street was quiet and no one was waiting at the stop for the early bus; but ironically, Sam felt safer alone in the open than in her own flat. There were more places to run. Outside, as she reached St Mary Magdalene's, it was so cold that it was starting to snow. She tried the church door and was surprised to find it open at this early hour. Pausing briefly in the pale morning light, she checked behind her before pushing at the heavy wooden door.

Sam wasn't sure what she was looking for, but she had made up her mind to return to the original crime scene and now was as good a time as ever. Some instinct told her that the police, the lawyers, the supposed professionals, were all missing something vital in the Leticia Joy case. This early in the morning, she had hoped she would have the building to herself so she could check every nook and cranny, but she was surprised to discover she was not the only one in the church.

There were three eager sinners, all sitting together by the feet of Christ, saying their rosaries as they waited for early morning mass. Sam could never understand the rosary thing that Catholics do, despite having been friends with Icey for so many years. As far as she was concerned, it was just repetitious prayer babbling. Icey had once told her that Catholics believed that, if you said your rosary daily, it would strengthen you to overcome temptation, and prevent you becoming lustful, angry and slothful. Sam had reminded her that habitual sin was part of daily life – and, after all, the ritual was hardly working in Icey's case. Her friend had laughed at the time and said it was because she wasn't as devout as she should be. But, as far as Sam was concerned, they could all go tell it to the mountain.

Standing in the church now, Sam felt awkward. She watched the devout three at prayer, curious about their convictions. How anyone could believe that there was a God was something that had always baffled her. She'd seen too much in her short life to believe in an all-powerful deity – too much suffering and inequality.

As Sam walked towards the altar, she suddenly sensed that someone else had entered the church. Looking over her shoulder to the back, she saw a large shadow thrown against the wall. The discreet lighting of the church – flickering candles and subdued halos cast from the intermittent electric light sconces that graced every other pillar – meant it was difficult to make out exactly who it was, but it was clearly the shadow of a person. Sam hesitated and then walked hastily towards the dark shape. As she closed the gap, she sensed rather than saw someone darting away. Sam quickened her pace, but by the time she reached where she'd seen the shadow, there was no sign of anyone.

She turned back to face the altar, where the faithful still prayed and the candles still burnt. Unsure now whether the intruder was just a figment of her overheated imagination, she made her way to the church door and peered cautiously around outside. It had started to snow more heavily, and was beginning to settle. The unusual sight momentarily threw her. Straining her eyes through the thick flakes of ice, Sam didn't see any sign of anyone about. She resolved not to let her imagination get the better of her.

She was about to go back inside when she noticed, in the car park, where the snow was already starting to settle, faint but fresh footprints making off towards the east end of the church. Pulling the door closed behind her, Sam decided to investigate. Following the track as far as it went, she came to an area overhung with trees where the ground was still clear of snow. The footprints died out and, as she stood there thinking what to do next, she realised how cold she was and cursed herself for not having worn a warmer coat.

In her anxiety she was probably deluding herself, she thought. The mystery shadow could have been an early morning worshipper who had simply changed their mind. It was ridiculous to think that someone was following her. After all, there was no way anyone could have known that she would pay a visit to the church at this unlikely hour. Suddenly feeling very tired and chilled to the bone, Sam hugged her coat to her body and headed back to the bus stop, picking her way carefully across the thin, slippery layer of snow. She wouldn't be any good to Icey frozen to death, and she would come back when it was lighter and she was more warmly attired.

When she reached the nearest bus stop, she immediately noticed something unusual. There was a piece of A4 paper folded in half and forced into a crack in the plastic cover of the timetable. Written on the outside of the paper in bold uppercase letters, Sam was astonished to see her full name. Automatically, she retrieved the note and opened it up, looking around her to see if anyone was watching. Inside there was a message in the same screaming capitals: 'MIND YOUR OWN BUSINESS, BITCH, OR YOU'RE NEXT!' Without thinking, she began to scrunch up the paper ready to throw it away before she came to her senses and slipped it into her bag. She looked around once again, but could see no one about.

The note changed things. She couldn't simply go home now so she retraced her steps to the church. As she stepped through the first of the outer doors, still thinking about the shocking note, she got an even bigger shock when she bumped into Iris Walker.

From what she'd seen of her in court and heard about her through talking to other members of St Mary's congregation, Iris was the sort of Catholic that everyone should avoid. She was a member of the lay apostolate, a thin-lipped, older woman with tight pipe-cleaner curls that stood a proud way from her haggard face. Sam stared at her, momentarily flustered and speechless. She'd been told that Iris was spiteful, judgemental and dangerous. She was in her fifties and spent most of her time at the church. She claimed she was doing charity work but, in truth, it seemed she had frightened some of St Mary's flock away with her hell and damnation preaching. The church would have dispensed with her services years ago but feared scandal if they did. She had exploited her position mercilessly.

'Good morning. You're here early?' Sam began as cheerfully as she could manage.

'I could say the same about you.' Iris sneered at her. 'This is no place for a whore!'

It seemed that everything Sam had heard about the poisonous Iris had not been an exaggeration. 'I thought sinners were always welcome, Mrs Walker,' Sam said politely, though her hand was itching to slap the woman's self-righteous face. 'Don't all Catholics believe in forgiveness?'

'Sinners rot in the eternal fires of hell,' Iris Walker muttered in reply. 'As you sow, so shall ye reap . . . That's what I say, and the same goes for your whore friend. The one doing time. The torment she's suffering is nothing to the pain that awaits her in hell!'

Sam was dumbfounded. 'Do you have any inkling what a vindictive, toxic old bitch you are? Hell's waiting for you, too. You say you're doing God's work here. You're more like a disciple of the devil, you old witch!'

Iris was not listening as she pointed her accusatory finger at Sam. Her voice was elevated; she was enraged as she spouted her own brand of the Christian message loudly: 'From the lips of an immoral woman drip honey, And her mouth is smoother than oil; But in the end she is as bitter as poison. As dangerous as a double-edged sword. Her feet go down to death; her steps lead straight to the grave. For she cares nothing about the path to life. She staggers down a crooked trail and doesn't realize it. Proverb 5.3'.

Sam raised an immaculately plucked eyebrow in response. 'You're so full of venom, I'm surprised you haven't poisoned yourself,' she retorted sharply. As she stepped forward to move past the spiteful woman, back into the sanctity of the church, Iris struck Sam across the face with a hard object she brought out from behind her back. Sam fell sideways against the wall of the porch and Iris struck her again with what Sam now realised was an oversized Bible. The blow landed across the front of her head and Sam fell to the floor, dazed. When she recovered sufficiently to get to her feet, Iris had already vanished.

Chapter Forty-Eight

Sam was still a little woozy as she finally re-entered the church. The left side of her face still felt a little numb and she cradled her smarting cheek in her hand. She noticed that organ music was now playing in a low tone, and the building felt warmer now compared to the snow and Iris Walker's icy reception outside. Father Luke Armstrong was also now in situ, talking to the three members of his congregation. Sam recognised him from Icey's trial. He had given evidence in an impartial way, not seeming to judge Icey. At the time, she had appreciated his honesty.

It was strange standing in the church and seeing the man to whom Icey had confessed all behind the wooden screen on the night of Leticia Joy's murder. In court, Sam's mind had been on other things and she had barely taken in what Father Luke looked like; but now with time to pause, she studied him more carefully. While she did not personally believe that God created Man, when she saw men like Father Luke, she was prepared to revise her opinion.

It was a shame he was a priest, Sam decided; it was rather a waste of his masculine good looks. Sam was lost for words. It was the same sensation that had washed over her when she met Paradissimo for the first time. Father Luke was taller than she'd first imagined – possibly six two, and probably in his early to mid forties, though he had a boyish smile and a full head of dark hair. Sam had always thought Icey had been drawn to St Mary's because of its name. Hadn't Mary Magdalene been a whore, too? But maybe Father Luke had also been part of the attraction.

She knew from talking to members of the congregation while she was handing out fliers that the priest had spent several years in the parish of Kensington and Chelsea. When he'd left, he had been sorely missed as everyone agreed that he was a first-rate priest. Compassionate, kind – though not as loving as some of the women would have preferred. The rumours were that Father Luke had tired of the constant sexual harassment and he'd actually requested to move to a deprived, inner-city, area.

St Mary Magdalene's had apparently been the first church to come up, and he'd accepted immediately. He was politically astute, ambitious, celibate, of course, and pledged to God. Sam waited until the last of the early morning sinners had departed and Father Luke was alone, and then she approached. He acknowledged her with a slight inclination of the head. Sam presumed he recognised her from court, but the knowledge that he remembered her pleased her.

'What brings you here at this early hour? My word . . . What's happened to your face?' he asked in shock as Sam drew closer.

'In answer to your first question: I couldn't sleep,' Sam explained, rubbing her cheek, self-consciously. 'And as to the second, I had a bit of a run-in . . .' Sam studied Father Luke's face and he met her gaze. 'Someone followed me here and left this at the bus stop.' She handed the note to the priest, who read it and raised an eyebrow. 'Whoever it was must have followed me here; because they couldn't have known in advance where I was going. I didn't even know myself. '

Father Luke scratched his rugged cheek and frowned. 'And who assaulted you?'

'I believe it was one of your most devoted church members. Iris Walker.'

'Are you saying that Iris placed this at the bus stop?'

'I don't know about that, but she's definitely the one who clobbered me!' Sam said vehemently.

'Then you should go to the police and report the matter. Why would she want to assault you?'

'I don't know, but I intend to find out. She is not exactly a good advert for Christianity, is she?'

'She has very strong views,' the priest answered diplomatically.

'Strong enough to kill, Father?'

'That's quite a leap, Miss Bailey, isn't it? I presume you're referring to Leticia Joy. As far as I'm aware, the police have concluded their enquiries. The jury have spoken. I know that it may be difficult for you, but you will have to accept what has happened and move on.'

'Can I confess something, Father?' Sam asked.

'Are you a Catholic?'

'Does it matter?'

'Do you believe in God?' the priest persisted.

'Not really . . .'

Father Luke had started instinctively to usher Sam towards the confessional but now, instead of going inside, he led her to the front pew and invited her to sit. 'Perhaps we should just talk?'

'Father, I believe that the wrong person has been convicted of Leticia Joy's murder. I'm determined to clear my friend's name. You were one of the last people to see both women on the night in question. I believe, Father, that you can help me.'

There was a pause before the priest replied, 'How do you think that I can help you or your friend? I told the police everything I know.'

'I know it's in your statement, but can you go over who else was in the church that evening?' Sam asked, taking her notepad from her handbag.

'Of course. It was my usual hour to take evening confession. I was inside the box for all of that hour. Elizabeth – your friend, Icey – was one of my last confessions of the evening.'

'Had anyone else booked in that night?'

'You're obviously not a Catholic! There's no booking system.' He sounded faintly amused.

'How well did you know Leticia Joy?' Sam asked, ignoring the gentle dig.

'She was a recent member of my congregation, but she'd started attending mass fairly regularly.'

'She was a local?' Sam queried.

'Yes. As you probably know, she was due to get married. The banns had been read.'

'You said in court that she also took confession that night. What did she confess? Was she worried about anything?'

Father Luke sighed. 'Sam, you must know I can't tell you that. I think we should stop now. I'm here to listen, not to answer questions. I can tell you that I didn't see anyone else but Leticia and Elizabeth when I came out of the confession box. I believe Iris was still here doing the flowers, but I didn't see her when I left. And that was long before Leticia was attacked. I only wish I had been here, but . . .'

'Is this what you always do, Father?' she demanded, cross that the priest was brushing her off. 'Walk away and abandon those in their hour of need? Is that what a man of the cloth would do? You can't help Leticia Joy now, but you could help Icey.' Picking up her things, Sam stood up and made to leave, but Father Luke stood, too, and put a hand on her arm to stop her. His voice was soft and almost inviting.

'I can't reveal what was told to me in confession, Sam. Not Icey's confession or Leticia's. I can tell you this, though; your friend was deeply troubled. I'm sure that doesn't surprise you.'

'We all have our problems, Father Luke,' Sam retorted. She resented the fact that the priest was implying that Icey was troubled enough to commit such a dreadful act. 'Even Leticia Joy must have done.'

'I suppose so . . . Look, this didn't come up in court because . . . well, no one asked and it never seems right to speak ill of the dead. But I can tell you that at the time of Leticia's death I believe the marriage had been called off. I presumed it might just be last-minute jitters on behalf of the groom – it happens more often than you might think. When I spoke to Leticia's parents, they seemed confident it was just a spat and would resolve itself in time for the ceremony to go ahead.'

'I see. And what did you think of the groom? Tom Padfield?'

'He wasn't much of a church-goer. I only met him a few times.'

'That's not really an answer, Father. What did you think of him?' Sam pressed.

'I . . . well . . . They seemed a somewhat unlikely match, I guess,' the priest said at last. 'Tom struck me as a slightly odd young man, but I have no reason to suppose he was responsible for her death, if that's what you're about to ask. And I don't know for sure who called it off.'

'Was he a member of your church?' Sam pushed.

'Oh no. I think he was a Protestant, or maybe nothing. I don't believe he was called as a witness at the trial.'

'The police only questioned him once,' Sam said, having subsequently learnt this through Harry's contacts. There had been no record of it in Frizzel's notes. 'He was apparently too distraught to say much. Later he was able to provide a statement, but the police didn't press him for an alibi, as far as I can make out. They'd already found their killer – for them it was an open and shut case.' She couldn't hide her bitterness.

Father Luke was silent for a moment, appearing to consider his next move. Finally he said, 'If you come with me into the presbytery, I'll have a copy of the banns, which will have Tom's address on it.'

'That would be a help,' Sam replied.

Father Luke led her through a small door at the back of the choir stalls. The presbytery was in a very untidy state. There were hymnals and prayer books stacked high on the floor, and the small desk was littered with paperwork as well as a dozen or so tall, unlit candles, which were scattered indiscriminately. Father Luke rummaged in a drawer and brought out a sheaf of papers. He flicked through them.

'Here it is.' He handed a copy of the banns to Sam. Padfield lived in Childs Square in Kennington. She made a note of the address.

'Thank you, Father. I'm sorry I was rude before. If you decide there is more you can tell me, please give me a call.' She handed him her card.

'I will. Take care, Samantha, and keep me informed of what's happening with Elizabeth. I'll pray for her, and you.'

'As you now know, I'm not a believer, Father.'

'Well, then, you need my prayers more than most.'

Chapter Forty-Nine

Sam was in a bad mood by the time she turned right into a discreet gated entrance, which led to a Georgian square of residential houses just off Kennington Road. Her disturbed night – and then early start – was beginning to catch up with her, leaving her tired and grumpy. Plus, her new boots were rubbing.

After leaving Father Luke, she'd spent an hour or two in a local café having breakfast, including two large cups of coffee in an effort to shake off her lethargy, and now she was ready to meet Leticia Joy's 'odd' fiancé.

As she made her way through the tall iron gates, she ignored a wolf whistle from someone in a van parked nearby. The central shared garden was excessively manicured and the flowerbeds were heavily planted, even if the bulbs were still waiting for spring. The five-storey houses were all painted white, and were immaculate. The balconies at the first floor levels were encased with black wrought iron, so polished it beamed in the glow of the weak morning sun, which had melted the remains of the snow.

Checking her written directions, Sam confirmed that the address she wanted was number 33, Childs Square. She was currently walking on the west side of the square, where all the houses had even numbers. Crossing over to the odd numbers, Sam made her first mistake. She cut across the central lawn, and bitterly regretted it. The elegant heels of her boots sank into the perfect lawn, leaving evenly spaced holes along her route. She was mortified as she looked back at the damage but there was little she could do to fix it. Number 33 was in front of her to the right. As she walked past number 27 and then 29, Sam opened her bag and took out a business card. Taking a deep breath, she strode towards Tom Padfield's door.

She checked her watch – it was still early, but not too early to make a house call. And besides, she noticed the light was on as she climbed the steps to the front door. As she pressed the bell, she also noticed movement in one corner of the bay window. Even so, no one came to the door. Sam waited a few seconds and then picked up the large knocker and rapped it twice. After the loud metallic bang, there was only silence. Stepping back two steps, she looked through the window at what appeared to be a living room and saw a pale man with a slim build. He had mid-length dark floppy hair but with a slightly receding hairline, and was sitting at the far end of the room in a large carver chair.

'Anyone at home?' Sam called as loudly as she dared, looking directly at the man through the window. He didn't move. He was sitting slumped in the chair and he brought a bottle of wine to his lips. His idea of breakfast, she assumed. As he wiped his hand across his mouth, he caught sight of Sam tapping on the window.

'Hello,' she called, cupping her hands against the glass and leaning forward to watch him. 'Can I have a word? My name's Sam Bailey. It won't take long.'

The man slumped forward and then his legs appeared to fail him as he slid to the floor. Sam watched in horror as he tried to pick himself up, but fell back for the second time. Sam hesitated and then turned to knock on the door again.

'Open the door, please, Mr Padfield!'

Quickly, she checked through the window again and saw him picking himself up, first to his knees and then standing up with a forward stoop as he made his way to the door. Sam then stepped back to the front door so she could watch through the letterbox as he slowly emerged in the corridor.

'Come on,' she muttered as he staggered towards the door. 'This way.'

Sam kept the flap of the letterbox open and after continued verbal encouragement, the door was eventually opened. Sam was greeted by a youngish man – late twenties, perhaps – obviously drunk, swaying in the doorway. He had no shoes on and was wearing what appeared from the state of them to be yesterday's clothes: suit trousers, a crumpled shirt and tie hanging loose around his neck.

'Mr Padfield,' she said by way of greeting, walking past him into the house. 'I am making a few enquiries,' Sam added, hoping her assumed police woman persona would work better on a drunken man than it had on the real thing.

He didn't acknowledge her. He just followed Sam through the hallway and back into the living room. Sam stopped and let him pass. He returned to his carver chair and she walked over and sat in the chair opposite him. To her left she noticed what appeared to be piles of financial paperwork, with bank statements and receipts scattered indiscriminately over the table.

Taking a breath, she said, 'I would like to ask you a few questions, if you don't mind?'

'What about?' he murmured, slumping back in his chair again. Despite being obviously the worse for drink, he had a voice of pure granite and Sam composed herself as she concentrated on the matter in hand.

'I wanted to talk to you about your fiancée, Leticia Joy. I'm sorry for your loss and I'm sure it must still be painful to talk about, but I need to ask you about her murder.'

'And?'

'And someone has been convicted of the crime. I believe wrongly convicted. I know you probably want to ensure the right person is punished for what they did to Leticia.' Tom Padfield's face didn't betray any emotion; Sam decided to change tack. 'I was just wondering if you could tell me a little about her? What kind of a person was she?'

His head was hung low and at first Sam presumed that he was still too upset to be any use as a witness, but she was surprised when he started laughing; a bitter, coarse sound that would have chilled the soul of any sleeping Catholic.

'Well, that's easy. She was a slut.'

'I'm sorry?' Sam's gaze snapped to Padfield's face. 'She was a *what*?'

'She was a slut – a tart extraordinaire.'

Sam watched Tom Padfield carefully as he sipped from his bottle of wine. She wasn't sure how to respond to his statement. Father Luke had hinted that the couple were having problems before Leticia's death; clearly Padfield thought his fiancée had been cheating on him. Steadying her nerve, she asked her next question.

'It was reported in court that you were about to marry?'

'That's a lie.'

'So you weren't engaged?'

'I didn't say that.'

'I don't understand . . .'

'We were about to get married.'

Sam stared at him. He seemed genuine and his pain was real enough.

'That was before she told me about the others,' he added.

'*The others?*' asked Sam.

'Yes. She said she didn't want to marry me without telling me the truth. She wanted to be completely honest with me about her past.'

'Go on,' Sam encouraged.

'That's when she told me that she'd worked as a prostitute. She said it was long before we met but that she had recently taken on a number of private clients to pay for the cost of the wedding. I was horrified.'

'Do you know who her clients were?' Sam wondered if it was possible that Leticia has fallen victim to a nasty punter. It was an occupational hazard for even the most careful of working girls.

'She wouldn't say. She said it didn't mean anything – that it was just business . . .' Padfield muttered miserably.

'I'm sorry, but when did she tell you all this?'

'Two nights before she died.'

Sam allowed the new information to sink in before continuing. 'It must have been a shock,' she began at last. 'I'm surprised this didn't come up in court and that the media didn't get hold of it. The press have portrayed you as a happy couple and Leticia as . . .' She allowed her words to trail off, not knowing how to phrase what she wanted to say.

'The bloody Virgin Mary! That's how they've painted her. I haven't spoken to anyone – and I'm not going to. What would I say – that my dead fiancée wasn't the innocent bride-to-be they claim? No one cares. It's a better story for them if she's some goody two-shoes,' he retorted, taking a gulp of wine.

Sam felt a chill in her heart. Tom Padfield's words echoed Harry's, but if Leticia had worked as a whore, what did that mean for Icey?

'I loved Leticia.' Padfield had started to ramble. 'It was she who wanted a big church wedding. I'd have been happy with just a small ceremony.' Padfield's head was hung low as he slipped into a stupor from which he didn't recover. Gibbering and incoherent, his eyes red with pain as he cried into his wine, Sam could just make him out as he muttered, 'She didn't have to sell herself to pay for the wedding . . .'

Sam got up and placed her business card on the table in front of him, deciding to leave him to his misery. He was oblivious to her exit. Pulling the front door closed, Sam's thoughts buzzed in her head. She wasn't exactly sure what Padfield's admission of Leticia's profession meant for Icey. Had they known each other after all? Icey had said no, and it wasn't as if there was some club where all of London's working girls hung out!

However, she realised that it did mean one thing: Tom Padfield had just made himself an obvious suspect; after all, with his obvious disgust and sense of betrayal, he had a very good reason for wanting his fiancée dead.

Chapter Fifty

Sam headed for the next address on her list at Streatham Common. She got off the bus on Alcove Close and walked towards the even numbers on the West Side. The large Victorian houses stood proud and the wind whispered around the Common. Leticia hadn't lived with Padfield. Her address in court had been given as the family home, number 16, which was the last house on the row. The three-storey house had seen better days. The burgundy paint had peeled back to the undercoat years ago, and the shabby door and splintered frame hinted at past violent encounters.

Sam knocked on the door and waited. There was a patter of tiny feet running across the hall and she heard a dog bark. A few moments later the lock turned and the door opened slowly. A large-bellied, buxom, middle-aged white woman appeared and forced her ample frame into the crack of the door. Barefoot and with pockmarked skin, she was barely five feet tall. Handing the woman her business card, Sam introduced herself. 'Are you Mrs Joy?' she asked with an air of authority.

'What do you want?' the woman hissed, without answering the question.

'Well, if I could just have a word . . .'

'No you can't "just have a word". What are you? Another journalist? Can't you just leave us be?'

'I'm not a journalist,' Sam said calmly. 'I'm investigating your daughter's death and, well, I spoke to Tom Padfield a little earlier and he said that he . . .'

'I am sure he told you a lot. That man is a liar. He never loved my Leticia. Now, if you will excuse me, some of us are still grieving.' She unwedged the door and stepped back.

'I have no wish to intrude . . .'

'Well, don't, then.'

The door slammed in Sam's face, which she thought was probably just as well. She hadn't fancied asking Leticia Joy's mother to confirm that her only daughter had worked as a prostitute. She pulled out her notebook and marked a tick next to Mrs Joy's name. She wondered if she might get a better reception from Mr Joy, but it seemed unlikely. She made a note, however, to try again when he might be at home.

As she walked back up the road to the nearest bus stop, Sam started thinking about the rosary bead the police had found in Icey's pocket. It still felt odd. It was the only piece of evidence that she couldn't really account for. She could see how Icey might have got Leticia's blood on her, and even how she might have picked up the murder weapon by mistake; but the rosary bead felt wrong, out of place, almost. But she didn't know what to make of it.

Feeling a vibration in her coat pocket, she checked her phone and found a missed call message from Irma. Sam smiled. If anyone would know about rosary beads, it had to be Irma. She was more Catholic than the Pope, more experienced than Mary Magdalene and more forgiving than Christ. Irma had promised her she'd find someone to talk to her about rosaries; it could be she was about to make good on that promise. Sam rang Irma's private number and her old boss answered straight away.

'Irma speaking.'

'It's Sam, returning your call. I presume you're about to tell me everything you know about rosaries?' she guessed hopefully.

'Well, what don't I know about rosaries . . .' Sam had to hold the earpiece at a distance as Irma's deep, rich voice boomed. 'You need to pay your respects at the house of Irma. We know all about religion here. You can be sure of that, girl.'

'I want to know the relevance of the beads of a rosary,' Sam asked.

Irma laughed, a warm, melancholy bawl that stopped suddenly as she cleared her throat. 'You have to think of the rosary as a prayer counter. The beads are to help you remember when you pray. Come see me soon and I'll tell you everything I know. Did I ever tell you that there was a time when I wanted to teach religion? I was a Sunday school mistress for a while . . .'

Sam smiled. To her knowledge, Irma had only ever been one sort of mistress but perhaps the idea of her as a Sunday School teacher was not as fanciful as it seemed; after all, you had to do as teacher said.

'You get down here as soon as you can, girl, and I'll find some good Catholics to explain the significance of the beads to you in person.'

'I've got a bit of work to do first, but I'll be round later, I promise.'

'I'll be waiting for you.'

As Sam hung up, she was suddenly aware that a car was following her. Pulling out her compact mirror, she pretended to check her face but studied the car in the reflection. She wondered if it might be an undercover police car, but nothing obvious gave it away. Or maybe someone else – her mystery note leaver from the church, perhaps? She paused next to a lamp post to put her mirror away. The car drew alongside her. There were a man and woman in the car, and the woman stared at her.

Sam continued walking and the car drew in behind her again.

A little further ahead, she saw that the approaching traffic lights were changing. She increased her speed and darted along the pavement as the lights turned red. The car stopped at the lights and, glancing back over her shoulder, Sam saw that the woman in the car was Iris Walker. She was pointing at Sam and gesticulating wildly. As Sam stared, Iris caught her eye and then pulled her hand slowly across her throat in a manner that left no doubt as to her meaning.

Up ahead on the other side of the road, a bus was just pulling into the stop. It wasn't hers and it was going in the wrong direction, but Sam decided she needed to make a swifter exit. Making a dash through the traffic, she flagged the bus down at the last second. It pulled over and she jumped inside. Standing by the doors, catching her breath, Sam looked back at the car. There was no mistake: it was definitely Iris inside. What did the woman want? She had already accosted her with a Bible, was she now following her – and, if so, why? And who was the man with her? The long-suffering Mr Walker, perhaps. As the bus moved forward, Sam went over the thoughts in her head. At the next bus stop she stepped off and disappeared into a crowd.

Chapter Fifty-One

Icey had a terrible night, not helped by two inmates in the cell opposite hers falling out violently. Before the screws arrived, most of the inmates were up and joining in, at least verbally. By the time the situation was under control, one had been removed to the isolation block, the other to the hospital wing with a homemade shank in her belly. Even before her very early wake-up call, Icey had tossed and turned all night. Whenever she closed her eyes, she had visions of her sentencing.

The scene played in Icey's head like a never-ending video on a loop. It was in her head day and night and sleep had become impossible. So she lay in the small square room, listening to her cellmate's snores and the commotion outside her door.

Icey hated prison, like she hated the cops and as much as she now hated lawyers. She had heard little about her appeal. Although Sam had visited her, there was only so much her friend could do and say. Icey was tired of waiting. She was tired of hoping and praying. During every service she repeatedly asked the question, 'Why me, God?' She got no answer.

One of the many terrible things about prison was the amount of free time available; so many hours in a day with nothing to do. So far, her routine was fairly standard. She was supposed to be out of bed at 6 a.m. every day. It was difficult to sleep on in any case when light soaked into the cell. Then she studied the copies of her appeal papers, looking for something that had been missed by the lawyers. On her good days she was determined to help Sam prove her innocence, but it seemed like every day was another disappointment. Association time was the only opportunity she ever got to meet the other women, aside from her near-mute cellmate. She exercised as often as she was allowed. At least it was a way of getting out of her cell.

Since she had been found guilty, the system now seemed to regard her as being in complete denial. They wanted her to show remorse, but how could she when she knew she was completely innocent and should not be in prison in the first place? She could hardly put the matter behind her and get on with her life. She couldn't go back and she couldn't go forward. She was stuck in the system, within the ever-spinning wheel of justice spinning out of control, but going nowhere in a hurry. Ironically, it was the Church that had always given Icey a glimmer of peace during her troubled childhood and teens. And it was in the Church everything had been taken away. The night of Leticia Joy's death she had gone looking for forgiveness and got set up. And now she was banged up without hope.

The room where they held the Roman Catholic services doubled up as a make-shift community chaplaincy office. Even so it was seldom that busy. Icey had been tempted to give up on God when she was first sentenced, and she still considered it when she was feeling low. But even at her weakest moments she enjoyed the peace and quiet of the place. Father William, who was Holloway's Catholic priest, had told her that if she was innocent then it was God's duty to put it right. Icey was relying on more than God but since Father William's words she had attended services twice a week during the time since she had been convicted, if only to remind God that she was still suffering.

Now she was waiting to make a confession. Father had

warned her – as he warned all of his prison flock – that he would not be able to keep quiet if she confessed to a serious crime, or if someone had been put in danger as a result of her confessed actions. Icey agreed to these terms.

When it was her turn, she stepped into the make-shift confession box, which was on old oak oblong box scratched with graffiti and coated in sin. It was very different to the last place she made confession. Kneeling down on the prayer mat, Icey found her voice.

'Bless me, Father, for I have sinned. It has been eight months since my last confession, and I wish with all my heart that I'd never confessed in the first place.'

Chapter Fifty-Two

The bus incident with Iris Walker only served to increase Sam's paranoia and preoccupation with her personal safety. She hadn't been sleeping well at night as it was. She knew she'd feel safer if she didn't have to keep relying on public transport to get around the rough parts of South London, so she'd already made her mind up to use some of her hard-earned petty cash on renting an alternative form of transport. Sam and Icey had learnt to ride a motorcycle when the local authority paid for both of them to take the certificate of basic training, which was then upgraded to a full licence course when Harry Kemp became their probation officer. He had argued that a full licence would increase their employability, but no job ever came as a result of their licences.

Coming to a sudden resolution, she stopped off at a second-hand dealership on the Embankment, Sam tested the Hayabusa CSX 1300S. She wanted a bike that was fast and easy to handle. The bike salesman described it as an iconic model with good balance and speed. The acceleration was effortless, with wind-cheating aerodynamics when it climbed up to seventy miles per hour. The three-way selectable engine mapping was an additional bonus. She agreed to rent the bike on a weekly contract with an option to terminate after fourteen days. The dealership threw in a helmet but Sam declined their offer of full leathers in favour of the jeans she was wearing and her own soft leather jacket.

She put the bike in gear and roared off. The wind lapped around her as she eased up into third gear. The bike was flawless as it sailed through the air. She arrived at work and parked up, feeling happier than she had for a long time.

At the office she opened and sorted the post and read the recent papers that had come in concerning Icey's appeal. Mr Frizzel was on a prison visit to one of his few remaining clients, and neither Oriel nor Flick were working for her today, so Sam spent the time following up on responses to her leafleting campaigning. Frustratingly, nothing meaningful seemed to have come of it but it was still a time-consuming exercise sorting through replies.

It was late evening when Sam locked up and made her way to Irma's. Riding the new bike, she arrived quickly at Soho Square. Taking care to chain the motorbike to the inside railings outside of Irma's discreet townhouse, she rang the old brass doorbell at the staff entrance, which was at on the side of the building.

A voice bellowed out from the intercom: 'Who's there?'

'It's me,' Sam said leaning towards the mouthpiece, 'let me in, it's freezing out here.'

Snow was beginning to fall heavily again now and Sam's short leather jacket and jeans combo was doing little to keep out the icy winter wind that was freezing her bones.

Sam heard a rustle, then the voice added, 'Anyone can be "me". Who's there?'

'It's Sam.'

There was a long pause and then the intercom went dead. She heard footsteps clack down the stairs and then the door opened, flooding the snowy footpath at the side of the house with light.

Irma stood there in all her glory. Despite being in her late forties, she was still a beautiful woman. Her crimson silk wrap hung loosely over her huge enhanced breasts. Her grey eyes had dimmed with age, but were still clear. She was statuesque, with fine features and good cheekbones. Even at her age she could still turn a man's head. Sam remembered her swearing to clients that her tits were organic, and then laughing in that huge bass laugh of hers. The boast was true, in fact; only the best organic soya oil had been used to enhance her cleavage, of which she was immensely proud.

'What gives, Sam, sweetheart? You come to hear all about the rosaries, then?'

Sam stepped inside and the hallway instantly brought back all the memories of her past life. Although Irma's house had been a relatively safe place to work, it was still, at the end of the day, a brothel; a place where Sam had sold her body for money. Though more often than not she and Icey had visited clients in their own hotels rather than being part of Irma's in-house team of girls. Between the two of them, they had slept with a lot of men, and while Sam tried not to judge herself too harshly she was glad she was no longer in that life.

Despite its uncomfortable history for Sam, Irma's house was warm and inviting. Irma led her across the huge hallway, the spacious reception area tastefully decorated with a stunning crystal chandelier, which bounced light onto the beautiful mahogany wood floors.

'Let me see you,' Irma said as she took Sam by the hand, looking her up and down before smiling. 'You look as beautiful as ever. Love the boots – are they designer?'

'No,' said Sam. 'They're a copy. There's a little shop in Kensington that sells designer shoes at rock bottom prices. It's not who you know, but where to go.' Sam laughed and Irma did, too. Both women felt at ease with each other.

'If you ever want your old job back, I tell you, you can have it back any time. You were one of my best girls.'

Sam smiled ruefully. While she didn't blame Irma for introducing her to the life all those years ago – it had ultimately been her choice to accept her offer, after all – she had changed since then, even if Irma hadn't. 'I've given up, Irma, time for me to go legit. I'm on the other side of the business now.'

'Playing detective?' Irma laughed again. 'Next time I get busted I should tell the police that I made more money playing cop than I ever made playing me. And I sure as hell never need a badge to control anybody.'

She led Sam further along the hallway. 'I'm serious, though, about the job offer. You really were one of my best girls. I still have clients ask after you, you know. Your regulars miss you.'

Sam smiled coolly. She didn't miss any of her clients or her previous career one little bit. 'Anyway, let's get down to this Icey business,' Irma said as she ushered Sam into her cosy lamplit snug at the rear of the building. Before she could do so, Sam heard a sharp cry of pain from a distant room, but even the noise felt strangely comforting – or at least reassuringly familiar. Although almost a year had passed since she'd last worked for her, it seemed it was business as usual at Madam Irma's. After all the stress, uncertainty and fighting Sam had endured in the past seven months, it was good to have a reassurance that some things stayed the same.

Irma shut the door to muffle the sound and settled into her comfy chair.

'Tell me everything,' said Irma. 'Flick told me about that poor girl on Clapham Common. Do you think the murder is linked to Icey's case? I thought the whole thing with Icey didn't sound right. Besides, while I can't say Icey's not the type to turn violent, I know our girl wouldn't kill anyone without just cause.'

'She's not guilty, Irma. She's been set up,' Sam said emphatically, sitting down on a sofa near to her old boss. 'This new murder feels like a godsend.' She paused. 'I know that sounds awful and I feel sorry for that poor girl, but the killing had religious overtones. She had her throat cut and a crucifix was found on her body. I do believe that both murders are connected. All we have to do is persuade the court of that, and then Icey can be freed,' she said optimistically.

Neither woman spoke for a few minutes and Sam let the room's familiar smell of jasmine – Irma's favourite flowers – settle her. 'By the way, I never thanked you for the law book. I'd also heard of one of the barristers you recommended. Ashley Towers. He's now been formally instructed, in fact, and I think things are looking up.'

Irma nodded in response. 'That's good. I don't believe Icey's guilty, either. And I've been talking to Flick and Oriel, too. We all want to make sure that she gets justice and will do all we can to help you. You can borrow Flick and Oriel whenever you need them.'

'Thanks, Irma, that's fantastic. There is one other thing I think you can help with. I know you have lots of religious props here for your, er, special interest clients. Can I go through the jewellery?'

'Do you have anything particular in mind? You mentioned rosaries before?'

'Yes, I need to find a bead that's similar to one found at the murder scene. I'm not sure how common they are or even if the lawyer for the prosecution was right that the bead the police found in Icey's pocket belonged to Leticia Joy's rosary.' It was something that needed further investigation.

'Well, Sam, as you know, we get more Catholics here than at

mass and we've got more rosaries than a nunnery,' Irma said smiling. 'So you're in luck. Come with me.'

She ushered Sam upstairs and showed her into a small room. As she snapped on the light switch, Sam saw that one wall was fitted with wooden wardrobes from floor to ceiling. She knew these contained all manner of costumes – from the traditional maid and nurse to medieval tunics, wedding dresses and ball gowns. An outfit for every fetish and fantasy known to man, in fact. Against the opposite wall stood a tall George I dressing table on which there was a large silver tray covered with every conceivable size, colour, length and style of rosary.

Irma swept her hand over to the tray and indicated the different articles to Sam. 'Rosaries, crucifixes and holy water we have in abundance. Some of God's finest have donated them over the years. God's finest sinners, I should say! Help yourself.'

As Sam started to sort through the rosaries, there was a loud knock on the door; it was Irma's personal maid, Belle, calling her boss away to answer a telephone call. 'I'll be back in a minute,' Irma said, swaying out of the room.

Sam fingered the religious artefacts. As far as she could tell there were at least eight different types of rosary on the tray, and they each differed in size, colour and design. She hadn't realised there were so many different options.

It took her a few minutes to find what she wanted: a yellow pearl with a white tint of irregular perfection. From her memory, it looked closely similar to the rosary the prosecution had shown in court; the one they said had belonged to Leticia Joy.

Chapter Fifty-Three

Sam went downstairs to find and thank Irma, but she had disappeared. She entered the kitchen to wait for her friend. The room was at the back of the house and had modern fitted units and large patio doors that led out to an icy terrace lit by garden lights. Sam could make out a line of large shrubs along the rear of the terrace, designed to try to block prying eyes. It was snowing hard now, she noticed, and she wondered if she'd been foolish opting to hire a motorbike rather than a car; but she liked the freedom of riding rather than driving.

As she stood there, looking around, a kitchen timer on the table went off suddenly. It made Sam jump and she silenced the timer with a quick thump. She looked to see if Irma was cooking anything that needed turning off, but the oven wasn't even switched on. Indeed, Sam doubted if it ever saw active duty, so she settled herself on a wooden kitchen chair until Irma finally returned and joined her. Irma busied herself with the kettle and made them both a cuppa. While they sat and drank the tea, Sam dug a hand into her bag and pulled out the note from the bus stop outside the church. She opened it up and showed it to her former boss when she returned.

'You got to be careful, dear,' Irma warned after she'd read the nasty warning.

Sam nodded and waited for Irma to say more on the matter, but the older woman handed it back and continued to drink in silence. A second cup was poured. Despite her reasons for being there, Sam felt comfortable. It was almost like old times – the good parts, at least – until suddenly Irma jumped up.

'Oh my God, help me! What time is it? That poor man will be dead.'

Sam put her cup down and watched the usually unflappable madam rush across the room. 'What's the matter, Irma?'

'Oh Lord,' said Irma as she fumbled in her pocket for the patio door key. 'Oh holy mother of God, I forgot the time.'

'Well, that's not worth getting upset about,' said Sam, baffled.

'Oh, Sam, help me. Come quick!'

Irma unlocked the patio doors and ran into the garden. She disappeared around a corner. Sam followed curiously, at first simply peering out from the warmth of the kitchen and then grabbing her leather jacket and following Irma out into the cold and dark. There, lying on the ground, was a body, a male body partially covered in snow, and completely covered in pink tape. Even in the evening gloom Sam could see his skin was blue – well, almost mauve – and he appeared not to be breathing.

'Help me,' repeated Irma as she grabbed hold of the man's shoulders, her silk gown slipping and her own skin goosebumping in the freezing cold. 'Help me get him back in the house,' she said urgently.

'Is he dead?' asked Sam, 'because if he is I'm not sure I want to get involved!'

Irma glared at Sam. 'Just help me, please, I have to get him back into the house.'

The man still hadn't moved. Sam noticed that his arms were handcuffed behind his back. His eyes were firmly shut and his eyelashes covered in flakes of snow. He looked for all the world like some kind of strange modern art sculpture.

Sam moved carefully to stand next to Irma and, after ensuring the heels of her boots were firmly wedged in the snow, she bent to help her lift the man. He weighed a ton; he was literally a dead weight, or at least she presumed he was. Awkwardly scooping him up, they managed with great difficulty to drag him in through the patio doors and onto the kitchen floor, where he ended up on his back with his knees partially in the air.

'He's dead,' said Sam, rubbing her fingers to warm them up before closing the doors, shutting out the blast of icy air.

'No, he's not,' replied Irma in a panicked voice. 'He can't be . . .'

'What did you do to him?'

'Nothing. Or at least nothing he hasn't paid me for.'

'Then what's his problem?'

'Quick, give me a hand – he's just cold. He hasn't even come round and he's gone all soft on us.' Irma looked fraught.

'You'll get done for murder. I hope he at least paid upfront?' Sam said, hoping a little black humour might lighten Irma's mood.

'If you want to help, shut up and give me hand!' Irma glared at Sam before bustling off to light the gas stove, igniting all four burners plus the oven, leaving the door open, and then turning the central heating up. She rolled the man onto his side and released the handcuffs and the ankle chains, but still he didn't move.

'Don't you have any blankets?' Sam asked.

'Trust me, we need to get his circulation going quicker than that. Hit him!'

'What?'

'Hit him!' Irma repeated as she herself began to slap the unconscious man about his arms, legs and torso. Having been told twice, Sam didn't need to be told again, so between the two of them they slapped and punched their 'dead' body for about fifteen minutes, at which point they finally saw the first sign of life. He opened his eyes.

'Thank God! It's working. Turn him over.'

As Sam turned him over, she was struck by a strange feeling. 'Who is he, Irma? What's his name?

'Mr Fisher. He's a regular client. Likes it rough – the rougher, the better.'

'He's not Mr Fisher. He's Mr Alfred Roma! He's the barrister who prosecuted Icey. He'll be up against her again in the appeal.' Sam stopped slapping the man and pointed at Roma's face as she spoke. She would never forget the man who had prosecuted Icey – and who had torn her to shreds when she'd been in the witness box. 'You should have left him out there to freeze to death.'

'Just shut up and help. What's it going to look like if he dies – especially if you're here?'

'I see your point . . .'

Both women continued to work, trying to pummel Alfred Roma back to life with their bare hands. Irma concentrated on the lower half of his body, and Sam on the upper half. As they struggled to raise him, he finally lifted his head and tried to speak. Sam bent down close to him to hear what he said.

'Oh, thank you, thank you,' he whispered.

Sam's anger boiled over. She doubled her fist and punched him in the face. Irma looked on and was about to intervene when Roma spoke again.

'Thank you,' he repeated, mumbling through a bloodied nose. 'I have never had such an enjoyable time in my life and now a threesome. What an unexpected pleasure.'

'You can't afford me,' Sam bit out. 'Get up now.'

Sam aimed an almighty blow at his upper body. It connected and winded him. He rolled over onto his knees and tried to get up, but the pink tape prevented him standing; he fell, onto his face.

'Oh, thank you, thank you,' he grovelled again. 'I can't thank you enough.'

Irma started to unbind him further from the pink tape and a naked Mr Roma squirmed on the kitchen floor before finally managing to pull himself to his feet. After Irma fetched his clothes, he took his wallet from his jacket and pressed several fifty pound notes into the madam's hands. He then retrieved his trousers and pushed one podgy and now bright pink leg followed by the other into the openings.

Before Irma could comment on the amount of money, there was calamitous noise as the front door was forced open. In ran a small army of police, both uniform and non-uniform officers. The Vice Squad had arrived.

Police officers piled into the room. Sam counted eight in all. She stepped into a corner close to a reproduction of the Mona Lisa. Roma struggled to compose himself as he hastily zipped up his trousers. He was flustered. A young man approached him.

'Are you all right, sir?'

Roma's torso was already beginning to show extensive bruising, and he had what appeared to be strawberry and cream stains smeared on his body. One eye was already starting to swell where Sam had punched him.

'Oh, I'm fine, just fine,' he said, more confidently than he could be feeling.

'Don't I know you from somewhere, sir?'

'No, I don't think so. Now if you don't mind, I'd like the rest of my clothes.'

'I'm sure we've met before, sir,' persisted the officer.

'I don't believe that we have.'

'I'll need your details, sir?'

'Certainly not,' Roma refused haughtily.

'Do you want to report any offence? Anything you want to tell me, sir? We had reports from the neighbours of a naked man in the garden, but you seem to have been the victim of a serious assault?'

'Absolutely not,' Roma snapped. 'I was just . . . er . . . visiting a friend, and now I really must be going. I have a meeting I need to attend,' he said importantly.

'Don't you owe these young ladies something?' said the officer. 'At least take your pink tape, sir, or is that on the house?' The officer's face was stony but Sam could see a twitch to his lips and she guessed he was trying very hard not to laugh.

Roma snatched the tape and walked somewhat unsteadily out of the room.

A female officer then took out some handcuffs and secured them around Irma's wrists.

'You load of tossers,' she shouted, although she didn't try to resist. 'You could have cost me big money. Why is it that every time I meet you lot, I nearly always lose a punter?'

Sam remained silent. She didn't wish to be arrested; she had far too much to do. Irma turned to her.

'Don't you be worrying about me. They come here at least once a month. For some reason they think I run a house of ill repute. But they can't prove anything. They are going to be up shit creek when my lawyer gets through with them.'

'What do you do, then?' another male officer asked Sam, eyeing her up and down, and openly leering at her legs.

'I am a private investigator and you have just violated this lady's human rights,' she replied, smiling as sweetly as she could.

The officer's gaze snapped up to her face. 'How so?'

'Well, if you're arresting her, you didn't caution her and you didn't tell her what you were actually arresting her for. And if you're not arresting her, well, you owe her a new front door at the very least. If I were you, I would let her go and leave before your bad mistake gets a lot worse.'

Before he could reply, Sam picked up her bag and walked out of the room. No one tried to stop her. Outside, she sucked in the cold night air and scanned the streets looking for Mr Roma while unlocking her bike. She wasn't overly worried about Irma; she could more than handle herself, and had more lives than the proverbial cat. The madam regarded arrest as an occupational hazard and, if she wasn't mistaken, the police would backtrack pretty swiftly from this incident given that the 'victim' was hardly likely to press charges. Roma had gone, but Sam knew they'd be meeting again in very different circumstances, and next time she would be more than ready to deal with him.

Chapter Fifty-Four

George MacDonald removed Martha Lewis's body from the fridge and unzipped the body bag. He knew instantly that Martha had taken some time to die. The teasing prods of the knife were evident all over the top half of her body. Around her nipple he counted five separate wounds inflicted with a sharp knife in a semi-circle, and an equal number on the left. It was as if the killer had tried to remove each, but had either been disturbed or given up.

Her legs were also extensively bruised, and between her legs her pubic hair had been shaped and trimmed into the shape of a heart. Tiny flecks of hair on her upper thigh indicated that this had been a recent act, but until they had the forensics back from where the body had been found, as well as from the victim's home, they couldn't know more. Even without closer inspection, he could also see that the killer had also inserted a crucifix into her vagina.

The woman's left upper thigh was extensively covered in blood where the shape of a cross had been carved out in eight separate places; similarly, there were nine crosses on the right thigh from high up to just above the knee. George knew at once that all of these incisions had occurred pre-mortem.

The puncture wounds to the upper torso indicated torture and control. Although supposition was never George's favoured method, he realised that her killer must have wanted her to suffer. He wondered if Martha Lewis had prayed for death long before her throat was cut.

DCI Paradissimo watched the autopsy from a distance. There were far better things he wished he were doing on a Monday afternoon, although at that moment enjoying a leisurely fry-up was not one of them. The stench of this room always made him feel queasy. It was a cross between sweet honey and raw meat that had been left out in the sun. Even though he had been in the job for many years, and had been present at more post mortems than he cared to remember, he never got used to it.

The stainless steel tables, refrigerators and washable floor coverings that extended halfway up the walls always reminded him of the slaughterhouse where he worked briefly in Australia during his gap year. He could still recall the odour of disinfectant that barely masked the stench of flesh; six weeks of dealing with guts and blood and animal carcasses had been enough for him.

Twitching his fingers, he continued to pace. His nicotine patch was not helping. He was beginning to feel stressed and was desperate for the real thing. He opened his jacket's top pocket and pulled out a packet of Marlborough Light. But even Paradissimo, hardened detective as he was, did not wish to show any disrespect to the dead; he moved out into the corridor and opened the fire exit door.

He paced up and down outside, lost in thought. He had thought handling Elizabeth Johnson's case might bring him the promotion that was long overdue, and it seemed he could be right. He'd been worried at first when it had brought him back into contact with Sam Bailey. He knew his superiors would frown on his behaviour if it ever emerged that his last serious relationship had been with a professional call girl. However, whatever Sam's thoughts about him now and the way he'd ended things with her, she clearly had no interest in telling all. And after he'd dodged that bullet, it appeared everything might fall apart anyway if it emerged that Martha's death was the work of the same killer. As he placed the cigarette between his lips and inhaled, he felt better immediately.

George finally emerged and invited Paradissimo back into the morgue.

'What's the position, DG?' he asked as he watched the pathologist drying his scrubbed hands. Like most of the coppers who'd known George a while, Paradissimo used his nickname. DG stood for Determination George. He was a gentle, mild-mannered man who only really came alive around dead bodies, especially interesting cases where the cause of death was unclear. He was one of the top pathologists in the country. If he determined the cause of death, it was rarely challenged, hence his nickname from his colleagues. It was a mark of respect, the same respect that George always showed to his work. He never treated anyone on his table differently. No matter what their rank or profession, he was always fair and precise.

'She was attacked from behind. There was a blow to the back of her head. Multiple stab wounds. Rigor mortis was present. As you know, it normally occurs around three hours after death, reaching maximum rigor after twelve hours. So I would put the time of death shortly before midnight on Thursday, the twenty-fourth of February.'

'The call came in after seven on Friday morning, so that would fit. So if you wrap it all up, what can you tell me? What does this mean?'

'It means that the time of death was about six or seven hours before she had been discovered. She had a total of twenty-three separate stab wounds – mostly, it seems, the killer's intent was to inflict pain, but not to kill her. He toyed with her. Once he had his fun, he wanted her to know she was going to die. After the first dozen jukes she'd have wanted to cut her own throat, I expect.'

'Is there anything else you can tell me now?'

'Yes.' Determination George scratched his face with one thick finger and Paradissimo couldn't help but remember where that finger had been only minutes ago. Despite George's scrubbings, he shuddered a little at the thought. 'She was strangled before her throat was cut.'

Paradissimo paused thoughtfully before asking, 'Why do you say that?'

'Well, she was dead before the knife was plunged into her neck. If you look at the left-hand side of the neck, you will see an incision probably made by a sharp implement.'

'Like a knife?'

'Like a knife. This incision was caused when the killer strangled her with a ligature, which he then cut from her neck and at the same time sliced into her skin. I found some fibres in the wound – what looks like cotton but I won't know for sure until we run some tests.'

'So the cause of death?'

'The cause of death was strangulation.'

'Even though her throat was cut?'

'Her throat was cut but, as I say, only after she was strangled. She was already dead.'

'Why would the killer want to strangle her first and then cut her throat?'

'Maybe because he wanted to conceal the real cause of death,' George speculated.

'Do you know what was used as the ligature?'

'She was wearing a pearl necklace, which was broken and

heavily blood-stained. Can't say for sure until I run tests but that could have been what he used as a ligature. From the impressions it left, though, I'd say we're definitely looking for something like that – see the indents here?'

Paradissimo leant forward nervously. 'Could it have been . . . a rosary rather than a necklace?' he said at last.

George eyed him curiously. 'Possibly.'

Both men were silent for a long time.

'Any chance it could have been consensual?'

George looked at Paradissimo in surprise. 'What are you suggesting?'

'Well, maybe it was a sex game gone wrong. She could have been a willing participant in some serious S&M. Some freaks experiment with hypoxia as a means of intensifying orgasm.'

'I would think it extremely unlikely that any young woman would consent to this!' George replied sharply. 'Besides, I can tell you that she put up a significant struggle. She has classic defence injuries on both hands. She knew what was coming and tried to protect herself.

'She must have suffered.'

'This was a sadistic, violent and painful death. Just look at the crosses carved into her thighs. That must have taken some time and the process would not have been an enjoyable one, to say the least.'

Paradissimo knew he'd been clutching at straws with the consensual idea. 'Did he rape her?'

'I've sent samples to the lab but I haven't detected any seminal fluid. I think your killer gets his kicks from violence rather than the sexual act itself. Look at the fact that a crucifix was inserted into her vagina.'

'What sort of man would do that?' Paradissimo asked automatically.

George studied him before replying. 'Why do you always assume that the killer is a man?'

'Do you think it could be a woman?'

'I make no assumption. Although it strikes me that whoever carried out the killing must have overpowered her quickly, which does in itself suggest a male, but not necessarily. There is one other matter which you might like to know.'

'Which is?'

'I found trace fibres in her nose and throat, consistent with a gag being placed in her mouth.'

'How does that fit in with strangulation?' Paradissimo asked, trying to piece everything together.

'I won't know for sure until I get the toxicology report back but my best guess would be that after she struggled she was drugged in some way to incapacitate her. There were traces of burn marks around her mouth,' George told him. 'I would hazard a guess – strictly off the record – that it's something like chloroform. Old-fashioned but effective. We'll know for sure when the lab gets back to me.'

Chapter Fifty-Five

Paradissimo left the morgue with more on his mind than when he had arrived. Martha Lewis's death had him worried. He couldn't ignore the similarities to Leticia Joy's murder. Both deaths appeared to have a sexual, religious aspect to it, but it was possible it was just his mind working overtime. The last thing he wanted was for some religious nut to compromise his only chance of real promotion. There were differences as well, after all. The main ones were that this felt like a much more violent episode. And in lieu of a rosary, the killer had left a crucifix behind.

He'd felt so sure that he'd got Leticia Joy's killer – it had all seemed so obvious. There was also gap of some months between Leticia Joy's death and Martha's. Too long for them to have been connected, Paradissimo reasoned in his head, ignoring the niggle that sometimes killers went months or even years before the impulse struck again.

Paradissimo was so deep in thought when he walked down the stairs and out of the building that he failed to spot Sam sitting in the bus shelter across the road. She didn't fail to spot him, though. When she was sure he had gone, she walked across the road and into the reception area of the coroner's office.

Determination George almost bumped into her as she hovered outside his office door, and he gasped in surprise. It was not every day that George MacDonald had female visitors, and rarely as attractive as Sam. She was delicious with a capital D. In fact, it was not often that he came across a living body in the hall, especially one so perfect.

Sam stepped up close and Determination George broke out in fine beads of sweat on his forehead. As he gazed at her womanly assets, one large drop of sweat ran from the edge of his nose. Sam removed a handkerchief from her pocket and handed it to him. Determination George's face turned a bright pink. 'Can I help you, miss?'

'I am sorry to disturb you, doctor,' she said as she closed in on him. 'I just want your help with a case I'm working on.'

Determination George was intimidated by the warm contours of her body. Patting his wet hair down on his greasy head, he was conscious of the fact that he was not looking his best. He was having trouble focusing through his large bifocal glasses, which he had failed to remove when she showed up.

'Have you performed the post mortem on the Clapham Common victim yet?'

'Yes,' George told her, flustered into the admission. 'Are you with the police?'

'You also did the post mortem for Leticia Joy, the woman murdered at St Mary Magdalene's Church some time ago, didn't you?'

'That's correct. How can I help you?' He sounded curious and eyed Sam up over the top of his glasses.

'Is there somewhere we could go to be a little more private?' she asked him smoothly.

'For what purpose?' he questioned.

'I'll tell you in a moment. Is there somewhere we can go?'

Alarm bells started to ring in his brain and he forced himself to focus on the situation. He took his job very seriously and he knew a fast one when he saw one. She didn't look like a police woman – he'd never seen her before. He presumed she must be a journalist. 'I don't believe there is, so if you don't mind . . . You shouldn't be here. It's not open to members of the public – or the media.'

Sam detected the change in him and knew she had been rumbled. Her charms had allowed her to sweet-talk her way past the security guard on reception, but they obviously weren't going to get her any further today. She would have to rely on her brain as well as her body. 'Well, doctor, I will come straight to the point. Are there any similarities between the two deaths? I'm investigating Leticia Joy's murder in order to help an appeal case. It would help me greatly if there were any leads you can give me.'

The pathologist was sweating as he removed his glasses to clean them, squinting in Sam's direction as he rubbed the steamed-up lenses with a handkerchief.' I am sorry, what is your name?'

'Sam Bailey,' she said, 'and I'm a private investigator. I have a card, here.' She reached into her handbag and handed it to him.

Determination George looked at the business card. 'Ms Bailey, I have to tell you that you're wasting your time here. What I've found is confidential and will only be released through official channels. If there is any information you want, I suggest that you contact the officer in charge of the case. Had you come a little earlier, you could have met him yourself.'

He dipped his hand into his jacket pocket and when he felt what he was looking for, he handed it to Sam.

'What's this?'

'It is the business card of the chief officer on the case. DCI Paradissimo will be delighted to help, I'm sure. Now if you will forgive me, I have work to do. Shall I have security escort you out or can you find your own way?' he said, fully recovering his equilibrium now. He escaped back into his office before she could try to work her charms on him again, although he was actually sorry he couldn't help the gorgeous young woman more.

Chapter Fifty-Six

Mid-morning on Tuesday, Sam arrived unannounced at the incident room at Camberwell Green. She was feeling a little rough and tired. After leaving the coroner's, she'd headed back to her own office to check on things. It wasn't strictly necessary but anything was better than her own company and memories of the nightmares of her past waiting to distract her from reality.

Dressed in her navy Chanel suit, a crisp olive blouse and thick woollen tights with knee-high boots, she approached the doors and produced from her bag a tube of shimmer gloss. She sealed her lips and pressed them hard together. Stepping into reception, she asked to speak to the officer in charge of the Clapham killing.

The old policeman behind the desk smiled nicely at Sam. He had seen her type before but even so he wasn't altogether sure. She was a looker but she seemed to have too much class to be a tom.

'DCI Paradissimo isn't here, I'm afraid; he's been called out on an emergency, but his second-in-command, Detective Constable Anne Cody, is about. I'm sure she'd be happy to have a word.'

'Thank you,' Sam replied, smiling back at him. She waited while he used his phone to summon Cody.

Sam spotted her the moment she walked into the hall. The thirty-something policewoman looked stressed and the tell-tale signs of excessive anxiety had taken their toll. Sam was a good judge of character and she could tell Cody wasn't a woman's woman at all. She was not so much straight-laced as laced straight. She was wearing a Gorray plaid red and black pleated skirt, mid-calf in length. Her blouse was mumsy rather than stylish, although Sam was sure that this woman had never been a mother. Her hair was slicked back into a severe ponytail – what Icey would call a Croydon facelift – which did her no favours whatsoever. She was everything that Sam never wanted to be and would try her utmost to avoid once she passed thirty.

Cody was also on observation duty. She had not failed to notice the elegance of the young woman at the reception desk, and recognised her instantly as the woman that Paradissimo had seemed so enamoured with at the Clapham Common murder scene last week. His old – though actually very young – flame. She was coolly professional as she invited Sam to follow her to an interview room, but it was obvious that she felt awkward as Sam sat cross-legged opposite her. The young woman clearly had natural style and Cody despised her for that. Most toms she knew were hardened street-walkers, all a little bit faded at the edges. She had never met such a high-class prostitute before. After seeing the effect she'd had on Paradissimo at the crime scene, Cody had looked up Miss Sam Bailey and discovered all about this ex-whore. She'd also asked around and the rumours were that she and Paradissimo had knocked around for a while before he had come to his senses and realised that a tart was always a tart.

Sam looked at Cody and knew what she was thinking. She was used to people judging her, first by her looks but always by her history once they found out how she used to earn a living. But as she tapped her heels on the marble floor, she couldn't help but feel pity for the female detective constable. She clearly didn't know any better and her dress sense was appalling. How could she have allowed herself to end up like that? But then again, it wasn't Sam's place to judge her, even if Cody was clearly judging her, looking at her with undisguised disgust. Sam tried to block it out; she knew nothing about the woman. And Cody was not the reason why Icey was in prison. Sam smiled and softened a little.

'I hear you want to speak to DCI Paradissimo?' Cody said at last as she handed Sam her business card. It was standard blue and red in colour with her telephone number in large upper case italics.

Sam took it and nodded. 'I do, but I understand he is not available at the moment.'

'Is it business or pleasure?' Cody asked with a smirk.

'It's business but I can do pleasure if he wants pleasure. As I'm sure we both can,' Sam said lightly.

Cody was not amused. She was agitated by Sam's response.

'Fire away,' she said, changing the subject. 'How can I help?'

'Well, it's about the Clapham killing. I believe there are similarities between that murder and the murder of Leticia Joy. My friend and colleague Elizabeth Johnson is currently serving a life sentence for Leticia Joy's murder; an offence she didn't commit. I'm also concerned that you've overlooked potential suspects in Leticia Joy's case. For example, Tom Padfield, Leticia Joy's fiancé. From the information I have gathered, you only interviewed him the one time and never even took him seriously as a potential suspect.'

Cody stared coldly at the presumptuous tart. 'So you're an investigator now, are you? What makes you an expert all of a sudden?'

Sam shrugged. 'It's a hunch.'

'Anything else, like evidence?'

Sam paused and studied the ugly police officer, and any compassion she had previously had flew out of the small barred window behind her. 'Well, in the case of Tom Padfield, he told me that he'd recently discovered that Leticia had been working as a prostitute – a fact that made him incredibly angry. He therefore had a motive to want her dead, something my friend never had.'

'Well, I guess it takes one whore to recognise another.'

Sam ignored the insult and carried on regardless. 'Leaving aside Tom Padfield, it's clear that in the case of Leticia Joy's death and that poor girl on Clapham Common, both were victims of a brutal attack. They were both young, pretty and found dead in roughly the same area. There were also religious overtones to both of the attacks: Leticia Joy attacked in a church and left with a broken rosary; and the killer left a crucifix inside the second victim. There's an obvious connection and since Icey was inside when the second murder took place, she can't be your killer.'

Cody's face was flushed and she looked momentarily stunned. 'How do you know about the crucifix inside the body? We didn't release that detail to the press.'

Sam once again ignored the question. 'You have to admit that the similarities are impossible to ignore.'

Cody observed Sam and knew that she had to be very careful. 'And you say you are investigating the murder. Why?'

'Elizabeth Johnson's appeal. I'm working to prove her innocence.'

'What's the name of your agency?' Cody snapped.

'Fleet Investigations,' Sam snapped back, handing her a business card.

Cody looked at the card in distain. 'Fleet Slappers, more like. Just because you and some other toms decide to get off the street, it doesn't mean that you're a detective,' she said scathingly. 'You should stop meddling in police business. If you continue, you'll get yourself arrested. Elizabeth Johnson has been convicted and I think that you should leave murder investigations to the professionals.' Cody stood up and held the door open.

'What if Icey's innocent?'

'What if? What if?' repeated Cody mockingly. 'What if you just stick to what you're good at, Bailey? S&M, I heard, wasn't it? Proper little Miss Whiplash, by all accounts. Your mate, too. Is that why she killed Leticia Joy? Is that how she gets her kicks?'

Sam struggled to maintain her temper. 'You know nothing about either one of us,' she said, forcing herself to stay cool. It was more important to get her point across than to score points.

'I know your sort all too well.'

'You need to listen to me. If this guy has killed twice in a short space of time, don't you think it's possible, even likely, that he'll strike again? Maybe he's already killed other women and you're too short-sighted to make a connection.'

'When I want to know about sex, perversion and whoring on the streets, I'll send for you. Now listen here, you jumped-up slapper. You open a knocking shop in the Temple and you think you're a detective? Now get out and don't come back unless you want to spend a night in the cells. Your sort isn't welcome round here – at least, not unless you're behind bars. Though I'll be sure to tell Paradissimo that his whore called, that's the least I can do.'

'You clearly have some personal issues with me,' said Sam with as much dignity as she could muster, standing up and walking to the door. 'But whatever you feel about me, I just hope you're treating Martha Lewis and Leticia Joy with more respect. They deserve justice.'

Despite her parting shot, Sam felt humiliated as she walked back to her bike. She was not Paradissimo's whore. She never had been, and that had been the cause of all the trouble between them. It was clear that Cody was buzzing with jealousy. Sam didn't know if she and Paradissimo were together now or if Cody just wanted to be, but either way, the other woman was welcome to him, as far as she was concerned.

Chapter Fifty-Seven

The memorial for Judge Certie was held in Temple Church at two o'clock. Those that knew him well thought that he had got himself into a little trouble – probably over a woman or debts or the like – and had taken the easy way out. Those that knew him best remained silent.

Mrs Certie had spent most of her life working with those less fortunate than herself. Now it was time to make herself her first priority. She had truly grieved for her husband and missed him bitterly, but it was now some weeks after his death and it was time to start rebuilding her life. He was not coming back. She was on her own.

When he was alive, she had been somebody. She was the wife of a judge, and not just any judge, a judge at the Old Bailey. She knew, even if he would not acknowledge it, that he could have achieved none of this without her. It was she who had made sure that his life was ordered and stress-free. It was she who had told him not to upset himself when the outrageously guilty had walked out of his courtroom. When he was infuriated almost to the point of heart attack by a jury decision or the behaviour of counsel, it was she who had persuaded him to calm down.

She had been happy to be an outlet for his frustrations. She always considered that the duty of a wife. They worked as a team, after all. Yet he had not thought of this when he took his own life.

It was more than a marriage he had broken. Of course, she was now entitled to a generous pension, courtesy of her husband's twenty years' continuous employment, but it did not compensate for the loneliness and the isolation she felt. It did not cure the embarrassment of being the widow of the judge who had thrown himself off the roof of the Old Bailey, right from the feet of the Statue of Justice. She'd had enough of friends avoiding her or skirting round the topic. It was time to move on.

Since handing over the judge's secret mobile phone to DC Haydn a few days before, she had begun to think that perhaps it was time to tell the police the whole truth about their marriage.

It had happened only a week or two before he had killed himself. Her husband had rung to tell her he was about to be made a High Court judge. Her mind had raced ahead at the time. He would be Sir Jonathan and she, well, she would be Lady Margaret. The wives of other High Court judges in Inner Temple would no longer be able to look down their noses at her. She would have to buy an entire new outfit for the swearing-in ceremony!

'There's something else I want to say,' her husband had said.

'Go on, what is it?'

'Well, I don't know how to say it, really. It's about something that I have wanted for a while, and I am sure you have, too, at times.'

Mrs Certie's mind had raced through ideas: a holiday? A new car? Something for the children? Nothing jumped out. 'I don't know what you mean. Just say it.'

'I want a divorce.'

The words had hit her like a slap in the face. 'A divorce,' she had whispered. 'What – who is she – some young thing at the Bar?'

'There isn't anyone else,' the judge had snapped.

At the time, she hadn't been sure if she believed that; and after finding the mobile phone, she'd believed it even less. Why would he have another phone she hadn't know about if not to call some other woman without her knowing? Why else would he have been seeking to destroy their marriage? But he had argued a good case at the time.

'I want a divorce and I am sorry to have approached the subject in this way, but I feel our marriage has been dead for years.'

'*Dead!* I have devoted myself to you. I have been utterly faithful to you and now you want a divorce?'

'I take it you don't agree.'

'No!'

'Calm down, Margaret'

'Calm down? How do you expect me to behave?' she had uncharacteristically screamed at him.

He had put down the phone and, strangely, had never raised the subject again, but life had changed for ever in the Certie household.

Then he had thrown himself off the roof at the feet of the Statue of Justice. Had that been to spite her? Were things in their marriage so bad that he'd rather take his own life than remain with her? He had humiliated her in front of the very people she'd always gone out of her way to impress. She'd wanted their respect and now, when they spoke to her, she could see the infinite pity in their eyes. They seemed to be thinking, 'Maybe you caused it.' Well, she was darned sure she had not, but she needed to find out what had.

Chapter Fifty-Eight

Mr Frizzel had booked a conference at Holloway with Mr Ashley Towers and Icey. They turned up at three o'clock to discuss the appeal, and Icey was furious. She had arranged to see Father William and had only been informed about the conference shortly after breakfast, singled out by a prison officer who told her the news. Why they wanted to see her today of all days was a mystery to her. Mr Frizzel, her waste-of-space solicitor, had not returned a single call since she'd got her sentence.

If Icey had her way, she would sack the pair of them and instruct Sam to argue the case herself. Sam was better than a barrel full of barristers. The thought made Icey pause. That was it. She had made her mind up. She was not going to attend the legal meeting, and demanded to be taken back to her cell.

Ashley and Mr Frizzel were informed by the prison officer on reception duty that Icey had exercised her right to refuse their visit. They returned a message that if she did not see them today, they would not return. By the time that reached her, Icey had simmered down and agreed to come down. It was obviously in her interest to see the lawyers.

When Frizzel and Towers entered the interview room, Icey was already sitting cross-legged at the table. Frizzel was oblivious to the slight chill in the atmosphere; Ashley, on the other hand, simply chose to ignore it. This was the first time he had met his new client and he was taken aback by her natural beauty. She looked annoyed but surprisingly healthy. Towers studied her curiously. She was very pale and delicate, but incredibly beautiful despite her grey, drab prison outfit and angry face.

They had good news and bad news for her. The sentence of life with a recommendation to serve thirty years was the correct sentence for the offence and was therefore unlikely to be appealable. If Icey wanted to try her luck, Towers told her, he would appeal the sentence itself, but he thought it would affect the appeal against conviction, because the judges might not think that he was serious. His advice was to appeal the conviction alone and leave the sentence as it was. Icey reluctantly agreed.

He and Mr Frizzel were reasonably confident that the appeal would get past the single judge. He explained to Icey that this meant that a single judge would look at the documents and decide whether there were any arguable points in favour of her case. If there were, he would refer the documents to a court of three appeal judges. At that stage, the lawyers would turn up at court, make submissions and argue her case.

Icey challenged them and then pushed them for answers, but Ashley would not be drawn on her chance of success once the appeal was before the full court.

'Sam is still beavering away trying to find fresh evidence,' Mr Frizzel told Icey, trying to reassure her. 'That is still our best hope.'

Icey glared at Frizzel. 'I think I have no bloody hope at all. I'm in here for the duration.'

'Courage, dear lady. Mr Towers is the man. He rarely loses a case.'

Ashley smiled modestly and waited for the Icey to react;

to at least concede that she had faith in him. But she barely acknowledged him. She wasn't ready to trust another barrister. She wasn't going to make that mistake twice.

Chapter Fifty-Nine

When George MacDonald was washed and scrubbed for the last time that day, he walked out of the mortuary. He was exhausted. It had been a long shift and he had seen enough of dead bodies for one day.

Every day he followed a set routine. First he would stop off for a pint at his local, and then home on the bus. If he was lucky, he would be home in time to watch the latest episode of *Law and Order*.

As he entered the pub today, he bought a pint and went to his usual table. The pub was quite crowded yet he felt isolated. His usual table was the only one that was free, and he settled down there as he did every day, facing the wall and its collection of horse brasses with a pint and *The Times* crossword.

Sam was sitting at a table just inside the door. She could see George but he couldn't see her. She was casually dressed in a blue and white tailored shirt with an open neck, fitted jeans and ankle boots. She looked at her watch before sending a short text message. Placing her phone on the table, Sam waited, watching the door. A short while later, in walked Oriel and Flick. As they looked around, their eyes settled on Determination George. Flick walked over to his table.

'Do you mind if we join you?'

'No,' said George, 'please help yourselves.'

Oriel walked to the bar, ordered two large glasses of red wine and brought them to the table.

George couldn't take his eyes off her. It was the second time in a long week that he had been excited by a living body. From the back she didn't seem to be wearing much of a skirt, and what there was fitted very well. The same applied to the pink lace blouse that accentuated her tiny waist. She would be high maintenance, he was sure of that. But she was perfect – and she was not the kind of girl he was used to seeing in the mortuary – even on his autopsy table.

'I hope you didn't mind us joining you like this?' Flick began smoothly.

'My pleasure,' he answered, wiping his hands on his trouser legs and grinning.

'I'm Rita,' said Flick, 'and this is Susan,' she said, indicating Oriel.

As George stared at the two women, he had a fleeting fantasy of taking them both to bed at the same time. One of them – Susan – caught his eye and he became embarrassed when she smiled at him. He had a feeling she knew exactly what he was thinking. It was not like him to stare and, at his age, he should really know better. The blonde one averted her gaze and caught his eye again when she looked back. Then she looked over her right shoulder and smiled at Sam, who was sitting in a corner watching the proceedings. Ever since she had first talked to the pathologist earlier in the week, she had kept an eye on his movements, or had one of Irma's girls do it. Since he was clearly not in the habit of providing information voluntarily, she would have to obtain it her way.

Determination George patted his hair down onto his slippery forehead and sipped his pint. He was not entirely sure, but he hoped that tonight he would not be left holding a dead body.

'What's your name?' asked 'Susan'. She had an accent that George couldn't identify but he found it charming, especially as she moved a little closer to him.

'My name is George.'

'Well, my friends call me Susie. What do your friends call you, George?'

'Some of them call me Determination George.'

'Why?'

'Well, it's to do with my job. I'm a coroner – a pathologist by profession. My job is to determine the cause of death.'

'Oh,' said Susie, running her fingers over one of his large podgy hands, 'that sounds creepy. But very important – you must tell us all about it. What have you been up to this week?'

At first George demurred to tell them more about his week – after all, he was a stickler for maintaining the confidential details of his autopsy. However, a couple of rounds later in their very charming company, he couldn't help but find himself confiding details about the poor girl he'd most recently had on his table.

Chapter Sixty

The police had put up a witness board on Clapham Common, requesting anyone who saw anything suspicious to come forward. They held case conference after case conference but they couldn't find any reason why anyone would want to kill the victim. All Martha Lewis's friends had been screened and, while she did not have a regular boyfriend, there were no suspicious contacts. Her flatmate Clare had given them the name of the bar she frequented in town. They had interviewed the regulars but there was no obvious suspect from there, either. It was noted that she had left the wine bar to go home alone that night, and had been less than ten minutes away from her flat when her killer struck from behind.

At the police station, Paradissimo and Cody convened to discuss the case. Haydn listened intently from his desk, curious to see Paradissimo in action.

'He had arranged her in an overtly sexual position,' Paradissimo said.

'But there was no evidence of rape?' asked Cody, pushing a dirty-blonde strand of hair off her forehead.

'No. There were no traces of semen, according to George's final report, or signs of penetration beyond the placing of the crucifix in her vagina. George said that occurred post-mortem,' Paradissimo replied, rubbing his newly shaved chin. 'The odd thing is that the killer wanted her to be discovered.

Someone – presumably the killer – fixed those lights so that they'd flash off and on automatically, to draw attention to her body.'

'But why?' asked Cody.

'Well, if we knew that we'd be closer to catching our killer.'

Haydn couldn't resist joining in at this point. 'But I don't understand. The killer could so easily have killed her and hidden her body under a bush or, to be on the safe side, he could have dumped her body in the pond. Had he chosen that option, he could have weighed down the body and it would have remained undetected for ever, or at least until the pond was cleared.'

'The killer wanted the body to be found,' said Cody, echoing her boss's words and shooting an annoyed look at Haydn.

'What are we missing?' asked Paradissimo. Cody watched him as he folded his muscly arms and perched on her desk. 'What about other forensics? Is there anything that might lead to his identity?' he added.

'No, everything's been checked – no fingerprints, no DNA, no nothing,' she said.

'Well, he must have walked along the path before he struck her; is there any evidence of that? Footprints?' asked Paradissimo.

'Nothing obvious. It's a footpath, there are lots of prints – and no way of guessing which belonged to the killer.'

Paradissimo pointed to Martha's picture on the incident room wall, with her body pinned down and spread-eagled, and a bright light illuminating her slit throat. 'We don't do guesswork, Cody.'

Cody blushed a ripe red and glanced away. He could be bloody annoying at times. He liked to crush her, especially when he wanted to bolster his own importance. She still fancied Paradissimo and had deep feelings for him, but he was beginning to leave a sour taste in her mouth. She still needed him on side, though, for the sake of her career.

'Well,' she said cautiously, choosing her words with great care, 'maybe we need to consider the religious aspects of the killing. The crucifix and the way he carved crosses into her thighs.'

'What about that?'

'It seems quite calculated,' she began. 'It makes me wonder if the killer has struck before. If that is a trademark.' Before anyone could answer, she rephrased her words. 'I mean, do we believe that the killer has struck before?'

There was silence. Haydn looked at her curiously and Paradissimo looked furious. She knew it. These hard-ball officers just sat on their arses, ducking the blame whenever the shit hit the fan. Once the press got hold of enough information, there would be a public outcry.

'What about the victim of the St Mary Magdalene's slaughter? Leticia Joy. There are some similarities between that case and this.'

'And the rest,' retorted Haydn in his lilting Welsh accent as he turned back to his computer and the case notes on the death of Certie.

'What do you mean by that?' Paradissimo's attention was on Haydn now and the elder officer wished he had kept his mouth shut.

'Well,' said Haydn slowly, 'from what I heard, we quite deliberately withheld some information from the media on the Clapham killing.'

'I know about the crucifix not being mentioned . . .' Cody began, but at Haydn's look she realised that wasn't what he meant. 'What else?' Cody looked confused. 'And why?'

'Because,' Paradissimo butted in angrily, 'we didn't want to make public too much detail about the killing. There are too many nutters out there and we don't want to encourage copycat killers or time wasters.'

'And what else was held back?' asked Cody, looking even more confused. No one spoke as she stared at the soon-to-be promoted DCI sitting there like a pussy. 'Is someone going to let me into the secret?'

'What the public don't know is that the Clapham Common victim was probably strangled before the killer cut her throat. George thinks some kind of pearl necklace was probably used.'

'And what am I supposed to read into that?' demanded Cody, none the wiser.

'Well, while it seems likely the killer used the victim's own necklace as a ligature, we can't currently rule out the fact that it could have been a rosary.'

The penny finally dropped. Cody stared at Paradissimo, whom she now realised was a complete prat. 'Are you telling me that the same person has struck twice and may kill again? Well, are you?' demanded Cody, suddenly recollecting more of Sam's words. Cody was speechless for a moment as she looked at her boss. 'Hold it one moment. If the same person killed both Martha Lewis and Leticia Joy, it means that the woman convicted of the murder of the St Mary Magdalene's slaughter is . . .'

'May well be innocent,' said Paradissimo, completing her sentence for her. 'But two courses don't make a dinner.'

Chapter Sixty-One

Icey was settling down to her prison routine but it was the lock-ins that did her head in, and so she booked up as much religious instruction as she could. The religious instruction class lasted a whole hour, but the whole process took up three hours because by the time she was breakfasted, then allocated an officer for mass, it took a good hour to get there and the same to get back.

On Friday, the topic was Catholicism, Christ and Christian shortcomings. Something that gave Icey a chill down her spine as she remembered the evidence in the trial and what got her into trouble in the first place. But curiosity won out, along with the need to learn as much as possible. She had spent too much time bunking off school and had never really fully embraced her religion. Although her fellow 'Christians' were clearly not terribly interested in religion, they were also not in a hurry to go back to their cells for a lock-in, so they too expressed interest in the teachings of Christ. A group of them sat in Father William's office as he began his lesson.

He spoke about the life of Jesus Christ and his mother, the Blessed Virgin Mary. Father William was no Father Luke; he was sixty if he was a day, though he had a voice like pure honey. It was dark and rich and his voice lingered long after he had moved on. Then he talked about how to become a better person. To be a good Christian.

'I was a blessed virgin once,' said Icey before she could stop herself. 'It was a long time ago and then after that I was paid to be the blessed virgin.' The homies started to laugh.

'Say what, so now you just a virgin?' asked one of them.

'Yeah that's right. Virgin on the expensive,' Icey said, smiling.

'I sure as hell think that you are verging on the ridiculous,' another inmate added, giving Icey a wink.

Father William was not amused. Such contempt coming from a group of women who had fallen very low indeed was quite extraordinary. 'Ladies, I think that is enough for one day. We will meet again next week.'

Icey looked at her watch; she still had another five hours to go until lock-in. She cursed herself and her big mouth.

Chapter Sixty-Two

Very few things took Sam by surprise, but she had not expected to find Irma and Father Luke Armstrong swapping stories in Irma's house on Soho Square. It was a Saturday morning and she was certain Father Luke should have been servicing the church and not risk being serviced by Irma.

As she made her way into the drawing room, she couldn't help but remember that it was as a result of her desire to go straight that Icey had gone to the church in the first place. Now here was a representative of God sitting in a brothel having a cup of tea. She had come across some very odd things in her young life, but Irma was full of surprises. Sam wanted to laugh out loud but she controlled herself; she would not ever wish to offend Irma.

'Come in,' Irma called out, moving a cushion out of the way. 'I have a very old friend that I would like you to meet. Father Luke and I go back a long time to when we were both at theology college.' Sam thought Irma had been joking about having been a religious education teacher but clearly her words had had some basis in the truth. She allowed herself a small smile as her friend continued, 'I told him that you were anxious to have a lesson on sin and redemption. Hips will also join us today.'

Hips was one of Irma's occasional girls and Sam had met her before, albeit briefly. Her real name was Hyacinth Whyborn. She was nicknamed Hips because she rolled her hips when she walked. This was because her left leg was half an inch shorter than her right. The fact that she was obese only accentuated the problem. She was mixed race with a heart-shaped, chubby face. She sat very still, and Sam was certain that her movement was restricted by her vast size. Sam nodded in her direction and then looked back at Irma. She was glad that the police raid didn't seem to have caused her any lasting issues. Maybe Sam's warnings to the officers at the time had hit their mark. Irma may have remained a free woman, but she'd clearly taken leave of her senses as she ushered Sam closer to God's messenger.

'I am sorry,' said Sam, holding up her hands in front of her as if to shield herself, 'I'm not remotely interested in religion right now.'

She turned and headed for the door and, just as she was about to reach for the handle, Father Luke spoke for the first time.

'We met recently at my church,' he said.

'That's correct, Father, but I don't see why or how you can help now.'

'I'm not sure, either, but I thought that we might take tea together.'

Sam looked from Irma to Father and then back again before shaking her head. The whole scene was unreal. 'My best friend is doing life for a crime that she did not commit. I have a detective agency to run, and you want me to take afternoon tea with you?'

Father Luke ignored her declarations and gestured for her to sit. Irma poured four cups of tea and nodded briskly at the space next to Hips. Out of respect for Irma, Sam sat on the edge of the sofa, clearly poised in readiness to leave. She felt very out of place but she was also feeling curious, even if she had little time to satisfy her curiosity.

'Hundreds of thousands of years ago, Christians were all

provided with rosaries. The word means rose garden or garland of roses, which in Latin is *rosariumi*.'

Procuring a rosary from his pocket, he handed it to Sam. On seeing the necklace she leant forward. He now had her complete attention. She realised she'd been too hasty; this had been Irma's intent all along. She had promised her an expert on rosaries. Who better than a priest?

Sam was about to pull a photograph out of her pocket, one she had pulled from the case notes of Icey's trial, but something told her to hold back. The timing was not right and, besides, she did not want to contaminate a messenger of God with a photograph of the slaughtering of the innocent. As far as the general public were concerned, Icey had killed one of God's own and was guilty as sin.

Instead Sam looked at the pearl rosary he'd given her and decided to question him and gain as much knowledge as possible.

'Why all this Latin, Father?'

'That is just the way it was back then.'

'But if the rose garden is about prayer, how does that work?'

'The rosary is really a set of prayer beads and helps you to keep a record of where you are in the prayer cycle. It has a very distinctive pattern.'

'Show me,' said Sam, holding the rosary up.

'The traditional fifteen mysteries of the rosary were formalised by the advent of the sixteenth century,' Father Luke explained. 'The mysteries of the rosary are grouped into three sets; they represent a mystery which is normally associated with a particular day of the week. The deeper purpose is to help the individual keep in their memory the principal events in the history of our salvation – the very tenants of our belief – and praise the Lord God for them.'

'A broken rosary was left in St Mary Magdalene's Church,' said Sam a little eagerly.

Father Luke glanced at Irma before replying. 'There may be no significance in that.'

'Is there any significance in a broken rosary?'

'I am not aware of any hidden meaning. Things get broken,' said the priest.

'Now,' said Irma, interrupting. 'Would you like another lesson on sin and repentance?'

This time Sam smiled. 'I think I know enough about sin,' she said, wryly, but she was glad she had stayed for the lesson.

Chapter Sixty-Three

Mr Frizzel had picked up on the third ring, which Sam hadn't expected at all. Even so, she could almost smell him down the phone line. So far she had repeated everything at least twice and was close to the end of her tether.

'Mr Frizzel,' she said, as slowly as she could manage before her patience ran out, 'I think the rosary bead could be key to saving Icey. It is really important that we ask an expert – not about the religious significance of it all but—'

'What do you mean, dear girl?' he slurred. 'The rosary bead was Leticia Joy's. It's a dead end.'

'But we don't know that for sure,' Sam persisted, biting her tongue to stop herself from screaming at him. 'During the trial we were caught out because there was no proof either way as to who the bead had belonged to, and the prosecution argued that it belonged to the deceased. We need a jewellery expert, not a priest.' The realisation had come to her as she left Irma's house, with Father Luke's explanations still turning over in her mind.

'If you say it's necessary, old girl, you have my approval, but just make sure that we can claim back the expense of instructing an expert.' His gruff voice told her all she needed to know. She wasn't sure whether he was sobering up or in the process of getting completely inebriated, but either way, he was not with it.

'Don't worry, I'm on it,' Sam assured him, resolving that if she was wrong she was prepared to cover the expense out of her own pocket.

She thanked him, closed her mobile and inhaled deeply. It was as if the imagined stench of Frizzel stayed with her, despite the fact that she was standing in the lunchtime light of a crisp March day in Soho Square, and Frizzel was festering in the gloom of his office.

An hour later, Sam fingered the string of fake pearls around her neck and stared enviously at the brightly lit window display of a very upmarket jewellers. The diamonds sparkled in the bright winter sun.

There were not many pearls – just a few strings at the back of the display – but if she was going to find a pearl expert, it was going to be in Hatton Garden. Clutching the rosary she'd borrowed from Irma, along with photographs of the court exhibits, she moved down the street to another window, which sported more pearls. She sighed. When the money came rolling in to Fleet Investigations, she and Icey would come down and buy their own real pearls – big as they could get, and maybe a diamond, too.

Glancing up at the shop's impressive front, she decided to try her luck in this shop. As she entered the stylish jewellers, she was glad she had dressed smartly that morning. She felt more at home here than she had in Irma's parlour with a priest. It was the kind of place she wanted to belong.

'Excuse me, I am looking for an expert in pearls.'

The young man behind the counter looked at her over his glasses. It was not that he looked her up and down, just down and down again until he had no choice but to acknowledge her. Apparently her smart clothes were not enough. For the first time in a long while, Sam wished she was someone other than herself; someone with real class.

'Buy or sell, madam?' he asked abruptly.

'Neither. I want an opinion for a law case. I need the best expert there is.'

'That'll be Father Goldman. He's at number 16a. Father Goldman is the best,' the assistant told her, seeming more respectful having heard the nature of her business.

'Is he a priest?' Sam asked in surprise.

'No, no. There's Old Goldman and Young Goldman. There are other generations behind them too. They know everything there is to know about pearls. May not do it, though. He's a grumpy old so-and-so. If he won't help, come back and see us.'

Sam stepped out of the shop and turned left. She wandered down the street past more brightly lit windows until she found 16a. It wasn't a shop, just a door. She rang the brass bell. There was a long pause and then the door opened a tiny crack.

'Yes?' came the gruff voice.

'Is Mr Goldman senior there?'

'Who wants him?'

'Me.'

'Who's me?' came the response, and Sam shivered with a sense of déjà vu.

She wondered whether she had come to the right shop. In any other situation, she would simply have walked out, but if what she'd just been told was true, this man was apparently the best in the business. 'I'm a private investigator,' she said in a firm voice. 'I need an opinion for a legal case.'

'You don't look like a detective.'

'Well, maybe you don't look like a diamond seller, but you are,' she retorted glaring through the gap at the edge of the door. 'I need the best expert on pearls and I've been told Mr Goldman is the best.'

Her flattery worked and the voice became friendlier. 'You're right, there. I'll ask him. I doubt he'll help, though. He's in a grumpy mood today. Wait there.'

Sam waited patiently as she heard the man descend some stairs. If this man thought Mr Goldman senior was grumpy, then she was in for a ride. After what seemed an age, he returned and the door opened fully. She saw now that he was a man in his late thirties, wearing a black skull cap. 'You're to come down.'

He led her downstairs to a brightly lit basement. A couple of young men were working on silver wire held in a vice. At the back, sitting at a desk, was an old man with an eye-piece, examining a stone. He had a long beard covered in spittle, making it look as if it were glued together. He did not get up nor offer Sam a chair, although he did take his eyepiece out.

'What can I do for you, my dear?' His voice was surprisingly young-sounding, and Sam instantly warmed to him.

'I am a private investigator,' she explained once again, 'and I need an opinion urgently on whether an individual pearl matches others on a string.'

'And why have you come to me?'

'I asked around the Garden and they said you were the man to come to on pearls.'

He chuckled, assuring her that she had definitely come to the right man. There was a glint in his eye and Sam had the feeling that if he'd been a few years younger, and alone in his workshop, he might have offered to exchange some pearls of his own for services rendered.

'My son says it's to do with a court case,' he said at last after he'd finished looking her up and down. 'What sort of a case?'

'A murder case.'

A straggling bushy eyebrow was raised. He shook his head.

'Please, please help,' she said in desperation. 'A friend of mine, Elizabeth Johnson, was convicted of a murder that she did not commit. Much of the evidence hung on the identity of a pearl from a rosary. The original pearl is with the court, but if you are willing to help me, then I could arrange for you to have access to the evidence.'

'When do you need my opinion?'

'I need it as soon as possible. It's not long to the appeal. Can you examine the rosary and provide an opinion as to whether a pearl found on the defendant came from the rosary?'

'Can't be done. Too busy.' He put the eyepiece back and recommenced examining the stone.

'Please, Mr Goldman. It's all respectable. I work for Mr Frizzel, the solicitor. He can vouch for it.'

There was a pause as he continued his inspection. Sam looked appealingly to the son, who held up his finger. 'Dad, I think you should help.'

There was no reaction. Sam decided to try again.

'My mate is doing life for something she did not do. She was set up, and I need to prove that.'

Still no reaction.

'If you won't do it, I will,' said the son. The father put down the eyepiece and stone, and looked at the son in surprise.

'What if you don't like my opinion?' said Goldman senior to Sam.

'That's up to the barrister to decide,' Sam told him.

'How much will you pay me?'

'Whatever the going rate is. If I have to, I will pay for it myself.'

'You sound very committed. Who is this woman whose life is at stake?'

'She's my partner.'

'*Partner?*' His straggly eyebrow shot up again.

'Business partner.'

The son moved forward and stood by his father's shoulder. 'Dad, I remember reading about this case in the paper. She's charged with killing someone in a church. If this lady says she's been set up, you should help.'

'Where are these pearls?'

'They are with the court,' Sam repeated patiently, 'but I have photographs and a similar string; they belong to another friend of mine.'

Sam fished in her handbag and pulled out Irma's string and photographs of the court exhibits – one of the single pearl bead found in Icey's possession, one of Leticia Joy's rosary and the other of Icey's own. The old man abruptly pushed Irma's string to one side.

'Those are no use. They may look the same to you, but you're no expert.'

Sam scooped the necklace back up, shrugging off his remark. It had been worth a try. He picked up the photographs and held them side by side.

'I think the single pearl was planted on my partner,' she said.

'I don't want to know what you think, young lady. What you think is of no importance. They do, however, look different to me. I will have to see the originals, though, before I can say for sure. Photographs can distort.'

Sam gave an audible sigh of relief. 'I can arrange for you to see the original evidence, or my solicitor can. We'll need a written report to give the judge and the prosecutor.'

'You ask a great deal, young woman. Arrange for me to

examine the originals and I will provide you with a report. Until then, you will provide me with the contact details for the person paying my fees.'

Sam was feeling light-headed by the time she came out of the shop. She scrolled through her mobile phone address book until she found the number of the BBC reporter who had stopped her outside the Old Bailey. He had given her his card and she had thought at the time that he might make a useful ally. The call went to voicemail.

'This is Sam Bailey for Daniel Giles. I'm sure you remember but I work for Fleet Investigations and I am working on the case of Elizabeth Johnson. I need to talk to you.'

She put the phone back in her handbag, but it rang back immediately.

'Sam?'

'Yes.'

'It's Daniel. Presume you're calling to tell me about the Clapham Common murder. I know all about it. Was thinking it felt a little similar. Got anything new?'

'The pearl bead that was found in Icey's pocket may not have come from Leticia's rosary.'

Giles paused. 'Is that kosher?'

'I have an opinion from Hatton Garden.'

'It is kosher, then!'

'It's only the guy's preliminary opinion. He's got to see the originals.'

'Keep me posted, soon as you get the final opinion. I'll try to get a teaser trailer on the news tonight.'

Sam hung up, and then she rang Mr Frizzel and Ashley Towers.

Chapter Sixty-Four

Ashley Towers settled back on his sofa and sipped at his Puligny Montrachet. He deserved spoiling, he decided. It had been a good day. Even the judge had given him a favourable nod when he closed his cross-examination. Win or lose (and it would probably be win), he had been the star of the show.

He switched on the six o'clock news on the BBC. There was a lead item about some further crisis in the Middle East followed by some more depressing economic news – another high-street chain had gone into liquidation. Then, to Ashley's astonishment, the familiar figure of Mr Frizzel appeared. Actually, not so much familiar as unusual. He looked abnormally smart. He had even combed his hair. That little prick Daniel Giles was interviewing him, and he could see the glamorous form of Sam Bailey standing behind them both.

'Yes, my firm is representing Miss Johnson but I do not want to comment on the likely outcome of the appeal.'

Ashley groaned, fearing Frizzel would go too far. Why hadn't they asked him to do the interview? He was an expert when it came to handling the media. Frizzel was, sadly, something of a loose cannon. It wasn't a live interview, though; maybe they would have edited out anything embarrassing. As he continued to watch, though, Ashley realised that he needn't have worried; for once the drunken solicitor restrained himself.

'Can I just say that my client was wrongly convicted and the truth will come out,' said Frizzel, swaying to the sound of his own voice.

Daniel Giles pressed ahead.

'I believe you have a preliminary opinion that the bead found on your client may not have come from Leticia Joy's rosary. Our viewers will be aware from our earlier reports of the significance of this possible finding. Can you tell us more now?' Giles asked, his face serious.

Ashley held his breath again. Sam had filled him in about her trip to Hatton Garden, and her efforts to discredit the evidence of the bead found on Icey. It was an important and delicate advance in the investigation, and he didn't want Frizzel to blow it. Once again, however, Frizzel managed to come good.

'Not at the moment. Fleet Investigations, the detective agency we use—' here, Frizzel gave a nod in the direction of Sam '—are still continuing to find evidence. They found our expert witness. Can't say more,' Frizzel said chirpily, before nodding once again, this time at the camera, before he no doubt disappeared towards the Frog and Duck.

Chapter Sixty-Five

Sam was back behind her desk at Fleet Investigations later that Saturday evening when she took the call on her mobile. It was Daniel Giles.

'See the piece on the box earlier?"

'Yeah, great.' Sam had hurried back to her office to watch the interview.

'Good coverage for you. Look, I've had a call from one of the powers that be. They want to run with this story right up to the appeal, mount a campaign, maybe do a documentary when it's over.'

'Fantastic.' This was just what was needed to highlight the injustice of Icey's conviction and add momentum to the appeal.

'Icey is your partner in Fleet Investigations?'

'That's right.'

'If the court quash the conviction, will you have her back?'

'Of course. She's a first-rate investigator.'

'But isn't this your first case?' Daniel asked, and Sam felt herself bristling.

'Yes, but . . . that is beside the point. She will be a first-rate investigator.'

'This whole thing hasn't been staged for the benefit of Fleet Investigations, then?' the reporter said, jokingly.

'Of course not.' Sam wasn't amused. 'This isn't a joke, Daniel. Icey is in prison. She has been convicted of murder. Why would we risk the possibility of adverse publicity?' Sam realised she was being led down a primrose path. 'Look, I really must be going. I've got a lot of work to do. I'll happily talk to you when it's all over.'

'Just checking. So the first case you're investigating is one of your own . . .'

Sam put the phone down without saying a word.

She had hardly done so when the phone started ringing. For once it wasn't a crank caller responding to her flier campaign but a prospective client. The woman had seen Mr Frizzel on the television, giving what amounted to a press release for Fleet Investigations and was keen to find out more. More calls followed – admittedly two were from former clients who had recognised Sam in the background of the interview and rang up asking for the current price of a blow job. But a few of the calls were legit. Finally Sam was seeing some serious possibilities for their agency.

By ten o'clock that evening, she was still in the office with the blinds drawn and the lights on low. The phones were now silent and she allowed herself a break to pour a large glass of red wine. From the information she'd taken over the phone from the three most likely clients, she was getting a sense of how their business would develop. The agency would specialise in missing persons, cheating spouses, lost souls . . . Given their own backgrounds, this would be right up their street.

But for now Sam was focused on just one case – Icey's.

Chapter Sixty-Six

Ashley Towers was deep in thought when the clerk rang through to his extension.

'Sir, I've got the Court of Appeal office on. They want to know where your skeleton argument is in the appeal of Elizabeth Johnson. They said something about the fact that you should have served it some time ago, and they can't list the appeal before the full court unless you serve the skeleton argument. They would like to list the case as soon as possible. Is there a reason why it has not been served, sir?'

'There is no good reason at all. I've been too busy. Bob, tell them they'll get it soon.'

'Sir, you should have informed the court in writing some time ago of the legal points you will argue at the appeal in your skeleton argument. You're running out of time.'

'Tell the court that we are waiting on a statement from a witness not previously called in the Crown Court. We will be making an application to call fresh evidence. As soon as we get it, I'll send one over the road. Tell them we will deliver it today by 4.30 p.m.'

'Very well, sir.'

In truth, Ashley wanted to hold on to the advice and skeleton argument for as long as possible before sending it to Alfred Roma, in the hope that Roma would not trouble himself too much to read it. If he had his way, Ashley would wait until the day of the appeal. Even if Roma had time to read the report, he would then not have time to digest its contents fully and formulate his submissions to the court. Elizabeth Johnson had a very good chance of having her conviction overturned, Ashley considered. But it would not hurt to use the little tricks he had learnt over the years. He hoped he could now prove beyond reasonable doubt that one and the same killer had murdered both Martha Lewis and Leticia Joy. But he was wise enough to know that you should never rely on things turning out as they should. It would take more than the obvious truth to convince the judges that Icey had been wrongly convicted of murdering Leticia Joy.

In fact, when the paperwork finally arrived, Alfred Roma started working hard on his response to the appeal. As counsel for the prosecution, he was beginning to have doubts about the correctness of the conviction. He had been here before over the many years he had been a barrister. It would all end in tears, and he would rather they were not his.

He was still troubled by the unfortunate business at Madam Irma's. He felt compromised – exposed in more ways than one – but he could hardly quit the case now. The trouble was, he also had to take his instructions from Lydia Watson, the lawyer of the Crown Prosecution Service, who was in charge of the case. She was nothing more than an overcooked slice of pastry – all flake and not enough filling. When she was in his chambers, he'd had the great misfortune to be her pupil master. It was the biggest mistake of his career.

For twelve months he'd had to suffer her stupidity, her inability to master a legal argument and her comprehensive failure to understand that she was not the greatest lawyer that had hit earth in the twenty-first century. When she was not telling how to conduct his trials, she was arguing with the clerks for not exposing her to other members of chambers. Everyone knew that the way to make a name for yourself was to be introduced to as many solicitors as possible in the hope that they would send work your way, but Lydia had an extraordinary talent for upsetting people, and Roma still couldn't believe she had got where she was today.

Back then, an extraordinary chambers' meeting had been held to consider her application for a place in chambers. Not one single member of chambers voted to keep her. Now, years later, she was telling him how to conduct his case. Twice she had returned his skeleton argument, requesting amendments when it was really none of her business. She was motivated out of sheer spite and a desire to humiliate him. Roma knew that he couldn't afford to lose the work she sent him. Not yet. Not now that she was his instructing solicitor and in a position to cause trouble, not to mention wreck his career.

The printer spewed out the final page. Clipping the corners together with a corner piece bearing chambers' logo, Roma read the document twice from start to finish before he placed his signature at the foot. He picked up the phone and dialled his clerk.

'My dear boy, the advice and skeleton argument in Elizabeth Johnson's case are now ready for collection. Would you be kind enough to make sure that it is copied twice and walked over to the Court of Appeal?'

Putting down the receiver, Roma felt deeply uncomfortable at the instructions he had received from Miss Watson. It had been quite inappropriate for her to instruct him to argue tooth and nail to uphold the conviction. He was not in the business of arguing to uphold a conviction that might be unsafe, just to win a case. Although with a little bit of luck and a sensible court, they would see the conviction for what it was without his help – completely unsatisfactory.

Chapter Sixty-Seven

Icey was in the prison yard when she lit up. She hadn't wanted to take up smoking again, but the pressure of her incarceration and pending appeal were stressing her out, big time. She had dropped six pounds in two weeks and was little more than skin and bones now. The weight loss was welcome because she always thought that she was a little on the heavy side. It did not matter to her that everyone else thought she needed fattening up.

The two screws on patrol had been pretty sympathetic. They had seen it all before. Pacing up and down, Icey wanted to enjoy her fifteen-minute smoke break, but her mind kept darting back to the thought of what would be happening in the appeal when it happened.

She was as prepared as she could ever be, though resigned to the fact that she would never get out of prison. The inmates were an interesting bunch of women with a good sense of humour. Some of the POs were compassionate but one or two had clearly slipped under the radar and were of a psychotic disposition.

Mr Towers had finally sent her a draft of his skeleton argument on the appeal against the conviction, and it looked good to her. Her team would call fresh evidence. They had solid information about a similar murder that had taken place while she was banged up, plus an expert would give fresh evidence about the rosary bead found in her possession. Icey strongly suspected that the new evidence was all Sam's doing. She wished that she had not been so lippy with Father William, as she could have asked him to explain the meanings of the beads. Although hadn't Sam said that it all came down to a question of design rather than any spiritual meaning of the Leticia Joy's necklace?

Pacing up and down, Icey spotted a small plaque in the corner of the hall. She stopped and looked at it. She'd never noticed it before. It was well worn and barely legible. Time had taken its toll, but as she struggled, she began to make sense of what was engraved. She lit up another cigarette as she continued to stare at the letters.

'That name, Ruth Ellis,' she muttered, 'I'm sure I've read about her.'

'I think everyone has read about her,' said the screw Betty, as she folded her matronly arms across her broad torso.

Icey had formed a good relationship with Betty. She was the mother of all screws. She had only taken the job when her children left home and went to university. Now she had a large extended family of Holloway ladies. She was a mother in every sense of the word. Her buxom bottom protruded outward in equal proportion to her bustline.

'Who was she again?'

'You mean, who were they, not who was she. There's a whole list of women up there if you look hard enough. All those ladies faced judicial executions.'

'What does that mean?'

'Well, it means that each of them were ordered to be executed on the day recorded. Ruth Ellis was the last woman to be hanged in this country.'

'Why was she hanged?' asked Icey.

'For murder, but when she was hanged, the public were not very happy about it and it strengthened public support for the abolition of the death penalty.'

'That's awful,' said Icey.

'It was. Did you know that the last hanging in this country was in 1964, but by then reprieves were commonplace?'

'Why didn't they reprieve Ruth Ellis?' Icey asked.

'Well, if you want my opinion, it was her lifestyle, really,' said Betty.

'What do you mean?' asked Icey, stopping in her tracks.

'Basically, she was a tart and she had shown a lack of remorse for the murder.'

Icey felt stunned and took a long drag on her cigarette.

'When you say she was a tart, do you mean a whore?'

'It's the same difference,' Betty said.

The remains of Icey's cigarette burnt her fingers and she stubbed it out, distracted. It was as if Betty was describing her. She was lost in thought. An ex-tart, maybe, but how could she show remorse for a crime she didn't commit? And couldn't even remember. She could imagine the noose around her neck as she stared at the names. She knew that God was not on her side and she would have to fight for her freedom.

'She was hanged on thirteenth of July 1955?'

'That's right,' confirmed Betty.

'But she is the same as me. I'm not be under a death sentence but I might as well be. I'll never get out of here. There is one law for the rich and another for the likes of me.'

'Oh,' said Betty. 'Welcome to the club.'

Stamping on the cigarette she'd dropped, Icey returned to the music block. She had recently signed up to attend a course in music appreciation. At first it had simply been yet another way of getting out of her cell, but she'd surprised herself by actually enjoying the sessions. This week the students were getting to grips with Puccini. They had drawn his name out of a hat. When Icey went back in, the music teacher started giving them a brief introduction to the composer. It was a welcome distraction from the horrors of Ruth Ellis's life and death, and Icey tried to push her story to the back of her mind. As well as religious instruction, she had signed up for every course that she could inside. Anything that provided a chance to take her mind of her worries was something she was interested in.

Icey was currently very interested in Puccini. He sounded like the kind of guy she would have liked to have met if he had been born later and in South London. He was the only bloke she knew who boasted about having a madam called 'Butterfly'. The teacher explained that there was no opera in the world that could match the tragedy and sorrow of Madam Butterfly. She was very much like many of the female inmates of the prison – a victim of circumstance. The opera was about a doomed love.

'Well, all I know about that,' said Icey, 'is that I was born as a result of a doomed love. Come to think of it, though, I ain't never heard of a love that wasn't ill-fated. What is it with these Japanese birds? Can't they handle a bit of rejection?'

'The fact that she was Japanese was, of course, very important. She, Madam Butterfly, is convinced that the man she loves, who is American, will return to her eventually,' the teacher explained.

'Ain't that illegal?' asked Icey.

'What?'

'Well, having a "madam". I know at least a dozen madams who ended up in prison. Maybe all they were doing was waiting for their lovers to return? That's what they should have . . .'

All the ladies started to laugh. Icey's mood had lifted.

'She was not a madam in that sense,' said the teacher.

'You just said that she was!'

'No, she wasn't a madam in charge of a brothel. It was just her title, like missus.'

'A madam called Butterfly waiting for her lover, who says she ain't a madam. Remind me to tell my mate. If it worked for Madam Butterfly, it might work for Madam Irma.'

'What happened to her bloke, then, miss?' asked one of the other girls.

'I mean, do we know about him? Did he end up doing time?' The girls giggled again.

'No, he left Japan and returned to America. He was actually an American naval lieutenant. He remained in America for several years, during which time Madam Butterfly remained faithful to him.'

'What, for several years?' said Icey astonished.

'Yes, and when he eventually returned, he brought his wife with him. This destroyed Madam Butterfly.'

'So she realised what we've known for ever. She didn't have to wait several years to find out that men are a waste of time,' said one of the ladies.

'No, she realised that loyalty is sometimes lost on those with fickle minds. It can also be an understated virtue,' said the teacher. 'When she finally realised that she had been betrayed by the man she loved, it all ended tragically.'

'What do you mean by that, miss?'

'Well, Madam Butterfly had fallen pregnant by her American lover and had a baby boy. The Lieutenant knew nothing about it and he went off and married an American woman. When he eventually returned, Madam Butterfly couldn't cope; she killed herself with her father's sword.'

'This is such a sad story, miss,' said Icey.

'It is tragic – it's one of the great tragic operas, in my opinion.

The blade of the sword bore the inscription "To die with honour when one can no longer live with honour."'

'Oh, miss,' said Icey, in tears, 'that's what I want.'

'What are you talking about?'

'I want to die with honour, miss. I don't want to stay in prison for the rest of my life.'

The class was stunned into silence. They all shared the same dream as Icey; no one wanted to be in prison. But for some there was no honour left to be had.

Chapter Sixty-Eight

It was Sunday and Mr Frizzel, typically, was asleep in his office when the bailiffs arrived. They had not given prior notice and Mr Frizzel was surprised by their assertions that he had not paid his bills. He stood up and then slumped back down. This was becoming a regular habit and Sam had made her views clear on the subject. He was certain he had not touched a drink that day, and was perfectly sober, although the night before he had been on a bender and was now suffering the king of hangovers. His brain would not catch up with what was going on, and for the first time in a long while he cursed drink.

The bailiffs served the formal paperwork on Frizzel. Two more men entered the tiny office and started to dismantle what expensive electrical equipment there was, with the intention of removing it to some safe location prior to auction. Rising from his chair once again, Mr Frizzel tried to prevent the removal of his chattels, shouting at the top of his voice for the men to remove themselves.

Sam was attending to a private client in her office next door. The lady was the first of a handful to approach her as a result of Frizzel's TV 'advert' for the firm. She was there to ask Sam to solve a personal problem, and Sam listened intently. She was about to get married but her best friend was convinced her husband-to-be was up to no good. The friend had said that the fiancé had made a pass at her, and Sam's client didn't know what to believe; but, before she went ahead with the wedding, she wanted to be sure her husband was going to be faithful. Could Sam help? Sam knew two girls who could more than test the fiancé's propensity for straying, and she replied that, yes, she could help. Privately, she thought the woman probably had more money than sense and also that, perhaps, the best friend was more jealous than concerned, but she wasn't in a position to look a gift client in the mouth.

Sitting at her desk, dressed in her Chanel suit and roll-neck jumper, Sam fingered the pearls around her neck out of habit, while taking down the client's details. She promised to do all she could to help her client know one way or another if she was about to make the biggest mistake of her life. As she went through the terms and conditions of their arrangement, Sam heard a commotion and thought Mr Frizzel was under attack. Making her excuses, she rose quickly from her chair and went outside to offer assistance. As she entered the office, she noticed that Mr Frizzel was standing on top of his desk, refusing to get down. Three burly men were trying to assist the old man, but Mr Frizzel swayed around precariously, preventing capture but possibly risking his own neck.

'What is this all about?' Sam enquired urgently.

'We're the bailiffs, love, and Frizzel here has not paid his rent. We have a court summons to seize his goods.'

'Mr Frizzel, we have spoken about this and you assured me that it would not happen again?' Mr Frizzel looked sheepish in response to Sam's telling off. She sighed and then turned to the nearest bailiff. 'How much does he owe?'

'Three and a half grand.'

Sam thought that sounded like a lot of money, but fortunately the 'more money than sense' client next door had just coughed up nearly a grand on retainer, and she also had just over two grand petty cash in the safe. She decided she would help Mr Frizzel, but as much for her own and Icey's sake as for his. Frizzel was putting Icey's future at risk with his unacceptable behaviour. Sam had had enough and, one way or another, Frizzel was fast outgrowing his usefulness, especially now that she had Ashley Towers on board. She might need him for now, with Icey's appeal pending, but she wasn't sure how much longer she could continue to prop Frizzel up.

As he performed the bailiffs' dance on the table, Sam spoke directly to them.

'Well, if you come next door, I will give you a cheque.'

'We don't accept cheques,' said Mr Muscle as he rolled his sleeves and took possession of the computer. 'We only accept cash.'

The screen went black as he pulled out a fistful of wires from the rear of the machine.

'Fine, wait here then and I'll come back with the cash in a moment,' Sam responded coolly.

Mr Frizzel stopped and looked at the bailiffs, who looked after Sam as she walked out of the door.

Eight minutes later, Sam returned, having made her apologies to her waiting client and leaving her with a magazine and a coffee. Counting out three thousand, five hundred and twenty-pounds on the desk, she requested a receipt. Mr Frizzel climbed down. The second bailiff (whom Sam had christened Baldilocks in her head) looked like a human bulldozer. He counted the money once and then again before he asked for some paper to write out a receipt.

Picking up the receipt, Sam noticed that the bulldozer had a problem spelling. After raising an eyebrow at him, she requested that the three men leave. They did, closing the door behind them. When they were alone, Mr Frizzel finally climbed down from the desk.

'I am sorry, old girl, for the financial mess I've caused.'

Sam handed him the receipt. He picked up a pen and wrote at the top 'I O U', and signed it at the bottom, 'For and on behalf of Mr Frizzel.' He handed the receipt back to Sam. She took it and walked back to her office without saying a word. She added this latest 'I O U' to the pile in her safe. There were seven in all. Mr Frizzel was getting to be a liability and seriously bad for business. It was time to make him an offer he could not refuse. But before she did so, Sam would talk to Harry over the coming days. His advice had always proved invaluable.

Chapter Sixty-Nine

It was a normal night for Sam: with lots on her mind, it was hard for her to switch off enough to sleep. For hours, she tossed and turned, closing her eyes and praying for sleep. But when it did finally come, once again her dreams were haunted.

She was a teenager again, lying in her bed, fearing the sound of footsteps outside her door. When her uncle Pete had been acquitted of all charges, her stepmother had allowed him to move into their home and Sam's childhood had ended.

She dreamt he was in her room, breathing down her neck with his fetid breath. 'Shush, don't say a word, my sweetheart. Uncle Pete is here,' he whispered into her ear.

'But Uncle Pete—'

'Shush, you'll spoil the magic. Go back to sleep. Uncle Pete will look after you, my darling.'

She had never wanted much in life – just a mother who loved her and a father who would look out for her, and here she was with Uncle Pete. He wrapped his arms around her. She pushed his hands away and then he did it again. The dreaming, grown-up Sam shouted at him. 'Don't do that!'

She turned round to confront him but he was gone. Sam was alone in bed with her thoughts once again. She was saturated in perspiration, her beautiful Victorian-style nightdress stuck to her slender body. The blackness of the room overwhelmed her. She reached over to switch on the lamp near her bed; her eyes were still heavy with sleep but she'd rather stay away than surrender to her dreams.

Her mind was dizzy with thoughts. She wished she could banish her 'uncle' from her dreams but he was always there, particularly in times of stress. In truth, it had been this as much as anything else that had ended her relationship with Paradissimo. She didn't want any man to get close to her; certainly not so close that she would have to confide the source of her nightmares. Bad enough that Gil was overly possessive and knew she was a tart; she didn't want him to know all her secrets, too. She suspected Harry knew about some of the more awful elements of her childhood – it would all be in her file, after all. There were times when she caught him looking at her in a way she thought betrayed his pity. But Icey was the only person she'd confided in at length since the aborted court case all those years ago.

Sam looked at the clock. It was three in the morning, too early even for her to make her way to the office. Instead, she lay there in her grown-up bed, waiting for morning to roll around.

Monday morning, Sam arrived at work later than usual after her disturbed night. Oriel and Flick were already there, as arranged, and Mr Frizzel had let them in. Both girls were casually dressed in jeans and jumpers. Sam had asked them to come in to Fleet Investigations a couple of days each week. The arrangement had begun with their help on Icey's case, but now Irma's girls were also making themselves very useful on the handful of new cases that had come in, and Sam had offered to pay them for their time. Irma had said she could 'borrow' the girls, but Sam insisted on compensating them for their out-of-pocket expenses at least. She needed and valued their help. On top of Icey's pending appeal, Sam was also dealing with an anxious mother concerned about her missing daughter, a handful of wives fearful that their husbands were cheating, plus their honey trap client. With no Icey on hand, Flick and Oriel were proving invaluable.

Business was beginning to pick up. Since the news report, Sam's diary had certainly been a lot fuller than it had been since she'd first gone legit, but yesterday's threat of eviction by the bailiffs was a chilling reminder that she had one other problem that couldn't wait.

Mr Frizzel was on the phone when Sam entered his office. Sensing trouble in Sam's brisk manner, he terminated the call. Pulling up a chair, she sat down next to him.

'I've been thinking about the future of our professional relationship,' said Sam, 'and I would like to make you an offer.'

Looking suitably meek, Frizzel moved papers around on his desk. 'What have you got in mind?'

'I would like to buy you out. I know you lease this property – and we sub-lease from you – but I can take over the lease. I can raise a loan, if need be. Harry Kemp has already said he'll invest in the business. In return, I will continue to honour all the bills and cancel your debt to me. You, of course, will continue to practice as before. Nothing will change apart from the fact that the bailiffs will no longer bother you.'

Sam paused to allow the impact of her words to sink in.

'I would like to think about it,' Frizzel said dejectedly. 'How much time do I have?'

'Take as long as you like,' Sam replied generously and more gently. She was grateful to the solicitor for allowing her to start up the agency, she reminded herself, and she would not rush him for an answer.

She spent the next hour dealing with a new client. She was a middle-aged woman who wanted low-level intelligence gathering on her husband. She had suspected him of having an affair with his twenty-two-year-old secretary. The woman seemed as annoyed at the cliché of it all as she was at her husband for cheating. The operation would start the next day for a period of fourteen days, and continue as advised. Reports and photographs of sightings were essential. The client had made it clear that, if he was seeing some other bitch, she intended to make him pay.

Shaking hands on the deal, Sam showed her new client to the door. While she wanted to give all her time to collecting evidence for Icey's appeal, the woman's case seemed relatively straightforward. Picking up the phone, she rang Irma. She needed an extra girl to help her man the office. As of tomorrow, Flick and Miss Oriel were about to take on surveillance for the next two weeks.

Chapter Seventy

Margaret Certie had aged badly since the death of her husband just over a month ago. It was the depression that she found the most difficult, and the nights spent in the house on her own were unbearable. Sitting at the table, looking out the window, and sipping brandy straight out of the bottle, she'd even begun to sympathise with her husband's baser instincts. What the point was of continuing? She was continuing to put off calling back the policeman. She knew she should be honest about the judge's state of mind at the time of his death, and tell the detective – Haydn, that was his name – about Jonathan's request for a divorce. In a way, she thought she might feel better if she actually told someone. Presently, it felt that her grief was getting worse not better, and her days merged into one block of pain and loss.

DC Haydn was surprised to hear from the judge's wife again. He was even more surprised to hear what she had to say. She told him about the phone call she had received from her husband requesting a divorce.

'I'm afraid he was a living a double life,' she said quietly on the phone. 'I suppose, deep down, I had sensed it for some time, and just chose to ignore the evidence.' Sighing, she finally began to admit what she'd previously tried to ignore, even in her darkest moments of missing her husband. 'There were telephone calls late at night that were abruptly terminated when

I walked into the room. He often arrived home late, saying he had been in some function at his Inn of Court. But there were frequent occasions when I called his clerk only to be told that he had left for home hours ago.'

'Thank you for telling me,' said DC Haydn, pondering the implications of this. 'Assuming for the time being that just one other person was involved, another woman, do you have any idea who it might have been?'

'I've no idea,' Margaret said sadly.

'Well, I'll follow this up, in any case.'

Margaret felt a sense of relief as she put the telephone down. She had bottled up her private affairs for too long, and it was all so unnecessary. It was not as if she had anything to lose. She had nothing left. She'd lost it all when her honourable husband jumped off the roof.

Walking from the kitchen to the drawing room, Mrs Certie carried a half-finished bottle of brandy in her right hand. Quite why she had not finished the bottle yet was lost on her. These days she was perfectly capable of polishing off a whole bottle in one sitting.

Slumping back down into her favourite chair, she reached for the TV remote control. It was extraordinary what repetitive rubbish was on the television. Flicking from the BBC to ITV and then Channel Four and back again, a story caught her attention. It was about the appeal of a convicted murderer; the approaching trial of a defendant called 'Icey' – Elizabeth Johnson. How could she forget that name? She'd been a constant support to Jonathan in his work, and she knew Icey's case was the last that her husband ever tried before he killed himself.

Elizabeth Johnson's lawyer was being interviewed but Mrs Certie's gaze was drawn to the young black woman also on camera. She was introduced briefly as Sam Bailey, a partner in Fleet Investigations – and friend of the accused. She had apparently found an expert who would give fresh evidence at the appeal hearing.

Mrs Certie made a mental note of the firm's name as she swigged from her brandy bottle. Then she dialled Directory Enquiries to ask for the number of Fleet Investigations. The operator connected Mrs Certie.

'Fleet Investigations. Can I help you?'

'That depends. My name is Mrs Margaret Certie. My husband was Judge Jonathan Certie. I believe we both have something in common. I have lost a husband and I understand that you have lost your friend. I'm afraid it was my husband's last case that sent your friend to prison. He tried her and found her guilty. Both events – his death and her imprisonment – occurred on the same day, and I have been wondering if there's a connection . . .'

Sam couldn't move. She sat stock still, completely stunned by the phone call, and it was not often that happened. In her determination to free Icey, she had barely acknowledged the suicide of Judge Certie; but she would never forget the man who had sentenced Icey to life with a minimum of thirty years in prison.

'How could I forget?' said Sam huskily. 'I'd like to talk to you in person. When can we meet?'

'I'll be in touch,' came the reply, before the phone went dead.

Chapter Seventy-One

DC Haydn visited Mrs Certie at her home in Chelsea the next morning, to follow up on what she had told him during their phone conversation. Sitting on the elegant sofa and politely sipping Earl Grey tea, he listened to see if she had any more details to add to her telephone confession. She certainly had plenty to say, and he made lots of notes as she spoke. He'd always felt that there was more to the case than just a jump from the feet of the Statue of Justice.

Margaret Certie walked with him to the front door. As he left the house, Haydn turned round to face her. 'I'll be in touch again. But there is just one other thing I wanted to clear up. On the day of your husband's death, you said when we spoke originally that you didn't phone him at work that day.'

'No, I did not,' Mrs Certie said emphatically.

'Do you perhaps have an unregistered mobile phone?' Haydn asked carefully.

Mrs Certie looked offended. 'I don't have a mobile phone of any sort. Ghastly things,' she responded icily.

'On the day of your husband's death, someone rang and was put through to his room. That person claimed to be his wife. Are you sure you didn't forget you called?' he asked, giving her one last chance to remember.

'As I told you before, DC Haydn, Jonathan always made it

clear that I was not to ring unless it was an emergency. I didn't call him.'

'Thank you,' said DC Haydn, nodding in acknowledgement as he took his leave.

As he walked down the front steps away from the house, he was deep in thought. He still hadn't solved the issue of the judge's second phone. He was also puzzled by all the calls and missed messages on the secret mobile. Why would Certie have a phone that not even his wife knew about? When he'd first interviewed her, she'd started off by saying that they had no secrets from each other, but clearly that was not exactly true. Now she seemed convinced that he had been using the phone to conduct some kind of extra-marital affair. From Haydn's perspective, the plain fact was that someone had called the judge just before he died claiming to be his wife. If it was not Mrs Certie, it was someone who was very much a person of interest.

The primary issue that needed to be resolved before any other was the identity of this mystery caller. He would have to seek prior authorisation from his superior officers to investigate the caller's details. He knew that such enquiries could only be sanctioned under the Regulation of Investigatory Powers Act 2000, which gave a statutory framework for the authorisation and conduct of certain types of covert surveillance operation. His experience had shown that a RIPA investigation normally took about eight weeks, but in this instance he would have to speed that up.

Arriving at the office, he picked up his phone and dialled, waiting for his boss to pick up. But it was late and his boss did not like to be disturbed unless it was an absolute emergency. He clearly wasn't going to answer now. He would try again in the morning.

Putting the phone down, Haydn sat back in his seat and

thought about the bigger picture – the questions he was no closer to answering. Why would a successful judge throw himself off the roof of the Old Bailey? Who was it that had called him and why did the judge have a secret phone? Was it Certie's mystery woman, if indeed there was one? Had she called things off, perhaps? Or had she even threatened to tell his wife? Maybe his colleagues? Or even the powers that be who had authorised his recent elevation to the High Court? Any of these possibilities could have driven a desperate man to take his own life. Haydn was determined that, one way or another, he would find out which reason was the right one.

Chapter Seventy-Two

Sam looked at her clock as Oriel and Flick checked their phones. Both were fully charged. They were now ready for their first morning of surveillance, and Sam could tell that Irma's girls were excited. They had already helped close one case. Sam had been surprised that the husband of her honey trap client had resisted Oriel's best efforts to seduce him yesterday evening. It was good news, though, and she was looking forward to telling her client later that day. Of course, it could be that Oriel just wasn't the man's type, but Sam rather liked thinking of it more optimistically: as proof that, contrary to how it sometimes seemed to her, there were still a few good men out there.

Now as she observed Flick and Oriel getting ready to leave, she envied their ability to see fun in the work but she had too much on her mind to share their excitement. On top of Icey's imminent appeal, she had her new clients to think about as well as earning enough money to pay the office overheads, having taken over Frizzel's lease. Her start-up grant still paid her own rent, but she couldn't afford simply to put her feet up. She certainly had a lot on her plate, she thought to herself.

As Sam gave the girls their final orders, the office phone rang. Flick answered but it was clear from her responses that the caller was refusing to give their name. 'They say they want a private word with you, Sam. I told her you're not available but she's not having any of it.'

Reluctantly, Sam took the phone from her outstretched hand. 'Sam Bailey speaking,' she said wearily, all the late nights catching up with her.

'Is that the owner of Fleet Investigations?' a quiet voice asked.

'Yes. I am Sam Bailey,' she repeated, trying not to sound impatient.

'It's Mrs Certie here. I have some information that might be of interest to you.'

'Mrs Certie? Thank you for calling back. You didn't leave me your number yesterday, and I've been eager to speak to you again. I'd be happy to meet with you at your convenience,' Sam suggested.

'Do you have a pen, my dear? I'll give you my address. Come today, if you wish.'

'Today is the one day that I can't do, I'm afraid,' Sam said with regret. 'Give me your contact details, though, and I'll check my schedule and let you know when I can come. In the meantime, can you tell me about this information?' Sam asked curiously.

'I'd rather speak to you about it in person, dear. Let me know when you can visit me,' Mrs Certie said, and then relayed her phone number and address.

Sam thanked Mrs Certie and replaced the receiver, still wondering what the judge's wife could have to tell her. Oriel and Flick had left during the call and Sam was now on her own. She had a full list of tasks for the day. The kettle boiled. Sam put the call out of her mind and made a cup of tea, carrying it back to her desk.

Chapter Seventy-Three

Pia Broom was shattered as she drove home from an unexpected late night out. It had not been her intention to stay as long as she had, but that was really no excuse. She was amazed at her own patience, actually. Normally she would have just got up and made her excuses, but it hadn't been that easy. Having accepted the invitation at the last minute from two of her work colleagues, Wendy Katlan and Gaynor Easby, it had felt a little awkward to leave early without causing offence. Both women were having personal difficulties, which needed extensive group discussion.

The Post Office was a very impressive new wine bar just off Fleet Street. The old Post Office had closed down three years earlier, and since then it had been an eyesore until a group of property developers decide to lease and convert the building. It was long, narrow and surprisingly spacious. The special concession during the opening week meant that for every bottle of wine purchased before 7 p.m., the second was on the house.

For her colleagues, Wendy and Gaynor, two women with nothing to do, no husbands, no partners and nothing waiting for them back at home, this was the perfect end to what would otherwise have been a lonely Tuesday evening. Wendy and Gaynor had arrived with the sole intent of getting plastered and wallowing in self-pity and cheap alcohol. At the end of the night, they'd had to be persuaded that it was time to go home, and the taxi called on their behalf almost refused to take them. It was only after they paid up front with a large tip that the taxi driver finally relented.

At long last, Pia – still cold stone sober – was on her way home and she was looking forward to her bed when she ran into trouble. As she approached the one-way system at the top of Wandsworth Road in her Volkswagen Polo, the car stalled to a halt. Turning the key again, the engine spluttered into life long enough for her to manoeuvre the car over to the side of the road, then it died again. It was hopeless. Looking at the dashboard, she knew instantly what the problem was. She had allowed herself to run out of petrol.

Looking over her shoulder and into her rear-view mirror, Pia saw that the roads were deserted. It was well past one o'clock in the morning on a work night. Most people were in bed. It crossed her mind to seek assistance from some kind-looking stranger, but there were none about. In any event, she was extremely cautious; you only needed to open the newspapers to read yet another story about young women being raped or sexually assaulted late at night.

Pia tried the engine one more time. It made the same spluttering noise as last time, but did not turn over, so she switched it off to prevent excessive pressure on the battery. Then she remembered that she had a spare petrol can in the boot of the car. Her recollection was that she had filled it recently, but she could not remember how recent that was. Stepping out of the car, Pia looked back along the street. The road was quiet and the hushed silence unnerved her.

Quickly, she walked back to the rear of the vehicle, leaving the driver's door open. She was such a ditsy woman, she thought; she could kick herself for landing in this predicament again. The last time it had happened, she'd promised herself –

and her worried mother – that it would be the last. But once again, she had been careless enough to run out of petrol and she had no one else to blame but herself.

The boot opened easily and the hatch flicked up. Pia peered blankly into the dark void for the petrol can in the boot. There was so much rubbish that had collected in the boot: old files, empty bottles, various clothes from nights over at friends' houses. The petrol can was nowhere to be seen. Looking through the rear of the car to the footwell, she thought she recalled placing it under the back passenger footwell, but it was not there, either. Checking the boot again, Pia decided she had no choice; she would have to ring the RAC.

Her membership card was in her purse inside her handbag, which was on the passenger seat. Closing the boot and returning to the driver's seat, Pia climbed in, closed the door and stretched over to reach her handbag. As she powered up her phone, she noticed someone on the west footpath approaching her. Her mind started working overtime. She thought the figure was male. He was tall – six foot, possibly a little taller. Maybe he could help get the car started. That was silly, she realised; there was nothing wrong with the car. The problem was with the lack of fuel.

Her phone powered up and then bleeped. Looking down at the screen, the message flashed 'low battery'. It was clearly not her night. As the phone flashed blank into the off position, Pia glanced up. The potential helper was now closer to her. She was able to make out his features. He was a she. Pia had been wrong. She was in her mid-twenties to late thirties, pretty, with a bob haircut and very little make-up apart from a heavy application of mascara. As she approached with her head down and both hands in her pockets, Pia decided against enlisting her help. She looked up as she passed Pia. They briefly engaged in eye contact before the stranger averted her eyes and walked on. She was now twenty feet away from Pia, her handbag swinging from her left shoulder as she presumably headed for home. Pia thought it was time to do the same.

Removing her handbag from the passenger seat, she got out of the car and closed all the doors with the flick of her central locking key. She could collect it in the morning. Pulling the collar of her coat up, she made a double knot in the belt to secure her coat to her body. Throwing her bag over her left shoulder, Pia looked hastily around. It was time to walk.

Across the road, the shops were all closed. She had hoped there might be a mini-cab office open at least, but Pia was not in luck. And she had not seen a single black cab pass her in all the time she had been stranded at the side of the road. Turning left at the top of Wandsworth Common, she walked briskly along the edge of the pond. Taking the next left, her mind darted back to when she was a child; when she had played in this very park, with its inner protected enclosure for kids. She had spent many happy hours there on the little swings, clambering through the tyres and climbing up the wooden structures. It looked very much the same now as then.

As she walked by the children's play area, she thought as she always did of the small scar on her forehead and how it had happened. She had been so stupid. It had been right there, just between the seesaw and the swings, where she had fallen off and caught her head on the edge of the swing. The scar was barely visible now. Taking her hand out of her pocket, she felt the old wound out of habit. Standing there thoughtfully stroking her scar, lost in memories, she didn't notice as she was approached from behind. She reacted with terror when a hand was placed over her mouth. She started to struggle as the chloroform dulled her senses. She looked up and saw a sight that was burnt on her memory for the brief remainder of her short life.

Chapter Seventy-Four

At 6.15 a.m. Mrs Francis thought that she was dreaming when she heard something scratching the outside of her front door. It might just be one of the neighbourhood cats chancing its luck – or local kids – but Mrs Francis lived in a hotspot for burglary and thefts from cars, and she was understandably wary. She had only recently replaced the items stolen during the last burglary, and now she convinced she was about to be targeted again. Switching on the light in the hall, she shouted at the top of her voice.

'Who's there?'

She could hear footsteps run from the door to the gate and then fade as they ran east. Moving to pick up the phone, she carried it with her to the front window to see if she could catch any sight of them. But this time she wouldn't take any chances.

'Police, please,' she said when prompted.

Looking to the east, she saw a car drove off at speed. She didn't get a long enough look at the number plate to write it down, but something else had caught her attention. Straight ahead across the road, sitting on one of the swings in the park, she saw a woman. The first thing she thought was that it was far too early for anyone to be out and about in the children's playground, especially without a child. Her second thought was that the woman was indecently dressed.

Two women police constables were just about to go off duty when the call came in, and they were not at all keen when they were allocated the job. It took them twenty-seven minutes to get to the identified location. There they spoke briefly to Mrs Francis before making their way to the Common. Mrs Francis was clearly an overanxious lady whom they'd dealt with before. Since her property had been burgled, she had made a number of calls to the police, all of which had been investigated and found to be of no significance. They hoped that, once again, this would be another false alarm.

There was a cut-through across some dense vegetation. It was known to the locals as pervs' alley. The view of the children's play area was clear to any person wishing to observe undetected. Many paedophiles in breach of their registration had been found in pervs' alley on observation duties of their own. Turning down the alley, they approached the play area from the rear.

At a distance of sixty feet, they could already see her. There was a naked girl sitting on the second swing from the right. She was swinging gently in the cool breeze of the early morning. Her head was inclined to the left and she was leaning towards the heavy chains. Both her arms were bent at the elbow and, from the way they were twisted, there seemed to be an obvious fracture to both her forearms.

She had heavy strapping applied to both wrists. Both of them were secured to the chains of the swing and both arms were positioned above her head. Her bottom was firmly on the swing and the seat was heavily covered in blood. Reaching for her radio, WPC Claire Wilson called for backup and an ambulance.

'Sierra Oscar to base, are you receiving me?'

'Go ahead, Sierra Oscar.'

'We are at the location. Require backup: ambulance, SOCOs and a coroner. This is a murder enquiry.'

'Support and ambulance on the way.'

Her companion, WPC Jean Hamilton, called her. Both walked with caution towards the victim.

'She's been hanging here for some time. She's turned purple.'

It was not just her clothes that she had been stripped of. Her back was covered in a criss-cross of tracks where the surface of the skin had been compromised. It looked like she'd been whipped. On the ground below her feet was an area of scarlet-red grass where the blood had drained from her body. Much of the blood had congealed around a pearl necklace, lying seemingly incongruously on the floor.

WPC Wilson joined her partner. The girl had been stabbed repeatedly in the upper torso as well. All of her clothes were in a neat pile on the floor. Her nipples were already dark blue and partially severed. The victim's eyes were open as if pleading, and it was as if she had a look of horror frozen on her face.

Most shockingly, on her head she wore a crown made of barbed wire with roses intertwined. The wire spikes had been forced down into her head, each one digging its own trench in her skull. The blood had dripped down her face and her upper body.

DC Anne Cody had good reason to be worried. When the call came through, she had felt queasy, and now, as she walked to the crime scene, there was only one voice in her head: Sam Bailey's.

The brief details of the recent murder that had come in over the radio were unwelcome news. She was more agitated than she had ever thought possible. Cody couldn't exactly recollect the conversation she'd had with Sam, but the woman had suggested the killer would strike again. And Sam Bailey clearly knew about men who got their kicks from violence against women. It looked like she had been right, and Cody knew the consequences for all of them would be disastrous.

Chapter Seventy-Five

DCI Paradissimo was in bed when he took the call. Rolling over onto his stomach, he listened to what Cody had to say. After her first words, he slid out of bed and reached for his trousers, which were on the floor where he last dropped them. They were crumpled and covered in carpet fluff. He brushed them down and tried to smooth out the worst of the creases with his free hand. He did not say a word, but the hairs at the back of his neck had started to rise. By the time the call ended, he'd finished dressing and was soon in his car and on his way to the new crime scene.

When he arrived, Cody was waiting for him. She was so predictable. She was wearing what he always thought of as her death suit. A funereal black, two-piece, below-the-knee tweed skirt with a matching high-neck jacket and a dark blouse. As he approached, he knew it wasn't going to be good. Cody was standing by a tree with an expression that Paradissimo knew only too well. She wanted to be left alone, gather her thoughts and consider the implications of the murder.

Looking over Cody's shoulder, he could see the latest victim was heavily blood-stained and her throat had been cut from ear to ear. From where he was standing, he could see that she had been tortured. He took in the crown of thorns, and the religious overtones of that alarmed him beyond measure. He walked over to his corpse and viewed the extent of the mutilation. He had been in the force a long time but there was something about this young woman, and something about the circumstances of her death, that sickened him to the pit of his stomach. He hoped that death had come quickly for her but feared the opposite was more likely.

The ambulance arrived quickly and the SOCO boys a little later. Life was pronounced extinct at the scene at 06.47 hours.

The victim's handbag lay open close to the swing, splattered in blood. Paradissimo could see a wallet sticking out. He put on surgical gloves and took it carefully between finger and thumb. Her cash and cards were still intact. A driving licence photo card informed him that their victim was called Pia Broom. She had been twenty-six years old when her life came to an abrupt and violent end.

SOCO were soon busy at work. A tent was erected in the play area and officers in their white overalls got down to retrieving samples and forensic evidence from the scene. Paradissimo looked at the corpse as the photographer snapped away, getting as many angles as he could of the dead girl who had not yet been cut down from the swing. Walking towards the pathologist, he came across Cody again. They both knew this time, without any doubt, that they were dealing with the same killer.

There were two dead girls, three if they counted Leticia Joy, and Paradissimo suspected now that they had no other option but to rethink all they'd presumed about the first case. This killer had to be caught, and caught quickly, if he was to stop the haemorrhaging of life. Young women were not safe, not while this freak remained at large.

Chapter Seventy-Six

All the papers led with the story of the Wandsworth Common murder. The salacious details – the ones the police had released, at least – were tailor-made for the tabloids. The body of a naked, attractive young woman, a crown of thorns . . . This time the media didn't shy away from linking it to the Clapham Common murder. A religious killer was clearly at large on the streets of London.

Ashley Towers was at the bar in the mess at the Bailey when the headline caught his eye. Alfred Roma was at the back, enjoying his usual full English breakfast, when he spotted the self-same words. At first Roma read as he ate, but by the time he had finished reading the story he'd lost his appetite.

Roma whispered under his breath, 'Shit.'

Ashley walked over to Roma and waited for him to look up.

'I will be asking for the appeal to be expedited in the Elizabeth Johnson case.'

'I thought you might.' Roma's voice was expressionless, but Ashley could see beads of sweat form on his forehead.

'Yes, I thought you might,' Roma repeated to Ashley Towers' departing back.

Roma immediately rang chambers. He needed an emergency conference with the CPS, though, of course, that meant speaking to the dreaded Lydia Watson.

Harry Kemp was in his office, waiting for his 9.30 appointment, when he came across the story of Pia Broom. She was a young, attractive girl and her death was nothing short of a religious sacrifice. As he read, his instincts told him that her killer had also killed Martha and Leticia – even the press were making the link to Martha, but there was no direct evidence of a link to Leticia Joy.

The killer was playing with the police. Harry knew it. With his years of experience on the Trident murder squad, followed by his criminology degree and probation work, his instincts about a killer's mind were usually spot on. The murderer wanted them to know that he was clever. This was a man who hated women. He regarded them as meat to be disposed of, and he took a great deal of pleasure in disposing of them.

While he waited for his client, Harry called a contact on the force to see what else he could find out about Pia Broom's murder. He waited until 10.15 for his client to appear. When there was no sign of his appointee, he made a note in their file and called Sam, arranging to meet her for an early lunch on Wandsworth Common.

Chapter Seventy-Seven

The bike went like a fantasy. Sam accelerated effortlessly along the Embankment and climbed up to sixty miles per hour before having to brake hard. The approaching police car flashed her twice and she brought the speed of the bike below the legal limit. Sam pulled over but the police car flashed on blue lights.

'You're lucky this time but the next time you'll get a ticket,' the officer said after Sam pulled her doe-eyed innocent act as best she could.

Even with the interruption, Sam arrived early at the café where she'd arranged to meet Harry for brunch. It was not often that she dressed down, but it was only Harry, she told herself, and she had nothing to prove. He was a friend. As well as her soft leather jacket, she wore a dust-pink cotton blouse, jeans, boots, pearl earrings and a double string of fake pearls wrapped loosely around her neck. She had just ordered Harry and herself the works with tea for Harry and coffee for herself when Harry arrived, laden down with newspapers.

He sat down and immediately passed the papers to her.

'Have you seen the news?' he asked at once.

Sam shook her head; she hadn't had time to turn on the television today, let alone pick up a paper.

'You need to read that,' he said swiftly. 'And that.'

He placed the *Sun* and *Mirror* in a pile on the table. Sam read through the headlines quickly. A grim smile spread across her features. But while she was horrified by the latest gruesome death, she realised the impact of what Harry was showing her at once. They would have to free Icey now. The killer was not just on the loose; he was out of control. The police needed to wise up and catch the real killer before any more poor girls fell victim. And she needed to get Icey out of prison.

When she had finished reading, she picked up her mobile and rang Ashley Towers. 'Have you read the papers today?'

'Yes,' said Ashley.

'And?'

'And I will be applying for the appeal of Icey to be expedited.'

'But it is less than two weeks away. Will they do anything sooner?'

'Well, it's Wednesday today; I will apply for the appeal to be heard next week. Let's hope the Court of Appeal take notice of me this time.'

'What about our expert?'

'We should have his report by then, but in any event I think we now have enough without him.'

Case conferences were the order of the day. DCI Paradissimo arranged one with DC Anne Cody at Camberwell. As a result of the Clapham and Wandsworth murders, they had been allocated more manpower.

DC Anne Cody was less optimistic. She had argued for a while now behind the scenes that the St Mary Magdalene's slaughter and the Clapham Common murder were both the acts of one person. Now there was a third death and they were getting no closer to discovering the identity of the killer. To add to her problems, she had brushed off Sam Bailey for suggesting what she had begun to suspect herself. Sam was a troublemaker and she would be back.

'What do you suggest?' said Paradissimo.

'Well, I think we all need to cover our arses,' said Cody as she looked around the room.

'We didn't know the killer would strike again!' said Paradissimo indignantly. 'And who is to say that Elizabeth Johnson is innocent of the St Mary Magdalene's murder? There was overwhelming evidence against her and the jury convicted her, didn't they?'

The two officers stared at each other long enough for Cody to know that Paradissimo had already started the process of protecting his back.

'What I suggest we do,' said Cody, backing down, 'is call a meeting with the Crown Prosecution lawyers. They are the ones ultimately in charge of the appeal. Tell them our concerns and pass the responsibility to them.'

Paradissimo liked that idea. The sooner he could pass on the responsibility, the better.

Cody noticed Paradissimo perk up at the idea of passing the buck, and for some reason it made her furious. He was shattering her illusions all over the place. 'In the meanwhile,' she said, 'I suggest we go back to the beginning and look again at all the murders. We need to go back, question every witness, put up information boards and report back by the end of the week.'

'In the meantime,' Paradissimo mocked, sensing Cody's disapproval, 'the press will have a field day.'

Chapter Seventy-Eight

DC Cody and DCI Paradissimo were retracing the final steps of Leticia Joy. Entering St Mary Magdalene's Church from the back entrance, Cody was immediately plunged into darkness. The smell of fresh roses and white Madonna lilies floated gently in the air, and the door closed after them. Roses were Cody's favourite flowers. They brought out the romantic in her.

It was a long time since Paradissimo had been in a church and he was not comfortable at all. He felt closed in and the way Cody seemed constantly to hover at his side did not help.

Two people were sitting in a pew together on the far side. Huddled up in winter coats, bowed in prayer, it was not possible to say at a distance whether they were male or female. Anne Cody dipped her finger in the bowl of holy water and blessed herself. Paradissimo didn't bother. Walking down the left-hand side of the aisle, they stopped by the statue of Christ and the first station of the cross. Along the transept, a bounty of candles was sparkling in the dim light.

Cody became aware of her loud footsteps on the concrete slabs. Tiptoeing forward to the front of the church, she counted her steps to the front pew. The confession boxes were situated towards the back of the church. Two still stood back to back in a dim unlit corner. They had previously been to the left of the front door when Leticia met her death, but had been removed for forensic examination. They'd obviously been returned to a different spot; the area on the floor was shadowed where the confession box had previously stood. Maybe St Mary Magdalene's remaining congregation was wary about confessing so close to where a woman had been brutally slain, Cody mused.

Christ was looking down at them from the cross and it gave Cody strength. She wasn't much of a Catholic but even a lapsed Catholic found it hard to turn their back on the lessons that had been drilled into them since birth. He was everywhere. Even if, in the cold sparkling light of the night, Cody felt like a sinner. Paradissimo had walked over to the original location of the confession box. Walking around the markings on the floor, he looked in the direction of the front entrance and then again to the feet of Christ.

The murder had taken place right here at his feet, near the altar. Icey must have walked the distance from the confession box to the feet of Christ. How else could she have got Leticia's blood on her? Paradissimo paced it out and counted to fourteen. Then he paced from there back to the front door of the church, where she had exited. This was a distance of roughly sixty yards. Why would Icey have walked all that way? Why would the killer – or Icey, if she were the killer – want to slaughter someone and then walk into the full glare of the light to be observed only to return to the scene of the crime? It simply did not make sense.

The attacker was making a point and that was what Paradissimo needed to get to the bottom of. In any event, anyone standing by the church door would not be observed, from the road, which meant that any witness would have to walk from the road into the church courtyard. Paradissimo didn't remember Sexton telling them this. There was something not quite right about the man's original statement, he realised.

He went back into the church and realised that if Icey had

been standing just outside the confession box, she would not have seen Leticia at all, given where they'd found her body. Maybe she had been telling the truth when she'd said that she'd noticed a couple struggling and had walked towards them before she realised exactly what was happening.

Cody observed from the back. She sat in the pew just behind the praying couple. Her closer observation had revealed a man and a woman. The woman was dressed in black. Her jacket hung loosely around her shoulders. The worn fabric was almost threadbare. Her head was lowered, almost stooped. Her black-gloved hands fidgeted as she prayed, moving the prayer beads between her fingers.

From the far right-hand corner, a figure moved across the altar, stopping only long enough to bless himself. He moved one step back and then, blessing himself again, walked down the aisle. He appeared deep in thought. He was oblivious to the people in the church. At the end of the pew, he turned right and then walked to the back of the church. Pausing in front of the confession box, he opened the door and entered. Closing the door behind him, the red light flicked on. A second figure appeared from the alcove. It was a woman in her forties with pipe-cleaner curls. She walked across the altar and approached the aisle. Cody stepped from the side and walked towards Iris Walker, but she was too late. Iris turned around and slipped through a side door, and by the time Cody reached the door, she had disappeared.

Chapter Seventy-Nine

Sam was sitting on her swivel chair in the office of Fleet Investigations, facing the back wall and its cork board display to which she'd clipped all the press coverage of the killings and relevant photographs and information from Icey's trial. How was Icey connected to the other two deaths? Why couldn't she remember what had happened the night of Leticia Joy's murder? Had she just been in the wrong place at the wrong time or was someone making sure Icey got caught up in this from the start?

Linked cards were placed above each of the bodies. As far as Sam was concerned, each of the victims had died a vicious and brutal death. Each of them was murdered in the middle of the night. They were tortured and stabbed repeatedly before death. But Sam also knew that if the police had arrested the right person for Leticia Joy's death, Martha and Pia would still be alive.

Sam had at first thought that Icey's memory lapse at the time of the murder had been down to her drinking, but what if something else had happened to her? After all, as Harry had pointed out when they'd had breakfast together on Wandsworth Common, the killer had to be subduing his victims in some way. Had Icey been drugged as well? It was a possible explanation for her loss of memory. She didn't like to think of the alternative, but was she clutching at straws in Icey's case?

Icey claimed that she couldn't remember much from the moment she spotted the mystery man to the time when she'd been found by the police with the knife in her hand. It did not make sense. If she put herself in the killer's mindset, why not just kill Icey? It would have been so much easier. Cut her throat, and leave her to die, along with Leticia Joy. But whoever had killed Leticia had wanted to keep Icey alive.

Sam thought this over. Why keep Icey alive? The only reason she could think of was that they wanted someone else to take the blame. But even that did not make sense. The killer had gone on to murder again. The police were no closer to discovering the identity of the killer; and, of his victims, only Icey was still alive to tell a tale. And she couldn't remember much of anything.

There was one other possible reason why Icey was still alive: the killer had been disturbed before he could eliminate her. Sexton had claimed he'd seen Icey at the church door, and perhaps that much of his statement was true. In which case, the killer might have thought that it was only a matter of time before the police arrived. That, of course, did not explain why no one – not even Sexton – had seen the killer leave the church; but it was more than possible that the killer had made good his escape out of another door before the police arrived.

Sam stared at the progress chart on her wall. The dead women were spread out like petals on the floor of a winter garden. The only thing left alive was Icey, and she had been lucky to escape with her life.

Sam stopped swivelling her chair. That was it. That was the clue to the killings. Icey was lucky. How could she have missed it? There it was, so obvious, and it was there right in front of her. Picking up the phone, she dialled the direct number on the business card DC Cody had reluctantly given her when Sam had confronted her at the police station.

'DC Cody, this is Sam Bailey.' Sam heard a curse as Cody remembered their meeting.

'You again,' came the reply. 'I thought I made myself clear the last time we met . . .'

'Please don't hang up. This will only take a moment.' There was a long sigh at the other end of the phone but Cody did not put the receiver down. Sam waited and listened as Cody's breathing returned to normal.

'Can you confirm that Martha and Pia were drugged before they were killed?' George MacDonald had told Irma's girls that he suspected drugs had been used in Martha's case, but they'd 'interviewed' him prior to him getting the toxicology reports back.

'Why do you want to know?' said Cody, exhausted. She'd had enough of this slapper-come-investigator sticking her nose in, and it was getting beyond a joke. She would have to go round to her home address and formally warn her that any more interference and she would be behind bars.

'The only reason I ask is because Icey has lost pieces of memory from that night and this was never followed up. Was she tested for drugs as well as alcohol when she was arrested?'

Cody could hardly contain herself. Closing her eyes, she counted to ten as a calming measure. It didn't work. 'Fuck off and don't ever phone this number again.'

As she replaced the phone, she looked down on to her desk and saw in front of her the two recent autopsy reports from Determination George. Flicking through them, half-intrigued and half in dread, Cody found the pages she was looking for and cursed. There in bold print it stated that both Martha and Pia had traces of chloroform in their systems, as did Leticia

Joy, she discovered when she then called up her file on the computer.

Growing increasingly alarmed, Cody also pulled up Icey's toxicology report on her computer. They'd assumed she was drunk at the scene – that much was obvious – and had had her breathalysed. Her blood had been taken for testing and had proved negative for any other drugs. But Cody's relief was short-lived; she noticed that Icey's blood sample had only been taken hours after her arrest. If she had been doped, then it wouldn't have necessarily been in her system.

'Where is Paradissimo?' she shouted. 'Where the hell is Paradissimo? We have finally got a breakthrough.'

Chapter Eighty

The horn sounded and Icey made her way out of her cell. Association time had started. She made her way down to the television room, where she found the two mules playing pool. Sandra spotted her at once.

'Hi, Icey,' said Sandra, leaning against her cue, 'you OK? You look a little pale.'

She half-heartedly shrugged her slender shoulders and plonked herself in front of the telly by way of response. Flicking through the channels, she settled on the evening news. As she did so, she noticed that a murder had taken place on Wandsworth Common. She flicked back again. Icey was amazed to see her photograph on the screen staring back at her. There were three other pictures of young women who also had question marks above the top of their photo. One was Leticia Joy. Turning up the volume, Icey listened intently as a sober, middle-aged reporter on screen began his report. The other women in the room started to gather in front of the television.

'A woman's body has been found on Wandsworth Common. She has been tortured and mutilated. There are reports that she was the third victim to die at the hands of a serial killer. The police confirmed that there were similarities between two earlier deaths. Doubts are now being raised as to conviction of Elizabeth Johnson, who was convicted for the murder of Leticia Joy, a young woman who was murdered at St Mary Magdalene's

Church in Camberwell last year in similar circumstances. Johnson is currently serving thirty years.

'Some prominent lawyers are calling for an urgent review of the case. Miss Johnson's lawyers have issued a statement in which they made clear that their client is the victim of a gross miscarriage of justice – and that far from being the killer, she had actually almost been the killer's second victim. The single Court of Appeal judge, however, had earlier refused leave to appeal.'

The reporter concluded by stating that they had invited someone from the Crown Prosecution Service to the studio to discuss the spate of murders, but they had refused.

Icey started to cry and then stifled her tears, holding a hand against her face and wiping her eyes. Someone might now listen to her when she said that she was not guilty. The mules were silent for once as Icey said in a hushed whisper, 'I told you I was innocent.'

Chapter Eighty-One

After Cody had hung up on her, Sam had decided to turn up at Camberwell Green Police Station unannounced and talk to Paradissimo himself.

Stepping into the reception, she asked to speak to DCI Paradissimo. This time he made himself available. From the moment he walked into the waiting room, he knew that Sam was going to be trouble. As he walked her to the conference room, he tried to keep the conversation light.

'I hear you want a word?' he said as he beckoned her towards the table and chairs. As he straddled one chair, he placed his arms on the backrest and rested his chin top of his right hand. Sam felt ill at ease. He was too close for comfort. His eyes settled on her legs and he did not once avert his gaze.

'How can I help?' he said.

Sam crossed her legs and unrolled the newspapers she carried; their lurid headlines screamed the story of the latest murder. She was silent as he glanced over the front lead stories. 'An innocent person is serving a life sentence for an offence that she did not commit and the killer is still out there. I think that about sums it up,' she said at last with cold fury.

'You shouldn't believe all you read in the papers. Didn't I teach you anything when we were together?' he said casually, tossing the newspapers aside.

'This is not about us.'

'What is it about, Sam? You come in here and you want to tell me how to do my job? You're acting like you're a real detective rather than a pretend one. Well, listen, love, I think you had better stick to what you're good at.'

'That was uncalled for.'

'Was it? You are good at your job, though, aren't you? You told me repeatedly that you were never an ordinary tart. Just look at yourself. All done up in your fancy clothes. But for all that, you're still as damaged as any street whore. I think you had better leave, there's nothing for you here!'

Sam did not respond but his explosion of anger shocked her. Perhaps it had been a mistake to come here.

'This is about Elizabeth Johnson,' she said through gritted teeth, trying hard to stay calm.

'It always was about Elizabeth Johnson. I wanted you in my life. I loved you. I was prepared to take the risk but you said no. You wouldn't even introduce me to your precious Icey!' Paradissimo said heatedly.

'That's not how I remember it. Besides, you're hardly one to talk on that score.'

'Well, tell me how you remember it, then, because my mind's not too good these days.' He could barely look her in the eye as he spat his accusations at her.

'Don't you raise your voice at me. We don't need to go down that route again.'

'I was prepared to put your past behind us, to commit to us, and you said no. You wanted your independence and you got it. Now you come strutting back into my life like a stray alley cat and you're surprised when I am not overjoyed.'

'Let's just stick to the reason I'm here, shall we? The three murders,' Sam said, not rising to the bait.

He wasn't listening, though. He grabbed her arm and pulled

her off the chair towards him. Sam lost her balance as he lost his grip. She fell partly to the floor but he pulled her up to her feet.

'A tom turned me down. It can't get much worse than that, can it?'

She shrugged off his arm and stepped back in alarm. 'I'm sorry I troubled you. I think I had better go.' She tried to walk to the door. He blocked her path.

'Do you always run away or is it the case that you just can't handle the truth, Duvet?'

'How many more times, Gil. Don't call me that.'

'What should I call you? Do you need me to pay me for your time now? What's your hourly rate these days?'

She looked at him sadly. 'I loved you once, Gil. But we both knew our relationship was never going to work. I was a working girl when you met me. And no matter that I'm not now, I'm still an ex-whore.'

'I regret calling you that.'

'But you were right. You're so right.'

'About?'

'About everything. I am damaged. You are the only man I have ever loved but we're too different. I should have known better than to get involved with you. When I am in a relationship, I'm at my most destructive.'

She was feeling emotional and exposed but she had said it, and now there was no going back. A part of her still loved him. She watched him warily, waiting for his response, but he remained silent. Then he shook his head at her, Sam wanted him to say something, anything. Instead, he began to give her a slow hand-clap, circling her with a sneer.

'You bloody actress. That was a good performance. What were you expecting? Did you really think I would fall for all that? "An innocent person is serving a life sentence for an offence that she did not commit. And the killer is still out there." Really? Elizabeth Johnson is a dangerous, damaged woman and you come a close second. You make an ideal couple. What makes you so sure that your friend isn't the killer? An impartial jury convicted her.' Paradissimo was biting back his own doubts for the sake of argument. There was no way he was going to tell Sam about the second thoughts he'd been having since Pia Broom's murder.

'That jury got it wrong,' said Sam without a second thought. 'You didn't even look for another suspect – just presumed that Icey was guilty. What do you think a jury would make of Martha Lewis's death or Pia Broom's? Is it true that the latest victim had a crown of thorns around her head? Did she have a rosary, too?'

'I think that you should stop meddling in police business. It's not for amateurs. If I were you, I would go now, unless you want to stay overnight in a cell,' he warned Sam with a sneer, determined to deflect her questions.

'But Icey is innocent.'

'She isn't,' he insisted, sticking to his guns.

Paradissimo walked over and opened the door. Sam gathered up her scattered newspapers as DC Anne Cody walked in. She was wearing a green and black tweed skirt, grey tights and black cardigan buttoned up to the neck.

'You again,' she said. 'How many times are you going to attempt to interfere with our investigation?'

Sam didn't answer as Cody stood directly in front of her. Despite her lack of respect for the woman, Sam was intimidated. Paradissimo walked back over to the window and leant his back against it, smiling smugly. He didn't have to say anything. He had already said enough.

'Why don't you leave the real detective work to us?' Cody said. The smirk on her face was menacing.

'Get her out of the station and if she comes back, arrest her,' ordered Paradissimo coolly before walking out.

Sam glared at the older woman. 'I told you that the killer would strike again, but you didn't believe me. If he kills again, it will be on your head.'

'There is no hard evidence to link these recent murders to Leticia Joy. It's all circumstantial,' dismissed DC Cody, concealing her own private thoughts. She had no intention of sharing her doubts with this woman. Cody had no respect for an ex-tom and she'd taken a personal dislike to Sam, although she would never admit even to herself that it was partly born out of jealousy. Sam's beauty, and her connection with Paradissimo, were two very good reasons for Cody to resent her.

'So you at least admit that there are similar circumstances?' Sam said, seizing upon the angry detective's apparent concession.

'We are too busy trying to catch a new killer. We don't wish to be distracted by a low-life whore with too much time on her hands.' Cody grabbed Sam by her upper arm, pulled her up and marched her out of the room to the front of the building.

'If you know what's good for you, you'll stay away from this investigation. If you've come looking to pull a copper, you've come to the wrong place. Wouldn't want you to end up like your friend Icey, would we? Or even Leticia Joy.'

She pushed Sam more forcefully that she intended, and the shove caught Sam off guard. She went reeling down the steps of the police station. The inverted pleat at the back of her skirt opened up, exposing her legs. The beret that was perched precariously on her head flew forward and landed close to her chafed hands. Her stockings were laddered and her knees were bloodied.

Sam was on her knees in the gutter, and it was not for the first time. She looked up to see Cody glaring down at her. 'That's right. Back on the streets where you belong. I wouldn't bother getting up in a hurry because you'll be back there before you know it. I really don't have the time to be messed around by a tom.' And with that, she turned on her heels and walked back into the station.

Sam felt humiliated. She cursed Cody as she got to her feet and slowly walked away from the police station. When she was sure she was far enough away and in no danger of being observed, she reached into her bag and pulled out a tape recorder. Checking it hadn't been damaged by her fall, she switched it off. Cody – and Paradissimo, too – would one day regret their intemperate attitude. Even though she had achieved what she'd set out to do with the confrontation, she was still uncompromisingly angry at the way she had been treated.

Chapter Eighty-Two

The next of kin had been contacted. Pia's mother had formally identified the body of her precious only child. Now it was 9.25 a.m. at the City of Westminster Mortuary on Horseferry Road, London SW1. Determination George unzipped the body bag and was overcome with a sense of purpose. He was excited that once again he could perform his magic and determine the cause of death.

Paradissimo stayed throughout the examination, together with DC Cody and WPC Claire Wilson, who was serving as exhibits officer, and Mr Nor, the Vietnamese photographer. DCI Paradissimo set the mood: he was anxious and fretting. Whatever the cause of death, it was going to be a disastrous day for him and his team. They had a serial killer on the loose and, despite his angry exchange with Sam, and his heated protestations to the contrary, even he was beginning to believe that Icey was innocent.

X-rays of the head, torso and upper limbs were taken prior to the examination. She was a well-nourished young woman of caucasian extraction. Age twenty-four. She was of slim build, five feet four and half inches tall. She was lying on her back inside a white plastic body sheet. There were clear plastic bags covering her head and hands. Her head was inclined slightly towards her left shoulder. Her left arm was flexed at the elbow, showing an obvious fracture of the left forearm, which lay alongside the body.

There was heavy blood staining inside the head bag and the right hand bag. There had been dried blood exuding from the nostrils and from the wounds to the right and left side of the face, and the top of the head was marked out by puncture wounds in the form of a circle around the head. She was naked. She had been scoured with a whip, which, as George had already surmised from the wounds, had pieces of something sharp embedded into the cord. It had clearly been designed to remove flesh quickly.

Once she had been stripped of her flesh, she'd been garlanded with a crown of barbed wire, which had punctured her head. The crown would have caused intense pain as the spikes had been embedded in her head pre-mortem. It was George's expert opinion that she'd taken some time to die. There were a number of stab wounds to the torso, none of which caused any significant vascular injury, with the exception of a stab wound on the front of the left upper chest. There was very little bleeding associated with the wound. The fact that there were 150 millilitres of blood in the left pleural cavity indicated that this wound was probably inflicted after the wound of the right side of the neck.

Pia had been stabbed repeatedly. She had an oblique 2.2 centimetre stab wound at the base of the right side of her neck, which then continued across the throat at an angle, before exiting at the left side. There was a puncture wound in the middle of the upper chest and a similar two centimetre stab wound situated at the top of the right breast. On the back of the torso, on the right lower chest, there was a group of stab and puncture wounds in an area measuring ten centimetre in the vertical and approximately eleven centimetre in the horizontal diameter.

There were in total a series of forty puncture wounds on Pia's body. The area of the breasts and the upper body had been targeted heavily.

Determination George turned to the officers and adopted an authoritarian tone.

'She was tortured before she died. Jucking – the shallow but repeated use of a knife on a victim – is a relatively recent practice. It is used to demonstrate power. The intention is to humiliate and disable temporarily. These injuries were not intended to be life-threatening, and they weren't. Her throat was cut and she was whipped when she was alive.' He paused. 'There is one other thing you should know.'

'What is that?' Paradissimo asked.

'The tests will have to confirm it, but it looks to me like the victim had been chloroformed. There are faint burn marks around the area of her mouth, consistent with exposure to chloroform. I'll know for sure in the morning. There's also this . . .'

Determination George handed to Paradissimo a bag containing a heavily blood-stained pearl necklace consisting of twenty-two pearls. It was broken and the eleventh bead was missing.

'What is that?'

'Her jewellery.'

That evening Determination George met up with 'Rita' and 'Susie' again. They were fascinated by the details of his new case, particularly the pearls. They also couldn't wait to hear more about his suspicion that the victim had been chloroformed, a fact he confirmed to them he had already learnt for sure about the first two victims.

Chapter Eighty-Three

Alfred Roma was pacing up and down in his room. The conference should have started three quarters of an hour ago, and he was getting more and more annoyed. He had read and re-read the case papers, and had made a precise note of the points he wished to raise. He was clear in his own mind that the conviction was not safe. As he rehearsed what he had to say, the telephone interrupted his thoughts. Picking up the phone, Roma was not best pleased to learn that Lydia Watson was not even on her way yet – she said she was just about to leave. She talked at him for three minutes exactly, and then she hung up. Roma was furious. She was an idiot and yet here she was giving him instructions. He breathed heavily and counted to ten, staving to remain in control of his emotions.

Replacing the phone, Roma gathered up his files and walked across the hall to the large conference room, situated above the clerk's room. The highly polished table reflected his solid bulk as he entered the room. Placing his papers and files at the head of the table, he stepped over to the first set of windows and opened them about ten centimetres. Moving to the middle window, he repeated the same task and then to the next. Before he returned to his seat, he glared at his reflection in the glass.

He was already sweating; his blue shirt sticking to his back and his armpits damp. He got up and made for the water cooler, gulping down a paper cupful of water. It was refreshingly cold.

He refilled his cup and placed it on the table in front of his files. Still thinking about Lydia, he pulled out his blue and white spotted handkerchief and used it to mop his forehead and wipe around the back of his neck.

A sound disturbed his thoughts, the distinctive noise indicating that the lift was on its way. Roma unbuttoned the third and fourth buttons of his shirt and quickly reached inside to pat his armpits with the handkerchief. Re-buttoning his shirt, he meticulously refolded his damp handkerchief and placed it in his pocket, then calmly waited for the conference to arrive.

Half a minute later, the lift doors opened and Roma heard a voice that sent a sharp stab of fear down his spine. It was a shrill, silly, little girl's voice. It brought back too many memories and Roma felt his breakfast rise to the top of his oesophagus. Pulling out his damp handkerchief again, he swiped his forehead one more time.

Miss Lydia Watson came through the door. Her eyes narrowed as she caught sight of Roma. She took the seat at the head of the table, casually knocking Roma's files along the table to a place further down. Roma felt like a little boy who had had his hand smacked. He was quietly seething. The case worker, Claudia Townsend, pulled a file trolley into the room and propped it up against the wall. Taking her seat to the left of Roma, she waited for the others to gather themselves. The DCI was the last to enter. He stood at the far end of the room, directly opposite Roma.

'Oh, do sit down,' said Roma, addressing the detective and looking most uncomfortable. Miss Watson smiled, said nothing and waited for Roma to open the conference.

'Well, I think we should all introduce ourselves from left to right for the sake of the record.' Roma glanced to his left, smiling in invitation.

'My name is Claudia Townsend and I am the case worker.' Claudia was a round woman who, like Roma, probably liked her English breakfasts a little too much.

'Detective Chief Inspector Paradissimo. I am the officer in charge of the case.'

'I am the case lawyer and my name is Watson, Miss Lydia Watson, and I am in control of the appeal,' Lydia announced from the head of the table. She glanced at Roma, who was busy nodding in agreement.

'And I am sure you all know me from when we worked together at the trial. My name is Mr Alfred Roma,' he confirmed, completing the introductions. There was a knock on the door and Catherine, Roma's secretary, entered with a tea trolley. 'Ah, splendid, splendid. Anyone for tea?' he asked jovially.

Catherine poured the tea, then placed the pot, together with a plate of biscuits, in the centre of the table before leaving the room. Opening his first file, Roma got started.

'As you all know, I asked for this conference because a number of matters have come to my attention since the trial of Regina versus Elizabeth Johnson, and these have caused me some concern. By the way, Detective Chief Inspector, thank you for popping in the note of the post mortem on Pia Broom. I am afraid it only increases my concern about the case of Miss Johnson.'

'I think it has caused us all some concern,' said Paradissimo, as he placed a cool mint into his mouth. He was only here to cover his back.

'The trial, as you all know, was a great success. The jury convicted in no time at all,' recapped Roma.

'That was probably due to the way the case was prepared,' interjected Miss Watson. As Roma looked in her direction, he saw that she was smiling a sickly sweet smile, which told him she was just waiting for him to step out of line so that she could slap him down.

'That is perfectly true,' agreed Roma, through gritted teeth. 'You and your team did a very good job preparing the case.'

'I am so glad that we were appreciated and recognised,' said Miss Watson, leaning back in her chair. 'The judge did compliment us.'

Roma smiled. Thank God he was just working with her on this case. Hopefully it would soon be over and he wouldn't have to work with her again.

Paradissimo popped another mint into his mouth and watched the interplay curiously.

'Since the trial,' continued Roma, 'there have been a number of developments. The first is that the new defence counsel, Mr Ashley Towers, appealed against the conviction and the single judge turned down the application. The application was renewed and I understand that the defence will now argue the case before the full court. They have recently asked for the court to hear the application sooner rather than later.'

'Why have they asked for that?' asked the DCI.

Roma looked questioningly at Paradissimo; surely the detective could be in no doubt of the subsequent events that had pushed a perfectly solid conviction to the brink.

'Well, as you know, since the trial there was the murder on Clapham Common. That was followed by the Wandsworth murder and the defence will argue the similarities of all three murders and that they were the work of one person,' he said, spelling things out.

'What has that got to do with the conviction of Miss Johnson?' asked Miss Watson.

Roma turned to her in surprise at the stupidity of the question, but backed down under Lydia Watston's practised glare. 'Obviously, if it is the work of one person, then Miss Johnson was wrongly convicted because the second and third murders occurred after she had been convicted of the murder of Leticia Joy and was in custody,' Roma said patiently, as if to a child.

'Well, what is your view?' Miss Watson asked abruptly.

'My view is set out in the advice I sent to the Crown Prosecution Service last week. It is the reason why I have requested this conference,' he explained quietly.

On cue, Claudia Townsend opened her file and removed copies of the document marked 'Urgent Advice'. She pushed copies in the direction of everyone in the room.

'My advice is that there are concerns. I believe that there should be a discussion so that we reach a consensus.'

Miss Watson sat and flicked through the advice, turning over page after page in a dismissive fashion. When she got to the final page, she turned the document over on the table.

'I have read this document twice now and I really don't see why you were so convinced about the position we took during the course of the trial, and yet now equally determined to reject it.'

Roma started to perspire again. He was feeling most uncomfortable. Pearls of sweat ran down the side of his face and his hair was beginning to stick to his head. For all his efforts to remain in control, he was not doing very well. Lydia Watson was officially in charge but he would end up carrying the can for any bad decisions that she made. After all, it was he who had to argue the points before the Court of Appeal judges. He could hardly tell them that he'd had major doubts but that he'd allowed this inexperienced fledgling lawyer to overrule him. He had always known that she lacked judgement. He wanted to return the brief, but that was unprofessional. He couldn't walk away from this, as much as he wanted to.

'The similarities between the three killings are such that there is a possible inference they were the work of one man. And what if he kills again?' Roma asked.

Paradissimo choked on his mint. Coughing and spluttering, he reached for the water. Removing the mint from his mouth, he concealed it in a tissue.

Roma went on, 'How are we going to explain away the religious overtones in each of the cases? Leticia Joy was murdered in a church with a bloody broken rosary left on her body. The killer etched crosses into Martha Lewis's body, as well as leaving behind a crucifix. Indeed, I believe you found a broken pearl necklace on her person, similar if not identical to a rosary. In Pia Broom's case, she was crowned with thorns and, again, she appears to have had a pearl necklace on her person. There are similarities that crop up in all three killings. Enough, I believe, to cast reasonable doubt against Elizabeth Johnson's original conviction.'

Roma sat back in his chair, satisfied that he had laid out his thoughts as clearly as possible.

'Pia was not wearing the pearl necklace, sir. One was found close by and we've never gone public on that or the fact that Martha's necklace was broken,' said Paradissimo, unruffled by the implications of Roma's words.

'What!' said Miss Watson. 'I wasn't told that.'

'Nor I,' said Roma hastily. 'It is in the file, however.'

Paradissimo felt his backside suddenly exposed. 'I am sorry,' he said. 'That was for perfectly good operational reasons. We did not want the killer to know we had picked up on it. Furthermore, this is perfectly normal practice when there is the possibility of a copycat killer.'

'Well, doesn't that mean that you're now assuming that the killer is the same person in each case?' said Roma, seeing an escape route.

Miss Lydia Watson was tapping her pen impatiently. She clearly wanted Roma to try to uphold the conviction. She had prepared the case for the earlier trial, and she had no intention of being made to look stupid now. If she were scorned, there would be no fury to match hers.

'Well, of course we think there's a link between Pia Broom's and Martha Lewis's deaths. There are obviously similarities there,' Paradissimo began carefully. 'But in the case of Leticia Joy . . . Elizabeth Johnson was caught red-handed and, while Leticia Joy suffered a violent death, it wasn't as violent as the other two victims.'

'There was an escalation of violence between Martha's and Pia's deaths too, though, wasn't there?' Roma asked, quietly. Paradissimo didn't answer. 'That doesn't really preclude a link to Leticia's murder. We shall have to disclose all of this to the Court of Appeal.'

'No problem,' said Paradissimo. 'I would expect that to happen. I will prepare a statement for the court and defence counsel.' He popped a fresh mint into his mouth and sat back in his seat. There was absolutely no way he or his officers were going to get covered with anything that hit the fan. This was down to the lawyers. They made the decisions. They prosecuted the case and ultimately they would take the blame, because he would see to it that they did. He leant forward across the table. 'If you want my personal opinion,' he said, 'I think Miss Johnson could be innocent,' he stated boldly.

'No one asked for your opinion,' said Miss Watson, irritated.

'Fine,' said Paradissimo, holding up his hands and sitting back in his chair. He'd made his point. It wasn't his backside that would be spanked. 'Do you think that Miss Johnson's conviction is still Court of Appeal safe?' he asked her.

'Yes,' replied Miss Watson firmly.

'Yes,' agreed Claudia Townsend.

Paradissimo inclined his head as if in deference to them.

'You're both being woossies,' said Miss Watson, glancing between Paradissimo and Roma.

'Hang on,' said Roma, 'I never said it was not safe. I merely wanted to explore the arguments.'

'Miss Johnson was found with the murder weapon in her hand. She was covered in the victim's blood, and she was still at the crime scene,' said Miss Watson. 'If she is innocent, then she must have been in the wrong place at the wrong time. The blood is explainable, perhaps, but that would mean the knife and bead must have been planted. Is that what we're supposing? Why?' she asked, throwing her hands wide.

'The pearl necklaces on the subsequent victims are a worry,' insisted Roma. 'And in each of the murders, the victim's throat was cut.'

'Only after she had been strangled, in the case of the Clapham Common murder,' Paradissimo chimed in.

'Correct, but the rosary and the pearls seem very significant, too. Is this the signature of the killer? Are you presuming the killer targets women wearing pearl necklaces of some kind, or that he brings the necklaces with him?' Roma asked curiously.

Paradissimo shook his head. 'We don't know.'

'Well, if the necklaces are not a signature, they're at least a calling card,' Roma commented.

'Well, how many signatures does the killer have?' Lydia asked angrily. 'A rosary is not the same as a pearl necklace. At trial, Judge Certie said that Icey was convicted on overwhelming evidence, and I still agree with him.'

'Events have moved on,' Roma responded as calmly as he could manage. 'We'll obviously have to put all this before the Court of Appeal. The point is that we are responsible prosecutors, and if facts subsequently emerge that undermine the previous conviction, we are duty bound to bring such matters to the attention of the relevant parties, and in this case the Court of Appeal,' he said earnestly.

Lydia Watson was turning scarlet with anger before his very eyes. She leant forward in her chair so that her bottom was resting on the edge of her seat. By contrast, Roma slouched back in his chair, watching her carefully, knowing what was to come. He had witnessed far too many of her terrible temper tantrums. She was at her crass incompetent best when she kept her mouth shut, but that was something that she had never been able to do, which is why she had always had difficulties throughout her career.

'Mr Roma!' she shouted at the top of her voice.

Paradissimo was about to pop another mint into his mouth but thought the better of it, and placed the packet back on the desk. He smiled. He was beginning to enjoy himself, watching the lawyers falling out.

Claudia Townsend was quite used to her boss and her explosive tongue.

'Are you suggesting I am not a responsible prosecutor?' Lydia questioned angrily.

'No, no, of course not,' Roma backtracked easily.

'I am responsible for the victims and their families – people you seem determined to overlook. How are they going to feel if we don't try to uphold the conviction?'

'I do see that, but I was beginning to wonder if we ought not to consider throwing in our hand. That's the real point.'

'Mr Roma, it is not for you to tell me, your instructing

solicitor, what the point is. Not only is it disrespectful, it is a classic example of you not recognising who is in charge here!'

'I do apologise,' said Roma, 'I was quite forgetting myself.'

'It seems to me that you are in the habit of forgetting yourself. I am not your pupil now, Mr Roma, do you hear me? I am not your pupil any more.'

Miss Watson's face was like an inflated balloon on the verge of exploding. Roma was looking at the creature that was his instructing solicitor. He had been absolutely right when he'd voted to refuse her a tenancy in his chambers. There was nothing that she had done before or since that had caused him any reason to doubt what he had always thought – she was just a very unpleasant bully with an insignificant legal brain.

'You are absolutely right that you are not my pupil, and I would add that you have not been for several years. But that is quite irrelevant. If I gave you the impression that I did not respect you as my instructing solicitor, I am very sorry. May I also apologise for any other offence I might have caused, since it is entirely unintentional.' Roma hated himself for doing it but he knew he needed to soothe the savage beast. His apology was obsequious as he toadied with all the sincerity of a rattlesnake.

Miss Watson had begun to deflate as if some sort of pressure-release override had just clicked into action. Paradissimo, opportunistic as ever, finally popped the mint into his mouth. At least he was in the clear. Miss Watson gathered up her papers.

'So, we go on as we were?' she said.

'If those are my instructions,' said Roma limply.

'They are,' she said firmly and swept out.

Paradissimo gave Roma a wry smile of sympathy.

Chapter Eighty-Four

Sam paid another visit to Tom Padfield. She knocked on the door. The house was in darkness. No one came. She bent over the railings and looked in through the drawing room windows. At the far end she could just make out the figure of Tom Padfield, sitting in his carver chair, in exactly the same spot as on her previous visit. But this time there were more empty bottles and rubbish littering the floor.

'Anyone at home?' called out Sam, as she stared directly at him through the windows.

He made no movement or sign of acknowledgement.

'Hello. Remember me? Can I have a word? It's Sam, Sam Bailey. It won't take long, Mr Padfield.'

Sam watched as Padfield slumped forward and, using the back of his hand, wiped his mouth. Sam studied the room through the window and was alarmed to make out a claw hammer lying on the small table next to Padfield's chair. Had that been there on her last visit?, she wondered. She felt sure she would have noticed it if it had. Undeterred, Sam knocked on the door again, and kept knocking until she saw Padfield finally stagger to his feet.

Looking back over her shoulder, she spotted the reassuring form of Harry Kemp, still sitting in his car, with the window rolled down. He had advised her against the visit to Padfield but when he'd been unable to dissuade her, a compromise was reached. He would drive Sam there and wait outside. His excuse was that he was concerned for her – even if Padfield wasn't their killer, he seemed to be somewhat unstable. Harry didn't want Sam to get hurt; and, besides, spending time with her was never a chore, although he hadn't told her that. He'd stuck strictly to the point of her safety. Sam had tried to reassure him that she didn't take risks with her personal safety; she was always armed with an illegal can of mace in her handbag, a legacy both from her teenage years living on a rough estate and her time spent working for Irma. Even so, she felt better that she had Harry as backup on this visit. Finally, Padfield came to the door.

'What do you want now?' His lack of personal hygiene was becoming invasive. His shirt and trousers were even more crumpled than previously, and his hair was unkempt.

Sam felt contaminated but she smiled and reached out to shake his hand. Padfield watched her in surprise, lifting his hand automatically, but then pulling back when she touched his limp, sweaty hand.

'My friend's appeal will be taking place soon and I just wondered if there was any more information that you might have that could help us,' she asked.

Padfield stood in the centre of the hallway, preventing her from going further. 'I wish your friend all that she deserves and more. Please send her my regards and tell her that maybe someday we can have a drink and she can tell me how Leticia met her death.'

Sam stared at him. 'Elizabeth didn't kill Leticia.'

'Maybe one day she can tell me that herself. Of course, if the real purpose of this visit is to rule me in or out as a potential killer, then please feel free.'

'Last time we spoke,' Sam said, ignoring his sarcasm, 'you

told me that Leticia was working as a call girl. Do you not have any idea who for? Did you ever see her with any men?'

'I . . .' Tom Padfield looked momentarily confused as Sam changed the direction of her questions so swiftly. 'There was a man, an old guy, he dropped her here one time. She said he was a friend of the family . . . She—'

'Did she tell you his name?' Sam asked eagerly, but as she watched, Tom Padfield's whole manner changed completely.

'She was a whore! It doesn't matter who she was doing it with! Now just leave me alone!'

'You must have been furious with her when you found out what she was doing?' Sam pressed.

'No.' He grabbed her arm and bundled her roughly down the steps of the house. 'I said, please leave.'

Sam walked back to the car. Harry Kemp was already out of his seat, watching the incident unfold and standing at the ready to intervene if Padfield got too physical. But he knew better than to say to Sam, 'I told you so.'

Chapter Eighty-Five

Sam was sitting in Ashley Towers' office in his chambers. She tugged uncomfortably at her jacket sleeves, feeling like lamb dressed as mutton in her formal pin-striped trouser suit. She was just too young to be wearing an outfit this severe, but while she was uncomfortable in her choice of clothing, she knew it was important to give the barrister the impression of maturity and wisdom beyond her years. She couldn't have Ashley Towers thinking she was a lightweight. Even so, she hadn't been able to resist wearing a pale pink silk blouse that softened the edge of her outfit. She had known very well that she would spend the day surrounded by men, and she did not want to give them any opportunity to think for a moment that she was anything less than deadly serious.

It was the first time she had actually been invited to Towers' chambers, although Frizzel often popped upstairs uninvited to see the barrister. In her imagination, Ashley's room had looked like something out of a legal thriller movie, one of the detective novels she loved reading or a Sunday supplement magazine: classy, elegant and traditional. She was disappointed with the reality. True, it was a large, dark-wood-panelled room. But there were also modern paintings hanging on the walls and a huge table made of glass. Piles of paperwork – other briefs, she presumed – littered the floor, and the side tables were covered with important looking documents.

Set in front of Ashley Towers were the two files she had 'helped' Frizzel prepare for the Court of Appeal. The first contained the original trial papers; the second was a comprehensive chronological file of all three murders so far, including media reports and all the information Harry had gleaned from his contacts. The St Mary Magdalene's murder was filed behind the red tab, the Clapham Common murder behind the yellow tab and the Wandsworth Common murder behind the orange tab. A page setting out the similarities between the three murders was behind the black tab. She had done a thorough job.

'So, what are her chances?' said Sam, getting straight to the point.

'We've got a strong argument, but I can't guarantee the Court of Appeal will let her out. They can be a funny lot.'

Sam frowned. 'What can I say to Icey?'

'Well, she knows the single judge previously refused leave, but it has now been referred to be heard before the full court,' said Ashley.

'Yes, but he didn't know then about the other two similar murders.'

'A cynical judge might say that it is speculation to say that they are similar,' Ashley replied.

'Only a lawyer could come up with such a stupid comment,' said Sam. She was becoming irritated.

'I think that we have a very strong appeal, but I have no way of guessing what the Court of Appeal will make of it. They may take a different view, but they will certainly be concerned about the similarity of all three murders – especially the religious slant to each of the crimes. That is all very well but they'll ask how does this similarity make the conviction for Icey unsafe – that's the question we have to be able to answer.'

'I've given you the reasons,' said Sam, indicating the files she had compiled. 'I've also got all the details of the Wandsworth post mortem.'

Ashley raised his eyebrows and looked at her approvingly. 'How did you get those?'

'Don't ask and I won't tell. The details seem to suggest that there's definitely a serial killer on the loose.'

'So who might that be?'

'I am still suspicious about Leticia Joy's fiancé, Tom Padfield. I paid him another visit. He claimed to have seen Leticia with an older man, but I don't know how reliable he is as a witness. Besides, if he did see her, it just gives him a reason to be angry with his fiancée. I know men, and he's definitely a bit screwy – plus he didn't want to talk to me. I'm more than surprised that the police never considered him a serious suspect.'

'Sam, hunches are not enough. You can't just go around accusing people of killing their girlfriends.'

It was the first time he had used her first name, she realised, and she was unnerved by it. She was Miss Bailey not Sam to him. But she knew he was right with his statement. She didn't have any proof against Padfield. She also realised that he had little motive to kill the other two victims, aside from her overall impression that he was a bit 'screwy'. She didn't want to raise any more objections than Towers already had. He seemed sceptical enough for both of them. However, she could see that while they could suggest that the three murders were linked, it might not be enough to secure Icey's release. Would it take actually catching the real killer to see her best friend go free? If so, Sam was committed to doing all that it took.

Chapter Eighty-Six

Margaret Certie was in her drawing room when she heard the doorbell. She was not in the mood to answer it, but she had a vague recollection that she had made an appointment and was expecting a guest. Sitting in her chair, she felt no urge to move. The house was a mess. Even in the dusk light she could see layers of dust upon layers of grime. She had dispensed with her cleaner shortly after her husband had died, and ever since then she'd become something of a social recluse. The dinner invitations had dried up. She was no longer invited to lunches for judges' wives. She was, after all, technically no longer a wife; she was a widow, and that status had brought shame and humiliation. The bell peeled again and Mrs Certie picked up her glass.

'Cheers, everybody. Cheers to all the judges that so honourably serve our country. Cheers.' Raising her glass, she drank her brandy in one go.

The bell sounded again and Margaret Certie stood up.

She called out, 'Just wait a moment, I'm coming. Good gracious me, how many times do you have to ring that bell? What sort of hour is this to call on someone? I heard you ring the bell the first three times.' She slurred and stumbled as she spoke. 'Who is it? What do you want? Go away!'

'Will you let me in, Mrs Certie? My name is Sam Bailey. You remember? You called me a few days ago, inviting me over. I couldn't make it but phoned you back this morning and left a message. You called me back and we made an appointment to meet now?' she reminded the older woman.

Mrs Certie leant against the hallway wall. 'I told you to go away. I'll call the police.'

'Mrs Certie, it's about your husband. You said you had information to tell me, remember? It really won't take that long.'

'I don't remember calling you. What about my husband? He's dead.'

'Yes, I know, and I'm sure you don't want to have this conversation in the street, unless you're happy for the whole of your neighbourhood to hear.'

Sam could hear fumbling on the other side of the door. One bolt slid undone, then another, followed by another. At last, an arm appeared from around the door, followed by a very untidy head of grey matted hair. The black polo-necked jumper Margaret Certie was wearing was heavily stained. Her colour was sallow and the loose skin hung like a spider's web off her fragile skeleton.

'Mrs Certie, my name is Sam Bailey,' she repeated slowly, taking in the woman's appearance. 'I'm just making some enquiries about your husband. You called Fleet Investigations twice,' she said pointedly.

Sam stayed on the top step by the front door as Mrs Certie fell against the wall, pulling the door wide open with her. She managed to lift herself upright but still stood a little unsteadily in the centre of the hall.

'I do remember you. You are the lady from the television. I called you some time ago.'

As Sam stepped over the threshold, a waft of stale air passed them in the passage. Mrs Certie tried to focus her eyes on Sam and then slumped back onto the wall. She was clearly drunk.

Closing the front door, Sam took hold of Mrs Certie and led her past the drawing room. Sam peeked in and saw that the surfaces were all thick with dust and the curtains were still drawn, even though it was the middle of the day. By the side of the sofa was a bottle of brandy, and next to an armchair was a further collection of bottles. Mrs Certie had clearly been having a party for one.

'You have been busy, haven't you?' observed Sam wryly, turning to look at Mrs Certie.

Mrs Certie grabbed Sam's arm and led her on towards the dining room. It was a grand room that also looked as though it had been untouched for the past couple of weeks. Flicking the light on, Sam saw a large pristine oak dining table with eight chairs and a candelabra positioned in the middle of the table. Two of the chairs were pulled slightly away from the table, and in front of them there were still two place mats.

'I'm so sorry,' said Sam, struck by the poignancy of the table set for two. 'I hope I'm not disturbing you.'

Mrs Certie slumped into one of the dining chairs.

'He's not coming back,' she whispered.

'Who's not coming back?' Sam asked quietly, although she guessed what Mrs Certie was about to say.

'My husband has left me. He's gone.'

'I'm very sorry for your loss,' Sam said, genuinely concerned. Before she could carry on, Mrs Certie continued.

'I should have known what he was going to do. I should have tried to stop him.'

'And why did he want to . . . take his own life?' asked Sam, bending down to look into an antique drinks cabinet. She had thought about making Mrs Certie a gallon of black coffee, but she needed her to talk, and alcohol seemed more useful for loosening her lips, she thought pragmatically. She reached in to take hold of two glasses and a bottle of Taylors 75. She poured Mrs Certie a large measure and a smaller glass for herself, and then sat down at the table next to her.

'He was a liar and a cheat. He wanted to leave me for a slut. He denied it but I knew . . . I knew.' Mrs Certie began to cry. Her body convulsed as she lowered her head and cried into her glass.

'Mrs Certie, do you know who your husband was seeing? Maybe you're mistaken,' Sam said gently, placing her hand over Mrs Certie's glass so that she couldn't drink any more. The alcohol wasn't quite having the effect she'd hoped. Mrs Certie was getting even more maudlin. 'It is possible that it was all in your imagination?'

Sam felt the judge's wife tense up. Mrs Certie released her glass and tried to stand but she was so unsteady on her feet that she lurched forward towards the table. Sam caught her before her face hit the polished wood top.

'Do I look like the kind of person to imagine things?' she demanded sharply, showing what Sam presumed was a glimpse of her character when sober. 'Do I look like the kind of person who has a difficulty distinguishing everyday reality from fiction?'

'I didn't mean to suggest that . . .'

'Yes, you did,' Mrs Certie replied, finally managing to stand unaided and walking unsteadily over to the sideboard. 'Oh yes, you did,' she repeated as she trailed a hand over what appeared to be a small wooden box bearing the initials HHJC. She picked up a corkscrew and grabbed a bottle of red wine from the cabinet. 'I have dedicated my entire life to that man, and then I discover I hardly knew him. I know more about him now that he is dead. He has shown me nothing but contempt and I will hate him for as long as I live.'

Mrs Certie seemed to be almost oblivious to Sam sitting at

the table as she walked back with the box in one hand and her wine and corkscrew in the other. Sam got the impression that Mrs Certie had rehearsed this speech before, whether to herself or to an audience she couldn't tell, but her guess was the former.

Sitting heavily back in her seat, Mrs Certie placed the box on the table and the bottle between her legs, wedging it inelegantly between her thighs in order to gain leverage with her corkscrew. She opened the bottle and put it on the table. She picked up her wooden box and stroked it fervently.

'I never thought he would cheat on me. Even when I had my suspicions, I pushed them to the back of my head. They say the wife is always the last to know.' Mrs Certie grabbed her bottle of wine but instead of pouring some into her now empty glass, she drank directly from it.

Sam remained silent. She wasn't sure whether Mrs Certie realised or even cared that she was still in the room.

'It was after he died that I found these when I was going through his things,' Mrs Certie continued after several long swigs of wine.

As she opened the box, Sam could there were at least a dozen piles of what looked like receipts, all clipped into bundles. Removing a random pile from the box, Mrs Certie slid it across the table towards Sam.

'Have a look at that and tell me whether you think that it is my imagination. My dear, dear husband, the Dishonourable Judge Certie, was having an affair.'

Sam picked up the pile and looked at the first bill. Then she looked at the next and then the third. Mrs Certie passed another pile of documents to her.

'Month after month he cheated on me and I can prove it – look!'

The receipts were clipped into monthly piles and showed a

slew of hotels and restaurants that were paid for on a Visa account in the name of J Certie.

Sam thumbed through the piles while Mrs Certie cried in pain at her husband's betrayal.

'These receipts are payments for dinner, lunch and hotel expenses.'

'And the rest!' said Mrs Certie.

'What do these receipts prove, Mrs Certie? It could have been that your husband was meeting with colleagues?'

Mrs Certie snorted unattractively. 'I don't think he was spending the night at the Hotel Florence with a business colleague – and it certainly wasn't with me!'

There were many receipts for bed and breakfast at this hotel over several years, specifying a double bed with breakfast for two, charged to the room. Champagne and strawberries seemed to be a particular favourite of the room's occupants. Sam didn't say anything but in actual fact the hotel was well known to her. During her working girl days, she had spent many hours at that particular establishment. It was well known as a haunt for gentleman seeking high-class action. And, in fact, for its after-noon tea. 'Mrs Certie,' she said softly, 'why don't I make us a cup of coffee?'

Mrs Certie did not look up, but through her tears Sam sensed that she was beyond help. 'Or is there someone I can call for you?' she asked.

'No,' she said in a voice that broke Sam's heart. 'There is no one to call.'

'There must be someone. What about a friend? A relative? Just someone to sit with you.'

'My children don't want to know, and I have no friends. They have deserted me ever since my husband died. I am a social leper,' she said, bitterly spitting out the words.

'Why don't I help you? Come on, let's get you into a nicer, comfier chair.'

Mrs Certie stood up, with a belated rush of pride. 'I would like you to leave, please,' she requested, slurring her words.

'Let me help, please. I'll just go and put the kettle on.'

'I would like you to leave now. You have been very kind but I would like to be on my own. You can take them with you,' she said, pointing at the pile of receipts. 'I have no need for them now.'

Without waiting to be asked twice, Sam scooped the receipts and placed them in her bag. 'Mrs Certie, I know this may be painful to think of but do you know of any reason why your husband would want to take his own life?' she asked, again as delicately as she could.

'Yes, I think I do, actually.'

'And what do you think was the reason?' Sam asked, realising she was holding her breath until Margaret Certie shared her theory.

'Me. It's my fault. I wouldn't give him what he asked for – a divorce!'

Chapter Eighty-Seven

The screws woke Icey up at 5.20 in the morning. They were the same prison officers that had processed her when she first arrived back to serve her sentence. At that time of the morning, most of the inmates were usually still asleep, but as the screws locked up there was a roar of noise that startled even Icey. It was like thunder. She realised that every inmate on her landing was banging on their door with whatever they could find – chamber pots, shoes, books.

'Three cheers for Icey.'

Icey stood rooted to the spot in her baggy prison slacks and worn-out grey T-shirt.

'Hip, hip,' shouted Sandra.

'Hooray,' stormed the response. 'And may we never see you again!' added one.

Icey was touched by their support and the send-off she was getting. Despite everything, she had made some friends on her wing, and some of them she would not mind seeing again, as long as it was on the outside. Maybe she might even be in a position to help some of them, given time. She'd made sure that all of them knew where to find her at Fleet Investigations.

The screws were unusually quiet and Icey even thought they were unlocking and locking doors a little slower than they normally did. Or maybe it just felt like it. They escorted her slowly down the corridor. The last walk to freedom. So she hoped. Icey was feeling good. She waved her hand behind her, even though she knew the inmates would not see it. She felt herself well up but she wasn't about to spill any more tears in this place.

As she walked, she thought back to when she first arrived. That was when she'd been given good advice: keep head your down, get a qualification. Just do your time. Chin up, old girl. It could be worse.

That prison officer, Smithy, had been right; it could have been a lot worse. If they had not got rid of capital punishment, she'd be rotting in the ground by now. Icey remembered the names of all the women who had been executed: Annie Walters, Edith Thomas and Ruth Ellis. She thanked God that she'd been born in a different time than they had, otherwise she too would be just another dead person with their name on a list. She just hoped to God that she would never see that grim plaque again.

Walking across the central association area, Icey followed the screw down the stairs. Once again the officer removed a bulging set of keys from her belt and opened the steel door. It groaned to a resting position. They walked through and it was locked shut before they made their way back to reception.

There were six other prisoners being processed, and another eight already sitting with their escort. Icey was due in the Court of Appeal, which had precedence over the magistrates and the Crown Court, except for the Old Bailey, where the judges got very short-tempered if the prisoners arrived late for their trial. On a number of occasions, the Common Serjeant had threatened to charge the prison service with wasted costs. Ever since then, the delivery of the prisoners had improved considerably.

Waiting for Icey in reception were two large plastic bags full of her belongings. Since there was a possibility that she wouldn't be returning to the prison, her personal property would be transported with her. By 7.15, she was processed and ready for transportation. She was given a Mars bar – her breakfast for the day. At the reception desk, the same woman who had processed her at the beginning of her sentence was on duty again.

'I was here when you came in, wasn't I?' Smithy said. Icey was not expected to answer. Looking down at her job sheet, the woman recognised her own handwriting. 'So I was,' she said pleased with herself. 'You're due up at the Court of Appeal, aren't you?'

'Yes.'

'Well, good luck. I hope it goes your way.'

'Thank you,' said Icey.

The handcuffs were snapped onto her left wrist and her escort snapped the other half onto her own arm, and together they walked to the displacement area. Icey was on her way.

As the horizontal metal bar was raised, the red light turned to green and the steel shutter doors rolled back. The meat wagon rolled forward. She removed the Mars bar from her pocket and unwrapped it. It wasn't her idea of a healthy breakfast but beggars couldn't be choosers and today she would need all the energy, and patience, she could mobilise in the short space of time left. Her appeal was due to be heard at ten o'clock.

Chapter Eighty-Eight

Sam had been waiting for this moment ever since Icey had first been convicted back in February.

She was up early, ready and waiting. The morning of Icey's appeal she found Mr Frizzel asleep at his desk, his head resting on top of his briefcase. She had worked for him long enough now to more or less accept that Frizzel lived in his office, but he evidently hadn't been home for days. His drinking had increased dramatically; it usually did around the anniversary of the massacre of his family, she knew. Mr Frizzel was slowly killing himself and she couldn't sit by and just watch it happen.

He looked like a baby, vulnerable and pitiable. Yet she felt like slapping him. Maybe just one hard bitch slap would bring him to his senses. But still she hesitated. He had been good to her and Icey over the years. In reality, the only person he had let down was himself, and he would ultimately pay the price. Alcohol had a habit of catching up with you in the end.

'Mr Frizzel,' she said, touching him on the arm. There was no reaction. He was dead to the world. Sam switched the light on and pinched his ears. This time he sat up with a start and stared blankly in front of him.

Walking into the kitchen area, Sam turned the radio on very loud as she made a cup of coffee for the both of them. Mr Frizzel rubbed his eyes and gathered himself together. If he had not actually been wearing his clothes, Sam was convinced they would have stood up and walked themselves to the nearest laundry.

'Here you are, Mr Frizzel, a nice cup of coffee for you,' she said, placing a steaming mug in front of him.

'And how did you get on the other day with the files?' he asked as he shook his head and moved his floppy cheeks from side to side.

'All done and delivered to counsel. And you?'

'You know how it is, old girl. I worked most of the night. I'm simply inundated with work.'

Sam looked around his tiny office. He was certainly inundated with something, but it mostly looked like empty bottles of scotch.

'Well, today is a very important day and I think that you need to concentrate and get ready. You will have to dress appropriately,' she told him, looking him up and down meaningfully.

Mr Frizzel looked at her, puzzled.

'Dress appropriately, old girl?' Sam had always dressed appropriately and he especially liked her dress that day.

'Yes. I think you should start now by taking your clothes off and changing your suit and shirt. Here, see, on the back of this door, I have selected the suit I would like you to wear, and the tie. If you won't do it, I'll have to dress you myself.' When Mr Frizzel did not move, she added, 'You are treating me to breakfast, so speed up.'

Mr Frizzel started to protest, but when he caught sight of himself in the mirror he was silenced. He did not recognise the old man looking back at him with a face like death and a body fit only for a morgue. Where had Mr Adrian Frizzel gone? Sam was right. It definitely was time for him to change.

He turned to nod his agreement at her, and on seeing his face in the light, she frowned, 'And I also think that you should have a shave.'

Sipping her coffee, Sam watched him as he removed his coat and jacket. He needed a shower too, but perhaps that was too much to ask of him for one day.

'And the rest,' said Sam. 'You have no secrets from me and you can rest assured that I am not remotely interested in your body.'

She reached into her handbag and grabbed the can of deodorant she'd bought on the way to the office. She handed it to him and turned her back as Mr Frizzel stepped out of his trousers.

'There is a clean pair of underpants on the side there,' she informed him, staring at his wall. 'Put them on and leave your dirty clothes in the plastic bag that's by the side of your desk.'

Mr Frizzel did as he was told and when he had liberally sprayed himself with deodorant and was dressed in his new clothes, Sam marched him to the greasy spoon café on the opposite side of Fleet Street.

She ordered a full English breakfast for both of them – sausages, bacon, mushrooms, a fried egg sunny side up, tomatoes, two slices of toast and coffee. She insisted on tucking serviettes into his collar to protect his clean clothes.

'What do you think will happen when we see Icey?' Sam asked as Frizzel got stuck in greedily.

He put down his knife and fork for a second and folded his hands together. 'My dear girl, if I knew that I would be a very wise man.'

Back at Sam's office after breakfast, Frizzel seemed more like his old self.

Sam took a deep breath; she had everything well prepared

and ready to go. The statements, maps, plans and all the exhibits were in order, along with the skeleton arguments from the prosecution and the defence. Mr Frizzel had delegated the task to her and it was just as well. She had read and re-read everything several times and she was now ready to guide Ashley Towers on any unexpected question that might arise. She had more faith in his abilities in court than their previous barrister, Mr Percival; but Sam knew everything there was to know about Icey's case, inside out. No one had given it more thought, time and attention than her, and for all Ashley Towers' fame, she was the real expert in this appeal.

'We'll leave in half an hour,' she said to Frizzel, smoothing out her ice-blue chiffon dress. He sat in Icey's desk chair and looked surprisingly scrubbed and sober in the new navy suit she'd bought for him. She said a silent thank you, as any other behaviour other than absolute cooperation that morning would have really annoyed her.

Oriel and Flick arrived at the office just after 9.30 in sexy tailored dresses and a cloud of exotic perfume, chattering and apologising for their lateness. The pair of them had made two stops on their way in.

First of all they had stopped off at a new patisserie on Fleet Street. It was called the Crème de la Crème and between the two of them they'd chosen a selection of bespoke gateaux, which Frizzel eyed greedily. There was a hazelnut and caramel mousse cake, which consisted of a hazelnut sponge encasing a caramel mousse, topped with glazed roasted hazelnuts in a cream and caramel sauce; and alongside this nestled a fresh cream gateau and six exotic tarts.

Their next stop had been a florist to pick up two-dozen long-stemmed white roses and a bunch of Madonna lilies. These were just a little gift from Irma and the girls. Sam had also arranged for the florist to send bouquets of pink hibiscus and white gardenias. By the time Sam grabbed her matching suit jacket and walked out of the office to the Court of Appeal, the Fleet Investigations office was a garden of pure perfection.

It would be a wonderful welcome home for Icey. The business was starting to do well. There was money in the office account and Sam had even reached a point where she was turning clients away. That was temporary. The problem would be resolved as soon as Icey was free and, together, they could concentrate on things other than ensuring her release.

Ashley Towers spotted the press as he walked across the zebra crossing towards the High Court. He checked his reflection in the glass doors at the entrance. He was looking good and he was glad he had decided to have his hair cut the day before, and chosen to wear his new red tie.

He soon became impatient with the queue at security. He turned left to the robing room, where he put on his wig and gown, had a precautionary pee and checked his appearance once again in the mirror. Staring at his own face made him focus on the case ahead, and he allowed himself a few minutes of silent contemplation.

Soon afterwards, he walked the length of the main hall, a high nineteenth-century gothic edifice. Originally the courts had been intended to lead off the hallway, but the judges had refused to sit on the same level as the hoi polloi. Now you had to go upstairs to reach the court. But before he did so, Ashley had a visit to make first.

The cells were in the corner on the far right. Pressing the buzzer, he introduced himself and waited for security to open the door. Icey was waiting for him in the pre-allocated conference room. She had changed out of her prison uniform into an outfit Sam had picked out for her, and she looked smart and demure in a designer navy blue two-piece suit. Although the skirt was a little loose at the waist, it worked perfectly with the white high-collar shirt and navy tights and shoes, and more than fitted the occasion.

As Ashley entered the conference room, Icey stood up automatically, too used to prison regime by now; and when he sat down, she followed his lead immediately.

'What are my chances?' she said after they'd exchanged cool greetings. At once he was struck by the similarity between her and Sam. They might be polar opposites in terms of looks, but they both got straight to the point.

'I am not a betting man, but I would say good. I am very hopeful.' He studied her pretty face. She had aged slightly during her stay at Holloway. She was still beautiful, but her looks were hardened and more angular now.

'Is Sam here?' she asked eagerly, her hands fiddling with her collar.

'I haven't seen her yet, but I'm sure she will be. She's never missed a conference. I am sure she will be waiting for you.'

Chapter Eighty-Nine

Mr Goldman was getting impatient. He was a busy man. He had turned up at the High Court at nine o'clock for a conference with the barrister Mr Towers and the solicitor Frizzel, both of whom should have been waiting for him in reception. They were nowhere to be seen and the longer he waited, the crosser he became.

He was eager to do his duty here and get back to his real work. The least he could expect was for counsel to arrive on time so they could get started. Waiting in his best suit and skull cap, he was not a happy man.

Ashley came out of the cells and headed for the reception area. He looked for Frizzel, but the man was nowhere to be seen. His expert witness, Mr Goldman, the jeweller, was easy to spot. He looked like he had spent his entire life looking through a magnifying glass. Although, currently, his expression was one of thunder. He obviously preferred to stay behind his desk than engage with strangers.

'Mr Goldman,' said Ashley, using his best disarming smile, 'I am so sorry that I'm late. I had to see my client in the cells. It takes for ever to get in and out.' Ashley held out his hand. 'Please accept my apologies,' he said smoothly.

Shaking it quickly but not falling for Towers' polished pleasantries, Mr Goldman snapped, 'I just discovered I went to school with the presiding judge.'

'I beg your pardon?' Ashley Towers was momentarily thrown and a little stung that his charm had not worked.

'I looked up the case on the list over there. The senior judge is Lord Justice Raleigh. Am I right?'

'You are, but he's an old Etonian?'

'So am I.'

Ashley could hardly disguise his surprise. 'Did you bring copies of your report with you as my office requested?' he asked in an attempt to hide his reaction.

Mr Goldman removed his original notes from his briefcase and handed over several copies of his report to Ashley. Ashley checked over the top copy.

'That's fine. We have to get permission to call you, but there should not be any problem with that.'

'Is it an issue that I went to school with one of the judges?'

'I don't think so, no. We'll have to disclose it, of course, but you are an expert and expected to be independent.'

Ashley's mobile rang. It was Alfred Roma. He excused himself to Mr Goldman and turned away to talk.

'Where the hell are you?' asked Roma. 'I am still waiting to see your expert's report.'

'I'm with the expert now. Sorry not to have got it to you before.'

Roma knew that Towers was not sorry at all. It was a typical stunt that lawyers employ; to serve reports as late as possible, to prevent your opponent from having enough time to read it and respond in any meaningful way. He saw right through these tactics.

'Where are you?' asked Ashley.

'I'm having breakfast over the road in Apostrophe. Could you slip it over to me?'

'I've already been through security once. I'll leave one on your lectern,' Ashley replied, hanging up.

He turned off his phone in case Roma called him again, and then made his way to Court Six, where he handed in copies of the report for the judges, and put another copy on Roma's lectern as promised. He sat in counsel's row and read the report again, marking up key passages.

Chapter Ninety

Court Number Six was a large ornate room lined with floor-to-ceiling bookcases, packed high with ancient law tomes. At the front of the court, on a high podium, were three empty chairs for the three judges who would hear the appeal. Facing them, there were several rows of narrow wooden tables accompanied by benches in front. These were for the barristers and, in front of those, were the seats for the silks – the Queen's Counsel, the senior elite members of the bar who wore silk gowns. Below the judges' podium, there was an area for the court clerk, the usher and the shorthand writer. In one of his rare moments of clarity, Mr Frizzel had described it to Sam as the engine room of justice, and the name felt right. As she admired it, the man himself walked over to the right and headed for a staircase.

'Let's hope for the best,' Frizzel said, as he disappeared up the carpeted stairs.

Sam began to follow him, her heels tapping on the marble floor, but checking her watch she knew they were early and she already needed a break from the doom-laden atmosphere of court. Bursting with nervous energy, her stomach in free fall, she walked back through the magnificent hall and stood on the steps outside. Despite the fact that the air was far from pure, mingled as it was with the fumes from the traffic, it was cool and helped to clear her head. As she watched the lawyers enter the great building, she allowed herself a small smile when she spotted a familiar face approach. He looked just the part in a very smart, black, double-breasted suit. He was carrying a smart red leather document bag over his shoulder.

Alfred Roma carried himself with all the excitement and bravado of someone in the final stages of a winning case. He was smart and well groomed. He looked up and saw Sam, and felt a wave of unease. He was sure that he had seen her somewhere else before; he couldn't quite put a finger on where, but something unpleasant niggled at his memory. Perhaps she had been a witness in one of his recent court cases. She was certainly striking-looking, and he thought he might have remembered such an attractive woman if he'd previously questioned her in court. But he saw so many witnesses, he found it impossible to remember all of them. Indeed, he tried to forget them as quickly as he could no matter how good-looking.

She was smiling at him now. It was nothing obvious, just the slightest of smiles. He acknowledged her with a half-nod of the head as he walked past, frowning slightly as he continued to look at her, trying to remember where he'd seen this beautiful young black woman before. As he stared, she pursed her lips and, quite shockingly, blew him a kiss. He glanced around to see if anyone had noticed – or indeed to check whether the kiss had even been directed at him. Then, deliberately averting his gaze, he continued on his way, his mind too preoccupied with what lay ahead to work out who she was and where he might have met her before.

Roma's mind was already rehearsing the legal submissions that would take the best part of the morning. He had spent the previous day assessing the strength of his opponent's case. They had a very strong submission with some good points. Roma had concentrated on his replies to the defence submissions. He knew he also had to get to the expert witness's notes, and hoped they weren't too long for him to digest in the little time he would have. He was, in fact, immensely irritated that he had not been given them before. He looked at his watch. He still had time. He would call Ashley Towers and have a firm word with him. Yes, that was what he would do; call his young colleague and give him a piece of him mind. So deep in thought was he as he walked through the entrance doors that he accidentally bumped into the person in front of him. With alarm, he noticed it was the brazen young woman from outside.

'I do beg your pardon, sir,' she said. Her face looked stern, but there was a glint of mischief in her startling green eyes.

'Quite all right,' came the reply, as Roma looked over his shoulder nervously. 'No harm done. Now, if you'll excuse me . . .'

'How's the weather, sir?' she questioned him with a cheeky wink, matching her stride to his and standing next to him as they both joined the queue to security.

'Fine, fine . . . It looks like it will brighten up.'

'Not too nippy for you, is it?' the young woman continued.

'Thank you for asking, but the weather is fine. It is March, after all,' he replied, half-turning round, puzzled and a little irritated by the woman's odd questions.

'You probably prefer it when it's a little cooler, though, don't you, sir?'

'My dear girl, what *are* you talking about? It's quite pleasant for the time of year.'

'The other week, though, you may remember, it was snowing?'

Roma frowned, wondering if the pretty girl was quite all there. He decided to humour her as best he could. 'I know it snowed a few weeks ago, but what's that got to do with anything?'

'Well, you nearly caught a chill, sir, and we were all very worried about you.'

Roma was more confused than ever as he moved along in the queue and passed swiftly through security. To his knowledge, he hadn't been anywhere where he might catch a chill, and the young woman was beginning to annoy him. He had more important matters to worry about than the weather. She was standing close to him as she made her ridiculous comments, he had had enough and turned around abruptly to face the young lady with the perfect body, his mouth open, ready to put her in her place.

'I do hope we didn't leave you outside for too long,' Sam jumped in before Roma could speak, closely following him through security. 'The other day, I mean. It was just that we got talking and didn't realise the time. So apologies for that . . .'

Roma did not feel well. 'The other day?'

'Yes, Mr Fisher, but no harm was done. As you said yourself, it was one of the best days of your life.'

'My name is not Mr Fisher.'

'You can call yourself what you like. You'd be surprised some of the names I've heard, sir.'

Roma visibly paled; it was all coming back to him. As he turned on his heel and attempted to walk off in the direction of the robing rooms, he increased his pace but still the young woman dogged his heels. 'You're mistaken, madam. We haven't met and my name is not Mr Fisher,' he snapped, veering away from her. 'And I would be very grateful if you could stop making a nuisance of yourself.'

'I'm happy to call you whatever you like, sir, but I want you to know that your secret is safe with me.' She gave him another slight wink, and followed closely as Roma walked down the stairs towards the robing rooms. 'There is just one other thing, sir, before I leave you,' she said.

'What is that, madam?'

'Madam Irma is running a bit low on pink tape. We used up a lot that evening. I was just wondering whether you know a good supplier round here?'

Roma waited for her to finish. He did not reply immediately. He needed to think – and fast. This attractive woman was trying to goad him, and he had no idea why.

'Who are you? Are you one of . . .?' He didn't dare finish the sentence, didn't dare to ask if she was one of Madam Irma's girls.

'My name is Sam Bailey.'

'*Sam Bailey*,' he echoed. 'Why does your name sound familiar?' he said, grasping at recognition just beyond reach of his overcrowded memory.

'You're the prosecution counsel in the appeal of Elizabeth Johnson. She's my partner in Fleet Investigations.'

'Your partner?'

'She's also a very good friend of mine, and we're both friends of Madam Irma. I will be watching the appeal very closely, Mr Fisher, or should I call you Mr Roma now?' She gave him a big smile. 'Either way, I'll see you in court.'

Chapter Ninety-One

Sam made her way back to Court Number Six, hoping that she'd made her point sufficiently to Mr Alfred Roma. Or at the very least, had thrown him off his game. She found Frizzel and took a seat next to him. Roma and Ashley Towers were deep in conversation in counsel's row.

Frizzel looked at Sam through half-closed eyes. There was something magical about her. She was always impeccably dressed, but today she had taken particular care with her appearance and the colour of her dress and jacket looked beautiful against her skin. Sam caught him looking at her. As she caught his gaze, she smiled. She was pleased with him, for once. He looked every bit the sober solicitor that he had once been. She reached over and touched him appreciatively on the knee. A tingle of pleasure ran up his leg and stopped short of his groin. He was acutely conscious that, for many years, his alcohol addiction had cost him dearly, in more ways than one. Frizzel smiled back. One day soon, maybe, he would give up alcohol and that would solve all his problems.

'When Icey enters the court she will come from the left into that steel cage over the dock,' Mr Frizzel began conversationally.

'Will she be able to see me?'

'I am sure she will.'

'All rise,' said the usher as the judges entered.

Sam looked at them as they walked in. They all looked the

same: grey and dusty with a hint of decay. She hadn't expected the judges to be in the prime of their lives, but they looked more dead than alive. The judge sitting in the middle was the most unattractive man she had ever seen. He looked like he'd had every inch of justice and fairness squeezed out of him years ago. Emerging beneath his wig were Dickensian sideburns that extended all the way down his mutton chops. His nose nestled into a moustache what was starched and twirled at the edge into a Victorian curl. He looked completely ridiculous.

Sam listened as it was explained that the first two cases were not ready to be heard. In the first, prosecuting counsel requested an adjournment to midday to resolve issues that had been raised by the defence. In the following case, counsel was not in the building and so the case was put back until he arrived. His absence seemed to put the judges in a bad mood.

The next case was Icey's.

Icey had been waiting for an hour and a half in the pits of the building. Her nerves were gone and she wished she could fast-forward to the verdict. She knew she was innocent, and she hoped she'd soon be free, but life had taught her that things did not always turn out as you wished. You couldn't expect to win just because you were innocent, as she already knew to her cost. They'd got it wrong first time round; she couldn't rely on them doing better this time. The truth did not always matter. If it had, Icey would never have been incarcerated in the first place.

The female escort, to whom she was handcuffed, was as broad as she was tall, with hands like shovels. As Icey followed her, she was mesmerised by the rhythmic thrust and tilt of her swinging rear end. It was indeed a remarkable sight. A map of the world bottom. The right cheek was on a different sphere and appeared to move quite independently of the left. In her head, Icey nicknamed her Double Edam.

As she climbed up the stairs in the dock, the first person Icey saw was Sam, looking smart, sexy and elegant in a beautiful dress suit. Icey felt a surge of hope at seeing her oldest friend.

Once in the dock, Icey's handcuffs were removed. She stood between Double Edam and a large black male officer. She knew she did not look like the monster that had slaughtered an innocent girl in a church. She hoped she looked like a young woman who had been in the wrong place at the wrong time.

Sam caught her eye and smiled warmly as Icey stood to attention. Once she had been identified, she made a slight bow to the court and then sat. She tried to establish eye contact with the judges who would decide her fate. But they were too experienced to make the mistake of meeting the gaze of the person in the dock, let alone identifying with them.

Chapter Ninety-Two

Ashley Towers got to his feet. 'May it please my lord, I appear on behalf of the applicant and my learned friend Mr Alfred Roma appears on behalf of the Crown.' His voice sounded assured and calm, and Icey watched him intently, impressed in spite of herself. 'This is an application for leave to appeal, following the refusal by the single judge this means that a judge on his own would consider the advice and the grounds and decide whether there is any legal argument that could be argued about the safety of Elizabeth Johnson's conviction. If there are or maybe arguable grounds the next stage would be for the single judge to grant permission for the case to be argued before a court of three judges. The applicant was convicted of a single count of murder.'

'Mr Towers,' said Mr Justice Longhurst, 'this is only an application for leave. If we grant leave, would you be content for this to be the hearing of the appeal?'

'Yes, my lord.' Ashley thought that a good sign. 'May I take it that the court is familiar with the basic facts?'

'You may.'

'The grounds of appeal are that the conviction was not supported by the evidence. Additionally, subsequent events suggest that the appellant is a victim of a miscarriage of justice. There is also an application to call fresh evidence.'

'Is this the expert evidence, Mr Towers?'

'Yes, my lord, and there is additional evidence as to subsequent murders of a similar nature which took place when my client was already behind bars.'

Mr Justice Elford then turned to Roma. 'What is the attitude of the prosecution to this appeal?'

Roma didn't reply instantly, taking a moment to think about the question. He was of the opinion that the conviction was unsafe, but that was just his opinion. As he thought about it, though, his conscience got the better of him. He knew he had to speak his mind.

'The attitude of the prosecution is that the conviction is entirely unsafe,' he stated softly.

There was complete silence in the courtroom.

'I am sorry,' said Lord Justice Raleigh, the most senior judge. 'Will you just repeat that? Did you say unsafe?'

Roma took a breath and felt beads of sweat begin to drip down his forehead. 'The attitude of the prosecution is that the conviction is entirely . . .'

Just at that moment, the court door flew open and in came Lydia Watson. She entered the court and took her place directly behind Roma. He watched her settle into her seat and then, once the noise of her entry had quietened down, Roma turned to face a hushed court.

'Mr Roma, what is the attitude of the prosecution?' repeated Lord Justice Raleigh.

'The attitude of the prosecution is that the conviction is entirely safe,' said Roma quietly.

'Oh,' said the judge, smiling and looking everywhere but at the woman in the dock. 'I misheard you at first.'

Icey had started to fidget. Cramp had taken hold of her legs and she had pins and needles in her left arm. She'd missed the exchange between the three judges and the fat sweaty man standing next to Ashley Towers. Her mind seemed unable to focus on anything but her legs and left arm.

Sam was also having problems hearing what was said. She cursed the mumbling Mr Roma. She could tell she had missed something important but when she turned to question Mr Frizzel, she saw he was doodling on his pad. She nudged him angrily.

Ashley sat in disbelief. He'd managed to have a brief chat off the record with Roma before the judges had arrived, and though the older man had admonished him for his late delivery of their new witness statement, he'd also led him to believe that the prosecution was not opposing the appeal. As he rose again to speak, he gave Roma the dirtiest of looks.

'My lords, may we start from the beginning. The conviction of the appellant is not only unsafe, it is completely unsatisfactory,' Ashley asserted. 'The defence at trial was that someone other than the appellant committed the murder and it is now apparent that the murder was indeed the work of a person who is still at large. Since the conviction of my client, two more murders have taken place in very similar circumstances. If there was ever proof of the wrongfulness of the conviction, then the subsequent events prove beyond reasonable doubt the appellant is innocent. Each of the three victims was a young woman, slaughtered at night. The patterns of injuries were similar. A knife was used in each case to torture the victim and cut their throats. Most significantly, there are religious overtones to all three murders: the first murder was in a church and a bloody rosary was found on the deceased. The second victim had a crucifix inserted into her person and crosses carved on her body, and the killer placed a barbed wire crown on the third.' Ashley paused, satisfied that he had presented clear and convincing details.

Mr Justice Longhurst glanced at his fingers as he spoke. 'Is it the appellant's case that these three murders were the work of one person?'

'My lord, yes. Most definitely. I thought that I had made that clear. I have handed up two comprehensive files covering the St Mary Magdalene's murder, the Clapham Common murder and the Wandsworth murder. The similarities in relation to each murder are clearly set out for you,' Ashley assured him.

'We appreciate your efforts, Mr Towers. It must have taken a great deal of time to prepare the files.'

'Indeed, my lord, I am grateful to my instructing solicitor Mr Frizzel and our investigator, Miss Sam Bailey.' Ashley turned, tipped his wig and acknowledged Sam. Surprised by Ashley's comments, Sam smiled at the three judges.

'We would like to hear from the prosecution again,' said Mr Justice Elford, the judge on the left, ignoring the exchange. 'Mr Roma, do you say that there is no connection between these three cases. If so, can you assist us with how you came to that conclusion?'

'My lord, the police led us to believe that there is a connection between the two most recent murders, but that the same cannot be said of the St Mary Magdalene's murder. There are some surface similarities, perhaps, but extensive enquiries have led the police to the conclusion that St Mary Magdalene's killing was not the work of the same killer.'

The judges appeared to be going through the file that Sam had meticulously prepared.

'Is it true that a rosary was found at the body of each victim?' Judge Elford asked.

'No, my lord, a rosary was found in the first murder only – it belonged to the victim. I believe, in the case of the second and third victims, a pearl necklace was found on the body or nearby in each case, but as I'm sure you're aware women often wear a necklace of some description. There is really nothing remarkable about that,' said Roma.

'And was the rosary or necklace broken in each case?'

'No, my lord.'

'And, in your opinion, Leticia Joy's murder was not the work of the same killer?'

'Most definitely not. No, my lord,' Roma stated clearly. 'The police believe the latter two murders are connected and may well be the work of someone who has read about the first murder – a copycat killer, if you will,' he explained, relieved to have finally calmed himself down enough to work in the seed of doubt. 'Crucially in the case of Leticia Joy's murder, the applicant was found with the murder weapon in her hand. The victim's blood was on her clothes and the pattern of the blood was entirely consistent with her being near the victim while she was still alive. She also left traces of her own blood on Leticia Joy's broken rosary, and a bead from the same rosary was found in her pocket. The trial judge observed that the evidence against the accused was overwhelming. The applicant could offer no explanation other than that she couldn't remember what had occurred. The case received a good deal of publicity, my lord,' Roma added for good measure. 'It may be that the murderer in the other incidents had read about and copied elements of the original crime.'

'Mr Towers,' said Judge Longhurst, turning to the defence counsel, 'what evidence it there that the St Mary Magdalene's murder is the work of a serial killer?'

Mr Towers went through a meticulous comparison. When he was finished, he sat down.

Despite the fact that it was her life they were making decisions about, Icey felt herself falling asleep. She had been up a lot earlier than anyone else in court, and the court technicalities made little sense to her. She thought Ashley was doing a good job but she knew her fate lay in the judges' hands.

Sam sat quietly, making notes on the proceedings. From her understanding, she also thought that the appeal was going well, although the mention of a copycat killing had worried her. But Mr Roma seemed unsure and out of his depth in prosecuting. Although she had no intention of blackmailing him, she hoped she'd done a bit to unsettle him before the trial. In comparison, Mr Towers had clearly anticipated his opponent's case. He was proving to be a vast improvement on his predecessor, Sam thought with satisfaction.

Chapter Ninety-Three

At midday, Mr Frizzel stepped out of court for some fresh air and came across a very irate Mr Goldman pacing up and down the corridor outside.

'I was told to be here at nine and now it is midday and I've still not been called. If I don't give evidence in the next fifteen minutes, I shall go. I have a business to run. My time is money,' the old man grumbled angrily.

'My dear sir, please accept my apologies. It's often very difficult to know how long these things will take. I'll just go and tell counsel of your problem. Your evidence is vital, absolutely vital,' Frizzel assured him.

He slipped back into the courtroom and scribbled a note to Ashley, who then turned to the judges.

'My lords, I have just been told that my expert witness has a prior engagement and is in great difficulty if he is not called immediately.'

'You require our leave before that can happen,' said the lead judge, Lord Justice Raleigh.

'Why was this evidence not called at the trial in the court below?' asked one of the other judges.

'My lord, the issue only arose when my learned friend invited the jury to compare the pearls themselves and conclude that the single pearl found on my client came from the victim's rosary,' Ashley explained.

'Did the Crown call an expert?'

'My lord, no.'

'Is this correct, Mr Roma? This is surely a matter of expertise?'

'The jury were only invited to note the similarity, not to conclude that the one pearl came from the string,' said Roma.

'But surely,' said Longhurst, 'the only reason for asking them to consider the point was the hope that they would reach that conclusion. You were asking them to speculate?'

Roma looked round at Lydia Watson, and then caught a glimpse of Sam at the back of the court.

'My lord, the Crown doesn't wish to be obstructive. If the court considers it in the interests of justice to call an expert . . .'

'Just a moment.' The three judges went into a huddle and then resumed their places. 'Mr Towers, you have leave,' Lord Justice Raleigh declared.

Roma rose tentatively. 'My lords, I only received a copy of the expert's report shortly before the court sat. I would welcome a brief adjournment to consider it.'

'No, Mr Roma. You raised this matter in the Crown Court and you really should have read the report before today. Let's get on. We have two other cases on our list today.'

'My lords,' said Ashley, 'I call Mr Isaac Goldman. I should say that he was apparently at school with my lord, Lord Justice Raleigh.'

'Don't remember the name,' muttered Raleigh. 'Wouldn't influence me in any event. You don't object, Mr Roma?'

Roma could hear Lydia Watson grumbling behind him. 'Of course, my lord, I know that your lordship would not be influenced by your knowledge of the witness, but maybe the public . . .'

By this time Mr Goldman had entered the witness box.

'Were we at Eton together?' asked Raleigh, turning to the expert witness.

'I was two years below you,' said Mr Goldman. 'We didn't have much contact. I remember you were captain of boats. I wasn't a rowing man myself.'

'Don't remember you from Adam. Let's get on.' And that was clearly that, and Mr Goldman was sworn.

'Would you please give your name, address and qualifications to the court,' said Ashley.

'I am Isaac Goldman. I am a partner in Goldman and Sons at 16a Hatton Garden. I have been in the jewellery business since I left school at sixteen. I am a Fellow of the Worshipful Company of Goldsmiths.'

'Do you have any special expertise?' Ashley asked to kick off his questions and allow this important witness to demonstrate his credentials.

'Diamonds and pearls.'

'Are you regarded as one of the leading experts in the world of pearls?' Ashley asked.

'I like to think so. I taught most of the others.' A modest ripple of laughter ran round the court.

'You have examined the two exhibits, is that correct?'

'Yes. Exhibits one and two,' Mr Goldman confirmed.

'Was exhibit one a rosary made up of pearls?'

'It was not complete. It was broken and there was one pearl missing.'

'Was exhibit two a single pearl?'

'Yes.'

'Were you able to make a comparison of the separate pearl with the pearls in the broken rosary?' Ashley asked, painstakingly working towards the key revelation.

'Yes.'

'What did you conclude?'

'I concluded that the rosary itself was made from Persian Gulf pearls. The solitary pearl is a Manar pearl,' Mr Goldman stated.

'How can you tell the difference?' Ashley asked the old man.

'Manar pearls come from Sri Lanka. Gulf pearls are not as white as those from Sri Lanka. Gulf pearls have a slight but distinct yellow colour.'

'Can you explain why that is?'

'Yes. The pearls are usually yellow because the fishermen in the Gulf have to wait for up to fifteen days for the shell to open in order to extract the pearl. During this time, some of the pearls lose their water and become putrid and yellow. The oysters of the Manar Strait open five or six days sooner than those on the gulf of Persia because the heat is so much greater at Manar.'

The three judges looked a bit lost, as did most of the observers. 'So what do you conclude?' asked Elford, to bring things to a point.

'The colour and texture made it clear that there is no connection between the single pearl and the pearl rosary covered in blood. They're not the same at all,' Mr Goldman said, putting it in a nutshell.

'Is it usual to combine pearls from the Gulf with those from Manar on a single string or within a rosary?' Elford queried.

'My lord, it would be highly unusual – most unlikely, I would have said. Both types of pearls are expensive and when it comes to real pearls, and this end of the market in particular, the homogeneity of stones would be important for any valuation. It is just as important as grading the size of the pearls.'

'Thank you, Mr Goldman,' Ashley said, taking his seat. 'Most enlightening.'

Roma stood up with the report in his hand. Ashley could see that his hand was shaking.

'Mr Goldman,' he began, 'would you look again at the two exhibits. I would suggest that the difference in colour is hardly visible?'

Mr Goldman glared at him in disdain and shook his head. 'Perhaps to an untrained eye, but even an apprentice jeweller could spot the difference. Someone who knew what to look for couldn't fail to spot it. Any expert in the country would give you the same answer,' he declared confidently, clearly not liking his judgement being called into question.

'You suggest that it is most unusual to combine Gulf and Manar pearls, but is there any way of telling where the pearls were originally strung?' Roma asked.

'No. There is nothing like a hallmark system for pearls. We often sell pearls strung abroad,' Mr Goldman replied.

'Do the standards of Hatton Garden necessarily apply abroad?' Roma asked, hoping to discredit this line of argument.

'Everybody worldwide knows that the homogeneity of the pearls on a string or on a rosary would affect its value. They would try to achieve it.'

'Mr Goldman, you cannot exclude the possibility that Gulf and Manar pearls were used in one string,' Roma said, growing a little agitated.

'I cannot exclude it, but it is highly unlikely. Mixing pearls of different kinds devalues the string as a whole considerably,' Mr Goldman responded calmly.

'Your reason for saying that the single pearl is a Manar pearl is that you think that it is whiter in colour?' Roma queried, trying a different tack.

'There is also the issue of texture.'

'Sometimes, presumably, a Gulf pearl may open as quickly as a Manar pearl?' asked Roma, finding his stride.

'It can happen, but it is unusual.'

'If it did, though, then the Gulf pearl could be whiter than usual?' Roma said, feeling that he might be getting somewhere now.

'Yes, but there would still be the same difference in texture.'

'Can you describe what is different about the texture?'

'Not really. You just come to recognise it,' Mr Goldman told him, with an impatient shake of his head.

'So you're making a very subjective judgement?' Roma commented, seizing his chance.

'Yes, but based on my many years' experience,' Mr Goldman reiterated. 'Anyone stringing these pearls would be likely to spot the difference and set the odd pearl on one side.'

'What if he did not have your years of experience?'

'He would be taught to look for the difference.'

'Thank you,' said Roma, returning to his seat.

'Unless your lordships have any questions . . .?' said Ashley, standing up to conclude matters with his expert witness.

'No,' said Lord Justice Raleigh, looking enquiringly at his fellows. They shook their heads. 'Thank you, Mr Goldman. We are very grateful. Count yourself lucky, if you had been a rowing man you might have had the misfortune to end up as a lawyer listening to these fellows all day.'

'I think the family business would have called, my lord,' Mr Goldman said, with a small smile to acknowledge the judge's humour.

'Very well, we'll break for lunch now. Two o'clock prompt, please.'

Their lordships rose and left the bench. Ashley looked across at Icey and smiled. She allowed herself to smile in return before she was taken down.

Outside court, Sam grabbed Ashley before he could disappear.

'How did you think it went?' she asked eagerly.

'Good. I think we're winning. We caught Roma on the back foot.'

'Only *think?*' Sam said, frowning.

'OK, better than think,' he said, grinning at her cross look. 'Come on, I'll buy you a sandwich in the Cock & Bull. I'll get my gear off and meet you in the entrance.'

Sam found herself smiling as she watched Ashley's back disappear. Her reaction to the conceited barrister caught her off guard. But then she allowed herself to smile again; Ashley was just doing his job, but they were both excited and happy to be on the way to freeing Icey.

Chapter Ninety-Four

After lunch, the judge to the left of Lord Justice Raleigh intervened.

'Mr Towers, your case is that your client cannot be guilty of the offence that she has been convicted of because of two subsequent similar murders committed at a time when your client was incarcerated?'

'That is correct, my lord.'

'Well, if that is the case, can you assist us with the state of the investigation into the other two murders? You're inviting us to assume the same killer is still on the loose?' Sam noticed a slight irritation in Elford's voice.

'Yes, my lord.'

'Mr Roma has invited us to consider the possibility of a copycat killer?'

'My lord, to look at the possibility of a copycat killer would be pure speculation,' Ashley said coolly.

Sam was confused. Surely it was obvious to anyone with half a brain that all three of the victims had been killed in a similar way. It was all there in the evidence; she had laid everything out for them in the file. What was all this nonsense about copycats?

'Precisely,' said the judge. 'In precisely the same way that you've invited us to consider that there is some other person, other than your client, who committed all three murders. Is that not also speculation?'

Sam watched Ashley. To everyone else's eyes, she was certain he looked composed and unflustered; but, because she was looking for it, she noticed a momentary hesitation in his answer and detected a twinge of uncertainty.

'It is not entirely speculative, my lord, because of the similarities between the methods of killing. Also, in each case, the necklaces offer a trademark or signature,' Ashley insisted.

'But only one of the victims wore a rosary. The other two wore pearl necklaces, which is very different,' Elford said thoughtfully.

It was now the turn of the judge sitting on Lord Justice Raleigh's right. His face was flushed and Sam thought he looked like a dried-up old strawberry.

'You have put your case very succinctly and we are indebted to you for clarity of your submissions. Apart from your client's assertions of innocence, do you have any additional evidence to submit in this case. For example, forensic evidence, any independent eyewitness?' Mr Justice Longhurst asked, raising his eyebrows.

'No,' said Ashley.

'Well, do you have anything more?'

'No, my lord,' said Ashley. 'But, my lord, the similarities between the three murders is such that the only logical conclusion must be that they were committed by the same person,' he reiterated staunchly.

'So you say,' interjected Lord Justice Raleigh. 'I think we have your point. Unless you have a further argument to submit?'

'The Crown submitted at trial that the single pearl came from Leticia Joy's rosary and they speculated that my client put it in her pocket as some kind of trophy. That proposition is blown sky high by my expert's evidence,' Ashley said, not liking this turn of questioning. Mr Goldman had sounded extremely convincing to him. He was frustrated to detect continued scepticism from the three appeal judges.

'Not quite sky high, Mr Towers,' Lord Justice Raleigh said moderately.

'My lord, if the bead wasn't from the same necklace, at the very least this suggests it's entirely incidental as a piece of evidence. However, it does also suggest that it could have been planted on my client by the real killer . . .' Ashley was getting a little desperate now.

'Again, Mr Towers, you have no proof of this. It's speculation on your behalf. But as always, you have put your case very clearly. We'll retire for a moment.'

Roma turned to Lydia Watson, who was looking even more smug than usual.

'Looks like we've won,' he said.

'I always knew we would,' she replied with that same grim confidence she always exuded.

Ashley gave a wry look to Sam at the back of the court. This did not look good. If the court had accepted his arguments, they would have called on Roma to reply. In his experience, a compliment from court usually meant you had lost. Lord Justice Raleigh was merely pacifying him in praising his technique. But maybe they would ask Roma to respond after they had deliberated a little. All was not lost.

A mere five minutes later they were back in their seats.

'We don't need to trouble you, Mr Roma,' said Lord Justice Raleigh.

Ashley's heart dropped. The senior judge started delivering the judgement of the court. He was reading from notes, but during the proceedings Sam had noticed that, while Ashley had been addressing them, none of the three judges had written down a single thing. The lead judge was now reading from notes he must have had with him before the hearing began. They had clearly all made up their minds even before the appeal was heard.

Sam smiled uneasily at Icey. Her friend look confused by what was happening, and Sam could hardly bear to think how she must be feeling.

Mr Justice Raleigh recited the basic facts. 'It is submitted by Mr Towers that similarities between this murder and two later ones, which occurred while the applicant was in custody, are so great that they must be the work of a single person who cannot be the applicant. There are indeed a number of marked similarities, but Mr Roma's argument that these were the work of a copycat killer has force. The religious overtones of each of the killings initially troubled the court. As did the statement that, in all three murders, either a rosary or a string of pearls was found on or by the victim. The Crown at trial invited the jury to consider that a pearl found on the applicant had come from the victim's rosary. Given the coincidences between the various murders, we thought it right to explore every avenue that might assist the applicant. As a result, we allowed Mr Towers to call fresh evidence.'

Sam leant forward to make sure she did not miss a thing. Her right hand moved frantically across the page as she took notes.

The judge continued. 'Today we have heard illuminating evidence from a leading expert on pearls, who has told us that the single pearl was of a different origin from those in the broken rosary. He was not, however, able to totally exclude the possibility that the single pearl did in fact come from the rosary. In the end, all the points that Mr Towers so ably made have an element of speculation in them. We have to set this speculation against the overwhelming evidence heard by the jury at the original trial.' He paused for emphasis. 'The applicant was found at the scene of the crime by the police with the murder weapon in her hand, blood from the victim on her clothing and a pearl in her pocket, which at the very least might have come from the victim's rosary. Mr Towers couldn't point to anyone else in the vicinity that could have committed this terrible murder. In conclusion, we are all convinced that this conviction was safe. The application for leave to appeal is dismissed. There is no appeal against sentence, Mr Towers?'

'No, my lord,' Ashley said dolefully.

'Thank you for your assistance,' Lord Justice Raleigh said formally.

Sam's gaze flew to Icey, who looked shocked and devastated, realisation of what was happening finally sinking in. It was like déjà vu, the original trial all over again. Sam stared at the judges in disbelief. 'What did he say?' she asked Mr Frizzel, her heart thumping in her chest. The judges rose to leave the court. 'What did he say?' she asked again, only louder this time.

'Is there a problem?' asked Lord Justice Raleigh, catching drift of Sam's words.

'No, my lord,' said Ashley, a little nervously.

'What do you mean, no, my bloody lord?' said Sam angrily, standing up.

Mr Frizzel stared at her, not sure what to do, but moving at once to her side. She had a point, so when Ashley indicated that he should hush Sam down, Frizzel ignored him and let her continue.

'I do have a problem,' Sam said loudly. 'You all made your minds up before you came into court. Not one of you took a single note during this session. You are the custodians of justice in this country. Did you not think that, when someone is serving life, the least that they should expect is that due consideration will be given to their appeal?' she said passionately.

The court clerk picked up the phone and asked for security.

'That is very observant of you,' said Lord Justice Raleigh, unruffled, 'but whether we wrote our notes before or after is completely irrelevant. We considered all the arguments. The appeal is dismissed.'

Lord Justice Raleigh had a way of putting people down in the politest way possible. His nickname was the Silent Assassin. It was, however, well known that the judges did sometimes make their minds up well before the actual appeal hearing. Sam was not necessarily wide of the mark in her accusations.

The three judges solemnly passed through the green curtain hanging over the exit from the Bench and disappeared. Sam shouted after them.

'You should all be ashamed of yourselves. You make a mockery of our system of justice!'

She was so furious that she really did not care if they locked her up there and then.

Chapter Ninety-Five

Ashley and Sam walked back down the steps to the great hall in silence. Both were too shocked to talk. Around them crowds jostled, and Ashley moved them quickly down the stairs. Mr Frizzel was nowhere to be seen.

Sam was still fuming, but she also felt deflated and defeated. As she got to the bottom of the stairs, she began to cry. She had let Icey down. The thought of her best friend having to go back to prison made her feel dizzy with anger, and she couldn't stop the tears from falling. She was also angry with herself. Maybe she hadn't done enough; if she had, Icey would now be free. The realisation was like a punch to the stomach.

Unsure of what to do, Ashley patted her shoulders and told her to wait while he went to the cells to see Icey. He wanted to hug Sam, but thought it would look unprofessional in the Courts of Justice.

The result of the appeal was not what he had expected. It had seemed to be going so well, too. Although Sam's outburst should not have happened, she had been right. The judges had indeed made their minds up before they came in. He knew it. They had kicked Icey around the court and then left her to the mercy of the odious Alfred Roma. And that bastard had not even had the courage to express in court the concerns he'd raised in private.

Every time they had discussed the case, Roma was full of

'Oh, dear boy, your client will be out by lunchtime,' when all the time the double-crossing toad knew that he never had a single intention of expressing any view other than complete support for the original conviction. One day very soon, Ashley Towers would get his revenge on his learned friend. Ashley never lost cases, and Roma had made him look like a tit.

Ashley soon discovered that, as a result of an earlier security incident, visits to the cell area had been suspended. A guy had tried to top himself with a necktie as a result of a knockback on his own appeal. Consequently, Ashley returned to Sam a lot quicker than she expected. Mr Frizzel met them and the solicitor hovered in the background, unsure of what to do.

Sam had also hoped to see Icey but it clearly wasn't to be. She wanted to give her a hug and tell her that, for as long as she had breath in her body, she would continue to work to free her. Instead of being able to comfort her friend, however, she now found herself loitering in the hallway, too stunned to decide what to do next.

She looked to Ashley, hoping for inspiration. He handed her an envelope. 'This is for you,' he said, coolly. 'Icey gave it to me earlier, in case we lost. She said that you should read it when you're on your own.'

Taking the envelope from his hands, Sam glanced at Ashley's face and assessed the barrister's mood. Ashley, normally so arrogant and controlled, seemed genuinely upset that he had lost the appeal. Even if his agitation was simply due to the fact that he now had a blemish on his otherwise spotless track record of victory, it was still reassuring to know that he cared on some level. She looked down at the envelope before tucking it into her handbag, feeling her heart sink as she pondered its contents, and then looked back at Ashley with a grateful expression. He had done his best for them, she knew that.

Sam wiped her eyes and took a deep breath to steady her nerves. She was no use to Icey sniffling by the steps to the court. 'Where do we go from here? What exactly do we have to do to get the conviction overturned?' she said briskly, trying to rally herself.

'I am afraid that this is the end of the line, Miss Bailey, unless we can find some new evidence,' Ashley said quietly.

'I don't accept that,' said Sam, and turned to stride off towards the exit. If she had to do this on her own, she would, she vowed to herself.

As she stormed out of the building onto the Strand, with Ashley and Frizzel trailing in her wake, she was caught in a blaze of flashing cameras and surrounded by a crowd of journalists who knew she was associated with the defendant.

'Look this way please, miss. This way!' they called out. Sam composed herself. It was important for Icey and for the credibility of their agency that she put on a brave face and look professional at all times. Nodding severely and staring into the cameras, she was glad that she had decided to use a waterproof mascara that morning.

'Any comment?' asked a reporter, as he thrust a mike in her direction.

'No comment,' said Ashley, swiftly and smoothly coming to her aid. Sam was glad to have him next to her; she was even grateful for Mr Frizzel's presence on her other side.

'No comment,' the solicitor echoed, firmly.

'I have a comment,' said Sam, making a sudden decision. 'Today the Court of Appeal refused to allow the appeal of Icey – I mean, Elizabeth Johnson.' Her voice carried clearly and the reporters followed every word with excitement at the prospect of a juicy quote. 'They said that the conviction is safe, but there is a mountain of evidence to show that it is not. They had made their minds up even before they heard the evidence,' she declared heatedly. 'This day marks a low point in our justice system. But this case will not go away. We will continue to fight to clear the name of Elizabeth Johnson,' she said, her voice ringing out across the crowd.

With her head held high but her spirits low, Sam walked down the steps of the High Court. Ashley Towers and Frizzel were left fighting through the cameras, and Sam did not pause to wait for them. She needed to be on her own to collect her thoughts and plan her next move.

She crossed purposefully over the road and walked back the short distance to Fleet Investigations. As she opened the door, the aroma of the flowers overpowered her.

'Welcome, welcome!' cried Oriel and Flick as they ran through from the back of the office. They fell silent when they realised that Sam was alone.

Sam looked around. The exquisite patisseries were beautifully laid out at the reception counter, and Irma's girls had arranged the flowers in vases that Sam did not recognise. She felt tears in her eyes.

'They refused the appeal. They said that the conviction was safe,' she explained quickly and succinctly to the girls. 'So we've got no reason to celebrate at all. We need to get down to work on the next stage of clearing Icey's name. But let's not let this delicious food go to waste. Let's have a drink and some cake, and we'll start again tomorrow, OK?' she said, determined to remain positive. At Sam's urging, they opened the champagne and Sam poured herself a glass. She asked the women to raise their glasses to Icey.

'Let's drink to her eventual release, and may the Court of Appeal judges rot in their mouldy beds.'

Flick and Oriel glanced at each other and then joined in the toast. Flick then offered a toast of her own: 'To Icey, soon may you be free.'

After demolishing some of the cakes and a second bottle of wine, Flick and Oriel sensed that Sam needed to be on her own, so at just after six the girls left.

Helping herself to some more champagne, Sam pulled Icey's letter out of her bag.

> *Dear Sam*
>
> *You have been the best friend that I could ever have. You stood by me when we both knew that I was in the wrong, and always when I was in the right. Your commitment to me is worth a thousand angels. Thank you.*
>
> *There is, however, just one more thing that I would like you to do for me. Please forget about me. Get on with your life. There's no justice for the likes of us. I no longer wish to be the unbearable burden that I have clearly become.*
>
> *Yours for ever.*
>
> *Love,*
>
> *Icey*

Sam was appalled. Far from being touched by Icey's affection and determination to save her from trouble, all she could feel was anger at her best friend. Icey was spineless. Instead of fighting her corner, she had crawled into a little hole to lick her wounds. Well, she wasn't going to get rid of Sam that easily – and she would get a piece of her mind when Sam next visited.

Scrunching up the note, she threw it into the bin and reached for the phone to call Harry Kemp. She knew she'd hit rock bottom and needed all the help she could get.

Chapter Ninety-Six

Icey was handcuffed to a new screw as she was led out the back of the High Court building into the rear holding area. She was still trying to get her head around what the judge had said when they turned down her appeal. She was not in shock. She felt nothing. There was one type of justice for the rich, and another for the likes of her. Had she really expected to walk out of court a free woman? She should have known better.

While she was waiting for the meat wagon to reverse, she counted the women in the van. There had been fourteen on arrival and there were fourteen returning. All had got a knock back. What did it take to win an appeal in this place? It seemed innocence was not nearly enough.

It took over an hour to get back to Holloway. The receptionist greeted her cheerfully, as if she'd been expecting her.

'Back so soon?' she stated. 'Well, at least you had a nice day out. I have a number of questions I need to ask you and that you are required to answer. Who is your next of kin?'

'Sam Bailey,' Icey replied tiredly.

'Are you on medication?'

'No.'

'Are you suicidal?'

'No.'

'I am sorry to have to ask the questions again, but it has to be gone through every time a prisoner is booked in. I also have to tell you that we have a service here called Listeners. They are like the Samaritans and are completely discreet, if you need someone to talk to.'

'Yes.'

'Now, do you want the good news?

'What?'

'You're off to Barbados. You've been re-allocated.'

For the first time, Icey looked the woman in the eyes and smiled weakly. 'I have always wanted to go there. I guess this is my lucky day.'

'This one is for Barbados L2R14, any takers?'

'Follow me,' said Beryl, one of the prison officers, as she walked off with the paperwork.

Icey did as she was told. She knew where Barbados was. It was next to Jamaica, where Sandra and Jean were. Maybe there were such things as silver linings; small ones, perhaps, but still in prison every tiny piece of good news was to be welcomed. It was a good wing to be on, most of the women there were mules and were relatively happy people in unhappy circumstances. Winding their way through the back corridors full of chipped wood and peeling paint, she tried to stop feeling sorry for herself. She needed to keep her chin up and her head down and serve her time.

But as Beryl came to a halt outside one door, checking the number against her list, Icey felt faint as she watched the prison officer turn the key in the lock. She closed her eyes and leant against the grimy corridor wall. She had to force her legs to carry her into the cell – at least she seemed to have this one to herself – and to the narrow bed, where she collapsed and curled herself up in a ball, blocking out the noise of the door being locked once again.

Her mind was working overtime trying yet again to

remember the night of Leticia Joy's murder. But still it was all a blank. She remembered Sam dropping her off at the church; she remembered the good-looking priest. She'd been drinking a lot in the weeks before the murder. She'd tried to hide it from Sam, but it had been getting worse. Even so, she'd been determined to quit – and to make a fresh start with Sam and the business. She badly wanted to go straight, quit drinking, quit whoring, all of it. Icey remembered longing to wipe the slate clean, but her stepfather's death still weighed heavily on her. Even if Jack Billings had deserved to be punished for what he had done to her as a girl, his death was still a stain on her immortal soul. As a dead man he haunted her dreams as much as he ever had when he was alive.

She'd gone to the church seeking solace. She wasn't sure whether she had intended to tell Father Luke what she had done. Had she told Father Luke about Jack Billings? That was one of the many things about that night she simply didn't remember. She thought she'd stayed in the church to pray, but she couldn't be sure. She remembered flashes from time to time of a figure attacking a young woman. She thought it was the killer attacking Leticia Joy, but, as with everything else, she couldn't be sure of it.

Had she really seen it or was it wishful thinking on her behalf? Whatever the case, the rest of that night was a blur. The more Icey tried to remember, the more it escaped her. And she only had herself to blame.

Chapter Ninety-Seven

On Monday morning, while Paradissimo was preoccupied with the appeal trial of Elizabeth Johnson, DC Anne Cody was on an early shift with DC Haydn. She'd agreed to accompany him to interview Margaret Certie in the hope that a female copper might get more out of the judge's widow than Haydn had been able to on his own. However, on their way to Mrs Certie's house, they were diverted to an emergency incident at the back of Brixton market. A member of the public had reported seeing a man running away with blood pouring from a wound on his arm. Gunshots were thought to have been exchanged. The Tactical Firearms Unit had arrived before Cody and Haydn, and the whole area had been cordoned off before they reached the scene. It was alleged that one of the two men had run into an abandoned building at the back of Railton Road, which ran adjacent to the railway line.

After a response and a standoff of seven hours, the police went in. The area was bombarded with tear gas in order to encourage the occupier to surrender, but it was in vain. Although he had entered the building, he'd left well before the Tactical Firearms Unit had arrived. While the fresh blood marks confirmed that someone was bleeding heavily, it did not necessarily support the various members of the public's assertions that he'd had a firearm. He had, in any event, escaped out the back and then across the railway line. It was clear that, whatever fate had befallen him, he didn't want to involve the police. The TFU retreated and went home. After their long and exhausting day, Haydn and Cody decided to leave Mrs Certie for the following morning.

On Tuesday they drove to the Certie family home in Chelsea. Haydn parked the car several streets away and they made their way on foot along Old Church Street, and then turned right. It was nearly midday and the sun was high in the sky. The townhouse was a very neat and tidy building on the outside, with a smart black door and polished brass. Cody rang the doorbell and waited. The curtains were drawn and they heard the bell echo at the back of the house. Cody rang again. DC Haydn moved forward and stretched over the railings to look through the basement window. The room was reasonably tidy. Cody rang the bell again and waited, but there was still no movement inside.

Bending down, Cody opened the letterbox and peered through. On the first step leading up the stairs was a bottle of brandy. It had tipped over and stained the dusty blue carpet that lined the stairs and the hall. The door to the rear rooms of the house was closed, as was the door leading to the front drawing room. Immediately below the letterbox on the hall floor, junk mail had piled up. There were at least a dozen letters, Cody could see.

'She's not in,' Cody said to Haydn. 'Looks like she might have gone away.'

Cody rang the doorbell again and took a closer look at the drawing room through the front window. There was something not quite right. She had a feeling in her gut and as a general rule her gut instincts were usually right, at least when it came to her cases.

'We could knock up the neighbours and ask them when they

last saw her?' Haydn suggested, and moved to the door to the left of Mrs Certie's house. Cody took the door on the right. Both knocked and waited. There was no reply on Cody's side. DC Haydn had better luck – he heard a noise from within, and the door was eventually opened. An Asian lady answered; she was dressed in an old-fashioned apron and a headscarf.

'Are you the owner of this house, madam?' enquired Haydn.

'She not here, I'm cleaner,' came the response, in broken English.

'Do you know when she might be back?' Haydn was joined on the doorstep by Cody.

'She gone for now. No back till later, I tell her you call.' She eyed Haydn and Cody suspiciously.

'Do you work here? At the house?' Haydn asked.

'Yes, I work.'

'Every day?'

'Every day.'

'We are making some enquiries about the lady who lives next door – Mrs Certie – have you seen her?'

'Yes, I see her all the time.'

'Have you seen her recently?' Haydn asked, to clarify.

'Yes. She gone out, come back later.'

'When did you last see her?' he persisted.

'All the time. She very sad. She gone out now. You come back later.'

'Thank you very much. We are sorry to have disturbed you.'

'OK,' replied the woman as she was shutting the door.

'Excuse me,' blurted out Cody just before the door closed. It swung open again. 'You say that you saw her recently, but she hasn't picked up her mail. When was the last time you actually saw her?'

'I see her all the time,' repeated the cleaner.

'Is there a way round to the back of the house?' Cody asked, growing frustrated with this line of questioning. 'How do we get access to the garden?'

'No access.'

'Well, thank you,' said Cody, admitting defeat. 'I am sorry to have troubled you.'

As the door closed, Cody went back to the front door of Mrs Certie's house and rang the bell again. She waited and then, looking through the letterbox one more time, she took a breath and realised at once exactly what she was missing. It was faint but present all the same: the smell of death.

'Give me a hand,' she shouted to Haydn as she braced her shoulder against the door. It didn't move, not a fraction. Real police work was seldom like the movies. Mrs Certie's door was bolted firmly into position. Haydn, meanwhile, had found that one of the basement windows was slightly ajar. He jumped the railing to take a closer look, and Cody could tell by his face that the news was not good. Pulling her phone from her pocket, she tapped in a number.

'I am at the Certies' house and we need someone to break the door down. I have a feeling that we are too late . . . But it might be a good idea to have an ambulance standing by just in case,' she requested.

As Cody ended the call, she bent down and looked again through the letterbox. Haydn came back to join her. 'Smell's worse down there. Can't see anything but I suspect we'll find she's been dead for a while,' he said sadly.

They found Mrs Certie's body lying on the kitchen floor. The timeline of her death was difficult to establish until the post mortem had been performed. Further questioning of the neighbour's cleaner established that she'd actually not seen her for a week. The forensic entomologist was more precise in his calculations. Examining the various bugs and insects in Mrs Certie's corpse, he was able to establish the minimum possible age of the oldest maggots that were taken from the body. He concluded that they were around six days old. In light of the evidence, the pathologist concluded that she died six days earlier, and the cause of death was a combination of alcohol poisoning and an overdose of paracetamol. The most probable explanation was suicide.

As a matter of routine, Haydn had contacted British Telecom to establish when Mrs Certie had received and made her last telephone calls. The last call was made from the house seven days earlier and the last call received was tellingly on the day they estimated Mrs Certie had taken the pills. Both the number dialled and the last number to call Mrs Certie were the same. The number was that of Fleet Investigations, co-owned by Sam Bailey.

Haydn shared this information with Cody and was surprised by her agitated reaction to the name. Why would Mrs Certie make and receive a telephone call to Fleet Investigations and then kill herself. Cody wondered. Sam Bailey's name kept popping up in their investigations, and it was making Cody increasingly nervous.

Chapter Ninety-Eight

It was several days before Sam had the heart to go back to the office. The day after Icey's appeal was refused, Harry Kemp turned up on her doorstep at home with take-out coffee and an offer of as much help and advice as he could give. He'd taken a leave of absence from his job as a probation officer – he was at Sam's service for as long as it took to get Icey free.

Gratefully, Sam let him in and together they started the laborious task of going through the court records again and again, looking for the slightest thing they might have overlooked. Harry had been in touch with his old colleagues around the country, but while there were plenty of unsolved murders, none of the cold cases seemed to fit with the three recent deaths in London.

On the third day, he insisted they decamp back to Fleet Investigations, and Harry held an early morning conference to set out their tasks for the day ahead. He refused to let Sam mope, even when she learnt that Icey was making good her threat to cut off all ties with her and was refusing visitors. Harry also seemed to take the presence of Oriel and Flick in his stride, and was soon including them in his efforts to help Sam keep the agency running. Oriel he set to work answering phones and, on learning that Flick had trained as an accountant, he set her the task of sorting out the company's finances. Sam had already been giving them modest payment, but now she increased their wages to reflect their extra time and commitment. She couldn't do without them.

She couldn't do without Harry, either. She was glad that she'd taken him up on his earlier offer to invest in the business. She continued to have a stream of new clients, and she was pleased with the increasing income. But the agency had large overheads, and she needed Harry's financial input. She also needed his help, she recognised, and she was happily surprised that he wasn't just acting like a sleeping partner. Sam was beyond grateful that Harry had stepped up to take a hands-on approach, even if it was only temporary during his leave of absence. With Oriel and Flick running the office, she and Harry could concentrate on taking on what clients they could easily manage, all the while keeping a firm hand on finding grounds for a fresh appeal for Icey. They were a team, and Sam liked how that felt.

Under Harry's tutelage, Sam was even starting to enjoy the work, even if it was mostly low-level surveillance on behalf of jealous spouses. She discovered she could be good at fading into the background, once Harry had got her to tone down her wardrobe a little, at least on nights when she was supposed to be unobtrusive. At times, Sam even felt guilty to be getting on with business while Icey was still serving life, but Harry was her rock whenever she faltered. He convinced her that, for Icey's sake as much as her own, she had to make a go of things.

Harry was also keeping his ear to the ground as regards to the two active murder investigations. He'd been impressed when Sam had told him of the way she'd managed to glean most of the coroner's findings via Flick and Oriel's charm offensive on Determination George, but he preferred his own methods of going for a drink with his old contacts in the Met.

'Besides,' he joked with Sam, 'I don't think my powers of persuasion are really up to that of your girls.'

By the end of the first week after the failed appeal, Flick had cut a swathe through the agency's paperwork and was standing by Sam's desk holding a bunch of receipts. She asked if Sam wanted them to be deducted from the monthly expenses. She had found an envelope of receipts on a shelf, and presumed it was Sam's way of collating her expenses on their ongoing cases, but she didn't know how to work out which case to assign them to.

Sam picked up a pink receipt from the top of the pile and looked at it blankly. It was vaguely familiar and she tried to remember where it had come from, but she had no idea. It was stamped 'For services rendered' and there was no company name on the bill. At first she thought that it might have been a non-office expense, but the total was five hundred pounds, which was rather a lot of money for her to have forgotten spending it. And then she looked at the envelope where Flick said she'd found the receipts, and she remembered. Mrs Certie had given them to her.

'It's funny, though,' said Flick idly.

'What is?'

'Well, the only person I know that gives out pink receipts with no company name is Irma.'

'Really? In my day they used to be blue . . .' Sam trailed off, thoughts suddenly clicking into place.

'No, this year she's gone for pink,' Flick said, before Sam grabbed the envelope out of her hand.

She began sorting eagerly through the piles of bills. As she worked through them, she noted that Flick had already sorted the bills into piles by month and in each 'monthly' pile a pink receipt for five hundred pounds plus sat proudly on the top. Sam picked up the phone and dialled a number.

'May I speak to Mrs Certie?' she enquired.

'Who is speaking?'

'Sam. My name is Sam Bailey. I came to see her some time ago and I promised that I would check in on her again,' she said, crossing her fingers against the little white lie.

'She's not available,' said the lady anxiously at the other end of the phone.

'Can I leave a message and perhaps she can call me back?'

'That will not be possible. I'm afraid she died a short while ago. I'm her daughter, Maria. Can I help you?'

Sam let out a gasp as she held the receiver close to her ear. Mrs Certie's words echoed in her head. 'We both have something in common. I have lost a husband . . . you have lost your friend.'

'I am so sorry to hear that – and for your loss. May I ask, what did she die of?'

'Well, we are not sure. The doctor said she'd been drinking and she'd taken rather a lot of paracetamol . . . But after my father's death, my brother James and I are convinced she died of a broken heart. How did you know my mother?'

'I . . .' Sam thought quickly. 'I knew your father and your mother. I saw her not that long ago. I'm shocked. When's the funeral?' she asked, genuinely upset at what had happened to Margaret Certie. She had struck Sam as a sad figure, and she'd felt sorry for her.

'It's already taken place. Yesterday, in fact. If there's nothing else . . .'

'I am very sorry to have troubled you,' Sam said sincerely.

She hung up the phone and called Madam Irma, who confirmed, after checking her books, that Judge Certie had indeed been a regular client.

'Mostly he liked to meet the girls in a hotel but occasionally he came to me,' said Irma. 'I was sad to learn of his death – he was a good customer over the years. Vanilla tastes, no trouble whatsoever. But what's it got to do with our Icey?'

Sam explained that Certie had been the judge in Icey's original trial; that he was the one who'd sent her to prison. She also expressed how she was sure that wasn't the whole story. But she *wasn't* sure what the rest of it was, yet. What could possibly be the connection between a dead judge with a hooker habit and Icey being convicted of murder? It was a shame she and Mrs Certie had never got to discuss it.

Chapter Ninety-Nine

Mr Frizzel was sitting inside his office. In front of him was a pile of papers – the latest case he had been working on. The office had the fresh smell of lavender with a touch of disinfectant. He was unusually upbeat.

After the second arrival of the bailiffs, when he had reluctantly signed over the lease to Sam, he was pleased that the fear of eviction was now gone for ever. But he was no longer his own boss. Sam had reorganised his office. Gone were the dark blinds that had obscured his excessive drinking. The empty alcohol bottles were gone, too. Sam had insisted that he now keep regular hours and he had been banned from sleeping on the table. Even so, as his new landlady, he sensed she was trying to keep out of his way and give him a modicum of independence. Frizzel was also aware that Harry Kemp was now in Sam's office on a daily basis. While the ex-detective hadn't said anything to him yet, he had a sense that Harry was just waiting for Frizzel to step out of line so he could slap him down.

Ashley Towers was moving on to other cases. He had done everything he possibly could on behalf of Elizabeth Johnson and it was not his fault the appeal had failed. He was as the end of the legal process and there was nothing he could do apart from refer the case to the Criminal Cases' Review Commission. He was not at all sure that they would even consider it. The more he thought about it, the more he convinced himself that the jury got the right verdict. The subsequent murders may have cast a shadow of suspicion, but they did not render the conviction unsafe. Reminding himself of this, he felt a whole lot better that the court had come to the decision they had.

Paradissimo and Cody were still dealing with their two ongoing murder investigations, but with no real leads about the deaths of Martha Lewis and Pia Broom to follow up on.

One night, Cody persuaded Paradissimo to join her for a drink in the Tudor. 'We work well as team,' she said as she rested her hand on his thigh. Her illusions about Paradissimo had been significantly tarnished lately, but she still found something about him irresistible. Maybe he was worth another chance.

'Sometimes,' Paradissimo said cautiously.

'I think we should celebrate,' she suggested coyly.

'Celebrate what?'

'The fact that we are good together.'

'Go on. What have you got in mind?'

'Supper.'

Paradissimo hesitated and studied Cody's face; maybe it was time for him to forget Sam Bailey. 'You're on. Where and when?'

'Supper at my place, soon as, and I won't not take no for an answer.'

Icey was still refusing to see Sam. It was not that she blamed her – far from it – but she meant what she'd said in her letter. It was better for Sam if they cut all contact. Even so, by the end of the week after the appeal, Icey began to fall ill. She couldn't sleep, couldn't face food. She felt lethargic, depressed and continually anxious.

It was a well-known fact that women in prison were more susceptible to illness than male inmates. Non-emergency medical appointments were available on Tuesdays and Fridays. Icey booked the next available slot and found herself sent to the sick bay. A psychiatrist was called out to assess whether she was suffering from a psychotic episode; in short, a mental breakdown. But he diagnosed depression and prescribed Icey pills that she refused to take. One of the few benefits of being inside was that Icey had been sober for months; she didn't want to start back down on the slippery slope of addiction. Unfortunately, this refusal marked her out as a troublemaker as far as the shrink was concerned. He decided to teach her a lesson and referred her to a second psychiatrist, threatening her with being sectioned under the Mental Health Act. He thought this would make her take anti-depressants, but Icey was made of sterner stuff; she still refused and an appointment was made for her to see another shrink in eight days' time.

The rebuilding of Holloway prison in the 1970s was based on the assumption that women in prison have high rates of psychiatric disorder. That defective line of thinking had led to much criticism at the way women prisoners were described as mad rather than bad or devious criminals. It had often led to the needless medicalisation of women prisoners. The resulting backlash meant that appointments for a second psychiatric assessment were often delayed for as long as possible within reason, provided there were no adverse repercussions to the patient.

The second psychiatrist was not as pill happy as the first. He was a brusque, no-nonsense chap who was less than sympathetic with her, though. Icey had no history of mental illness. She was a convicted murderer and it was not unknown for some women facing long stretches in prison to try it on in order to get sent to a 'softer' institution, or even to try to escape en route to a psychiatric hospital. This doctor seemed convinced that he had Icey pegged; nonetheless, she was ordered to remain on the sick bay where she continued to refuse all medication. Her next of kin, Sam Bailey, was informed in writing and by telephone of Icey's mental state. All requests to visit Icey were declined. When Sam complained, she was informed that it was Icey's expressed wish. There was not a great deal Sam could do except write to her every day and encourage her to lift the embargo.

The peace, tranquillity and isolation of the sick bay improved Icey's mental state far more, she believed, than the original shrink's 'happy' pills would have done. Finally, the second psychiatrist, after a period of observation, allowed her back to her wing. When she was well enough, she was placed on light duties. She found herself moved from the kitchen into a new role in the library, ostensibly cataloguing the prison's collection of books and music.

Icey surprised herself by finding enjoyment in her new job. It gave her the opportunity to listen to music she'd never been exposed to before. Previously she had joined in the music appreciation classes simply to get out of her cell for a while. Now she was discovering a genuine love of music. She found a classical piece called 'The Lark Ascending' by Vaughan Williams. Somehow, the soaring violins gave her hope, as if one day she too might soar above the prison walls with the birds. To her, it expressed freedom; a life without incarceration. In her head and heart, she was free at last or had, at the very least, made peace with her current situation.

Chapter One Hundred

Poppy Withers was in no mood to be reasonable as she stepped out of the underground station into the pouring rain. With no umbrella to protect her, her short black hair was soon sticking to the sides of her face, and she had to squint her eyes against the harshness of the wind. Her pretty short dress provided no protection, either, and she hugged her thin raincoat tightly around her body.

It was a Wednesday night – a work night – and she would rather have been home on the sofa watching trashy television. But her best friend, Fergie – Louise Fergurson – had rung in distress about the break-up of yet another relationship. Poppy did the only thing a friend could: she offered to meet her for a drink.

Shillings Wine Bar was on the corner of Essex Street and Fleet Street. It was full. She'd had to squeeze her way past the usual crowd spilling out onto the pavement. Inside were the forever lonely and the soon-to-be coupled-up brigade, and the lights were down low as candles flickered on the tables.

Poppy had spotted her friend in the mirror to the left of the bar. Fergie had stood up and waved Poppy towards her. She had clearly been drinking for some time. Her make-up was already smudged. Her mascara was clotted and the streaky lines down the side of her face told their own story. Fergie had been given the boot earlier in the evening. She had taken this latest rejection very badly. Why could she never keep hold of a man? It had taken two bottles of red wine and a bottle of carbonated water (Poppy had insisted on the latter) to get Fergie to feel sufficiently unburdened. Three hours had passed before Poppy considered that she had done her duty. She had listened and said all of the right things. He wasn't worth it. She would find someone else who really appreciated her. She kissed Fergie goodbye and promised to ring her to let her know she'd got home safely.

Thirty minutes later she was back at the Oval station. Pulling her navy blue raincoat around her slender body, she pulled the collar up against the howling wind. Stepping across the road, Poppy caught her breath as the wind whipped around her legs. At the last minute she crossed the road and slipped through the gap in the fencing of Kennington Park to take a short cut. But as she walked on past the sandpit, Poppy began to get the feeling that she was not alone.

Standing still, she waited. At first, there was no sound apart from the whispering wind and the pitter-patter of the rain on the ground. But then she heard it again: a faint rustle in the bushes, perhaps? Maybe there was a fox or, more likely in London, a rat in the undergrowth. Where was it coming from? Peering into the dark, Poppy didn't get a chance to listen for longer. The noise, she realised, was behind her; but by then it was far too late.

Chapter One Hundred and One

Riva Bell was a self-declared yummy mummy and she was about to meet her fellow mums in the local park for their weekly Thursday meeting. Gathering her two children together, along with Polo the Labrador Retriever, she checked her pockets. When she was sure that she had not forgotten anything – keys, purse, sweets in case the kids got fractious – she closed the door and walked the short distance to Kennington Park. When they had safely crossed the road, the children ran ahead. The One O'clock Club was an informal group that met – weather permitting – by the sandpit in the park. Here, while their assorted kids played, the happy mothers discussed world events, which normally centred around an update on the latest gossip about the unfortunate affairs of the not-so-happy mothers. Cassandra, the blonde, was already there, as were Bluebell and Grace.

Luckily, the weather today was fine. Although it was well into March, it wasn't too cold and Riva's daughter, Mandy, was the first into the pit, followed by the other children. They began to fill their buckets with sand. Jumping up and down to level the sand, Mandy fell slightly to the left. There seemed to be something under the sand, which made her lose her balance, especially in her new wellies that she insisted on wearing everywhere. Brushing off her knees, she walked back to the spot where she had taken that fall, and jumped again. Riva Bell watched her determined daughter with a smile as once again she lost her balance. But this time she did not get up. With her small hands she swept away the sand directly in front of her. Polo let out a bark and then began to whimper as he joined Mandy in the pit. Mandy suddenly stopped digging and stood up as the dog began to paw wildly at the sand.

Riva looked on with increasing horror as she walked towards her daughter and saw that the sand was red. The young mums began to usher their children away in a panic. Frantically, Riva grabbed Mandy's hands and pulled her tightly against her own body, but Polo refused to leave. He continued barking and scratching until Riva had to physically lift him out of the pit. A park attendant arrived and called the authorities before he secured the area. He knew he should wait for the police, but instinct prevailed and he fell to his knees and started to dig with his bare hands in the unlikely event that the poor creature buried in the sand could somehow be saved by his efforts.

DC Cody and DCI Paradissimo were in the office, catching up on recent events. A major player in a drug ring had been caught after years of avoiding detection, and Paradissimo was personally delighted. Cody was feeling smug, too, even though she had nothing to be smug about. Her date with Paradissimo had yet to happen. She hoped it was just a matter of timing – they were both busy with cases, albeit that they'd had little in terms of real breakthroughs in either of their active murder investigations. The killer hadn't left much behind by way of forensic evidence – no fingerprints, no DNA, nothing.

As regards to Leticia Joy, she and Paradissimo had long since dismissed any thought of responsibility for Icey's incarceration. She was history. The Court of Appeal had said it was all OK, so OK it was. When, however, they got the call about the body in Kennington Park, they both had a certain feeling of foreboding. The sensation of dread washed over them in a wave that knocked them sideways.

Walking through St Angus Place, past a gaggle of traumatised mothers and children – a subdued One O' Clock Club gathering – they approached the sandpit area of the children's playground. A patrol car was already on the scene and officers were putting up tapes round the crucial area. The head and part of the neck of a young woman protruded from the sand. Putting on gloves – although it seemed that the crime scene had already been severely compromised – Cody placed a finger on the side of the woman's neck, and ascertained that she was definitely dead and had probably been so for some time. The rest of her body was not yet visible, and, tempting though it was to keep digging, Cody waited for the SOCO boys to arrive.

As she waited, Paradissimo approached her from the left. A gust of wind blew a sliver of sand from the woman's neck, exposing what Cody had first presumed was the beginning of a necklace. It was not. She could now see clearly that it was, in fact, a rosary. Cody felt sick. As she reached forward, she stumbled. A flood of nausea engulfed her. She closed her eyes. When she eventually opened them, she looked over in the direction of the approaching Paradissimo. He had moved closer towards the sandpit but all of his focus was on the victim's neck. 'I guess I'm not seeing things,' he said at last. 'Just tell me . . . Is it broken?' he asked Cody quietly.

Cody looked carefully and realised that it was. She started to count the beads. Like any good Catholic, she knew that every rosary was made up of sixty beads. The necklace was broken in the middle and as she counted it looked to her as if the eleventh bead was missing, leaving a gap on the string. 'You can't tell me now that this isn't the work of the same killer,' she began, but Paradissimo's wounded look silenced her. It was clear he was haunted by the same thoughts.

The SOCO boys arrived just before the ambulance. Life was pronounced extinct at the scene. A forensic tent was erected over the sandpit and the whole area was fully sealed off. A handbag was found nearby, and it seemed reasonable to suppose that it had belonged to the victim; from its contents, the woman was identified as Poppy Withers.

Cody stayed semi-slumped against a tree as the crime scene photographer took his final roll of film before the body was transported to the morgue. The news would break in the press almost immediately, and she was not looking forward to that. Not one little bit.

Chapter One Hundred and Two

Sam heard a rumour about Poppy Withers' death before the news broke officially. Daniel Giles, the reporter, had called her and told her there had been another murder. She called Harry to let him know, and together they watched the early evening news on a television in her office.

A young woman had been found brutally murdered in a similar way to the three previous female victims in the London area over the last year. Significantly, a rosary had been found around her neck. Her body had been discovered in a sandpit in Kennington Park by local children.

Sam watched thoughtfully, and then turned to Harry. 'How many more before they release Icey?' she asked simply.

'We need to look into this,' Harry said calmly. 'Why don't I head over to Kennington and see what I can find out?' He hoped he might run into someone he'd known on the force; someone willing to talk to him for old time's sake for the price of a pint or a coffee.

Sam nodded her agreement. 'I'll call Towers,' she called after him, as Harry headed out of the door. She hurried over to the phone and picked it up, muting the sound on the television as she did so.

Ashley Towers was in the conference room on the ground floor when the phone rang. He was surprised to hear Sam Bailey's voice at the other end of the line. It was some weeks since they had last spoken.

'Mr Towers,' said Sam. 'Good afternoon. I am calling because of an item on the news today. Did you get an opportunity to see it?'

Ashley Towers was intrigued but acknowledged ignorance. 'No, I am afraid I've been in meetings all afternoon—'

'There has been another murder,' Sam cut in briskly. 'The body of another young woman was found stabbed to death, this time in Kennington Park.'

'What has that to do with me?' he said flatly.

'Well, they're reporting that she had a rosary round her neck.'

Sam put the phone down and almost immediately it rang. It was Flick. 'Have you seen the news?' she asked without preamble.

'Yes. Harry's gone to Kennington to see what he can find out,' Sam told her. 'I don't want to get my hopes up, but they're saying the killer left a rosary on his victim this time. The police have to see this murder is not only linked to the two previous cases as we've argued in court, but also to Leticia Joy's murder! Flick, now that your little surveillance project is behind you, I think I have another job for you and Oriel . . .'

Chapter One Hundred and Three

Inside the City of Westminster Mortuary, Determination George was unzipping a body bag. DC Anne Cody identified the body as that found in Kennington Park. Cody stayed throughout the examination, together with WPC Claire Wilson as exhibits officer and Mr Nor, George's assistant and photographer. X-rays of the victim's head, torso and upper limbs were taken prior to the examination. George could see that the body was that of a well-nourished young caucasian. She was naked, of slender build, five feet six inches in height. She was lying on her back inside a white plastic body bag. Clear plastic bags currently covered her head and hands to preserve evidence until George was ready to examine her fully.

It was a scene becoming painfully familiar to them all.

George carefully removed the bag covering the victim's head, revealing moderate blood staining inside the bag. She had obviously bled extensively from her injuries. Around her neck, she wore a pale ivory beaded rosary, which was damaged: counting from the right, the eleventh bead was missing. She had been stabbed repeatedly and the manner of the wounds was similar to those of the three female murder victims the police suspected might be connected, and which George had autopsied during the last twelve months.

There were a number of stab wounds on the torso, none of which caused any significant vascular injury. She had an oblique

2.3 centimetre stab wound at the base of the right side of her neck, below the right collarbone, and a series of small puncture wounds in the middle of her upper chest. There was a similar 2.5 centimetre stab wound situated at the top of the right breast, and the fact that George discovered 120 millilitres of blood in the left pleural cavity indicated that this wound was probably inflicted before the fatal wound to the right side of the neck.

It looked like this victim, too, had been tortured before death.

In his report, George noted a total of fifty-five separate stab wounds, including what he presumed at first to be the fatal wound to her neck. A substantial proportion of the wounds were situated on the upper body, particularly around the breasts. She had also been struck at least twice over the head to the region of the right ear.

To George, the most interesting thing about this case was the way her throat had been cut. He surmised that a sharp knife had been drawn from left to right across her neck, severing her carotid artery. It was very similar to the way Leticia Joy had met her death. And at first he concluded that she had bled to death, until he discovered that Poppy Withers had sand in her lungs. He doubted whether she had lasted for long, but she had certainly been breathing when the killer had buried her.

Having sent off all the evidence he'd collected to the lab, a washed and scrubbed Determination George made his way to his local for a quick pint as per his regular routine. As he ordered at the bar, he noticed that his usual table was occupied by the two girls he had met some weeks ago. He smiled warmly at them.

'Come and join us,' said 'Susie' as she moved her coat and patted the seat next to her.

'Goodness me,' said 'Rita', 'we've not seen you for a while. We missed you. I bet you have been busy?'

Determination George smiled and smoothed his hair down. 'I've been extremely busy,' he told them, a touch boastfully.

'Well, all work and no play makes George a dull boy!' teased Rita with a smile. 'What have you been working on?' asked Susie in her charming accent as George took a seat. 'Anything interesting?'

Chapter One Hundred and Four

The weekend papers all carried the same tragic story of Poppy Withers – a sand princess, they called her, resurrected by a group of young children. All carried the story of a serial killer striking again.

A select few of the more liberal papers had begun to make the connection to Leticia Joy's death. Perhaps some diligent journalists had dug up footage of Mr Frizzel's TV interview all those weeks ago, along with reportage of Sam's heated outburst on the steps of the High Court after Icey's failed appeal. If they had, this would certainly have given credence to their theory and encouraged them to express such outrage. A killer was still at large, they protested, while an innocent victim was serving a life sentence for a murder that she had not committed. Sam couldn't have put it better herself. How many more? the headlines asked. In the text below, Sam saw listed the names of the relevant victims: Leticia, Martha, Pia and Poppy; each followed by a question mark.

Sam breathed a sigh of relief. Was the tide beginning to turn in their favour? The girls had told her of George's initial findings. She was pleased that the press were finally catching up with the connection between Poppy Withers and Leticia Joy, and the other two victims. If the newspaper editors were asking questions, then surely it was only a matter of time before the authorities listened and Icey was released?

*

Alfred Roma had yet to see the papers. He was just stepping out of the shower when he heard the news story about Poppy Withers on the radio. Turning up the volume, Roma caught the tail end of the story. A young girl had been found tortured to death. She had a broken rosary around her neck. The death was linked to three earlier murders. One woman called Elizabeth Johnson was serving life for a murder that many now thought she had not committed. Roma dried himself in silence as he digested the news. The conviction of Icey was about to try him once again.

Ashley Towers read all the Sunday papers and then called Mr Frizzel at home. It took a while before the solicitor answered and when he did, Frizzel sounded surprisingly sober. Ashley guessed this was Sam's doing, and he felt a flash of admiration for her.

'Have you seen the papers today?'

'No,' said Frizzel. 'Why, is there something that I should know about?'

'There's been another murder. The victim had a rosary around her neck. We'll have to go the Criminal Cases' Review Body. Let's meet tomorrow.'

'In the Frog and—' Frizzel began. Perhaps he wasn't as much of a changed man as Ashley had thought.

'No,' Ashley interrupted, 'First thing Monday, in my chambers.'

Chapter One Hundred and Five

Icey was in the music department when she came across the talent of Koko Taylor – born Cora Walton in Bartless, Tennessee, USA, on twenty eight September, 1928. She had been nicknamed Koko by her sharecropper parents, Icey found out, due to her love of hot chocolate. Like Icey, she'd received little formal education. Instead she was obliged to pick cotton until she'd been discovered.

Icey read as much as she could find about the blues singer and immediately felt a connection with her. She'd known injustice, and she'd been a fighter. Icey listened to her music and she understood the spirit of her songs. Koko had fought all her life and not once had she given up. She knew what it meant to be the underdog; to have little hope and yet to rise above it all. Icey felt that Koko would have understood the injustice of her situation now, but Icey herself was not prepared to forgive or forget. How could she in her heart forgive a God who had been instrumental in her incarceration?

It was while she was listening to Koko's music that a screw approached her and told her that she had a phone call.

Icey was still refusing to let Sam visit, but she knew that she should probably start reaching out again. As the screw escorted her to the nearest phone, she mentioned in passing that she'd recently seen Icey on telly.

Icey eyed her curiously. 'Are you sure? What was it about?'

The screw shrugged without explaining, but was quite taken aback by the calmness of Icey's tone and manner.

It was Mr Frizzel on the phone. 'Icey, there's been another murder and I would like to renew your appeal,' he said, coming straight to the point. 'Would you like me to go ahead?'

Icey was stunned. She'd been hoping to speak to Sam, and here was Frizzel who had been promising her freedom ever since she'd been charged; and now he wanted her permission to appeal when she shouldn't be here in the first place.

'As far as I am concerned, you can bugger off,' she told him bluntly.

Icey hung up the phone and requested to return to the music library. She'd had enough of lawyers to last a lifetime.

Back in what was fast becoming her sanctuary, she turned over some other tapes. One was 'Nessun Dorma' sung by Luciano Pavarotti. She'd heard of him. She seemed to recall the song had something to do with football, but when she pressed the play button, and listened to it through her headphones, it was simply heaven. She was completely captivated by the music. Tears welled up at the back of her eyes as she was catapulted into emotional overdrive. It was one of the most beautiful and exquisite pieces of music she had ever heard. It came close to Puccini's 'Madam Butterfly', she thought. Closing her eyes, Icey rested her head in her hands.

As she swayed to the power of Pavarotti, she hardly registered the first slap. The second was hard enough to bring her to her senses. It smacked her headphones off her ears and they bounced off the table. Opening her eyes, Icey at once focused on Andrea, an obese, androgynous-looking screw with short, crew-cut hair, an eye for pretty girls and a reputation for being a bully. She was standing in front of Icey, all sixteen stone of her squeezed into her tight regulation uniform of grey trousers and a light sky-blue shirt. Her fat fingers were red from the slap she had just executed. She was indecently close to Icey as she fingered her baton speculatively. It was the latest telescopic truncheon, called an asp, and was capable of inflicting serious injuries. As Icey looked up, she could see Andrea debating whether or not to use it, which prevented Icey from responding instinctively to the violence with a blow of her own.

'Solitary,' said Andrea cruelly. 'Three days.'

'What for?'

'Sleeping on the job. You're here to work, not sleep,' Andrea told her harshly.

'You're a bitch. You know I wasn't asleep.'

'Don't back-chat. It'll be another seven days if you argue.'

Icey laughed. 'I can do the time, bitch, but what about you? I'm in here for life but even that wouldn't be enough time for you to become human. You're just a sad and lonely screw. The boys don't like you and the girls don't like you and you've only yourself to blame. The only way you can get your kicks is imposing solitary on prisoners you want to get off with.'

Andreas's face started to colour. Beads of sweat formed in a tight row around her flabby neck.

'Are you suggesting that I'm abusing my authority?'

'Are you denying it?'

'Solitary,' repeated Andrea loudly, her expression nasty.

'Is that with or without you?' said Icey, as she laughed and placed Pavarotti back on the shelf and made her way towards solitary.

Three days without seeing a soul. For Icey, it was hardly a punishment. She would do her time without complaint, but she made a vow to give that screw a wide berth when she got out. And just maybe she'd return one of Sam's calls.

Chapter One Hundred and Six

While they waited for the official autopsy report on Poppy Withers, DCI Paradissimo and DC Cody paid another early morning visit to St Mary Magdalene's Church. At this hour, it was almost in darkness, apart from some lateral light from the street lamps outside. The smell of fresh roses and Madonna lilies was still present, but the church was empty.

Once again, out of habit, Cody dipped her finger in the bowl of holy water by the door and blessed herself. Once a Catholic, always a Catholic. She was worried. They'd clearly missed something all along in the Leticia Joy case, and the proverbial was about to hit the fan. Cody also realised that her behaviour towards Sam Bailey had been unprofessional and disgraceful. It had really arisen out of frustration – and personal jealousy, she now acknowledged. Now Cody was frightened and Paradissimo was, too, although he would never admit it. Sitting at the back of the church, she did what came naturally to a good Catholic girl. She started to pray.

Paradissimo didn't seem to notice Cody; he was busy looking for inspiration on who might have killed Leticia Joy. Without even acknowledging it to himself, he also knew he was looking for signs of Elizabeth Johnson's innocence.

Cody had finished her prayers and was still sitting in the pew when she noticed Iris Walker. She was by the altar replacing the flowers with her back to the front of the church. She was unaware of Cody's approach. When she was close enough, she tapped Iris on the shoulder.

'Hello, Iris, remember me?'

Iris ignored her as she continued to split the stems of the Madonna lilies.

'You disappeared the last time I was here. Was there a reason for that?' Cody asked.

Gripping the handle of her scissors, Iris continued to stab at the flowers, but she was clearly nervous, her eyes darting around. 'I don't have to answer any of your questions.'

'That's correct. But you were here, weren't you, on the night of Leticia Joy's murder?' Cody asked.

'I can't remember.'

'You gave a statement that you had been here earlier, doing the flowers like you always do. Try to remember?'

Iris turned to face Cody. She held the scissors tightly in her right hand and Cody stepped back out of instinct. She was reassured when she sensed Paradissimo approaching from out of the shadows.

'Yes, tell us about the night of Leticia Joy's murder, Iris?' he requested.

'I was here, yes, but earlier in the evening. You've asked me this before. It's all in my statement,' Iris said impatiently.

'Well, we're asking you again,' said Cody. 'What time did you leave the church that evening?'

'I can't remember. It was a long time ago.'

'Did you know Leticia well?' Cody asked, realising that she or Paradissimo should have questioned Iris Walker in the first place, but they'd been so sure they'd got the killer bang to rights that they'd allowed one of their newer recruits to take her statement. With hindsight, it had been a mistake.

'She was a whore,' Iris snarled back.

'She was a victim,' Cody replied.

'She was a whore and was judged by her God.'

'Do you have a problem with whores, Iris?' Paradissimo asked sharply. 'Look at me, Iris. Do you have a problem?'

Iris averted her eyes. She began to tremble as the two coppers waited for an answer.

'She was a whore judged by her deeds. The Bible says that you reap what you sow.'

'Is that right, Iris? So you're saying she had it coming to her?' Paradissimo was standing only inches away from Iris, and didn't take his eyes off her face.

Iris did not answer.

'Where were you again on the night of the murder? Just remind me?' Paradissimo instructed.

'I was here.'

'And what time did you leave?'

'I don't remember. It was early evening.'

'And do you have an alibi for later on that evening?'

'I went home – my husband was there,' Iris said belligerently.

'Really? How convenient! Did you kill Leticia Joy?' he asked suddenly, his tone more insistent.

'No, but I wish I had. Her sort is not welcome in the house of God.'

'And do you decide who's welcome, Iris? Is that your job? You seem to have had a problem with Leticia Joy.' Paradissimo's gaze was burning into the nervous woman's eyes.

'I . . .'

'We may need to ask you some more questions. We know where you live, but where's the best place to get in touch with you?'

'You can find me here, mostly . . .'

'Really?' Paradissimo said sarcastically. 'We'll be in touch.

You don't need to bother to show us the way out. I'm sure God will guide us.'

'Is she for real?' Paradissimo asked, even before they were out of earshot.

'I am sure she is. She's a fanatic,' Cody replied in a matter-of-fact tone.

'I'd say she's sectionable!'

'But is she crazy enough to kill?'

'Well, let's make some more enquiries. We can talk to her husband, for a start, but what's the betting he'll say his wife was home all evening even if she wasn't!'

Chapter One Hundred and Seven

On advice from Harry, Sam had called a conference meeting at Fleet Investigations with the two of them along with Flick, Oriel – and Hips. After the judges' attitudes last time, she knew she needed all the help she could get if they were to get Icey grounds for a new appeal. Besides, a conference seemed like a very good idea when Harry suggested it. She also liked the way it sounded: professional, thorough; business as usual. In future, she decided – when Icey was free, in other words – she would call a case conference meeting once a week as a matter of routine.

Today, Sam was dressed in a black skirt and an orange blouse and loose cardigan. Even without make-up she was beautiful. Harry was the first to arrive. Sam was pleased to see him and smiled broadly at him as she handed him a cup of coffee.

'You must be delighted with the media coverage,' he said after he had sat down.

Since the latest murder, Sam had been interviewed by various newspapers. Over the weekend one of the more popular weekly women's magazines had spoken to her at length for an in-depth feature about Icey's case they were planning on running next week. She was due to be interviewed by the BBC in the next couple of days as well. She'd told Harry about her forthcoming interview, as well as the magazine feature.

'I must admit I was a little apprehensive at first about how they would deal with the fact that both Icey and I are ex-call girls,' Sam admitted, sitting next to Harry, 'but obviously I can see why they needed to mention it. It makes for a juicier story after all, and that's what will get us the publicity we need. I'm glad, though, that by and large the media coverage has been balanced and fairly comprehensive. But we can't afford to sit back and become complacent,' Sam said seriously.

'There is no chance of that, Sam, is there?' Harry replied, a little dryly.

Sam started to laugh. Harry's good-natured humour was infectious, and she thought again of how supportive he'd been throughout Icey's trial. He was a lovely man and, while she'd always regarded him as her unofficial mentor, as she stared at him now she felt an unfamiliar flutter of something else. He wasn't a handsome man – not like Paradissimo – but his face had a lived-in charm and she liked the way his smiles were usually matched by the sparkle in his eyes.

Today, it also seemed as if he'd made a special effort with his appearance. He was wearing a smart navy suit with a light blue open-neck shirt. He was clean shaven, but Sam noticed a small speck of blood on his chin where he'd nicked himself with his razor. She resisted the urge to dab at it; to take him in hand. Harry needed a woman in his life, she thought, not for the first time. But what surprised her was the second thought that came unbidden – that she could see herself in that role in his life.

Was she confusing gratitude with attraction? He was a lot older than her, of course, but then she'd always found herself attracted to older men – something she was sure any shrink would have a field day with, given her father had always been in and out of her life due to his all too frequent stretches in the nick. She had no idea how Harry felt about her, especially knowing how well acquainted he was with her past. She also knew that she didn't want to do anything that would ruin their relationship and, based on her track record with men, it was probably better that they just remain friends.

Harry, aware of her staring at him, flashed Sam a curious look. 'Penny for your thoughts?'

'Oh, sorry, I was miles away,' Sam said, flustered. 'I was thinking about Icey,' she lied swiftly.

Oriel and Flick interrupted the moment, arriving together. They were both dressed in jeans, jumpers and high heels, and were merrily gossiping about some reality TV show they'd both watched the night before – gypsy girls in big lit-up bridal frocks, it seemed. Their chatter subsided as they entered the office.

Hips arrived soon after. Irma had said she was the smartest of her girls, and Sam needed her wisdom more than ever. She was also a devout Catholic and, as an unbeliever, Sam didn't think it would hurt to have her insight on the religious aspects of the case, even if she didn't quite see the use of the prayers Hips assured her she was constantly saying for Icey.

Sam had prepared carefully for the meeting. She had borrowed a couple of chairs from Frizzel's office so that they could all sit and peruse a copy of Icey's file. Despite needing his furniture, she had not thought it useful to invite the man himself. Each of the folders contained a summary of the four murders, listing the similarities and the differences between them. She had clipped pictures of each of the victims from the papers. She had also bought a white board, which she'd fixed to the back wall of the office. On the board was a photograph of Icey, taken in happier times. She was smiling out at the camera, looking beautiful in a pretty ice-blue dress and jacket. Also on the board were photographs of each of the four victims. Above the head of each victim, Sam had been unable to stop herself adding a question mark in blood red marker pen, just like in the newspapers.

Hips was busy reading the files that had been provided them. While she had been aware of the subsequent murders ever since Icey had been sent down, she hadn't until this point read all the facts. The killing of Leticia Joy was bad enough, but then there was Martha in very similar circumstances, followed by Pia Broom and now Poppy Withers. Each one of them had met a particularly gruesome end.

'May I speak?' Hips said at last, looking up from the file in her hands. Everyone turned to look at her.

'No one's stopping you,' said Sam directly. 'You've got a voice. What do you want to say?'

'Well, I was just thinking that these deaths, they are all connected.'

The room was silent as Sam stared at Hips, trying and failing to hide her disbelief at the obviousness of the statement.

'Is that it? We kind of got there before you.' Everyone laughed except Hips, who looked embarrassed. Sam relented. 'I'm sorry, Hips, what were you about to say?'

'The surname of the first victim was Joy?' she questioned, though she clearly knew the answer to that, given her avid perusal of the case file and the fact that she was now standing next to Sam's whiteboard.

'Yes, Leticia Joy,' Sam confirmed.

'What day of the week was she murdered on?'

'Does it really matter?' Harry answered wearily.

'It might do,' Hips told him.

'She was murdered on a Saturday night,' said Sam, eyeing the larger girl curiously.

'And the reports say that there was a bead missing from her broken rosary?'

'That's correct.'

'Do you know which bead?'

'Yes, the fifth bead of the necklace,' Harry said at once, not needing to check his notes.

'Is that relevant?' said Sam, leafing through her file, trying to second-guess where Hips was going with this.

'I'm not sure yet, but the fifth bead is part of the Mystery of Joy,' Hips said slowly. 'What about the second victim, Martha?'

'What about her?' Sam asked.

'What day of the week was she killed on?' Hips replied a little impatiently. Surely they could see what she was angling for.

'Thursday,' said Sam, checking her calendar.

'And she was found with a pearl necklace, not a rosary?'

'Yes, that's right.'

'It wasn't broken?'

'No, it wasn't.'

'How many beads were there?'

'Martha's necklace wasn't all pearls – it was a silver chain with pearl beads on it. There were six beads, I believe,' Sam said, flicking through her notes.

'The sixth bead is part of the Luminous Mysteries.'

'Is it associated with any particular day of the week?' asked Harry, his interest caught now.

'Yes. Thursday.'

Hips counted to herself up to eleven, and made a note on her file. 'I thought so, and Pia Broom?'

'Pia Broom died on a Tuesday, and she had a pearl necklace which was found close by,' Harry answered comprehensively.

'And the necklace had twenty-two beads. But the eleventh bead was missing,' Sam added, and Hips nodded her head.

'I am sure that Poppy Withers died on a Wednesday,' she said. 'Am I right?'

Sam checked through the file and double-checked the date of the death against the calendar on her computer.

Frowning, she said, 'Wednesday it is. How did you know that?'

Hips ignored her and carried on. 'So,' said Hips, 'Joy died on a Saturday night, Martha on a Thursday, Pia on Tuesday and Poppy on Wednesday. That is the mystery.'

Flick, who had been uncharacteristically silent until now, stood up suddenly. 'Are you mad, girl? You've just mentioned four different days of the week and are telling us that's the connection? Have I got that right?'

'You have,' Hips said calmly.

Sam was still leafing through the file but she suddenly gave Hips her full attention. 'What is it, Hips? What are you on about? Explain, please.'

'Well,' said Hips, picking her words carefully, 'it's the mystery of the rosary.'

'Well, it will remain a mystery if you don't get on and explain it,' Harry said sharply.

Hips didn't appear flustered by Harry's tone. She took her time and explained. 'The rosary is divided into decades. Each decade represents an event in the life of Jesus. There are four sets of "Mysteries of the Rosary". Set one is the joyful mysteries; set two, the mystery of light; set three, the sorrowful mysteries and set four is the glorious mysteries. The Mystery of the Rosary contains a total of twenty mysteries, each of which is associated with a particular day of the week; a day when you're supposed to say that prayer. Joy died on a Saturday at the feet of Christ. The mystery associated with that day is the joyful mystery. I don't think her name is a coincidence. She may have even been targeted because of it. The second victim, Martha, her name was, right? She died on a football pitch on a Thursday, yes?'

'What does that mean?' asked Sam, concentrating hard to follow what Hips was saying.

'Well, Thursday is associated with the luminous mysteries.'

'I don't see how her death fits in with the luminous mysteries,' said Flick.

'There are five different events that happened, which are all part of the luminous mystery. The fourth event is a transfiguration by light.' Hips spoke as if reciting a lecture; in truth, the mystery of the rosary had been one that had been drilled into her since she was very little, coming as she did from a deeply religious family.

Harry sat up straight and looked at Hips with a sudden spark of excitement in his eyes. 'Martha died on a football pitch that was illuminated by floodlight,' he said eagerly.

'What about Pia Broom?' Sam questioned. 'Whoever murdered her left her for dead on a swing with a crown of thorns embedded into her head,' she added.

'Well,' said Hips, 'the sorrowful mysteries of the rosary include the crowning of thorns. "And platting a crown of thorns, they put it upon his head, and a reed in his right hand," Matthew 27.29,' recited Hips.

'She was also severely beaten,' said Sam, 'and left in a pool of blood. How does that fit in with your theory?'

'The Agony in the Garden,' said Hips without hesitation. '"And being in an agony he prayed more earnestly; and his sweat became like great drops of blood falling down upon the ground," Luke 22.44.'

'You're scaring me now, Hips,' said Sam, but in truth she was on the edge of her seat and eager to know more. 'What does that mean?'

'Like I said, all these killings are connected.'

'So what about the most recent murder?' Harry asked. 'Poppy

Withers. How does her death fit with your rosary theory?'

'The glorious mystery occurs on a Wednesday or a Sunday. The mystery is about the resurrection of Christ and, well, maybe our killer is getting more metaphorical. Maybe he saw his victim as being resurrected from the sandpit,' she speculated. 'I'm not sure.' Hips had clearly run out of ideas, but what she had suggested so far was more than enough to digest.

'Each bead represents a particular mystery,' Hips told them, bringing it back to the common factor of the rosaries. There was silence for a few moments while everyone allowed the information to sink in.

'Well,' said Harry at last. 'Thank you, Hips. That's a lot to take in, but if you're right about all this, then it seems to me that the killer has to be a Catholic. Presumably only a Catholic would know the details of the rosary so well, and attach so much significance to the mysteries?'

'That doesn't exactly narrow it down, Harry,' complained Sam with a sigh. 'Do you think the police have figured this out already? Presumably they have experts looking into it?'

Harry rolled his eyes in response. 'I very much doubt it. I'll give my contact a call, unless you want to talk to the officer in charge and tell him Hips' theory?' he asked Sam, carefully watching her reaction to the suggestion. Although they'd never discussed it, he knew a little about her past relationship with Paradissimo, but he couldn't say that he'd ever approved of it. He'd never worked with the man but from what he'd heard he was an arrogant bastard. He'd always thought Sam could do so much better.

'I think they'd take you more seriously than me,' Sam replied swiftly, remembering her recent encounter with both Paradissimo and his sidekick, DC Cody, and not relishing another confrontation just yet. 'Besides, our priority should be freeing Icey, not helping the police. Let them do their own investigating. They're the experts, that's what they both told me,' she said disparagingly.

'Unfortunately, I think it's going to take finding the real killer to get the authorities to reconsider their verdict and admit they got it wrong where Icey is concerned,' Harry warned with a sigh. 'We need to give them somewhere else to look – someone else to consider.'

Oriel, who'd been silent so far while Hips was recounting her knowledge of the rosary, gave a nervous cough before speaking. 'Mrs Sexton said her husband was a religious nut. That he went obsessively to church. He's a prime target?' she suggested.

'Isn't he in a mental institution, though?' countered Sam.

'Yes, but his wife said he makes a habit of breaking out, and he always comes back to South London looking for her. He's obviously a devout Catholic,' Oriel explained.

'Well, that in itself is not a crime,' Harry said wryly. 'But I agree we should talk to him. He has an obvious connection to the first murder – he was a witness. Maybe his presence at the church that night wasn't as innocent as it seemed. He's a local and a member of St Mary Magdalene's congregation, and as such he probably knew Leticia.'

'Well, if we're following that line of thinking, there's also Iris Walker. She fits "religious nut" to a t. And she attacked me in the church. It wouldn't surprise me if she was the one behind that threatening letter left for me at the bus stop, too. She obviously had a problem with Leticia and with me.'

'Maybe with sinners in general?' Harry said, and Sam looked at him sharply before she saw that his eyes were sparkling.

'Thank you, Harry.' Sam smiled back at him. 'And let's not forget Leticia Joy's fiancé.'

'Though from what Father Luke told you, Tom Padfield isn't a Catholic, is he?' Harry recalled.

'No, but Leticia was and Tom had reason to be angry with her,' Sam added.

No one spoke for a while as the recent revelations hit home. Harry was the first to break the silence. 'I think we should revisit Iris Walker, Sexton and Padfield. The witness first, I think – let's find out what else he might have seen the night Leticia Joy was killed.'

'I can handle Sexton,' Sam said, with more confidence than she felt. 'Perhaps you can track down Iris Walker, and then we'll tackle Padfield together. Flick and Oriel can hold the fort here. Great work, everyone,' Sam said, proudly concluding her first case conference.

Chapter One Hundred and Eight

Paradissimo and Cody were looking at the morning papers in Paradissimo's office when he got the call. As he picked up the phone, he realised at once that his Chief was in a foul mood.

'I suspect that you know what this is all about,' Smithers snapped without introduction.

'Well, sir, not really.'

'It's about being hauled over the coals by the media. They say we're doing nothing to catch a killer – that we've even got the wrong person in prison for one of the murders. All the while you insist that there is nothing to worry about.'

'If you're talking about Elizabeth Johnson, the Court of Appeal decided that case firmly in our favour. They concluded that it wasn't the work of the same killer.'

'Yes, that was based on your assurances that there had been a thorough investigation and the police were confident that there was no link.'

'There is no link, sir.'

'Well, so you say. Have you assessed the evidence in relation to all four murders?'

There was a slight hesitation as Paradissimo thought about his answer. 'I have considered the evidence in relation to three of the murders. In relation to the latest victim, that information is not available to me yet.'

'Well, the evidence is available to me and I would like to review it asap. Shall we say ten o'clock this morning?'

'Yes, sir,' Paradissimo agreed, looking at his watch. It was 8.46 a.m. already. As he placed the phone down, he started to shout at no one in particular. 'Will someone get me a file on all the available information on Poppy Withers, and I want it now!'

Cody did not respond. She had recently told Paradissimo in private of her increasing concerns about Leticia Joy's murder investigation, and he had ignored her. Now, as the officer in charge of the case, he would have to accept the responsibility for that.

Paradissimo immersed himself in the available files on his desk. At 9.45 precisely, Cody walked into his office, dropped an advance copy of Poppy Withers' autopsy report on his lap and walked out. She had had enough of bailing out officers who brought trouble upon themselves. But if Paradissimo went down, she had no doubt that he'd try and take her with him. She had to give him something, but even so he deserved to have his life made a little difficult.

It was after eight o'clock in the evening when Anne Cody arrived home. Slipping off her coat, she walked into the bathroom and ran a bath. She was feeling stressed and tired. She needed a good soak. Walking through to the kitchen, she pulled a bottle of Chilean wine from the fridge and poured herself a large glass.

She filled the bath to the max, allowing for a liberal amount of bubble bath. She looked at the bottle: Snow Flake, the remains of a Christmas gift set. The suds began to relax her aching muscles and caressed her skin from the moment she stepped into the tub. It had been a difficult day, but she had come through. Paradissimo was in the clear. There would be an investigation, of course, but their boss had given them the nod that DCI Paradissimo would come out of that smelling of roses. The official report would not contain a shred of evidence that he had been incompetent, despite any personal concerns his colleagues might have. And if Paradissimo was in the clear, they all were.

Stepping out of the bath, Cody felt a little light-headed. She grabbed the wine bottle on the way to her living room, leaving a trail of bubbles and wet footprints behind her. She felt refreshed as she reclined on the sofa in her dressing gown, with the TV on low. She was almost dozing off, in fact, when the picture on the screen caught her interest. It was Sam Bailey. She was wearing impossibly high heels and a chic midnight blue chiffon coat and dress. She looked more like a celebrity than an investigator. Cody couldn't help but notice that every aspect of her was immaculate, but she was drawn in particular to Bailey's manicured hands. She was holding a large manila envelope on which Cody could just make out enough letters to guess that it had her own name on it.

Bailey was being interviewed by Daniel Giles from the BBC. She was complaining about the police investigation of a suspected serial killer and the wrongful conviction of Elizabeth Johnson. Cody did not take her eyes off the envelope in her right hand. Sam Bailey was giving it her all. Complaining as usual about the injustice and wrongful conviction of another tart.

'I warned the police that there was a serial killer who would attack again, and they ignored me. I was thrown out of the police station and told that if I returned I would be arrested.'

'And who told you that?'

'The officers involved in the investigation. I have a recording of the conversation.' She held up the envelope.

The camera turned to Daniel Giles.

'Miss Bailey is calling for an investigation into why an officer apparently threatened her, and why the police have failed to see the similarities of the four murders. She claims that as a result of incompetence, innocent women have lost their lives. The officer in charge of all four cases, Detective Chief Inspector Paradissimo, was invited to comment but declined.'

Cody's mobile rang. It took her some time to find her handbag, and then locate her phone inside it.

'This is Chief Superintendent Smithers. You'll know what this is all about?'

'The Leticia Joy case, sir.'

'What do you know about a private investigator being thrown out of the police station?'

'She was not exactly thrown out, sir. She was escorted out. And she's not exactly a detective, she's a former tart,' Cody couldn't resist saying.

'What about the recording that she says she was thrown out?'

'That might be a little more difficult, sir.'

'I want you in my office first thing tomorrow. Eight o'clock sharp.'

Laying her phone aside, hands trembling slightly, Cody was grateful that Sam had not yet chosen to name and shame her publicly, but she was conscious that it might be only a matter of time before Bailey played that trump card.

Icey was in recreational time with the mules, sitting on the sofa. Her feet were crossed beneath her as she watched the news. To her amazement, her photo flashed up on the screen. She was astonished. Andrea the nasty screw had taunted her about being on TV, but actually seeing herself on the BBC was a shock. It was weeks since her failed appeal, and she was in the news again. What was going on? Having cut herself off from Sam, she was also cut off from the outside world, she realised.

The whole room fell silent as the inmates watched the latest on Icey and the London murders. The item suggested that she had been the victim of a miscarriage of justice. Slumping back into the chair, Icey couldn't let herself get excited. She had been down that road before and the only thing she'd got from it was a nasty headache. She had absolutely no faith in the judicial system at all. If the world was a safer place as a result of her incarceration, it clearly had not stopped three subsequent murders. But she'd got her hopes up before. She wasn't going to do that again in a hurry.

Mr Frizzel was watching the same programme. He was sufficiently alert to contact Ashley Towers. Towers was wide awake. He helped himself to a large vodka and tonic as he watched the news and ignored his ringing phone. Icey was news again. He would spend the rest of his life haunted by the only case he should have won, and lost – though it seemed that it might yet make his name once and for all.

Chapter One Hundred and Nine

It took four hours to travel to Tranquillity House in Kent. Sam had always intended to make the trip earlier, after Oriel had failed to track Sexton down at his house, but she'd been distracted by other events. Besides, she'd thought at the time that Sexton wasn't going anywhere – her calls to the facility had confirmed that he was in no risk of being released in the immediate future. And when she'd phoned this morning, she'd learnt that Sexton, for once, was exactly where he was supposed to be. She'd decided to take the train to Canterbury and a cab from the station, but as the taxi pulled in, she wondered at first if she had come to the right location.

The facility was truly in the middle of nowhere but its grounds were extensive and the main building was old and rather beautiful, set in a well-manicured garden. From the distance it looked like an old manor house. Its name was well chosen, Sam thought, except for the fact that she knew that it housed some of the most dangerous patients detained under the Mental Health Act: the seriously psychotic, the acutely paranoid and a small number of patients judged to be a serious risk to themselves and others. It also acted as an overflow for some prisoners who were no longer considered dangerous but were waiting to be reallocated to a less secure unit. Sexton, she had learnt by charming the male nurse who'd answered the phone earlier, had been waiting for some time. Other residential units had refused to take him because his religious views were often extreme and offensive to other patients and staff. He did, as Oriel said, fit the brief as a 'religious nut'.

They swept up the drive and the taxi stopped parallel to the security door. Sam stepped out of the taxi and walked into the first of three reception cubicles. She felt a little underdressed in jeans, jumper and leather jacket. Pressing the bell once, she waited for someone to answer. The heavy glass doors shut tight behind her, creating an air-tight vacuum. The steel and glass mesh doors creaked open as she stepped through into the second reception bay.

'I am here to see Mr Sexton. I have an appointment.'

'Who are you?' asked a tired-looking, middle-aged woman behind the reinforced glass. She wore a violet cardigan, which clashed unfortunately with the pink-rimmed glasses perched on her nose.

'I am a friend of his wife. I visited her earlier and I told her that I would visit her husband. I called here, too. I think he's expecting me.' Sam felt uncomfortable. She was never very good at lying, and while she hated herself for it, there was no alternative in this instance. The end had to justify the means.

'Ward 2C,' the receptionist muttered. 'Can you sign in?' She handed Sam a visitor's badge and pointed at a guest book. 'You'll need to disinfect your hands before they let you on a ward,' she told her as Sam signed in.

Sam did as she was told. A nurse then appeared and, by a terse nod of her head, indicated that Sam should follow her down the corridor. The walls were lined with a selection of large, bold finger paintings hung at precisely the same height and distance apart. Sam found the child-like daubings vaguely soothing.

The nurse led her to another reception area and then

abandoned her. Sam waited a few moments and then looked around for another member of staff. She introduced herself to the staff nurse on Ward 2C, a big burly man who could have been a bodybuilder, although he seemed friendly enough, far friendlier in fact than the female staff she'd encountered so far. Sam explained whom she'd come to see, spinning her story about being a friend of the family.

'He is in a good mood today, but he has been a bit volatile recently. If you have any trouble with him, pull the emergency cord. Second room on the left, you'll find him in there.'

He walked briskly away, leaving Sam standing by the door of her mystery witness. She looked in through the small window in the door before knocking twice. Sexton was lying on the bed. He half-opened his eyes, but did no more than squint. She knocked again, which caused Sexton to grunt and turn over to face away from the door. Sam waited but there was no sign that he wanted a guest. Turning the handle, she stepped into the room. He did not move.

'Mr Sexton, may I come in?'

'No,' was the response.

'Mr Sexton, your wife has told me to tell you that she will be in to see you as soon as she can.'

Sexton rolled over onto his back and then onto his side. He was a big man and his huge bulk wobbled as he shifted himself. When he was facing Sam, he opened his eyes. Dribble stains marked out the borders of his chubby cheeks. They made their way down his cheeks and onto his T-shirt. Sexton was a disorderly mess. His stubble was fast becoming a beard and his greying dark hair was naturally greased back.

'You're a liar,' he said. 'My wife has never visited me here.'

'I am sure she said that.'

'I am sure she did not.'

Sexton evidently had enough of his faculties to know that Sam was lying. 'You are right. I'm sorry that I lied. I only said that to see you,' she said, coming clean.

Sexton beamed a smile – a full smile full of black holes, missing teeth and cracked incisors. 'Get out!' he snarled at her.

'Well, before I do, I would like to talk to you about a woman called Leticia Joy, who was murdered in St Mary Magdalene's Church. Do you remember the death of that young woman? You gave a statement to the police?'

'No.'

'Here, let me show you a photograph. Perhaps it will help you remember?'

'No.'

Sam pulled out the tabloid photo of Leticia Joy. She handed it to Sexton as he scratched his belly. 'Have you seen that woman before?' she asked, sitting down on the chair nearest to the door.

'All women are the same,' sneered Sexton. He lowered his right hand and leered at Leticia's picture.

'What about Elizabeth Johnson?' Sam pressed on. 'You might remember her as Icey. You went to school with her, remember? Here, have a look at this photograph.'

Sam handed Sexton a photograph of Icey. He took it and stared at it for several minutes without speaking.

'You claimed that you saw her on the night that Leticia was murdered. Can you tell me what you remember of that evening?' Sam said at last, trying to judge the best moment to broach the subject.

Sexton looked at the photograph and smiled. Placing his hand inside his tracksuit bottoms, he began to rock. Sam watched as he manipulated his organ to his rhythmic beat. She was torn between wanting to leave and needing to hear whatever

Sexton had to say, no matter how disgusting his behaviour. Men were such pigs, she thought absent-mindedly, but if he thought he would shock her into leaving him alone, he had reckoned without Sam's steel core. Besides, he was no more disgusting than the average punter she'd had to deal with at Irma's – though at least then she had been well paid to watch middle-aged men get their rocks off.

Sam waited for Sexton to become a spent force. He was taking his time so she moved forward and pulled her friend's photograph from his grasp. But, as she turned around to make her way back to her chair, Sexton grabbed her and pulled her backward by the neck.

'Your friends are all whores. All women are sluts,' he hissed at Sam, as he dragged her by the hair down onto his bed. She struggled against him but his hand over her mouth prevented her from crying out. The alarm cord was an arm's length away, but she couldn't quite reach it. She was an idiot. She had no right to be in his room and now it was going to prove to be her undoing.

'All women are sluts,' he said as he pushed Sam onto her back and rubbed his belly against her. He was lying on his left-hand side with his left hand around Sam's neck. His right hand was still submerged inside his tracksuit as he rolled his belly on top of her. His right knee was between her legs.

He'd removed his hand from her mouth but Sam still fought to resist the urge to scream. She realised that this might be her only opportunity to question a key witness in Icey's original trial. Even though she knew she was in trouble, she couldn't give up her quest for the truth. She would have to grit her teeth and endure this horror. 'Her name was Leticia Joy, did you know her?'

'She was a slut, the mistress of God. She was God's whore.'

'Do you know what happened to her that night?'

'She was God's whore,' Sexton repeated. 'She deserved to die.'

'And who killed her?'

'Forgive me, for I know not what I do,' Sexton muttered.

'What have you done? What do you need forgiving for?' Sam asked, trying to manoeuvre herself away from Sexton. Before she could break free, he grabbed her by the neck and squeezed tight. Sam tried to push his arm away – anything to relieve the pressure on her neck – but it was useless.

'Let me go,' she managed to gasp as she implanted her long, sharp nails into the back of his hand. 'Please stop.' She wriggled against him but could not shift his bulk with her slight form. She did, however, manage to free one of her knees and brought it up sharply into his groin.

Sexton slumped forward. His right hand was still between his legs, and that had protected him to some extent, but he was still winded by Sam's sudden brutal attack. The pressure on her neck, however, eased at once. Sexton rolled onto his back and started to whimper. Sam used the opportunity to extricate herself from his clutches, catching her breath as she squirmed away. Her body was pumping with adrenaline and she looked down at the man in disgust and pity. Was this their killer? It seemed unlikely, although he was certainly screwed up enough, it seemed, turning violent without the slightest provocation.

When her racing heartbeat had calmed down, Sam looped back to the ward and sweet-talked the burly nurse enough to pin down the timings of Sexton's recent escapes. Only the night of Leticia Joy's murder coincided with one of his walkabouts. On every other occasion, Sexton had been safely locked up in Tranquillity House, where the only person he could harm was himself. Or idiot ex-tarts who think they're detectives, Sam berated herself softly.

As she walked out of the main reception, she noted the time on the clock. She had been with Sexton for no more than ten minutes, and at the facility less than an hour, but it felt like a lifetime. His wife had described him accurately. Religious nut indeed. But even if he'd been there on the night Leticia Joy was killed, he had a solid alibi for the other three murders. She wondered if he'd told the police everything he'd seen that night at the church, but it was fairly obvious they'd get little out of him.

Something he had said bothered her, though. He'd called Leticia the mistress of God, which seemed an odd thing to say, even within the context of his wild ramblings. Was Sexton implying that Leticia had had an improper relationship with someone at the church? It might be a stab in the dark, but Sam thought of Father Luke and his boyish good looks. Was that who Sexton meant by 'God'?

Chapter One Hundred and Ten

The death of Poppy Withers continued to cause an uproar in the national press. She had died, according to one of the more liberal rags, because the English judicial system was not fit for purpose and had not been working for a number of years. One of the more right-wing tabloids took a different slant: if Poppy Withers had been a foreigner and on benefit, the police might have taken the trouble to investigate the death with a little more care; but she was English and she had a job.

The *Daily Mirror* was the most robust in its coverage. It asked how many more victims there would be before the authorities realised that a serial killer was on the loose. It ran a long feature on Elizabeth Johnson, not stinting on the details of her call girl past but making it clear that here was a woman who had been on the verge of turning her life around before she'd been wrongly convicted of murder. At the end of the piece the readers were invited to sign a 'Save Elizabeth Johnson' petition, calling for the release of this tragic English rose who was wilting in prison.

The *Guardian* was more measured. The piece about Poppy Withers was not an emotional affair. The murders of Pia Broom, Martha Lewis and Leticia Joy made grim reading, and you did not have to be the Home Secretary to see that the cases were linked. The *Guardian* wondered why it was that the Court of Appeal, the police and the Crown Prosecution Service were all in denial about the obvious connections.

The CPS called a conference in the wake of the media onslaught. They received a letter from defence solicitor Mr Frizzel, asking again whether it was still their case that the conviction of Elizabeth Johnson was safe and satisfactory or whether, in light of the recent events, they were prepared to concede that the conviction was unsafe. He had made it clear in his letter that he would be pursuing all available avenues and would not rest until his client was free.

Chapter One Hundred and Eleven

In the wake of the coverage, Sam called another case conference with Harry. This time, though, she asked Irma to come along, too, hoping for a fresh perspective on what next steps to take. Irma wasn't a legal expert but she was wise in the ways of the world, and Sam trusted her judgement on people.

Harry arrived first, as she had expected he would. She gave him the bare bones of her meeting with Sexton, leaving out the fact that he'd attacked her. She knew that would only make him angry, and she didn't want him to nag her again about taking chances with her safety. Harry had little to report – he'd yet to track down Iris Walker at either her home or the church, and according to her neighbours and fellow parishioners she was rarely anywhere other than those two places.

They were standing close together, perusing Sam's whiteboard, when Irma arrived. It was her first time at the agency as well as meeting Harry, and she inspected both curiously.

Harry took a piece of paper out of a manila file. On it he had written three names: Sexton, Padfield and Iris Walker – their three suspects. Sam took the pen from his hand and struck a line through Sexton: he had proved to be a dead end after all. Irma smiled knowingly at the easy way the two of them interacted with one another.

'There's a connection to all the murders, and we need to find it,' said Harry. 'Hips gave us some excellent insights about the significance of the rosaries, and clearly that ties the cases together in one way. But what we need is a link between the victims; something to point us to a suspect,' Harry summarised.

'Well, I think Tom Padfield has to be our chief suspect,' said Sam. 'Didn't you tell me that most murders are committed by someone who is close to the victim? Padfield clearly hates women because of something Leticia did – or was.'

'Woman's intuition,' said Irma, frowning as something on Sam's whiteboard caught her eye. She stood up and pulled a pair of ornate designer glasses from her handbag before leaning in to take a closer look. 'Who's the girl on the left? She looks familiar.'

'That's Leticia Joy,' said Sam in surprise. 'The first victim, the one Icey was convicted of killing. You must have seen her picture before, it was all over the news. . . .' She paused, aware that Irma had a life-long aversion to watching the news or even reading the papers.

'Well, you know me, Sam. I hear things; I listen to people talk. I got the gist about Leticia Joy but I'm not much of one for real life or watching the news when I make my business out of other people's fantasies. But this girl looks familiar, though.'

'Her picture's been everywhere – on TV, in the papers . . . You're bound to recognise her face,' Harry chipped in.

'That's not where I recognise her from,' Irma said emphatically.

'You know her?' Sam asked in astonishment.

'I'm not sure . . .'

Sam handed Irma a copy of the newspaper clipping about Leticia Joy's death that she'd pinned to her board. It was the photograph all the papers had run of Leticia; the one where she looked fresh-faced and innocent, the very picture of a virgin bride. 'Her face is very familiar . . .' Irma repeated. 'She looks a little like Lottie, one of my girls who quit a while back, but . . .'

'But?' Sam questioned eagerly.

'But Lottie was a redhead and wore a lot more make-up.' Irma sniffed. 'And far nicer clothes. Maybe she just has one of those faces but I could swear . . .'

Sam's thoughts raced. 'Irma, could she have been one of your girls? Her fiancé said she was a working girl in the past. That she'd recently taken on some clients to help pay for her wedding . . .'

'Well, you know I have a lot of girls on my books and they come and go. Lottie didn't work for me for all that long – and rarely at the house. The last time I spoke to her, she said she'd come into some money and was quitting.'

'Maybe Leticia's working name was Lottie?' Harry suggested. 'After all, it's quite common for working girls to use different names.'

'Do you think Leticia Joy is your Lottie, Irma?' Sam asked her former boss carefully.

Irma studied the newspaper photograph again, 'Well, I can't be a hundred per cent sure but I'm sure enough. Leticia Joy with red hair and a makeover would be Lottie's twin.' Irma paused and then looked up from her file excitedly. 'Sam, one of Lottie's regular clients was Judge Certie!'

Sam and Harry exchanged surprised looks. 'And she'd come into some money before she quit?' Harry asked. Irma nodded. He turned to Sam. 'Given what we know about the late judge's call girl habit, I always wondered if he was being blackmailed. He certainly left himself open to it.'

'You think Leticia could have been blackmailing the judge? I guess that might explain her death and his suicide.'

'Hold on a minute, Sam. I wouldn't go that far. You're not

suggesting that the judge might have killed her rather than risk being exposed?' Harry said with a frown.

'It's possible . . .' Sam began.

'It doesn't make sense,' countered Harry. 'If he killed Leticia, what about the other dead girls? Who murdered them? Certie was long dead by then. Or are you suggesting there are two killers out there, when all along we've been trying to prove there's only one and it's not Icey?'

Sam was getting flustered, which was unusual for her. She was embarrassed that she had made such an obvious and elementary mistake in front of Harry. She needed to think more like a private investigator.

'What about the other girls, Irma?' she said to cover herself. 'Do you recognise any of them?'

Irma walked over to Sam's board and they viewed the photographs together. Irma stared at each photograph in turn before she finally shook her head.

'No, I don't recognise any of the others.'

'I was thinking more that we had a reason for the judge deciding to top himself than a reason why Leticia was murdered,' Harry explained patiently. 'But I do think it's a bit of a coincidence that the very priest that she might have confessed to about her profession is also in the habit of taking tea with a madam. You did say that you met Father Luke at Irma's house, didn't you, Sam? In which case, the question that I have in my mind is . . .'

'Did Father Luke know the judge?' Sam said. There were times when she could read Harry's mind like a book. Sam and Harry turned to face Irma, who looked alarmed by their sudden interest.

'Well, Irma, did Father Luke ever meet Judge Certie at your place?' Harry queried.

'No, I don't think so. Father Luke and I were at college together, as you know. But Certie was just a client – he seldom came to my house. You think Lottie was blackmailing him? I vet my girls carefully and they're paid well; they know better than to push their luck.'

'Well, maybe it wasn't Leticia/Lottie who was doing the blackmailing?' Harry said at last.

'Then who?' questioned Sam. 'And how does this all help Icey?' Something was niggling at her, though. Something Sexton had said when he was attacking her at the asylum. He'd called Leticia 'God's mistress', and at the time it had made her think of Father Luke. But that hadn't been all he'd said. She was stupid not to remember it at first but he'd said Leticia was 'God's whore'. It was a strange phrase for him to have used. She recounted his words to Harry and Irma now, as well as her fleeting thought that maybe Leticia had had an improper relationship with Father Luke or someone at the church.

Irma looked shocked. 'The Father Luke I know wouldn't dip his wick with a member of his congregation! You know he moved to Camberwell in the first place because he was being harassed by some of his congregation?'

Sam nodded. 'Yes, I heard that from someone . . .'

'Well, just because he doesn't screw his flock doesn't mean he doesn't get his jollies somewhere else,' Harry interjected. He'd always been a bit suspicious of men who claimed to be celibate. 'If Father Luke knew that Leticia was a working girl, then maybe their relationship was more, well, business-like?'

'You mean they were tart and client?'

'He isn't a client,' Irma insisted, but Sam and Harry ignored her.

'I'm not sure I'd put it quite that way, Sam, but it's possible.' Harry turned to look at Irma. 'I presume that sometimes girls have clients that don't go through you, off the books, like?'

Irma wanted to deny it but she was aware that it happened, although she didn't approve of it at all. She gave a slight incline of her head and sighed. 'Though I don't believe the man I went to college with would do something like that. He wouldn't compromise his position in that way.'

Sam gave her a small smile. 'Well, you know him best. Though even priests have human weaknesses, don't they?'

'The only weakness Father Luke Armstrong has is a certain fondness for the finer things in life . . .'

Harry looked at Irma curiously. 'Really? Well, maybe he wasn't Leticia's lover or her client . . .'

'That's what I'm trying to tell you,' Irma began, and then stopped when she saw Harry's face. 'But that's not what you meant, is it?'

'Harry?' Sam asked curiously.

'Well, maybe Father Luke is Leticia's co-conspirator.'

Irma looked blank but Sam got it at once. 'You think he might have been the one blackmailing Judge Certie with something he learnt at confession?'

'Or he was working with Leticia. You said she'd come into some money?'

Irma shook her head violently. 'Priests aren't allowed to do that,' she insisted.

'Well, they're not allowed to do a lot of things but it doesn't seem to stop them,' Harry said at last. 'But this is all a bit of speculation, based on the ravings of a mad witness.'

'It is, isn't it?' Sam gave a heavy sigh but then an idea struck her. 'I think maybe we need to get a fresh perspectives on all of this.' She smiled at her two friends. 'You know, I feel this sudden need to go to church.'

Chapter One Hundred and Twelve

Harry and Sam had made plans to meet at St Mary Magdalene's Church early the following morning, but when Sam arrived in Camberwell at 8.50, Harry was nowhere to be seen. It was unlike him not to be early for one of their meetings. She grabbed two take-out coffees from the nearest local café and sat on one of the wooden benches in the grounds of the church, anxiously checking her phone for messages while she sipped her own hot drink. By 9.10, she'd finished her coffee and was beginning to feel frustrated. Something must have come up, she realised, but she felt a little let down that Harry hadn't let her know he couldn't make it. With a heavy sigh, Sam abandoned Harry's now tepid coffee in the nearest bin and made her way to the main entrance of the church.

It was surprisingly quiet that morning, too late for early morning mass and not yet late enough for the casual worshipper to drop by. Despite herself, Sam felt a fleeting tingle of apprehension on entering the main area of the church. It was a grey, wintry day and the church was mostly shrouded in darkness. It was almost as if she sensed fear in the air as she waited just inside the doors while her eyes adjusted to the poor light. Stepping forward, Sam stumbled slightly on one of the uneven flagstones and had to pull herself up. She looked around for a switch to turn on some of the church's electric lights, but found nothing. She moved into a murky pool of daylight cast from one of the nearby windows, but before she could fully get her bearings she found herself knocked to the floor.

Iris Walker stood in front of her, dressed in a dark funereal dress. Her face was scrubbed clean apart form a shard of red lipstick that had been bluntly applied across her pencil-thin lips. In her hand was the large Bible that she had hit Sam with before. It was clearly Iris's weapon of choice but before Sam could get to her feet, the older woman began to snarl at her.

'Do not prostitute thy daughter, to cause her to be a whore; lest the land fall to whoredom, and the land become full of wickedness.' Iris quoted from the Bible as she struck Sam about the head with the good book.

Sam was momentarily dazed. 'Iris, stop!' she pleaded as the darkness stretched out in front of her. She scrabbled to her feet and began to stumble towards an open doorway behind the altar, but Iris pursued her.

The whores will suffer eternal damnation. Repent, sinner, for the Kingdom of Heaven is nigh!'

Sam was struck across her right cheek with the Bible, knocking her against one of the pews before she hit the solid cold floor again. Iris Walker then struck Sam repeatedly across the back of her head as she continued to chant verses.

Sam remained rooted to the floor as Iris raised her foot and stamped on her face. She screamed out in pain and rolled over to protect herself.

'Whore! Your sort are not welcome in God's house!' Iris bellowed, continuing to rant.

Before Sam could react further, Iris disappeared into a dark alcove to the right of the door. Sam was still lying on her stomach when she heard footsteps approaching. She lifted herself up onto her elbows and noticed that it was Father Luke.

'My dear child, let me help.'

'Thank you, Father, but I can manage,' said Sam as she managed to stand up, and – with the priest's help – make it into the nearest pew. She looked around for her handbag and spotted it a few rows behind, but it was too much effort to go and get it. She could feel a trickle of blood running down her face.

'What happened?'

'You really should try and control Iris Walker. One day she will kill someone,' Sam said, her face burning with pain as she spoke.

'Did she attack you?'

'I think she tried to kill me,' replied Sam, half in wonder, half in disbelief. Vaguely it occurred to her that she really should report the attack to the police this time, but she was still too shocked to think coherently.

The priest handed her a handkerchief and waited while Sam dabbed at her face and took deep breaths to calm herself. 'What brings you here?' he asked at last, after Sam had composed herself a little.

'Well, Father, I really wanted to ask you some questions about Leticia Joy.'

'Again? I'm not sure that I have anything new to add, I'm afraid. You know I can't tell you anything she said to me in confidence.'

Dabbing the back of her head with the handkerchief, Sam couldn't help but notice that the priest seemed a little uneasy. Maybe he was wary that Sam was about to cause trouble for his church and force him to do something about the distinctly unChristian Iris Walker. Or maybe Harry was right and the priest did have something to hide. She'd noticed that the handkerchief he'd given her was silk and monogrammed. Maybe it had been a gift from one of his besotted parishioners, but she remembered Irma telling them that Father Luke liked the finer things in life. No paper tissues for him, it seemed. 'Did you know that Leticia Joy had gone back to her old ways?' she asked him.

'What ways? I don't understand.'

She knew the priest realised her meaning. Why was he being deliberately obtuse? 'You knew she was working as a prostitute. Either she told you in confession or you knew because you saw her at Irma's. Did you see Judge Certie there, too, Father, or did Leticia tell you he was one of her clients?' He did not answer. Sam continued. 'Just tell me if I have got it wrong. Did they ever meet here? Is that how you knew? Was that when you started to blackmail him?' she said, taking a risk.

Father Luke did not respond. There was not a flicker of unease in his controlled expression. Sam waited nervously for an answer. His words, when they came, were measured and cold.

'I don't know what you're talking about. Leticia was one of my parishioners, that's all.'

He began to stand, at the same time reaching inside his robes, and Sam watched in shock as he removed a rosary. She couldn't stifle her gasp, even though she realised at once that, of course, a Catholic priest would carry a rosary. Even so, when Father Luke turned back to look at her, she knew in an instant that what Irma had called her 'woman's intuition' had been correct. But Father Luke was not just a lech or a blackmailer; there was murder in his eyes as well as the recognition that Sam had guessed his basest instincts. The priest began to advance towards her. 'Why, Father?' Sam whispered. 'What did Leticia Joy ever do to you? What did any of them do?'

Father Luke gave no reply; instead, he fingered the beads of his rosary and muttered to himself. Sam found it hard to make out his words at first, but as he repeated them in a slow liturgy, she caught his meaning. 'I forgive you for you know not what you do. Women, you are all the same. You turn your God-given beauty into the ugliness of self-righteous pride. You come in here asking for forgiveness. The epitome of wanton wickedness. A stealer of the hearts of men. You deserve to die.' Before Sam could protest, he grabbed her around her neck and dragged her up from her seat towards the altar of the church. 'This way,' he murmured crazily. 'All are welcome in God's house.'

As she screamed out, he placed his hand over her mouth. 'Shush,' he said with icy calm. 'This is a church, after all.' Forcing her into the choir stalls behind the altar, Father Luke pushed Sam so that she sat down heavily. He placed his arms almost tenderly around her shoulders. Anyone witnessing the gesture might have mistaken it for the comfort of a priest to a straying member of his flock, but Sam knew differently now. Despite his calm demeanour, Father Luke's eyes were wild. He whispered in her ear, 'Let us pray.'

He reached again into the pocket of his robe and turned to face her. It was then that Sam saw the glint of something silver in his right hand. Frozen with fear, she was taken completely by surprise when he used his left fist to strike her, the sudden blow catching her between the eyes. Sam screamed and tried to get up, but the priest was bigger and stronger. She instinctively raised her hands to protect her face from his rain of blows as he lashed out at her like a demented spirit in a house of evil.

'Quiet in God's house, have some respect,' he said.

The light from the stained glass tinted the blade of the knife blue as Father Luke raised his right hand. Sam heard herself scream as she slid to the floor. Surprised to discover she was momentarily out of the priest's grasp, she scrambled to her feet. She knew she couldn't get to the main church door without him catching her, so she ran in the same direction Iris had disappeared moments earlier. Father Luke was still close by.

She could hear him behind her. She managed to slip through the door to the vestry before him, and slammed it shut behind her, using her body weight to keep the door closed until she realised there was a key in the lock. She turned it quickly and breathed a sigh of relief. She might have locked herself in with Iris Walker, but she'd take her chances with her over Father Luke any day. Though with her ear to the door she could still hear him on the other side, cursing and ranting.

Then it occurred to her that he might have another key, and she stepped backward in alarm, finding herself in a connecting corridor. Feeling her way along the wall, Sam kept going until she reached what she guessed to be the priest's quarters. She slipped inside. The hall was dark and gloomy, but strangely warm despite the flagstone floor. In spite of her caution as she explored her new surroundings, Sam's heels clicked loudly as she walked. She recognised Father Luke's study from her first visit to the church, when he'd given her Padfield's address. Now she noticed a set of low stone steps leading up to a mezzanine floor. Sam edged her way up the short staircase but the mezzanine level yielded no surprises; it led to nowhere, merely a blank wall.

Turning her back towards the dead end, Sam stepped down onto the second step and waited. The air had been still but now she felt something; a faint gust of air prickled her skin and she felt a draught coming from the wall. How could that be? Stepping back up onto the top step, Sam pressed her ear up against the wall and listened. She could hear nothing but as she placed her hands on the stonework, she felt a slight impression in the plaster. She pressed harder, pushing her full weight against the wall, and felt something move. There was a door in the wall, hidden to most prying eyes but now opening to reveal a small dark room behind. It was an old church but still Sam was surprised to discover it had a secret room. She inched forward nervously, worried in case she had discovered Iris Walker's hiding place. 'Iris?' she whispered. There was no reply so cautiously she stepped through into an area that was no bigger than a small cupboard, about six feet by three. She fumbled for a light switch, which, once turned on, revealed that at least Sam was alone. The area was empty apart from five monochrome boxes set in a neat row on a shelf on the far side of the wall. Maybe this was just an old store room, but it seemed odd to store so little here; besides, most store rooms she had encountered didn't have such an obscure entrance.

Sam reached for the first small black box. It was no bigger than a few inches square. Inside was a solitary bead. Sam's brain was in a whirl but she tried hard to concentrate. It looked very much like a bead from a rosary – a rosary similar to the one Leticia Joy had owned. She snapped the box shut and opened the next. Inside was what looked like the tip of a knife, stained with blood. Sam resisted the urge to touch that, too. Instead she opened the remaining boxes. The third and fourth boxes were empty and the fifth box contained a broken SIM card. She could hardly guess what that meant so turned her attention to scooping up the three boxes that each held something, before making her retreat, her heart beating to a staccato rhythm as she made her way out of the room.

As the door pivoted back into place, Sam stumbled down the stairs back into the dark hallway, where she collided with Iris Walker. This time Sam was prepared. With her hands full she couldn't hit Iris, so she kicked her in the stomach. The force sent Iris flying backward against the wall and she slid to the floor, howling in pain. Sam didn't wait for her to recover; instead, she carried on running down the hallway, desperately looking for another exit from the vestry.

She couldn't find another way out and, while the last thing she wanted was to unlock the door to the church and face Father Luke again, it seemed there was no alternative. The key turned easily in the lock and Sam nudged the door open, ready to run. The church was suspiciously quiet, peaceful almost, bathed in candlelight and the jewelled hues of natural light beaming through the large stained-glass window behind the altar. It depicted the crucifiction but Sam noticed now that there was a weeping woman shown as well, holding the bottom of the cross. Mary Magdalene, she presumed.

Slowly, Sam edged her way down the aisle to the side door of the church, determined to make her escape with the evidence contained in the boxes intact. She suddenly saw her bag tucked under one of the pews ahead of her, and ran towards it. She searched desperately for her mobile phone, her hand shaking as she also stowed the three boxes carefully in her bag. She was not aware of the shadow behind her until a hand brushed against the nape of her neck.

Sam let out a gasp and prepared to scream, but the hand clamped down hard on her mouth, preventing her from making a further sound.

Chapter One Hundred and Thirteen

'Hush, Sam . . .' The voice, when it came, was not what she expected. It was not the harsh rasp of a demented priest but a deep, world-weary voice she would recognise anywhere. Sam looked up into kind brown eyes and the face of a man she knew would never hurt her.

'Harry . . .' she managed to whisper when he withdrew his hand. 'I thought you didn't make it—'

'No time now, Sam, we need to get out of here. It's Father Luke . . .'

She nodded. 'I know, but how did . . .' Her voice trailed off as she looked, really looked, at Harry's dishevelled form. There was blood on his collar but more worrying still was the blood already seeping from the knife wound to his stomach, turning his white shirt red. 'Harry, you've been stabbed!'

'We need to get out of here now, Sam. In case he comes back.' Sam grabbed her bag with one hand and Harry's arm with the other, and together they part-ran, part-stumbled towards the side door.

Outside in the graveyard that surrounded St Mary Magdalene's, Sam helped Harry to the bench she'd sat on earlier. She searched her bag for anything to staunch the blood flow, remembered the scarf she was wearing and pressed it ineffectually to Harry's stomach. 'You need an ambulance, Harry.'

'On its way. I've called the police, too. I got here early so I thought I'd talk to the Father first.' He smiled wryly, though his breathing sounded laboured. 'Big mistake. Let's just say he didn't take too kindly to my line of questioning. I think I must have passed out for a bit but then I dialled 999. That was just before I saw you come back into the church.'

Sam could already hear sirens in the distance. At first, she'd thought it was just wishful thinking on her part, but they were getting closer now. It was almost over. Father Luke was their killer. She looked around as people passed by the church going about their business. It seemed surreal that she and Harry were sitting there unnoticed, recovering from violent encounters with a psychopath, while Joe Public went shopping. She eyed the church door warily. 'Do you think he's still in there? I thought there might be another exit, but I couldn't find one in the vestry.'

'Not our problem now, Sam.' Harry nodded at the unmarked police car that had just pulled up, Paradissimo in the driving seat. A trail of flashing blue lights followed in his wake.

Sam explained quickly and emotionlessly to Paradissimo what she and Harry had discovered at the church, then handed him the boxed evidence, all the while keeping an anxious eye out for the ambulance. As it arrived and the paramedics made a quick examination of Harry, Sam realised she'd forgotten to tell Paradissimo about Iris Walker. But by then a paramedic was asking her if she wanted to accompany Harry to the hospital, and she was forced to make a split-second decision. Watching Harry limping towards the ambulance, supported by another paramedic, the choice was easy. The police were here; they could take over. Even now, as she watched, a team of armed officers had the building surrounded. Father Luke was caught, or as good as. Iris Walker, too. It was Harry who needed her.

Chapter One Hundred and Fourteen

Paradissimo entered the church by the back door in the vestry that, in her panic, Sam had been unable to find. The armed unit had found Iris Walker hiding between the statues of John the Baptist and the Virgin Mary. She was quickly bundled out of the church, and placed in police custody.

Father Luke proved harder to track down. The police began a finger-tip search of the premises. Mindful of what Sam had said about hidden passages in the building, Paradissimo ordered Cody and officers with sniffer dogs to find a schematic for the building, but got impatient waiting and went on his own exploration.

He found Father Luke in one of the crypts beneath the church. The priest was on his knees, praying, with a bloody knife in his hands.

'It's the police,' said Paradissimo, as armed officers trickled in to deal with the killer. 'You are under arrest for the attempted murder of Harry Kemp and on the suspicion of the murders of Leticia Joy, Martha Lewis, Poppy Withers and Pia Broom. You don't have to say anything, but anything that you do say will be taken down and may be used against you,' Paradissimo intoned once Father Luke had been relieved of his weapon and handcuffed. It was only then that they discovered that the priest's vestments weren't just covered in Harry Kemp's blood but also his own. He had turned his knife on himself, slashing his wrists. Questions would have to wait until their suspect received medical treatment at least.

Chapter One Hundred and Fifteen

As Harry underwent emergency surgery at St George's to repair a deep laceration to his stomach, Father Luke ended up in the same hospital, but it soon emerged from a preliminary examination that the priest's wounds were superficial. He had killed four women that they knew of in extreme, brutal, sickening ways, but it seemed the good Father had baulked at turning his knife on himself with any serious intent, even when it was clear he would not escape justice.

The blood on the knife tip was confirmed as bearing traces of Leticia Joy's blood. The nooks and secret crannies of St Mary Magdalene's gave up more of the priest's secrets. In the crypt they found traces of a recently excavated stone at the base of one of the tombs; in it they found reams of notes, scribbled down on faded notepaper, about the fall of Eve, Delilah and Jezebel. Good women who had gone bad when they broke God's moral law. Clearly, these were the demented ramblings of a madman who had taken to punishing all 'fallen' women who crossed his path.

As Sam waited at the hospital after having her own superficial wounds checked out, she heard that Father Luke had been brought in on another floor. Driven by her anger on behalf of Harry, Icey and the other victims, she made her way to where the priest was being held in a private room, only to find her way barred by two burly policemen. She realised her charm would only get her so far this time. She also needed to call Frizzel and Ashley Towers in any case, to discover how soon they could expedite Icey's release now that the real killer was close to being charged. As she turned to leave, she bumped into Anne Cody and eyed the WPC warily. She expected the older woman's usual wrath but instead Cody smiled, albeit a tad warily, and offered her one of the coffees she carried in her hand, gesturing to some seats further down the corridor.

Sam declined the coffee – she still didn't like or trust the detective, and wasn't about to accept any peace offerings – but she did follow her to the waiting area, where she looked around curiously, expecting to see Paradissimo and dreading his arrival.

Cody correctly interpreted her look. 'He's not here,' she said calmly. 'He's been taken off the case.'

'Really?' Sam was surprised. He'd clearly been in charge at the church, what could have happened so quickly to change things? 'Why now?'

Cody shrugged, still clearly not wishing to trust Sam that much with the intricacies of police politics. While Paradissimo hadn't had his knuckles rapped too severely over the Leticia Joy case, in the wake of Father Luke's arrest the top brass wanted to be careful. The media were now watching every move they made. The senior team wanted Paradissimo out of the way while they made their case against Father Luke, even if it seemed likely that his defence might legitimately plead insanity in his case. 'I get to question Father Luke,' Cody said briefly, nodding back along the corridor towards the private room.

'Has he said anything yet?'

'He's been ranting and raving. Did he say anything to you?'

Sam shook her head. 'Not really.'

'What about Harry Kemp? Did he tell you anything?'

Sam sighed, 'He didn't really get the chance.' She bit her lip nervously. 'He's in surgery now.'

'I know. We'll have some questions for him when he's well enough, but we've found a lot of evidence at the church.'

'Like what?'

Cody didn't reply and Sam sighed, realising that she'd get no details from her. 'But you don't have any doubts that he's the killer?'

'No, not this time,' Cody said ruefully, and the two women shared a pointed look. Sam got up to leave, only to have Cody call after her. 'I'm sorry about your friend . . .'

Sam glared back in return. 'Which one?' she said sharply, not ready to forgive and forget that this was one of the people who had helped put Icey behind bars in the first place.

Cody shrugged and met the harsh glare of Sam's rage for a few seconds before looking away first.

Chapter One Hundred and Sixteen

While the police built their case against Father Luke, the media had already tried him and found him guilty in a series of front-page exclusives under lurid headlines.

It was the *Mirror* that ran the first story, making the connection between Sam and Harry leading the police to the priest in the first place. The paper accused the judiciary of astonishing incompetence and gross arrogance. It had taken two private investigators, operating from a tiny office in the heart of the Temple, to pursue the killer. In the wake of the coverage and Towers finally doing his duty by Icey, the Crown Prosecution Service announced that they would not resist a further appeal on behalf of Elizabeth Johnson. She would be free within twenty-four hours.

Sam greeted the news from Towers calmly. Harry was out of the woods but would be spending a few days on a ward before they'd let him home. Harry had been visited in hospital by several of his old colleagues, one of whom had let slip that Iris Walker had been released without charge.

'You could pursue assault charges, you know, Sam,' Harry suggested from his sick bed.

Sam shook her head. 'I think I got off fairly lightly compared to you, Harry.' She was still a little bruised and battered from her encounter with Iris, but nothing that time wouldn't heal.

'Besides, I think the police have their hands full at the moment . . . Did your contact say anything about Judge Certie? Was Father Luke blackmailing him, do you think?'

'I don't think they've made that connection yet,' Harry replied, struggling to sit up straighter as Sam leapt to his side to adjust his pillow. She'd already insisted that Harry be her house guest while he recovered from his injuries. 'Though, between you and me, I wonder if it wasn't Iris who was doing the blackmailing. It might explain why she was so wary of us asking questions.'

'I guess we'll never know for sure,' Sam concluded. 'And we've got other things to think about, too – getting you back on your feet and Icey's coming home.'

Chapter One Hundred and Seventeen

The door to Fleet Investigations was open when Icey arrived. She switched on the light, still holding her plastic bag of belongings clutched to her chest. She had been a little surprised that Sam had not met her at the prison on her release. Instead, a local mini-cab, arranged by the prison service, had dropped her here.

It felt like years since she had seen the ash-grey office, and then it had been newly painted and pristine. Now it looked like a working office, the shelves full of files and piles of paperwork covering the desk, all signs of an office life that was totally alien to Icey. She looked around nervously. Sam wasn't anywhere to be seen but Icey did spot an envelope, addressed to her, on the big burgundy leather desk. She recognised the handwriting before she read the contents of the card inside. It was from Sam and it simply said: 'Welcome, partner, to the belated opening of Fleet Investigations.'

Replacing the card, Icey checked her watch. She had anticipated that Sam would be here to meet her at least, but walking towards the back of the office Icey felt stupid. She had thought that her best friend would wish to celebrate her freedom, but she was obviously mistaken.

The phone rang in the rear office. Icey walked towards the noise, sure that it was Sam with a ready excuse. The phone stopped as she opened the door, and the office erupted. Sam,

Irma, Hips and two pretty, smiling girls she didn't recognise were all crowded into the space behind the door. On the desk was an assortment of patisseries, sandwiches and champagne. Sam was the first to step forward and embrace her while the others raised their glasses to celebrate her freedom. Irma greeted her like a long-lost child.

Icey was stunned and felt tears prick her eyes. One minute she had been doing life with no hope of freedom, the next she was free and drinking champagne. It was almost too much for her to cope with.

The celebrations continued for several hours, during which time Icey was introduced to Flick and Oriel, and learnt of their part in her release. She hugged the women warmly, grateful for their help. But it was Sam who got the biggest hug. Without her determination and persistence, Icey would still be locked away. Freedom tasted sweet, but her friendship with Sam was sweeter.

Ashley Towers popped his head around the door and had one drink before making his excuses, clearly somewhat overwhelmed by the lively atmosphere, a far cry from the sort of parties he usually attended. Mr Frizzel had not been invited, and Harry was still resting up in St George's.

Sam was on top of the world. Icey was free, Harry was on the mend and that was all that mattered. They could now get on with the rest of their lives as they had planned before Icey got arrested.

She sipped her champagne, the gentle fizz bubbling deliciously in her mouth. Looking around for a bottle to offer refills all round, she thought she could hear a phone ringing. Sam stood still and listened more intently. She was right. It was definitely ringing. Stepping into the front office, Sam closed the door behind her and walked over to pick up the phone.

'Fleet Investigations.'

There was no reply but she could hear someone breathing at the other end of the line. Not loudly enough for her to automatically think it was a dirty phone call, but clear enough to know there wasn't a fault on the line. Perhaps they couldn't hear her. 'Sam Bailey speaking, can I help you?' she said a little more forcefully.

'Hello, Sam, how's my favourite little girl?'

'Sorry, who is this?' she asked, feeling the tiny hairs at the back of her neck stand on end.

'It's been a long time, sweetheart. I saw you on telly.'

'Who is this?'

'It's your old uncle Pete, sweetheart.'

Sam felt an icy chill shiver through her body. 'I am not your sweetheart!'

'You will always be my sweetheart.'

Without waiting to hear more, Sam hung up the phone in alarm. She could almost smell him in the room with her. Just a few words, a couple of minutes, and she'd been transported back to the frightened child she'd once been. He was in her hair, on her clothes and, when she closed her eyes, he was in the room. The stench made her want to heave.

The phone rang again and Sam thought about pressing the button to switch the calls to voicemail, but something made her pull up short. She wasn't that frightened child any more, she was a grown woman, strong and independent, and if the man who had terrorised her childhood thought he could just slime back into her life, he had another think coming. She picked up the phone defiantly.

'Sam—'

'Listen up, you pervert,' Sam interrupted, cutting him off.

'You need to lose this number. Don't even think of trying to contact me again. The court may have believed your lies, but I know what you did to me and if you come near me again, then you better believe I'm going to make sure the punishment fits your crimes, you sick bastard!'

With that she hung up the phone again and stood for several minutes in the dark office as she tried to compose herself. She would not allow him to get to her, not now, not when things were going so well. She hoped that he'd got the message, but if 'Uncle Pete' did try to weasel his way back into her life, she knew that her threat was not an empty one. Over these last months, she'd learnt a lot about her own strength of will. She would make him pay for what he'd done to her. Her biggest hope was never to hear from him again, but part of her almost wished he would force the issue. Throughout her whole life, she'd never run from a fight, and with everything that had happened to Icey she'd proved to herself that she could take on any challenge. Maybe it was time she confronted her demons.

She took a sip of her champagne, feeling her mood pick up, silently toasting herself and the thought of finally getting her revenge on her abuser. A hundred different scenarios ran through her head, but now was not the time for such plans, she thought, as Icey appeared in the doorway, a look of curiosity on her face.

The big smile Sam gave her friend was genuine, her green eyes sparkling with joy and confidence, and she held her head high as she walked over to give Icey a long hug before, together, they rejoined the party.

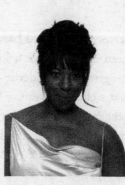

An exclusive interview with Constance Briscoe:

What was your inspiration for The Accused?
I have to credit, Tony Arlidge, with the initial idea. Though, as a lawyer I am able to draw on a lot of my past experience for plot inspiration but Tony – who's also a barrister – has been great for brainstorming plot ideas!

I also read a lot and for this book read a lot about serial killers. Most of all, though, I really wanted to write a readable, entertaining book that people would enjoy.

You combine your writing career with being a barrister and a part-time judge, how do you find the time to write? Which do you enjoy most?
Actually, I have to set time aside every day to write. It's usually in the morning for a couple of hours. I do enjoy writing and I'd love to be able to write full time. Maybe, one day . . .

The Accused doesn't exactly offer a glowing picture of the British legal system, what with its depiction of uncaring barristers, corrupt police and dismissive judges do you think Icey would have got a fair trial in reality? Would you have defended her?
It is true that I have tried depict the dark side of my profession but it is fiction and I am certain that Icey would have

received a fair trial. I certainly would have given anything defend her and I am sure I speak for a lot of my colleagues. She'd be a challenge – given the evidence against her and her attitude at times. What a client!

I'd also like to meet Sam – I like the fact that she's not prepared to compromise, speaks her mind and is very in your face, as well as glamorous.

Your non-fiction books Ugly and Beyond Ugly have been phenomenally successful. Did you have any idea when you first started writing that your books would prove such an inspiration to others?
I had absolutely no idea at all that the books would be that successful and I am very glad about that. The inspiration to others came as a bit of a surprise. I have never seen myself in that light before.

Which classic novel have you always meant to read and never got round to?
War and Peace.

What are your top five books of all time?
Tristram Shandy, Laurence Sterne
Our Mutual Friend, Charles Dickens
Pride and Prejudice, Jane Austen
The Adventures of Huckleberry Finn, Mark Twain
Middlemarch, George Eliot

What book are you currently reading?
I am currently reading *Dream of Ding Village* by Yan Lianke, which is a brilliant novel about the price of progress in modern China.

Do you have a favourite time of day to write? A favourite place?
Yes. In Vandrach, France, on the balcony in front of the millrace. Tony and I found the place about three years ago and it's magical. Though mostly I write in London which has its own – if very different – charms!

Which fictional character would you most like to meet?
Tristram Shandy.

Who, in your opinion, is the greatest writer of all time?
Either Charles Dickens or Laurence Sterne.

Other than the law and your writing career, what other jobs or professions have you undertaken or considered?
I would like to try my hand at gardening. I think I would be a good TV presenter but I have not had any offers as yet . . .

What are you working on at the moment?
At the moment I am working on a sequel to *The Accused*. In my professional life, I can't talk about my current cases, but I do find myself handling a lot of sex crimes and cases involving extreme violence. It can be harrowing but incredibly rewarding, too. And of course, in terms of research for the next novel, all very useful . . .